For Gail, with love, as always

Also by David George Clarke

The Dust of Centuries

Quincentenarian

The Delusion Gambit

Fatal Consequences

The Cotton and Silk Thrillers

Irrefutable Evidence

Remorseless

The Cambroni Vendetta

An Imperfect Revenge

Non-Fiction

Hong Kong Under The Microscope

A History of the Hong Kong Government Laboratory 1879–2004

DAVID GEORGE CLARKE

THE CAMBRONI VENDETTA

A COTTON & SILK THRILLER

clarkeFiction

THE CAMBRONI VENDETTA

goccia
Italian noun [feminine] /ˈgot:cha/
drop; droplet

If more than one person knows a secret,
it is no longer a secret.

Cosimo Graziano Rosselli, Assassin

Part One

MAURIZIO CAMBRONI

Chapter One

Incarceration in a high-security prison in the foothills of the Apennines, fifty miles south of Rome, had taken an uncompromising toll on Maurizio Cambroni. Frail and in permanent pain, the seventy-four-year-old former art dealer was dying, a wasted caricature of the scheming fraudster who had accrued millions peddling high-quality fakes. His waxen skin bore the craquelure of a Renaissance painting, while a hideous array of liver spots disfigured the crown of his bald head. Apart from gnarled, peasant hands that shook to a beat of their own creation, he lay motionless for hours on end in his bed in the drab prison clinic; moribund, his life force spent.

Yet even as his body continued its unwavering decline, his mind still roiled and plotted, consumed by an unquenchable rage. And when that rage boiled over, as it did every few days, his hooded eyes would flash open, the bitterness radiating from their black pupils like twin beacons of hatred. Someone had betrayed him, and in the sinister world of organised crime that permeated Maurizio's life, there was no greater sin.

Bedridden since his imprisonment, Maurizio had trawled through his memory, painstakingly recalling every moment of every day of the months leading up to his arrest. He had reviewed and catalogued every client, every visitor to the gallery and every employee for any evidence of duplicity. No one escaped scrutiny, his son Ettore included. Day by agonising day, he had doggedly hung on to life, determined to solve the riddle of his downfall.

Slowly, one by one, he eliminated his clients from consideration, trusting his insight into their characters and an instinct honed over many years of double-dealing them.

As for the forgers themselves, the craftsmen sequestered in a secret workshop above the main gallery, what possible gain could there have been for any of them in betraying him when his ruin was theirs too? And ruined they were when, to a man, they pleaded guilty to forgery. If they ever plied their trade again after their release from prison, it would be on the streets earning a pittance.

Apart from Maurizio and his son Ettore, there were only three other employees in the main gallery. The first, the large African guard called Thompson, was like a faithful hound, his loyalty guaranteed by his generous salary. Earning more in a month than he had previously made in a year peddling fake designer goods in the Piazza della Repubblica, he was the Cambronis' man. Maurizio was sure he could discount him.

Of the other two, it seemed ridiculous even to consider Maria Renzo. A trusted old retainer, family almost, she had been part of the gallery for over forty years and was familiar with every one of the Cambronis' devious schemes. It was true that the prosecutors had dropped the charges against her, but was that in return for information? Maurizio did not believe she was capable of such treachery. More likely, once the case against Maurizio became ironclad, the prosecutors had lost interest in her. You could only expect so much from state employees. No, Maria was above suspicion; she had to be.

Which left only one person: the young woman employed to take up Maria's duties when her failing health took its toll; the art expert with the refined Milanese accent who in no time had become indispensable, achieving record sales during the time of her employment. Ginevra Mancini.

Had she really only been with them for a few months? It seemed so much longer; she had become part of the furniture. Maurizio had agonised over the personable young woman for many weeks, reviewing every moment of her employment before he could finally admit the obvious to himself: Ginevra Mancini had insinuated herself into his life for the sole purpose of betraying him. It hurt his pride to do so, not to say his self-esteem, but once he had capitulated to the notion, the young woman consumed his thoughts.

How had she passed the rigorous scrutiny of his security team? They had bugged her apartment with hidden cameras and microphones, screened her belongings and checked her background numerous times. And every one of those times she had ticked all the boxes so perfectly that her very squeaky cleanness should have raised doubts. Instead, her flawless performance had fooled him as completely as it had Ettore and Maria. And as for the clients, they had loved her.

Once Maurizio had convinced himself that Ginevra Mancini was his nemesis, he got word to his security team. But when they broke into her apartment, they found it empty. Mancini had disappeared, evaporated, vanished, leaving nothing to prove she had ever existed.

But Maurizio didn't need proof of her existence. She *had* existed and must still exist. The right person could find her and inflict the ultimate punishment. Knowing he was dying, Maurizio was determined to set the wheels of his revenge in motion. He wouldn't live to receive the joyful news of Mancini's execution, but knowing the score would be settled was satisfaction enough. No one crossed Maurizio or his kind and got away with it. A vestige of his former power and a few contacts remained. He simply needed to issue the instructions.

The fate of Ettore Cambroni was altogether different from that of his father, owing largely to his choice of lawyer. Trusted by the mob and with links to a labyrinthine network of favours and hypocrisy, the astute Silvano Da Maggio knew the Art Fraud Squad's main target was Maurizio. He also understood that given the choice between a fight that might see the entire case collapse or the old man's head on a platter in exchange for Ettore's freedom, they would choose the latter. Ever philosophical, the urbane Commissario Massimo Felice, head of the Art Fraud Squad, had been around long enough to be content with Maurizio Cambroni taking the fall and his empire collapsing.

Not that Ettore was celebrating. His days in the art world finished and his reputation with the mob destroyed, he was a beaten man, his self-esteem in shreds. The grand family villa in the Chianti hills he had once occupied now forfeit to the State, he passed his miserable days cloistered in the seclusion of his modest Florence apartment.

Ettore only ever left the apartment when his father summoned him to his sick bed in the prison clinic, an order he hated receiving. The prison filled him with foreboding. Every time he went there, its very walls seemed to close in on him and the threat that someone would contrive a reason to keep him there was an ever-present and taunting demon in his mind. His father only summoned him rarely, but when he did, he had no choice but to obey. And now that Maurizio had finished his deliberations, the final summons arrived.

"Babbo!" Ettore gasped in shock when he saw his father's skeletal features, the shape of the old man's emaciated frame hardly registering beneath the bedcover. In the three months since Ettore's last visit, the decline in Maurizio's condition was profound.

Cambroni senior's eyelids flickered open, his eyes locking onto his son's. With the slightest twitch of the index finger of his left hand, he instructed Ettore to move towards him. Ettore took a tentative step forward, his deference to the power of the old man as strong as ever.

Maurizio moved his head impatiently. "Closer," he rasped. What he had to say to his son was for no one else's ears. Suspicious of everything and everybody, he assumed the room was bugged. Why wouldn't it be? The authorities wanted to listen to everything.

Ettore bent over, turning his head so that his right ear brushed his father's lips. No microphone could now register what Maurizio said, and Ettore's head blocked Maurizio's mouth from the view of any camera.

The message was a simple one, the two whispered words a barely audible hiss.

"Ginevra Mancini."

Ettore straightened, his eyes falling once more on the wasted shell of his father.

Satisfied he had his son's attention, Maurizio lifted his hand towards his neck and with a slow but unambiguous gesture, dragged his extended index finger across his throat.

"I'm surprised he took so long to work it out," declared Maria Renzo.

Bolstered by cushions, she was sitting in a chair close to an electric heater in the sitting room of her apartment, a room Ettore considered was already unhealthily hot.

Maria's relief when no charges were laid against her had been immense: she was old and her health would have suffered irreparably. However, she had followed Maurizio Cambroni's trial with a heavy heart, despairing over the daily flow of scurrilous minutiae from the ever-salivating gutter press.

"I always suspected that girl," she lied, knowing full well it was her approval that had persuaded Maurizio to accept Ginevra Mancini.

"You never said anything," said Ettore, his tone accusatory.

"Not my place," the old woman retaliated.

"Then why did you say she was perfect?" snapped Ettore. "I remember your exact words. You said nothing about any doubts."

"She fooled everyone, not just me. I saw your eyes roaming her body. She was the perfect honey trap for you both. Madonna, men are so gullible." She crossed herself in case she had offended the Virgin.

Ettore sighed his resignation. "We were all to blame. She was so convincing; I think she understood more about art than any of us. Wherever did the police find her? I can't believe someone so talented works for them."

Maria nodded. "I've been thinking about her a lot and wondering. I remember that when she spoke English to clients, the rich American woman, for example, she sounded very English. Not that I know much English but I've seen other Italian women speaking English to foreigners, and they have an Italian way of doing it. With Ginevra it was different. I can't put my finger on it but I'm wondering now if when she was with us she was acting a part."

"You think she might have been English?" said Ettore, the surprise clear in his tone.

Maria's shoulders lifted in an exaggerated shrug. "I don't know," she said. "It's possible."

Ettore stood up and paced the room. "I have to find her, Maria. Babbo insists. It's his dying … I was going to say wish, but it's an order. He wants her dealt with. And if what you've just suggested is true, it makes the search even more difficult. She might not even be in Italy."

Maria's embittered mouth tightened, her meagre lips disappearing. "Of course, Ginevra Mancini won't be her real name. That fop of a commissario will have given her a false identity. The bastard. What sort of mother allows her son to become a police officer?" She crossed herself again.

Ettore stopped pacing. "I will try to call in what few favours I have left. I need someone to find her, someone who is also competent to take the job to its required conclusion. Someone good. But I need *something* to tell him. Anything."

Maria's head bobbed with sudden animation. "The American woman!" she said, sounding pleased with herself. "Ginevra got on well with her. She only sold her genuine paintings, the sort we used as sweeteners. She didn't want the woman to waste her money."

Her eyes roamed the room while her ideas took on flesh. "I'd bet on a saint's bones the American woman used her real name. She had no reason to fake it. Find her and you'll find a way to Ginevra."

For the first time since entering the room, Ettore's shoulders relaxed as a malevolent sneer formed on his lips.

"Connie Fairbright," he said. "The rich American's name was Connie Fairbright."

Chapter Two

Ten days after Maurizio Cambroni tasked his son Ettore with finding and killing Ginevra Mancini, the old man was dead. He had held on for almost two years, determined to solve the puzzle of his betrayal. But once he had made his final decision, once he had rejected all other possibilities, once his ire had focussed to a white-hot pool of hatred and he had issued his final instructions, he sensed an immediate response from his body, its inexorable rate of decline shifting up a gear as his life's spirit prepared to leave.

The funeral was sparsely attended, with only a few reluctant family members pressed into service by Ettore. At one time, Maurizio's fame as an art dealer would have seen many of his wealthy clients crossing continents to pay their respects. But the trial had changed all that. Most of those wealthy clients now knew they were the owners of a good number of brilliantly executed fakes for which they had paid enormous sums. Few people would now cross the road for the man, let alone a continent. Even Maurizio's mob contacts were mostly absent, wary of who might be watching and secretly filming them. Mostly absent, but not completely. There was one. A strutting young man of around twenty dressed in attitude and a snappy suit. He was fodder for the mob, disposable and deniable, although he wasn't bright enough to know it. He was there for one reason: to place a wreath that concealed a small sealed envelope.

Given the number of his men compromised by Maurizio Cambroni's trial who were now serving long prison sentences, the strutting young man's boss had considered sending a bomb rather than flowers. But business was business. Ettore's requirements demanded specific talents. Expensive talents. There was money to be made.

When Ettore had made contact the day after Maurizio issued his instructions, he was told to meet an intermediary in a faceless backstreet Florentine bar. All pretence at niceties ignored, Ettore went straight to the point. "I have heard you have someone who is clever, someone good enough to trace a woman I am looking for and resourceful enough to kill her while making her death seem like an accident."

The intermediary's eyes, cold, lifeless orbs that revealed nothing, were fixed on Ettore's.

"It will be expensive," he said, finally.

"I will pay whatever is necessary."

The man grunted. "Someone will contact you."

He stood and walked to the door, his coffee untouched on the counter.

The small envelope in the wreath contained a scrap of brown paper folded into quarters. Written on it was a mobile phone number. In the seclusion of the study in his Florence apartment, Ettore stared at the number and memorised it before burning the piece of paper. He knew little of modern technology, but enough to know that phones could be tracked, so he wasn't stupid enough to call the number from his regular phone. Instead, he retrieved one of a number of anonymous burner phones from a wall safe and took a walk to a quiet backstreet where he knew he would not be overheard.

The number answered after two rings. "Pronto." The voice was refined but accented. Possibly Sicilian.

Ettore knew the form.

"Alvino gave me this number," he said, using the nickname for his mob contact, a name that reflected the man's reputation for fearlessness, a man who had guts. Use of the name was a signal to the responder that Ettore was genuine. "I need the full extent of your services," he added.

There was a pause. Ettore pressed the phone to his ear, but he could hear nothing.

After a long full minute, the voice at the other end barked a question.

"You are using a burner phone?"

"Of course."

"At precisely eight this evening you will receive a text message on your phone from another number, not this one. Do not call this number again; it will not work. The message will be an address. Be there at noon tomorrow and be sure to take all the usual precautions. When you enter the building, go up one floor, turn right at the top of the stairs and walk to the door at the end of the corridor. Go inside, sit down at the table and wait. Once you have received the text message, delete it and destroy your phone."

Before Ettore had a chance to respond, the line went dead.

The room in the featureless, backstreet building was in darkness apart from a desk light pointing straight towards the single chair where Ettore sat as instructed. The light was dazzling, but that was the point: Ettore was not expected to see the facial features of anyone else who entered the room.

After ten minutes, he was beginning to wonder if he had made a mistake when a voice pierced the darkness from beyond the lamp.

"Relax, Signor Cambroni, you were not followed, I have confirmed it." The voice was the same one he had heard on the phone the previous day, the slightest Sicilian lilt hidden under layers of refinement.

Ettore's eyes widened in shock. He had heard nothing; no door opening or closing; no breathing apart from his own. Had the man been there all the time?

He decided he should exert a little authority, not just be putty to this man. He was no novice.

"Of course I wasn't followed. I took every precaution. I—"

"You didn't spot my man, Signor Cambroni." The interruption was a calm yet authoritative statement. Not a question. "He watched you all the way from your apartment."

Ettore gulped; he had seen no one.

"Tell me everything you know about the woman you want found."

Ettore drew a deep breath. "There's not much. The police took all the records from the gallery, all the photographs, all the CCTV footage." He paused, realising how inadequate he sounded. "I only have the name she used," he continued. "Ginevra Mancini, although it must be false. She was well educated, sophisticated and she spoke with a Milanese accent. A refined one."

"Age? Height? Looks?"

The words cut critically through the air, increasing Ettore's feeling of inadequacy.

"Her documents gave her age as twenty-nine. She was about one metre seventy and she was pretty with an oval face. Her hair was dark, not long, not short. Well cut."

"Eyes? Weight?"

"Her eyes were, er, light brown, I think—"

"You think?"

"I … Yes, light brown. I am sure. She was slim; looked fit."

"Like a police officer?"

"Yes. No." Ettore paused, his head shaking. "No, she had none of the manner of a police officer. She was just … thoroughly charming. And very knowledgeable. About art, I mean." He paused again before adding, "Maria, my associate at the gallery, thought she might not have been Italian, although it never occurred to me."

"What did she think she was?"

"English; she thought she might be English. Maria has a good ear for accents, better than mine. It's just a possibility."

"It's not much to go on. Is there nothing else?"

"Not on Mancini, no. But there is someone who might know her. An American woman."

"Tell me."

For the next five minutes, Ettore repeated all he could remember about Connie Fairbright and her English companion, Diana Fritchley, the one immensely rich and charming, if somewhat guileless, the other, the English woman, cold and humourless, her lack of interest in art clear to Ettore from the first moment he met her.

When Ettore had finished speaking, the room fell quiet, the only sounds meaningless creaks and rumbles from elsewhere in the building. With nothing to interrupt his unease, Ettore thought maybe his interrogator had left, although he had heard nothing.

Then, with no warning, the man's voice shattered the silence. "I will find this Ginevra Mancini woman and kill her. How I do it is no concern of yours. It will look like an accident."

There was a pause followed by a sigh of false regret, the sigh of a man used to bargaining. "It will be an expensive mission, probably lasting several months. The price is two hundred and fifty thousand euros."

Ettore gulped. It was twice what he had expected to pay, but he felt in no position to argue.

"I agree. How do you want it paid?"

"Everything up front. Taped to the underside of the table in front of you is a piece of paper on which are written details of a bank account. You will transfer the full sum to that account in the next twenty-four hours. Once I receive notification of payment, I shall begin."

"And if you …"

"If I what? If I fail?"

"Y-yes."

"I do not fail. Once I have a photograph of Ginevra Mancini, I will contact you for confirmation that I have the right person. After that, you will hear no more until I have completed the assignment."

Ettore waited, but there was nothing more. Several minutes passed and although he sensed he was now alone, he felt he shouldn't move, not without approval. After a further five minutes, there was the clunk of a terminal switch being thrown somewhere distant, somewhere beyond the darkness. The room flooded with an intense light. Once Ettore's eyes adjusted, he saw that the room had another door beyond where he was sitting. His interrogator must have arrived and left that way.

He felt under the lip of the table for the piece of paper and carefully pulled it from where masking tape was holding it in place. He stared at the bank account details. A quarter of a million euros; he hoped it was worth it. Sighing, he turned the piece of paper over and saw a handwritten message.

You may leave.

Part Two

JENNIFER COTTON

Chapter Three

Jennifer Cotton pushed open the door to the office space in the Metropolitan Police Art Fraud Squad she shared with the three detective constables now under her command and headed towards her new desk in the corner. Only one of her three colleagues was there; the other two were in the Midlands following up enquiries at auction houses. Detective Constable Pete Whitacombe looked up from where he was sitting in front of his computer screen.

"Morning, *sarge*," he said, grinning. "Can I get you anything? Tray of cakes, real Colombian coffee? I've plumped up the cushion on your chair, just as you like it."

"Shut it, Whitacombe," snarled Jennifer, half closing her eyes and injecting a liberal dose of mock menace into her voice. "Remember who's writing your appraisals from now on."

"Couldn't be any worse than my last three," countered Whitacombe. "I'm surprised the Met still employs me."

"You and me both." Jennifer floated her most supercilious smile towards him as she plonked her bag on her desk and slipped her jacket onto the back of her chair. "From what I heard, you can count yourself lucky we have our full complement of cleaners."

"Not my skill set, sarge, you know that." He held up both hands, palms outwards. "Couldn't countenance the thought of sullying these delicate mitts with menial tasks."

"So your wife tells me. I must let her know about your cushion-plumping skills; she'll be most impressed."

"Rather you didn't. She'll accuse me of brown-nosing and she hates that sort of thing."

"Would she consider your offer of real Colombian coffee brown-nosing too? It sounds the perfect way to start the first Monday morning of my new incarnation."

Whitacombe pushed back his office chair and stood. "Your wish is my command, dear leader. I'll head off immediately to supervise the grinding of the beans."

"As long as you don't have to go to Colombia. I've got some great files to fill your day with happiness."

"No, just Coco's Coffee House round the corner. Ten minutes, tops."

"Then what are you waiting for?"

Whitacombe turned as he stopped to pull open the office door.

"By the way, Jennifer, congratulations, once again. You really deserve it; they kept you dangling for far too long."

"Thanks, Pete, appreciate it."

"Mind you," he added as he stepped through the doorway, "it's going to be hard getting used to calling you ma'am."

"Don't even thi—" began Jennifer, but she was talking to a closed door.

Smiling to herself, she sat back in her chair. Detective Sergeant Cotton. Whitacombe was right; it had taken far longer than she thought it would. She should have known that rules, procedures, exams, appraisals and review panels could be glacial in their progress even with the meritorious service awards she'd notched up.

But now she'd finally made it and she had remained in the squad. Was that a good thing? Did she really want that? She pursed her lips. At times she missed the immediacy of serious crime investigation, but she also enjoyed the cachet of being assigned to the Art Fraud Squad, of making constructive use of her broad knowledge of the art world in her daily routine.

The undercover assignment at the Cambroni Gallery in Florence had been an unusual one for the squad, one for which

Jennifer, with her fluent Italian, was uniquely qualified. It had been an outstanding success in spite of the unexpected arrival on the scene and attempt on Jennifer's life by her bête noire, the crazed ex-police officer and serial killer Olivia Freneton.

That Freneton had ended up as the victim of her own bomb was down to Jennifer's father Henry Silk's quick thinking, but Jennifer's questionable step of adding to Freneton's already fatal injuries still haunted her, in spite of her attempts to relegate it to the deepest recesses of her mind. She had taken another person's life, and even though that person was only minutes away from death, with no possibility of survival, she had still done it. Nothing had been said, although she was sure that Henry had seen her do it. How could he not?

Suspecting nothing, Massimo Felice had organised the removal and disposal of Freneton's body without the formality of a detailed autopsy. The cause of death had been obvious: multiple fatal injuries from the motorcycle accident. For Felice, maintaining Jennifer's anonymity had been far more important than any inquest. Freneton was an insane serial killer being hunted across Europe who had conveniently managed to kill herself. Game over.

Jennifer sighed, sat up and switched on her computer. Just as she did, the office door swung open and a distinctly more flustered Pete Whitacombe than the one who had left minutes earlier appeared. Jennifer frowned; he couldn't possibly have had time to fetch the coffee.

"Jennifer. Sorry, I completely forgot. Paul wants to see you. Told me to tell you that as soon as you arrive you're to go to his office."

Jennifer dropped the corners of her mouth dismissively. "Probably just wants to congratulate me."

"Could be, but he didn't look happy."

"Shit, Pete! He'll be even unhappier if he thinks I've been dilly-dallying here."

"Sorry, Jennifer."

.   .   .

Unlike the detectives' squad room, Detective Superintendent Paul Godden's office had been recently renovated with a floor-to-ceiling glass wall and glass door, the result being that unless Godden closed the blinds, he could be seen by anyone approaching his office.

As Jennifer hurried along the corridor, she saw her boss looking impatiently at his watch as he reached for his telephone. When she tapped on his door, he immediately dropped the handset back on the cradle and waved at her to come in.

"There you are, Jennifer," he said, pointing at the chair opposite him for her to sit down. "I was beginning to think something had happened to you."

"Sorry, Paul, I—"

"It doesn't matter. You're here now."

He paused, staring at the old-fashioned blotter on his desk, his eyes avoiding hers.

Jennifer waited, wary of interrupting her boss's thought processes. She was familiar with Paul Godden's meticulous ways and knew it was better to wait than ask questions, no matter how strong her urge to do so. A moment of self-doubt reared its head as she looked at Godden's deeply furrowed brow. Had her promotion been cancelled? Had they changed their minds, the powers-that-be? Could they even do that at this stage? It was true she was, in theory, acting in the rank, but that was for some stupid bureaucratic reason; it didn't impinge on the reality of the process. She had been promoted; she had the letter.

Godden coughed and looked up, now fixing his eyes on hers.

"I'm afraid that we have a problem, Jennifer, or at least I do."

"I don't understand," said Jennifer, her voice little more than a nervous whisper as the self-doubt developed legs and began to march mockingly around the office. "Is it … is it my promotion?"

Godden frowned again, this time in confusion.

"Promotion? No, it's nothing to do with that, although in my view they should have bypassed the rank of sergeant and promoted you straight to inspector."

"Can they do that?"

"In practice, no, they can't, but you know how things are. If they wanted to, they would find a way. But no, it's not about your promotion."

"Then …"

He pointed at his computer monitor. "An email from admin arrived first thing. It was waiting for me when I logged on. I had no idea they started so early." He paused. "I'm sorry, Jennifer, but you've been transferred out of the squad, as from the first of next month. Two weeks' time."

"Transferred!" Jennifer was horrified. "Why? Where?"

"Back to your old squad in Nottingham. The Serious Crime Formation. It seems that the DCS there, Peter Hawkins, heard about your promotion and made a play. He's wanted you back forever, in fact he didn't want to let you go. It was only your injuries following the first Freneton attack on you in Harlow Wood and the lengthy nature of your recovery that weakened his resolve. He saw your posting here as an extension to your convalescence."

Jennifer snorted in derision. "Cheeky bugger. Some convalescence that turned out to be; Freneton nearly bumped me off again."

"Yes, well, at least there can't be a third time, thanks to her being dead and buried. No, it seems that the long-time sergeant in the SCF is about to retire."

"Neil Bottomley?"

"Yes, Bottomley. Given that his departure creates a vacancy and the fact that you are experienced in the Formation's work, Hawkins has pulled strings. And unfortunately his strings go far deeper into the fabric of the police hierarchy than mine. As far as he's concerned, it's game, set and match."

Jennifer sat back in shock. She had not seen this coming. She had just spent the weekend in Nottingham with her long-term boyfriend Derek Thyme, a black, elite track athlete and detective constable in the SCF, and he hadn't even mentioned Neil's retirement. If he'd known anything, if he'd had the slightest inkling that Jennifer was about to become his immediate boss, he would have said something.

"I don't know what to say, Paul," she said. "Having filled your vacancy after so long, you've got to start all over again."

Godden was shaking his head. "That's the other thing that left me helpless to complain. They've completely out-manoeuvred me. It seems they've found another young DC just like you in a squad in Manchester. She's been in the force for four years and has a degree in art history. Apparently she's dead keen to transfer here, sees it as her career goal."

"Don't tell me she speaks Italian as well."

"Not Italian, no, but she is fluent in French and Russian, so …"

He raised his shoulders in submission before continuing.

"The only concession I got from on high is that if another case arises that needs your particular language skills and ingenuity as a detective, I can apply to have you temporarily transferred back for the duration of the case."

"Hmm," grunted Jennifer. "Of course, if this young superstar turns out to be a crap detective …"

From Godden's weak smile, she could see the idea was a non-starter. "By all accounts, she's excellent, as well as being extremely personable. A senior officer who will remain nameless described her as a clone of you but with two foreign languages instead of one."

"Actually, that's not correct. I speak French, Russian and German as well as Italian."

"But unlike your Italian, the other three are not native speaker level, as I recall. This young lady is a mother-tongue speaker of both her foreign languages."

"Then you shouldn't trust her. She's probably a Russian spy inserted into the British police by Putin's lot to undermine the system."

Godden laughed. "Good try, Jennifer, but her parents were dissidents in Moscow. Her mother is French and her father a Russian economics professor. They had to leave Russia in a hurry after the KGB started to flex its muscles again."

"Cover story," countered Jennifer.

"Sorry, but she's been screened at the highest level. She's kosher."

"Will I get to meet this wonder woman before I head for the sticks? By the way, what's her name?"

"Sofie Lukina. That's Sofie with an f, I'm told. And yes, you will meet her. She's arriving on Thursday, so you'll have just over a week to show her the ropes."

"Does she use ordinary methods of transportation or can I expect her to teleport into my office? And what about my post? She's not getting that as well, surely?"

"No, of course not. For the time being, Pete Whitacombe will be acting. He's got good reports, obviously not as good as yours, but he shows promise. Don't tell him I said so."

"May I say anything to him about my transfer, given it's imminent and I was about to start taking over organising the allocations."

Godden exhaled heavily. "Good point. I'd better tell him straight away. Could you send him in, please?"

"He popped out to get us both coffee from that real coffee shop round the corner. We gave up on the poison the machine on the next floor churns out a while ago. Once he learns I'm not going to be his boss after all, he'll probably charge me for it."

Chapter Four

Jennifer sat at her desk and stared at the wall on the far side of the room as she mulled over the surprise Paul Godden had just sprung on her. Transferred back to the SCF in Nottingham, her first CID posting, but as a detective sergeant. She smiled. She'd be Derek's boss, unless someone decided to transfer him as well. But knowing the big boss Pete Hawkins' tactics, she was pretty sure Derek would be staying exactly where he was.

Nevertheless, it had come out of the blue, and despite Hawkins' connections, he had chosen his moment carefully, which meant he must have been following her career far more closely than she realised.

Although she had no real choice in the matter, given she wasn't married and had no family considerations that might be grounds to object to a posting, she thought through the pros and cons and decided the time was right to move. She had enjoyed her time in the Art Fraud Squad, but it was a small team with limited career prospects for its staff. The two inspectors had years of service ahead of them, as did Paul Godden, and Jennifer certainly didn't want to remain a sergeant for the rest of her career. In addition, opportunities such as the one that saw her working undercover in Florence were rare. For much of the rest of the time, the work, although fascinating, hardly stretched her as a detective.

And if she were really honest with herself, she would have to admit that after every trip back to her apartment in the smart residential district of The Park in Nottingham, she was increasingly reluctant to leave and return to the bustle of London, even though for most of the time she had the luxury of having her father's house in Hampstead to herself. No, it would be good to be back, good to spend more time with Derek.

Her thoughts turned to the young DC who would be making up the numbers in the Art Fraud Squad. "Let's see what we can find out about you, Sofie with an f," she said, as she keyed a set of instructions into her computer.

She knew many of the personnel listings for the various police forces were confidential, especially to officers at her level. Her own name, for instance, was simply listed against her rank, but no personal or posting details and not even a photograph were shown. The Art Fraud Squad rated anonymity an important factor in its work. However, for less sensitive postings, more details were sometimes listed.

She clicked on the Greater Manchester force, went to CID, and typed Sofie Lukina into the search. To her surprise, the information was as scant as her own, with only Lukina's rank listed against her name. There was no posting data and no photograph. So either she was already in a sensitive job or personnel had been unusually efficient and removed her details ahead of her transfer.

She closed the screen, drumming her fingers on the desk. She had no direct contacts in the Manchester area, but she did know someone who had transferred from there two years before. It was unlikely her close friend Detective Superintendent Trisha McVie would have come across Lukina directly, but she might know someone who had. She reached for her phone and dialled a number.

"McVie." The tone was no nonsense but without the irritation that so many senior officers injected into their voices, as if the caller were interrupting something of national importance.

"Trish. Hi, it's Jennifer. Have you got a moment?"

"For you, Detective Sergeant, on your first day in command, of course. I've just sent an assistant commissioner off with a flea up his backside, so I'm all ears. How's it all going in the dark and mysterious world of art fraud?"

Jennifer laughed. It was always refreshing to talk to Trisha. She was always upbeat, always positive in spite of her inability to stay in a relationship for more than a few months. When their paths had first crossed soon after Trisha's transfer to the Met nearly two years before, even with the difference in their ages and ranks, they had immediately bonded. Cotton had quickly become Jennifer, and out of the office environment, ma'am became Trish.

It was a mutual love of art that initially set the two women on a path to friendship. Trish was passionate about paintings and sculpture, with a particular interest in the nineteenth century, but now, thanks to Jennifer, her passion had expanded to include Renaissance art.

"Turned out to be the shortest command on record, I reckon," replied Jennifer.

"Why? What's happened?"

"Well, the first ten minutes were up to expectation, but then I was told I've been transferred out, back to regular CID."

"What! You must be joking. What the hell do they think they're up to? They can't mess you around like that. You should complain to the union rep. Where are you going? I've made it perfectly clear to those who control these things that if you ever get moved anywhere, it will be to my squad. It's been promised, for Christ's sake. Bloody hell, Jennifer, I didn't see that coming. I'll be having words."

"I didn't see it coming either, not a hint, but despite it being a kind of weird thing to do, I'm not too dismayed."

"Really? Why? Where the hell are you going? I hope it's not out of London; our girls' nights out are far too important."

"I'm going back to my old squad in Nottingham, the SCF. Pete Hawkins, the DCS there, planned the whole thing, pulling rank and connections on Paul in the process."

"Nottingham? Well, it could be worse, but it'll be a bit of a schlep when I need a shoulder to cry on the next time my love life falls apart, which, incidentally, I think it's about to once again. And

I'll miss getting pissed with you in Henry Silk's magnificent mansion."

"Ah-ah!" Jennifer was shaking her head. "No way. There'll always be Hampstead, I promise you. Henry's even started ordering your favourite vintages."

"God, I love that man. Why is he so fond of that billionairess when he could have all that I can offer him? You know, impossible work schedules, dates called off at the last minute, interruptions in the middle of the night to leave his bed for some grimy scene. I mean, her life is so boringly predictable."

"I can't imagine you as my stepmother, Trish."

"Don't tell me he's marrying her! I like to think I still have a chance."

"Not that I know of, no, but they seem pretty together."

"I know. I'm not jealous or anything, as you can probably tell from the sound of grinding teeth. When are you off? Not today, I hope. We've got to have a swansong bender somewhere."

"You're a bad influence, detective superintendent, I'm supposed to be getting fit for a half-marathon."

"Christ, you're so fit, you could run it right now."

"Maybe, but you're not, and we are running it together, if you remember."

"No problem, as long as you don't mind carrying me for at least half the course."

"Only half? You must have been secretly training."

"Watch your lip, detective sergeant! Anyway, you didn't answer my question. When are you off?"

"Not until the end of next week. There's a young DC replacing me who's reporting for duty here on Thursday. Actually, she's partly why I called. I was wondering if you know her or know someone who might. She's rather intriguing."

"Mmm, I don't know too many DCs outside of my own lot. Plus a few from my Manchester days."

"It was those days I was thinking of. She's currently posted to a CID unit somewhere in Manchester, but I don't know where. She's pretty young, but I think she's been there long enough to have over-lapped with you."

"What's her name?"

"Sofie Lukina. Sofie with an f."

"Lukina? That's an unusual name. You know, I think it rings a bell."

"It's Russian."

"Russian! We're employing Russians now?"

"Russian father, French mother. Fled here as dissidents."

"Really? And I think I have a hard time. We don't know we're born, Jennifer. How old is this young woman?"

"Not sure. Mid- to late-twenties, I think."

"With an unusual name like that, I shouldn't have much difficulty tracking her down. I'll call you back. But it will cost you."

"2008 Premier Cru?"

"Smooth-talking bitch. You knew one mention of that and I'd be putty in your hands."

"Thanks, Trish."

"Call you back later. Oh, God, the assistant commissioner's hovering again. Must want his hair shirt changing for something rougher. Where did I put that horse whip?"

Ten minutes later, Jennifer was still smiling to herself about her conversation with Trish when a bewildered Pete Whitacombe came into the office carrying two take-away coffees in Coco Coffee House's own reusable china mugs.

"These are fresh ones, Jennifer, I went to get some more. The others I got earlier went cold."

"Thanks, Pete. You didn't buy new mugs, did you? We've got quite a collection sitting in the cupboard. Any more and we can have a car boot sale."

"I know. I keep forgetting to take them with me, but I'd prefer to buy new ones than use the disposable plastic ones."

Jennifer pursed her lips, not convinced of the logic. However, she was grateful for the coffee.

Pete placed both mugs on Jennifer's desk and turned around to grab a chair.

"What's this sudden posting all about?" he said, sitting down to face her. "I just don't get it. For one moment, a very brief one, you're this unit's sarge, and the next, I'm acting and you're off to the Midlands. Did Paul wake up this morning with this week's great idea or is it something that's been brewing for a while?"

Jennifer picked up her coffee and took a tentative sip. "Wow, that's hot!" she said, and put the mug down again. She pulled a face. "You know, Pete, I think this whole thing blindsided Paul as much as it has us. I trust him; I don't think he's playing some daft game. No, it's Pete Hawkins, the DCS in Nottingham who's engineered everything. Did Paul tell you about my replacement?"

"Sofie Lukina? Yes. Said she'll be approaching your standard once she's learned the ropes. Do you know anything about her?"

"No, but I'm on to it. I have my faithful superintendent at Scotland Yard on the case. She'll be calling me back soon."

As if on cue, the phone on Jennifer's desk rang.

She smiled. "That could be her now."

Chapter Five

Jennifer lifted her phone's handset.

"Cotton."

"You know, your surname, stated like that, always sounds like a secret password I'm supposed to reply to with something equally obscure," announced Trish.

"It is. You're supposed to say, 'Egyptian or Indian?' and then I say, 'What took you so long? It's been all of ten minutes since you set off on your quest for information'."

"Yes, *sooo* sorry about the delay, but after extensive research involving half the Manchester Constabulary, I think I've got the answers you need."

"I'm impressed. What have you found?"

"Well, what you've been told already is correct: she's a clever girl who's impressed her bosses. Contributed some excellent input in a couple of difficult cases, but apparently she's dead keen on joining your lot. Can't think why, given it's such a dead-end job with none of the excitement of regular CID work. I mean, when was the last time you had to risk your neck undercover to expose some shady art dealer?"

"Confidential information, even at your level, ma'am, I'm sorry to tell you."

Jennifer smiled to herself at the look of incredulity on Pete Whitacombe's face as he listened in on the conversation.

Trish ignored her remark and continued. "Ticks all the boxes and apparently she's far less lippy than the bird she's replacing in your squad."

"Sounds too perfect to me; I still reckon she's some kind of Mata Hari, but I'm confident she'll break under my subtle interrogation. A week will be more than enough."

"Her mug shot is on its way to me. I'll send it over as soon as it arrives."

The following Thursday morning, Jennifer was fifteen minutes early when she walked into the high-rise in Canary Wharf that was home to the Art Fraud Squad. She wanted to be ready and waiting in the office to greet DC Lukina. However, after passing through security and heading towards the lifts, she saw a woman of about the right age and build ahead of her waiting in the lift lobby. Jennifer looked at the woman's reflection in the wide stainless steel panels surrounding the lift doors and recognised Lukina's face from the photo Trish had sent her.

She stood back to cast her eye over the new DC while they waited. Lukina was about an inch shorter than her, allowing for a slight difference in the heels of their shoes. She was slim and had the relaxed stance of someone who trained regularly, while her hair, shorter and a lighter brown than Jennifer's, was well cut and augmented with a few highlights. Tailored black trousers, an expensive-looking brown leather jacket and the long strap of her bag slung casually over her shoulder all gave the impression of a young, outgoing executive or media type rather than a police officer. She would blend in well in many of the situations in which the squad members found themselves. From Lukina's overall poise, Jennifer felt that here was a young woman who hadn't just dressed up for the day to impress her new boss and colleagues; there was money behind her, over and above a detective constable's pay. With a film star father and a stepfather who was an internationally famous fashion designer, Jennifer herself was in a similar situation and she looked forward to finding out more about her new short-term colleague.

By the time the bell pinged to announce the arrival of the lift, two other people had joined them. When they walked in, Jennifer moved to the back of the car, noticing that Lukina did the same and was now standing to her right. One passenger got out on the third floor while the second left on the fifth. As the doors opened on the sixth floor, both women walked forward. Jennifer turned her head and smiled.

"I think you must be DC Lukina," she said, and held out her hand. "DS Cotton," she added. "Jennifer."

Sofie Lukina's eyes smiled warmly along with her mouth as she took Jennifer's hand.

"I'm delighted to meet you, er … is it all first names here?"

Jennifer nodded. "In the Art Fraud Squad, yes, unless you're on the carpet for something. It makes for a good working relationship in a small team."

Lukina shook Jennifer's hand. "Sofie," she said, letting go and reaching to block the doors that were now threatening to close. "Whoops!"

She held the door back for Jennifer who exited the lift ahead of her.

"I'm pleased to meet you too, Sofie. Welcome to the squad. The others should arrive over the next ten or fifteen minutes. Paul is pretty relaxed as a boss, but he is something of a stickler for punctuality."

"I'm pleased to hear he's relaxed; I was concerned that I've been thrust upon him against his wishes. I mean, I applied for a transfer to the squad ages ago, but I was told that vacancies are few. So it was a bit of a shock last week to be informed that I was moving."

"Well, it could be serendipitous in that we all get what we want, although I must admit it's sooner than expected."

"I don't understand."

"As so often happens in the force, it's a game of musical postings, and if whoever is controlling the music gets it right, no one's nose is put too much out of joint."

She caught Sofie's still-puzzled expression as she pushed open the door to their office.

"Here we are," she said. "Home sweet home. Your desk is over there, for the time being, at least." She pointed to a corner away from the row of windows.

"For the time being?"

"Yes. Once he takes over on Monday week, Pete might want to juggle things."

"But I thought you were the sarge; that I'd be working for you."

"You are until Friday of next week, then I'm off to Nottingham." Jennifer paused and laughed. "This whole thing started because my old boss in the SCF in Nottingham, who it turns out is a DCS with a far longer reach than I ever imagined, wanted me back. He plotted and planned and then sprung his scheme, for which you proved to be a perfect find. With your qualifications, no one could object."

"Oh, well, that's all very flattering, but I was hoping to learn from you."

"You'll learn plenty from the others; they've got years of experience and I know they'll be supportive. They're good guys, believe me, and Paul's a caring boss." She stopped and put her bag on her desk before turning back to Sofie. "You don't look convinced."

Sofie shrugged. "I suppose I was looking forward to working with a like-minded woman. The force is still very male-oriented and from what I've heard about you, I just knew we'd get on."

"Tell you what, after a year or two, if you've had enough and want to go back to nitty-gritty CID work, you could always apply to join me in Nottingham."

"You think I'll have had enough after two years? I was thinking of it more as a long-term posting."

"It might well be, and good luck if it is. I'm just saying, that's all. I know when I started, I felt a bit like that, and my first assignment couldn't have been more exciting. But that was exceptional. A lot of the work is routine, although you do get up close and personal with a lot of really amazing art. Some days when I've been doing that, I've had to pinch myself, unable to believe my luck that someone was actually paying me to do it."

Sofie moved over to her desk, hung her jacket on the chair, took a deep breath and turned back to Jennifer, smiling. "I can't believe I'm here. Two weeks ago, I had no inkling."

"Nor me, I can tell you. However, if you want a bit of female company to let off steam with outside the office, I've got a friend on the force who's totally into art. I'll introduce you to her. In fact, you might have heard of her; she used to work in Manchester. Trisha McVie."

"Detective Superintendent Trisha McVie?"

"The very same. She works over in the Yard, but she's always looking for excuses to sniff around here. We get on really well; in fact, she's become a great friend. And outside of work, she's a total pisshead. We've had some great nights out."

"A DC, oh sorry, a DS and D Super? Unusual."

"Yeah, it is a bit. But it's probably because we're women up against the fellas. I doubt there are many equivalent male friend-ships. Not at our sort of age, anyway."

"How old is she?"

"Nudging forty and something of a high-flyer, in that she's already been a super for four years."

Sofie eyed the large pile of files on Jennifer's desk. "What about cases? Are you busy at the moment?"

"Oh, yes, we're always busy. And there's some good meat among this lot. I'll—"

She paused as the phone on her desk rang.

"I'll bet that's Paul wanting to meet you."

She picked up the receiver, listened and grinned towards Sofie.

"OK, Paul, I'll bring her through."

After almost two days of showing Sofie the ropes and observing how at ease she was in dealing with people, Jennifer felt confident that her replacement would fit in perfectly. The two got on well and Jennifer was already regretting that she wouldn't get much chance see Sofie in action as a police officer.

With Pete Whitacombe tied up in the law courts, waiting his turn to give evidence in a case involving a team of scammers who had been working several galleries, and the other two DCs still in the Midlands, Jennifer and Sofie were alone in the office. Jennifer had more or less finished her notes on the files she would be handing over to Pete and she looked up at her new colleague. So far, she had kept their conversation on a professional level, but now she wanted to learn a little more about DC Lukina.

"How's the hotel, Sofie? I forgot to ask with Pete getting a fit of nerves about his court appearance. Presumably you're at the Ibis down the road we've all been in at one time or another?"

Sofie closed the file she'd been reading and sat back in her chair. "No, I didn't use the hotel; there didn't seem much point. My parents live in Chelsea and it's an easy commute. They are delighted to have me back home, but I think I'll be looking for a place of my own pretty soon."

"Don't you get on with them?"

"We get on fine. They're lovely, but always busy with their work. And I've been used to my own independence for a long time now, so I don't want to return to the nest. I think it would soon cramp my style."

"Chelsea must be nice, though. What's the work that keeps them so busy?"

"They're both academics. My dad is an economics and politics professor and my mum has a chair in applied linguistics."

"Hence the languages I've been told you speak?"

"Partly, yes, but my dad is Russian and always insisted I speak it as much as possible at home, while my mum is French, and was also insistent that she got her time too. No sooner was I back than we were having these ridiculous three- or four-language conversations, none of the languages being English."

"Surprised your English is so good then," said Jennifer, laughing.

"What about you?" asked Sofie. "You're fluent in Italian, aren't you? How did that happen?"

Jennifer smiled. "Long story, but basically I was brought up in Milan by my mother and stepfather. Then, well, since you are now part of the squad, you'll probably hear bits and pieces of this from the others even though it's confidential. So please, what I'm about to say doesn't go beyond these walls. OK?"

Sofie nodded. "Of course. It sounds intriguing."

Jennifer pursed her lips. "Not so much intriguing as an attempt to keep the press at bay and also to help me retain my usefulness should I go undercover again. I'll keep it short. A few years ago, soon after I started with the SCF in Nottingham, I arrested a famous actor for murder who turned out not only to be innocent but also to be my real father. Of course, I didn't know the second part when I arrested him. In fact, I didn't believe a word of it until a DNA test proved it."

"Wow! Who is he, this actor? Will I have heard of him?"

"Probably; he's become pretty popular in the last few years. It's Henry Silk."

"Heavens, that certainly has been kept quiet. I'd no inkling of any connection."

"We try to keep it that way."

"I remember him being arrested and then exonerated. Do you get on with your newly discovered father?"

"Yes, brilliantly. He's amazing, not at all like the TV persona he once had, or the tough-guy type that Hollywood tends to make him. I'm lucky since I also get on with my stepdad in Italy. And Henry has this great house in Hampstead he seldom uses, where I've been living."

She paused to tidy the pile of already tidy files on her desk.

"In fact, are you doing anything this evening? Trish McVie is coming round, no doubt to cry on my shoulder about the state of her love life, but also probably to fling theories around about her latest case. I'd like you to meet her; I know the two of you would get on. If you'd like to join us, Hampstead isn't too far from Chelsea, and if you want to stay, there's plenty of space. Trish often stays over rather than being found drunk in charge of a pair of high heels."

"That would be brilliant, thanks, I'd love to. Can I bring something?"

"Don't even think about it. We're slowly working our way through Henry's wine cellar, which is difficult since he keeps replenishing it. I thought that since it's the weekend, you might be off seeing a boyfriend or something."

Amused by the unsubtle fishing, Sofie laughed. "No. I'm between relationships at the moment, as they say. Actually, it's difficult. As soon as men find out I'm a police officer and that I speak Russian, they get the wind up. Think I'm a secret agent."

"Whereas we, of course, *know* you are."

"Bugger it, rumbled by Cotton of the Yard," muttered Sofie in fast Russian.

"I was on to you from the outset, comrade," replied Jennifer, her Russian almost as fast. "Jenniva Godunova is nobody's fool."

"Molto impressionante, signorina," countered Sofie.

Jennifer raised her eyebrows. "Italian too, DC Lukina?"

Sofie's eyes flashed in amusement. "I went out with a junior diplomat from the Italian embassy for a while who insisted on trying to teach me his-a beautiful-a langer-widge."

Chapter Six

At nine o'clock that evening, Jennifer was opening a second bottle of a vintage French red she had fetched from the climate-controlled basement beneath the kitchen in Henry Silk's house. Sofie had arrived an hour earlier with a selection of cheeses, salami and rice crackers, ignoring Jennifer's insistence that she bring nothing. Trisha had bustled in half an hour later muttering darkly about an unscheduled briefing her DCS had demanded regarding a gruesome double murder for which she was the senior investigating officer.

"The pwess won't stop pestewing me, Twisha," she mimicked in a gross exaggeration of her boss's speech defect. "That wetched senior weporter fwom the Guardian seems to think that one favouwable article about the Yard and we're beholden to her."

"I can sympathise with him," said Jennifer, laughing, "Paul is forever fobbing off reporters with long explanations that say nothing. He's very good at it, but it must be wearing."

"Wery wearing, dahling," sniggered Trisha. "Sorry, Sofie, we're not here to talk shop, at least not for the first five minutes. How are you settling in?"

"Er, fine, thank you ... Trish. Sorry, it seems odd addressing senior officers by their first name. It didn't really happen where I was in Manchester."

"It's simple, Sofie. Here, I'm not a senior officer; I'm just a friend, and I can assure you, I value evenings like these immensely. If your career takes you up through the ranks, believe me, the kudos is all very well, but friends can become thin on the ground. You'll find many of those from years ago change when they get married, have kids, pets, go through messy divorces and so on, and as soon as they meet you, they just moan on about speeding tickets like they expect you to have them all cancelled. In avoiding them, it can be all too easy to get stuck with a group of mainly male senior officers, the joy of whose company socially is right up there with haemorrhoids.

"Finding Jennifer and I had a common love of art was brilliant and then finding out we were in many ways kindred spirits and got along like the proverbial blazing house was icing on the cake. Of course, her old man having one of the best wine cellars in Hampstead adds a little value too."

She raised her glass to them both. "Here's to art and to Hollywood."

"Mind you," she added, the corners of her mouth dropping, "every silver lining has a cloud trying its best to shred it. Jennifer has been dragging herself back to Nottingham almost every weekend for months to see her gorgeous hunk of muscle-bound boyfriend, and now she's moving there permanently. I can't think what he sees in her."

She stopped and eyeballed Sofie, her face serious. "I suppose there's a Mr Right lurking in your life, too, Sofie. You're too much like Jennifer here for there not to be. God, this is so depressing." She took a theatrically large slurp of her wine.

"Actually," laughed Sofie, almost spilling her own wine, "there's no one in my life. Not at the moment, and there hasn't been for a few months. I don't seem to have the time."

"You mean half the Manchester force wasn't queuing at your desk wanting to have their evil way with you?"

"Is that what they were after? And there was I thinking they wanted to practise their French. No, I'm sorry to say that they were a nice enough bunch, salt of the earth and all that, but I didn't fancy any of them. In fact, with all due respect," she added, glancing at Jennifer, "I don't think I want a relationship with another cop. We'd talk about nothing but work."

"Not true!" objected Jennifer. "We talk about lots of things apart from work. Like working out, marathons, iron man. Even art, on rare occasions."

"It's not the talking that interests me," growled Trisha, "and all that other stuff sounds far too knackering. But here's to you, Sofie, you seem pretty grounded." She raised her glass again.

Jennifer reached for the bottle to top everyone up. "Talking of relationships, how are things going with, er, what was his name, Trish? Steven?"

Trish took another large swig. "Lurching along. Usual mixture of sex and slanging matches. He's sweetness and light until he's had a few, then the inner demons get the better of him. I think it's only because he knows I excel in unarmed combat that he keeps his fists to himself."

"So hardly the man of your dreams."

"No, but he's got plenty of money so we get to some pretty fancy restaurants, and he's talking about a cruise on his boat in the Greek islands. Maybe I'll kick him overboard and sail away into the azure-blue yonder."

"Self-made man?" asked Sofie.

"Now, now, DC Lukina, your CID antennae are showing," said Trish, waving an index finger at her.

Sofie laughed. "Can't be too careful. One of the DCs in my squad in Manchester almost found herself the equivalent of a gangster's moll. Fortunately for her, when he was busted, her particular gangster did the honourable thing and kept quiet about their relationship."

"You're right, of course, Sofie," said Trish, "but in Steven's case, it's old family money." She paused and gave them a mischievous grin. "Although I have to confess I ran a surreptitious check on him just to make sure there was nothing dodgy going on."

Sofie stood up from the bar stool where she was sitting. "Where's the nearest loo, Jennifer?"

Jennifer pointed through the door. "Down the hallway and on the left, just before the front door."

Trish watched her go. "Seems like a nice kid," she said to Jennifer once Sofie was out of earshot. "Do you reckon she'll fit in well in your squad?"

"My soon-to-be ex-squad, you mean," replied Jennifer, pulling a face. "Yes, I do. She's enthusiastic, clever and from our discussions over the last couple of days, she knows her stuff. You seemed to have clicked with her, too. Funny how quickly you can tell, don't you think?"

"Yes, I think she might be a good carousing partner when you're stuck up in the darkest Midlands. I—"

She was interrupted by a loud yell from Sofie in the hallway. "Jennifer!"

This was followed immediately by an equally loud shout, but this time it was a man's voice. "For Christ's sake!"

Jennifer and Trish's heads shot round.

"Henry?" they both said, and ran for the door.

About halfway along the hallway, they skidded to a halt, roaring with laughter as the wine got the better of them.

Ahead of them by the front door, Sofie had Henry Silk pinned against the wall in an armlock.

"Jennifer," she panted, "I came out of the loo and walked straight into this burglar strolling in like he owns the place. Do you have any handcuffs?"

"It's all right, Sofie," called Jennifer as she wiped her eyes with the back of a hand, "you can let him go. He *does* own the place."

"What!" squealed Sofie as she released Henry's arm and jumped backwards. "Oh my God, I'm so sorry. You took me by surprise and I just reacted automatically."

"I'm glad the British police don't carry guns," said Henry ruefully as he rubbed his arm. "In the US they'd be calling the coroner's meat wagon by now to cart me away. I take it you're a plod like these two?"

"Yes, I … oh, gosh, I'm so sorry. Have I hurt you?" She reached out to take his arm, but Henry waved her away.

"It's fine, don't worry. I'm pleased to find my house is in safe hands." He held out his right hand. "Henry Silk, I don't think we've met."

"Sofie, Sofie Lukina. Are you sure you're all right?"

"Nothing a glass of wine won't cure, assuming those two giggling soaks haven't drunk me out of house and home."

"Henry!" cried Jennifer, finally getting herself under control. She rushed along the hallway and threw her arms around him. "What a lovely surprise. What are you doing here?"

Henry gave her a squeeze and held her out at arm's length.

"I've got a break in filming and Connie's tied up over some business thing with her team of accountants. Reckoned it would take all weekend, so I borrowed the Fairbright bus to pop over and surprise you."

"How did you know I'd be here and not in Nottingham?"

"A certain DC Thyme spilled the beans. We're in cahoots, you know; we have your every move charted."

"I must have words," said Jennifer. "Can't have my junior officers giving out confidential information." She took him by the hand. "Come on, we're just about to eat. Are you hungry or did you have Connie's cordon bleu chef on board?"

"No, it's his weekend off. There were only sandwiches, so I'm starving."

"Hello, Trish," he added as Jennifer marched him past her. "How are you? It's been ages." He stopped to give her a hug.

"All the better for seeing you, Henry, my dear heart-throb. Didn't bring any of your young supporting actors with you, I suppose?"

"'Fraid not, Trish, you'll just have to keep drinking."

Twenty minutes later, they were all seated around Henry's dining table enjoying Sofie's cheese and biscuits along with some salami, prosciutto and tomatoes Jennifer had extracted from the fridge. Henry had insisted they eat at the table rather than the large island unit in the kitchen, claiming that after a long flight, he felt the need to stretch and be civilised.

Henry's current favourite soprano, Pretty Yende, was entertaining them in the background, but most of her exquisite high notes were lost as the conversation danced around the table.

Jennifer had brought her father up to date with her new posting and was now explaining Sofie's transfer to the Art Fraud Squad. When Sofie mentioned her parents, it turned out Henry had met them at a gala reception in LA the previous autumn.

"I remember them so well," he said. "Your father and I were both crying on each other's shoulders about the loss of our beloved daughters to the grimy world of crime investigation. He must be delighted that you're moving into something more cerebral."

"There's nothing cerebral about forgers in backstreet workshops churning out fakes, Henry," chided Jennifer. "They are still criminals."

"I thought you were quite taken by that young man at the gallery in Florence," said Henry.

She smiled. "Tonino Varinello. Yes, he was great eye-candy and a brilliant artist. His forgeries were superb."

"Where is he now, this Adonis with a paintbrush?" asked Trish, her eyes flashing interest.

"Still serving time, I'm afraid," replied Jennifer. "He got a reduced sentence, thanks to Massimo Felice pulling some strings, but I think he's still inside. Anyway, Trish, he wasn't your type."

"You don't know everything about me, Jennifer Cotton. There might have been a hidden spark too subtle for you to see."

"I'll get word to his boyfriend and ask him what he thinks, if you like. He's a lovely lad who's waiting patiently for Tonino to get out."

"Bugger," said Trish.

"Exactly," giggled Jennifer.

Trisha sighed with exaggerated despondency and turned to Henry. "How's the lovely Connie?" she asked.

"She's in great form, thanks. Sends her love," said Henry, a slight hesitancy in his voice. He flashed a glance of concern at Jennifer.

Jennifer smiled as she tilted her head towards Sofie. "It's OK, father dear," she said. "Sofie has been inducted into the inner circle. She knows about you and me and is sworn to secrecy. She might as well know about Connie, too."

Sofie held up both hands. "There's no need to tell me anything if it's sensitive," she protested.

"No problem, Sofie," replied Henry. "As part of the Art Fraud Squad, I'm sure it will be included in your briefing. Connie and I are, I suppose you'd use the phrase 'an item'."

"An item!" chortled Jennifer. "I prefer Connie's description."

"OK," said Henry, reddening slightly. "Connie prefers the word 'lovers'."

Sofie clapped her hands. "How delightful!" she cried. "That's so romantic."

"Hmm," grumbled Henry, feeling outwitted by the three women. "Anyway, we keep it quiet. Connie's obsessive about her privacy and being linked to someone like me can rather swing the spotlight on you, if you know what I mean. The press can be relentless."

"I'm sure they can," agreed Sofie. "But surely a girl would enjoy the kudos? I know I would."

"Hey, DC Lukina. Back off!" barked Trisha, but her eyes betrayed her amusement. "There's a pecking order for those making a play for the attentions of this here film star, and I'm at the front of the queue. And anyway, you'll need to be more subtle than that."

It was Sofie's turn to blush. "That's not what I meant," she mumbled.

Jennifer laughed and reached out to touch her arm. "It's just that Connie's loaded, lucky lady, but wealth can bring its own problems, especially if you're not the socialite sort, which she certainly isn't. She's far too sincere."

Sofie was nodding, having thought through the conversation. "So the Fairbright bus is, what? A private jet?"

Henry nodded.

"Connie Fairbright," continued Sofie. "My parents have mentioned her, or at least my dad has. I think they've met. Something to do with a charitable foundation."

"Small world," said Henry, "but that sounds about right; Connie's involved with so many of them, I can't keep up. She has a whole team devoted exclusively to charity work. Anyway, perhaps you can understand why we prefer to remain under the radar."

"Definitely," agreed Sofie.

The following morning at eight, Sofie shuffled into the kitchen to find Jennifer sniggering over a note she was reading. As she looked up, she pulled a face in sympathy.

"Oh dear, DC Lukina, you look a little delicate. Is all that drumming coming from your head?"

Sofie grimaced. "Massed marching bands. An endless parade of them."

"Paracetamol?"

"Just water, thanks," said Sofie, reaching for the fridge door.

"Actually the stuff out of the tap is fine," said Jennifer, nodding towards the sink. "It's not the usual London poison, loaded up with all the chemicals the government thinks are good for us. It's been filtered, resin-exchanged and purified to within an inch of its life and is now on a par with the best of mountain springs."

Sofie ran the cold tap, filled a glass and drank it down. She nodded in approval as she refilled it.

"Impressive. From a different universe. The stuff that emerges from my parent's taps is so full of chlorine it's like drinking swimming pool water, which is why I'm forced into buying bottles."

Jennifer waved the note at her. "Trish sends her love. Apparently, there was a development in her case overnight, so she had to leave early for the office. If her head's like yours this morning, I pity anyone who comes within biting range, junior or senior. She doesn't take prisoners unless they're bad guys."

Sofie swallowed down her third glass of water. "The other face of Detective Superintendent McVie, eh?"

"Yes, when she switches into professional cop mode, you wouldn't recognise her. She keeps threatening to have me drafted onto her team, but I'm not sure how it would affect the dynamics of our friendship. That's one reason I'm pleased about my move to Nottingham; I'll be beyond her reach for the time being."

"Do you know the D Super in the squad you're moving to?"

"Hugh Gregson? Yes. Well, I've met him. Jovial, but far too overweight for his own good. Derek says he's a great boss. He came in to fill the void left by Freneton and the SCF is now a far happier place. She was a tyrant, even ignoring her serial killer proclivities."

Sofie walked over to the island unit where Jennifer was standing and sat on a bar stool.

"Jennifer, thanks so much for a wonderful evening. I hope I wasn't slurring too much by the end. It's lovely of you to welcome me so warmly and of course to meet your amazing dad. Connie Fairbright is a lucky lady."

Jennifer's smile was warm. "It was fun and I'm delighted you and Trish have hit it off. I need someone to keep an eye on the human, more vulnerable Trish when I'm not around. And, yes, Connie is lucky, but she's a pretty special lady herself. So unaffected by her vast wealth. I've met a lot of super-rich types through my work with the Art Fraud squad and none of them was as grounded as Connie."

"Do you have any plans while Henry's here?" asked Sofie. "Oh, I forgot, you can't go anywhere together, can you?"

Jennifer's raised her eyebrows in amusement. "You're right. Jennifer Cotton and Henry Silk are not seen together in public. But Jennifer Cotton and her favourite uncle Erasmus, well, that's altogether different. There's nothing to stop them heading off to an exhibition at the V&A, say, if they wish to. Nothing at all."

"Erasmus!" Sofie clamped a hand to her mouth. The name had come out louder than she intended.

"Did somebody call?"

Sofie's head shot round in time to see a man in his mid-to-late sixties walk into the kitchen. She gasped. She knew instantly it was Henry, even though all the visual clues her eyes were feeding her told her otherwise. This man seemed not only shorter and more rotund but also his whole bearing was the antithesis of Henry's. At that moment, it occurred to Sofie that acting was far more than speaking lines with conviction; this man was playing the part with every fibre of his body and yet doing it so naturally that the illusion was perfect.

Jennifer laughed at the look of confusion on Sofie's face.

"Sofie, meet Uncle Erasmus. He flew in with Henry last night, but Henry keeps him hidden in his suitcase."

"Mean bastard at the best of times," muttered Uncle Erasmus.

Sofie laughed in delight. "What a brilliant performance. Even your voice has changed completely."

Erasmus leaned his head towards Jennifer. "What's the girl talking about, young Jennifer?"

"No idea, Uncle Razzy. She's seems confused."

Erasmus stood up straighter and transformed physically, if not visually, back into Henry.

"Pleased to know I'm not losing my touch, Sofie. Can't afford to be complacent."

"I'd love to have some lessons for when I'm working undercover," said Sofie.

"Hmm," replied Henry, pulling a doubtful face. "A few years at RADA, a few more working rep, films and TV, plus an innate, God-given talent. Shouldn't be a problem, Sofie."

"Be sure to keep working on the modesty, too," cautioned Jennifer.

"Overrated, dear daughter. Now, get a move on. It takes your old uncle a bit longer to get around than his sprightly brother."

Chapter Seven

For Jennifer, returning to the Serious Crime Formation was bittersweet. When she walked into the squad room with Derek on her first Monday morning, the team of DCs and civilian officers gathered around to welcome her and escort her to an empty desk next to Neil Bottomley's. Neil, reluctant to retire after so many years, had stretched out his time to the limit and was due to leave in three months.

"Not quite ready to give up my desk, lass," he said, "even though there's no one else I'd rather give it to."

"I can wait, sarge," she said, automatically addressing him as she always had.

"It's no longer sarge, lass, not now you've begun moving up the ladder, and especially after everything we went through together in the name of crime detection."

Jennifer's smile was tinged with sadness. "I know, but I reckon I'll always think of you as sarge."

She looked around the room. "Looks much the same as it did three years ago, just a few different faces." She could almost hear echoes of DI Rob McPherson's gruff Scottish growl. She shuddered briefly before smiling at the assembled group.

"Yes," said Bottomley, checking his watch. "And as usual, there's one missing. It used to be Thyme here who was always almost late. We didn't call you Justin for nothing, laddie, before

Jennifer here took you in hand," — he shook his head in weary resignation as he nodded at Derek — "but you had nothing on DC Brooke. If his surname was Thyme, we'd be calling him 'Never On'."

There was a general muttering of amused agreement, at which point the door to the squad room flew open and DC Gus Brooke marched in, seemingly oblivious to his situation until he saw that all eyes were on him.

He paused mid-stride. "Er, morning everyone," he said, trying to sound casual. "Sarge," he added, his eyes finding Bottomley's. "Sorry to be late. Bloody car let me down again. Took ages to start." He lifted his shoulders and pulled a face.

"Time you got it sorted, laddie. If that pile of junk you call a car lets you down on the way to a call-out, you're going to find yourself in big trouble. Anyway, it won't be my problem for much longer. Let me introduce you to your new boss. DS Cotton, this is DC Brooke."

"Great to meet you at last, er, sarge," said Brooke to Jennifer, a half-smile on his lips as his eyes fixed on hers. "Derek's told me all, er, mentioned you, of course."

"You too," replied Jennifer, hoping her answer was suitably ambiguous. "It's Gus, isn't it?"

"Yes, sarge, it is," he replied, tilting his head in an obvious expectation that Jennifer would offer her first name. She didn't. Derek had already briefed her on the new office Romeo. She could understand why he thought himself something of a catch: he was good looking in a muscular, rugby-playing way, and at around six two, the same height as Derek. His vivid green-blue eyes, almost aquamarine, sparkled as he continued to look into hers. *I hope his wife keeps him on a short rein,* she thought. Looks could be deceptive, she knew, but even without Derek's heads-up, her antennae would have been sending out warning beeps.

"Anyway," said Jennifer, glancing around the group. "Don't let me keep you. I think I should report to the big bosses."

"Quite right, DS Cotton, so you should," boomed a voice from behind her. "Come on, let's go through to my office."

Jennifer turned, smiling as DCS Pete Hawkins' familiar East

Notts accent filled the room. "Yes, sir," she said, but she was already talking to his back as he marched off in the direction of his office.

Jennifer winked at Derek as she walked past him. "Nothing changes," she whispered, from behind her hand.

"Take a seat, Jennifer," instructed Hawkins as he threw his coat onto a chair in the corner of his large office. "Good to see you, lass. Thought I'd be drawing my pension before we got you back here. Happy with the move?"

"Yes, sir, I am. It took me by surprise, I must say, coming immediately after my promotion, but, yes, I've been hankering after some regular crime work even though I thoroughly enjoyed working in the Art Fraud Squad."

"You did well in the undercover case, lass, and catching Freneton, well, that certainly took us by surprise. You must tell me the inside story one day; I get the feeling there's more to it than what's written in the reports."

Too right there is, thought Jennifer, but I'm never coming clean on that one, not when I'm technically guilty of murder. You'll only ever hear an edited version.

"Yes, well, there's only so much goes in a report, sir, as you know. The real hero of the day was Henry. I wouldn't be sitting here now without his quick thinking, and nor would he be sharing Connie Fairbright's luxury life with her."

"Who'da thought it, eh, Jennifer? He was marched in here on suspicion of murder, turned out to be your old man, and then proved his worth in Italy."

"Yes, he was far more deserving of the medal they gave me than I was," said Jennifer.

"Don't be so modest, lass. There was a lot of bloody good, old-fashioned detective work in there from you too. Don't sell yourself short. Any road, we've got plenty here for you to get your teeth into. Hugh Gregson's waiting to bring you up to speed, and Len Crawford will be your DCI. We never filled Rob's post, told we had to cut back, but I'm still working on it. Got to have a chain of command."

He paused, a cloud of concern drifting across his face. Jennifer wondered if he also still felt the echoes of the late Rob McPherson.

"Something wrong, sir?"

"It's probably nothing," he replied, his voice dropping uncharacteristically to little more than a whisper. "I'd like you to keep an eye on Hugh Gregson; I'm concerned about his health. He's extremely overweight and not the fittest super around. Seems a bit breathless lately. I've tried to raise it with him, but, you know how it is, men like Hugh don't like a fuss, tells me he's fine. He's a first-rate cop, really knocked the place into shape after the chaos of Freneton and her murderous spree. Christ, she was after the lot of us, could've succeeded too if Neil hadn't stood up to her. But Hugh, he works all hours, total dedication …" Hawkins little speech drifted away to nothing.

Jennifer sighed inwardly. Men of Hawkins' generation were so closed, bottling everything up, never giving vent to their emotions except when they were bawling people out. It was little wonder so many of them were unhealthy.

"I'll do that, sir. I've been looking forward to working with Detective Superintendent Gregson; he has quite a reputation from his days in the West Mids. I'll let you know if I think he's overdoing it or hiding something."

"Thanks, Jennifer. Knew I could rely on you. Well, no time like the present. He'll be waiting for you in his office."

Jennifer stood up and turned to leave. As she reached the door, Hawkins called out again. "Jennifer?"

"Sir?"

"It's good to have you back."

"Thank you, sir. It's good to be back, believe me."

"Come in!" Hugh Gregson called in response to Jennifer's knock on his open door, his West Midlands accent in vivid contrast to Hawkins' and most of the other officers in the SCF.

As he stood to greet Jennifer, she suppressed a gasp. She

remembered him as being a large man, but nothing like the unhealthy specimen now facing her. His face had a pasty pallor and there were beads of sweat across his forehead.

"Detective Sergeant Cotton," he said, panting breathlessly. "Jennifer. Delighted to meet you again." He waddled around the end of his desk and held out his hand.

"You too, boss," replied Jennifer. She paused for a moment before taking the plunge. "Is everything all right, boss? You look a little unwell. Would you like me to fetch you some water?"

Gregson looked in her direction, but she wasn't convinced his eyes were focussing on her. "I'm fine, Jennifer, thank you. I'm just … it's a bit, what, airless in here, don't you think?"

No, thought Jennifer, I don't.

"I'll fetch some water, boss. Perhaps you should sit down."

She turned and started walking towards the door, but she had only taken two steps when she heard a deep grunt from behind her. She spun around and was horrified to see Gregson had slumped across his desk and was sliding off as his knees searched the floor for purchase.

"Boss!" she yelled. "Help! Someone! Emergency!"

She ran towards Gregson, grabbing his arm in a vain attempt to ease his fall, but he was too heavy. Jennifer stumbled and fell with him, but was quickly back on her feet. She needed to turn him onto his back. She reached for an arm and pulled with all her strength. "Come on! Anyone!" she yelled. "I need help in here!"

The door burst open and Derek rushed into the office followed by two of the other detectives from the squad. Hawkins was right behind them followed by the DCI, Len Crawford.

"What happened?" bellowed Hawkins.

"He just keeled over, sir. I think it's his heart."

With Derek's help, she had turned Gregson onto his back and was searching for a pulse in his neck.

"Christ!" she yelled through clenched teeth. "I can't feel anything. Derek, we need to give him CPR. Someone call an ambulance!"

"Already done," said a voice Jennifer didn't recognise. "They're only two minutes down the road. Let's see if we can get him breathing."

One of the detectives was leaning on Gregson's chest and pushing it rhythmically and firmly. "Get the defibrillator," he yelled, "it's in the squad room."

But their frantic efforts were in vain. Gregson's heart had given out in one massive attack. Later, after the postmortem, the pathologist would comment to Hawkins that for the man to have continued for as long as he had defied all logic; there was nothing anyone could have done.

"Bloody place is jinxed when it comes to superintendents," muttered Neil Bottomley once the ambulance had taken Hugh Gregson's body away. "No one's going to want to apply for that job. First we get Freneton and now poor Hugh. Bugger it."

Jennifer had never seen him so emotional. He was fighting back the tears as he sat fidgeting at his desk, at a loss as to what to do.

"Was he married, Neil?" she asked softly, laying a hand on Bottomley's arm.

Bottomley responded by chewing his lip and nodding. "Joan," he said, eventually. "His wife's name. They are our neighbours. In Southwell. I'd better go and break the news. Pam will be devastated. They'd become good mates."

"I'll come with you," said Jennifer. It was a statement, not a question. She didn't want him to drive in such an emotional condition.

He looked up. "Thanks, Jennifer, you're a good lass."

Chapter Eight

The entire staff of the SCF was in shock at the sudden death of Detective Superintendent Hugh Gregson. Much admired, he had been the boss for almost three years, his combination of dedicated professionalism and instinctive detective skills lifting them from the doldrums following the gutting of their ranks by Olivia Freneton. They knew his jovial informality was a veneer that hid a ruthless tenacity when dealing with suspects, a skill they all attempted to emulate. They also knew he would always have their backs, his support a solid foundation for their hard work.

But life had to go on, as did work. When Pete Hawkins heard that Jennifer was about to take Neil Bottomley to break the news to Gregson's wife, he overruled her.

"I'll take him, Jennifer. For a senior officer like Hugh, it's the only respectful way. And anyway, the Gregsons are friends; my wife and I see quite a bit of them. You stay here lass. The team needs you and I also want Len Crawford to get you up to speed."

"You OK, Jen?" asked Derek as Jennifer walked towards her new desk, her legs leaden. She had yet to sit at it, stow her stuff, examine the in tray and fire up the computer. She didn't answer immediately; she just squeezed his hand as she passed him before slumping into her chair.

She took a deep breath, sat up straighter and lifted her eyes to where he stood waiting. "No, not really, to tell you the truth. It was a hell of a shock, but it could have happened to anyone here. Being with him when his heart gave up, I mean. The first moment I saw him, I wanted to sit him down and call an ambulance. How long had he looked like that?"

Derek shook his head. "Not long, just today really. I mean, he's looked dodgy for a while and I think he was getting a bit pissed off with people asking him if he was OK. But nothing like the way he looked when he came in this morning. Things must have deteriorated over the weekend."

"What was the stupid man thinking of?" lamented Jennifer, her voice choking with frustration and anger. "It's a job, for Christ's sake, not a religious calling. If he'd taken a little more care of himself, he'd have had more years with his wife. If I ever get like that, so single-minded that everything else falls by the wayside, I give you full permission to drag me out of here by the hair no matter how much I kick and scream. Got it!"

"My mind boggles at the thought bu—"

"Have you got it!"

"Yes, Jen, I've got it."

"Good. Because I'd do the same to you; don't think I wouldn't."

Derek glanced around the squad room, aware of a heavy silence in response to Jennifer's unintended raising of her voice. "I'll get back to work," he said, quietly.

He turned and made to walk away but Jennifer called to him.

"Derek. Sorry. I just …"

"I know, Jen, it's OK." His eyes lifted to somewhere beyond her as a movement caught his attention. "Here comes Crawford. Probably wants you."

"I hope he's healthy," muttered Jennifer.

DCI Len Crawford stood at the door and looked around the room.

"Right, everybody. I know how gutted you all feel. Hugh Gregson was a helluva good cop and a great guy. We'll all miss him. But I know if he'd had the opportunity to say one more thing to you all, it would be 'get on with your work'. This team, all of you, are what he lived and in the end died for, and he wouldn't appreciate it if we stood around moping instead of getting on with all the cases he and all of you have invested a lot of time in. Sorry if that sounds heartless, it didn't come out quite right, but I think you get my gist."

There was a general mumbling of assent from which one voice spoke up.

"We're on it, boss, don't worry." It was Gus Brooke, the newest addition to the team and the least invested.

Crawford wasn't worried and neither was he impressed. He glanced coldly towards Brooke before addressing the room. "I've no doubt we'll be finishing a bit early today, depending on the DCS, but even if we don't, I suggest that we meet for a drink after work. In the meantime, DS Cotton, I'd like a word in my office, please."

He turned towards the door. As Jennifer stood to follow him, she noticed heads getting together as the team continued to come to terms with events. However, no one's head leaned towards Gus Brooke.

"Sit down, DS Cotton," said Len Crawford, pointing towards the chair by his desk. He was altogether different from Hugh Gregson, a man less confident in his role, and like many in that situation, he wore a protective veil of formality. He had the reputation of being thorough and fair, if somewhat dogmatic, but less able to listen to others' points of view. At least he looks fit enough, thought Jennifer.

"Thank you, guv," she said, sitting down.

Crawford sat opposite her, still wearing the buttoned jacket of his tired dark-grey suit, his tie neatly pushed against the collar of his white shirt. He ran a weary hand through his short and receding salt-and-pepper hair.

"A somewhat unfortunate start to your new job, Cotton. Let's hope it only gets better from here on." His attempt at a smile was through closed, thin lips.

Jennifer said nothing as she watched him wringing his hands.

"I want to give you a rundown on how things work here, at least bring you up to date. But before I do that, I just want to say that I'm aware that you and DC Thyme are, what …?"

"A couple, guv," replied Jennifer, bristling, her response emerging as more aggressive than she intended. "We're a couple. A serious, long-term couple. But I should like to put your mind at rest, in case you are concerned. I'm now Derek's immediate boss, and here, at work, I'll treat him exactly like the others. We're both perfectly capable of separating our professional and personal lives. It won't be an issue."

Recoiling slightly at the sharpness of Jennifer's tone, Crawford decided to drop it. In his heart he was against couples working in the same team and he hadn't been looking forward to broaching the subject, but at least the elephant he perceived in the room had been dealt with.

"That's good, DS Cotton, very good; I'm pleased to hear it. Nevertheless, I think as a working procedure, routinely, that is, when you go out on a call and you're not with me, if you are the lead officer, I'd prefer the accompanying DC to be someone other than DC Thyme, unless it's unavoidable."

Jennifer wanted to scream. Stop bloody waffling man, she thought. Get to the point.

"In fact," continued Crawford, "I'd like it to be DC Brooke. To be frank with you, I'm more than a little concerned about how he's fitting in. As you know, he has only been in the SCF for a few months. Previously he was in the West Mids in the same squad that Detective Superintendent Gregson came from, although they didn't overlap. The transfer was approved because Brooke's wife has been moved here with her job and neither of them wanted the commute.

"Anyway, the point is I'm concerned that Brooke isn't a team player. He seems to have an inflated idea of his own abilities and he needs knocking into shape. His attitude towards women is, well, I think chauvinistic is the word. It occurred to me that having a well-respected female officer such as yourself immediately above him in the chain of command, someone grounded and sensible, would be better than having a man in the role, for many reasons. Apart from anything else, he came with a reputation of being something of a Romeo. I don't care what he gets up to off-duty, as long as it's legal, but I don't want it happening when he's at work."

"Is that what's been happening, boss? Has he been doing the rounds?"

"Not overtly, no, although the female staff haven't taken to him even though he is, apparently, a good-looking man. But you know how sensitive people are these days about anything that could possibly be construed as harassment."

Jennifer steepled her hands and put her lips against her fingers. She wasn't happy with the arrangement but since Brooke was a member of her squad, she had to deal with it.

"There may be a way to integrate him, guv," she said. "I've been told he's a fitness nut, like DC Thyme and me. Perhaps I can persuade him to join us in some training."

Crawford nodded, encouraged. "Yes, he's certainly a fast runner and he has already distinguished himself in chasing down a youth who was getting away in a major drugs operation. There was a dilemma since we badly wanted this youth and the easiest way would have been for the undercover DC we had in the drugs gang to arrest him. But that would have compromised his cover. DC Brooke didn't know who he was and simply acted instinctively. So he's got the right tools; he just needs grooming."

Jennifer looked up from her own thoughts to find Crawford sitting back, his hands folded over his belly beatifically. He was more than happy to have passed on the problem.

Although Jennifer had no appetite, at 12:30 she stood and went over to Derek's desk, bending down to his ear. "Lunch," she said, quietly. "Somewhere the guys don't use."

Derek cast a rueful glance at the pile of papers in front of him. He hadn't planned on more than a sandwich, but something was obviously up.

"OK," he said, grabbing his jacket. "There's a new Pret up near Canning Circus they haven't discovered yet. Let's go."

"You mean I might get some coffee that's not made from a toxic powder that glows in the dark?"

"Coffee's brill; so are their wraps. Come on, you can treat me from your enhanced senior officer's stash."

As they both sat down with their wholemeal wraps filled with brie and rocket, Derek looked across the table at Jennifer and grinned.

"How did the meeting go with Crawford? What did you think of him?"

"Odd bugger, like you've always said. I'd say he has an inferiority complex. Hardly in the same league as Mike Hurst."

Derek chuckled. "Being five foot six in his heels doesn't help, either. I always try to slouch a bit around him, but I notice Gus always stands too close and stretches himself up to his full height."

"I'll bet," said Jennifer, laughing through a mouthful of leaves. "Mind you, dear old Rob McPherson can't have been much more than that and it never bothered him. Crawford seems to have a bit of a thing about Brooke, and I must say I'm not over impressed with him either. Wants me to keep a special eye on him, use him as my oppo when I go on call-outs, rein in his flirting."

"Good luck with that, although I doubt he'll try it on with you. He knows I'd deck him if he did."

"Now, now, DC Thyme," replied Jennifer, looking at him over imaginary spectacles and wagging the remains of her wrap at him. "I won't allow fisticuffs in my squad room."

"Not even over a matter of honour, ma'am?"

"Certainly not. Take him down a dark alley."

"Actually, I dunno what his problem is," said Derek. "I've met Mo, his wife, and she's lovely. You'd certainly get on with her. Trouble is, I think he's always been something of a player and at the moment he gets too much free time. She's away a lot with her work even after her transfer here, which was the reason for his move in the first place."

"Yes, Crawford said as much."

"Seems to think he's got a permanent pink ticket. Of course, it could be all harmless bluster; I'm not aware of him trying it on with anyone in the SCF."

"What does his wife do?"

"She teaches sculpture, but she seems to have courses going on all over the place, so although they've moved up here, she's hardly ever at home, except at weekends, sometimes not even those if she's overseas somewhere."

"Art again," said Jennifer, "I can't seem to get away from it. Do you think the others will be happy with me going on calls with Brooke? I don't want them to think I'm favouring him."

"I think they'll be delighted. They mainly try to avoid him if they can; reckon he's a bighead. Anyway, the pairs that have formed up existed under Gregson before Gus arrived and they're well established. Two DCs going out is fine unless something needs a senior officer. Seems to work, so if you're keeping him out of their hair, they'll be happy. And you might even manage to deflate that ego a bit."

"You've set me a challenge now. How long before I have him lapping at my feet?"

Derek grinned. "I think he'd do that immediately if he thought there was a nice prize at the end of it."

"That's not what I meant, DC Thyme."

Part Three

COSIMO GRAZIANO ROSSELLI

Chapter Nine

ONE MONTH LATER

Connie Fairbright was sitting in Bar Fulvia in the Tuscan hill town of Castiglion Fiorentino with Henry Silk, the man who two years before had appeared out of nowhere and rescued her from the maniacal serial killer Olivia Freneton, the man who had saved her life.

An immediate spark between Connie and Henry had quickly cemented into a comfortable permanence, but there were two problems, the first of which was distance. After many years in the wilderness, Henry's star was shining brightly in the movie world; Hollywood had beckoned and Henry had answered. He now spent much of his time filming in studios all over California while Connie spent much of hers in the high-security confines of her villa in the hills outside Castiglion Fiorentino.

The second problem was that Connie shunned any form of publicity. An intensely private person, she wanted no mention of her personal life in the press or online media, or anywhere else where she might attract the attention of another Olivia Freneton. There were plenty out there, perhaps not as murderous, but she had no doubt they would be just as single-minded in their pursuit of her fortune. Obsessive about keeping her relationship with Henry as low profile as possible, she never accompanied him to the glitzy, narcissistic bonanzas of self-importance at which Hollywood excelled, not to parties and not even to expensive and exclusive restaurants, no matter how discreet the management. There was always the risk of eyes and phones that might point in their direction, and once tempted with the scent of a story, the pursuit of the celebrity-press hounds would be relentless.

Henry was only too pleased to comply with Connie's wishes, and not just because he was totally smitten by her. He had his own issue of privacy with his daughter. To maintain her effectiveness as a detective, Jennifer's anonymity was essential. Throughout the aftermath of the Cambroni trial and the death of Olivia Freneton, she and Henry had managed to keep their father-daughter relationship known to a trusted few. If they went out together in public, Henry would adopt a disguise, but otherwise they met well away from prying eyes in places such as Connie's villa or Henry's house in London.

The happy exception to Connie and Henry's self-imposed rules of privacy was found in the rural backwaters of the Tuscan countryside, and morning coffee and pastries at Bar Fulvia was a ritual whenever Henry arrived from Hollywood. They both loved the old town square's unhurried ambience and the noisy babble in the bar among groups of earnest, retired men arguing the finer points of Italian politics over their cups of caffè corretto. But most of all they loved the freedom of being themselves, of being unmolested, part of the furniture. It was true that they were foreigners and always would be, but in the parochial eyes of the locals, the entire population of nearby Arezzo qualified as foreigners, let alone the rest of Italy. However, these two foreigners were accepted, particularly Connie. The American signora was always polite and friendly and, more importantly, she had injected plenty of cash into local pockets with her villa conversion.

Connie squeezed Henry's hand. He had flown in four evenings earlier, arriving in time for sundowners and a cosy dinner. By the following morning he was completely relaxed, a world away from the madness and tantrums of the studio.

"It's such a pity you're off again tonight, Henry; there's nothing I like better than sitting here in this magical place with my lover."

Connie's eyes crinkled with amusement at the word she knew would provoke a response.

"Lover?" questioned Henry, rising to the bait of the familiar refrain.

"Yes, Henry. Lover. It's what you are, isn't it? What *we* are. Lovers. I like the word; it has an air of intrigue about it. And what else do I call you? I can't stand the word 'partner', it has too many connotations, and the last companion I had tried to kill me. Surely you don't think 'boyfriend' is appropriate; you're almost fifty-three."

Henry tossed his head theatrically. "Fifty-two and a half. My birthday is almost six months away. What about beau?"

"What about it? You're not filming a remake of Gone With The Wind, are you?"

"Fancy man?" persisted Henry, undaunted as he sought alternatives. "Swain? Yes, I like swain."

"I'm afraid you're missing one qualification for swain, my darling."

"Really? What's that? I think it rather suits me," said Henry, striking a pose.

"Youth, my love, youth. Swain has a connotation of youth about it."

"OK, then. Fella. I'm your fella."

"And I suppose I'm your bit of stuff."

"Cor-shew are, darlin'," said Henry, putting on an Eastenders accent. "That's certainly how I describe you when asked if I'm seeing anyone."

Connie laughed. "Fortunately, I know full well that you maintain an enigmatic silence to all around you when it comes to our relationship. Long may it continue, although I know it's inevitable that one day some spotty hack will happen upon this bar when we're in it, recognise you and find out who I am."

Henry leaned closer to her. "Would that be such a bad thing? It's been two years now since Olivia Freneton met her demise. I'd love to be able to wine and dine you publicly. I'd be the envy of hordes of eligible bachelors and the talk of Hollywood."

"No, thank you. I do not want the Val di Chio invaded and ruined by paparazzi, our every move recorded and spread across the Internet. The people of this town would never forgive me."

She paused, smiled warmly at him.

"I never realise how much I miss you until you're back here in our special place. And although I hardly seem to have paused for breath since you were last here, it's been lonely without you."

Henry laughed. "You sound like a script from one of the soaps I used to be in."

Connie poked her tongue out him. "Hey, Mr Romantic, you're supposed to be living up to that debonair Hollywood image now you've hit the big time. You should be melting my heart with one casual but passion-loaded glance."

"Give me a break; I'm off duty. One of the many appealing things about this place is I'm just another foreign face. I can be myself and walk around without someone asking me to pose with them for a selfie."

Connie pulled a face, pouting in mock petulance. "Do you really have to fly back tonight? The time's been so short."

"'Fraid so, but I'll be back in no time. And you don't have to keep sending a private jet for me every time, you know. I'd be perfectly happy slumming it in first class on some sordid commercial airline."

"Henry. You know what airports are like these days with all the security; they're zoos." She shuddered. "I hate flying enough without having to do it with other people. And for as long as I'm fortunate enough to have the wherewithal, I'll make the travel arrangements for both of us."

Henry sat back and smiled. "Far be it from me to sound ungrateful. I must say there's something eminently civilised about being picked up in a limo at the studio, whisked to a private airport, cocooned and painlessly transported to Perugia and then limo'd to your villa."

He paused and glanced around, his eyes resting briefly on one of Connie's minders sitting two tables away. He leaned forward and lowered his voice.

"I'm pleased to see you're still taking your security seriously. It's reassuring to know you are in safe hands when you're out and about."

Connie nodded. "My brush with that insane woman was some wake-up call. The thought of what she nearly achieved and how she went about it still leaves me shuddering."

Henry took her hands in his. "We were all lucky that day, you, Jennifer, and I. And even Derek, although he wasn't there at the end."

"No, but she could have tried something at the agriturismo the night before."

"But she didn't, my love," reassured Henry, "and here we are in our post-Freneton future. No point in dwelling on it all, turning over the same old horror stories. I think it's time to accept that everything associated with the delusional, psychopathic world of Olivia Freneton is dead and buried with her. I know it hasn't been easy; it hasn't been for Jennifer either, but I think she has finally drawn a line under it. She now regards it as she does any case she's been involved in. Once the trial is over and the evidence and paperwork catalogued and stored away, that's it. The baddies are out of harm's way and the goodies can carry on with their lives unmolested."

Nico Terzi and Benno Papadopoulos were the two professional minders from Connie's team on duty that morning. She had chosen the team carefully, vetting the many applications with her US head of security and her two PAs, one Stateside and an Italian one based in Rome, until she had fine-tuned her list to a squad of eight. She paid them generously and expected the best. Of the eight, Nico and Benno were her favourites, her invisibles as she called them, for their skill in blending into the background.

Seated in the car outside the bar, Benno constantly scanned and assessed every passing individual and vehicle. Nico, by contrast, relied more on his ears than his eyes. Seated in the bar and apparently glued to his newspaper, he tuned into every conversation. While Connie and Henry enjoyed each other's company, Nico was listening, filtering and cataloguing, leaving nothing to chance. That was his role: tune in, assess, plan, repeat.

To escape Nico's rigorous scrutiny would require someone with exceptional skill; someone in a league of their own. Someone like Cosimo Graziano Rosselli, the man sitting two tables behind him. Referred to somewhat melodramatically in the circles who used his talents as *l'ombra*, the shadow, Rosselli was an assassin whose abilities were second to none.

Disguised as a greying pensioner in his sixties, Rosselli gave the impression of being a man absorbed with his newspaper while listening through earbuds plugged into an iPod. From time to time, he would stroke the head of the pug dog seated on the chair next to him, but his focus behind his heavily tinted sunglasses was entirely on Connie and Henry.

Chapter Ten

Constantly mindful of their security and privacy, Connie and Henry had developed a habit of speaking in such hushed tones that even with the state-of-the-art sensitivity of the directional microphone concealed in the iPod, Cosimo Graziano Rosselli was hard pushed to pick up everything they said.

It was the fourth morning Rosselli had sat in the bar watching and listening, and from what Connie had been saying, Henry was about to return to the US. However, far more importantly, their conversation that morning had already added significantly to the fragments of information Rosselli had picked up during the past four days.

It had taken time for Rosselli to reach this step of his research. He had started by searching Google for the name combination of Ginevra and Mancini, both irritatingly common Italian names. There were many and even though his experience told him that none would be the young woman he was looking for, he had to follow up each one.

Of the Ginevra Mancinis he found, he could eliminate most as non-starters. They were either too old or too young; too fat or too thin; too short or too tall; or their facial features differed too much from Ettore Cambroni's description. And of those he shortlisted, many were married with children or unsuitable owing to their education or employment. This still left seven women of around thirty, all of whom had Facebook accounts with photographs of themselves showing them to be dark-haired, attractive and slim. Three even came from Milan and might therefore have the accent that Ettore Cambroni had described. He had studied the photographs carefully, trying to see inside each woman's head. But a second clandestine meeting with Ettore to show him their photographs confirmed his thoughts: none of these women was the Ginevra Mancini he sought.

In the double-glazed tranquillity of the book-lined study in his modern Rome apartment, Rosselli had sat in his favourite swivel leather recliner as he considered his next move. From the nature of the sting operation against the Cambronis and the information from the trial, he knew the Rome Art Fraud Squad of the Polizia had been involved. However, a few discreet enquiries quickly saw him backing off. The head of the squad, Commissario Massimo Felice ran a tight ship. The squad was a closed shop, Felice being the only public face, and he was known to be incorruptible. And to make matters worse, when Rosselli talked to a long-time source in the lower levels of the Polizia, he was told that casual enquiries to colleagues had been met with suspicion. Given the last thing Rosselli wanted was to alert the squad, he immediately instructed his contact to make no further approaches.

At this point, like Ettore Cambroni before him, Rosselli accepted that the better route to Ginevra Mancini would be through the rich American, Connie Fairbright, and the companion Cambroni had mentioned, the Englishwoman, Diana Fritchley.

Another Internet search for these two threw up some interesting results. There was plenty of business-related information around the name Connie Fairbright, the mega-rich widow of billionaire businessman Brad Fairbright who had been killed several years previously in a plane crash, but nothing at all on Diana Fritchley. This puzzled Rosselli until he researched the surname Fritchley and found that not only was it rare but also that among the few Fritchleys he found, none was called Diana.

Rosselli knew from Ettore Cambroni that the Fairbright

woman's restored villa was somewhere near Castiglion Fiorentino in Tuscany. Using a contact in the Arezzo Carabinieri, one of many around the country on whom he had compromising information, he quickly gathered what he needed to move forward.

There were only two calls involved, the first from Rosselli using a public phone to make contact with the officer, the second from the officer to an untraceable number Rosselli had given him to hear the results.

"It's Beppe, signore," announced the police officer, his voice hesitant. As always, he was concerned about crossing a man he knew to be dangerous.

"You have something?"

"Si, signore, a little, but I hope it will be useful to you." He paused, worrying about how to explain what he had to say to this enigmatic man.

"Well?"

"Allora, signore, the villa of the American woman, Signora Fairbright, is in the hills above the Val di Chio, east of Castiglion Fiorentino. It's called Villa Brillante and is about three kilometres from the main road that winds up the side of the valley and heads over to the Nestore Valley, and it is, apparently, impregnable. I know the senior police officer there, the maresciallo in charge of the zone. He has been instructed by his superiors not to go near the villa, that all matters of security are to be handled in-house by the woman's security company. It is rumoured that the villa houses many priceless paintings, but I can find no one who has actually been inside to see them first hand."

"Does the Fairbright woman live there full-time?"

"Apparently not, signore. According to the maresciallo, she flies frequently to and from the US in a private jet she keeps at Perugia airport."

"What about her companion, the Fritchley woman?"

"The information about her is … confusing."

"What does that mean?"

"Well, again according to the maresciallo, Signora Fairbright's companion was killed in a motorcycle accident about two years ago on the steep main road near the villa. It seems she just drove over the edge on a corner."

"Suicide?"

"Possibly, signore, but it is not certain. You see, there is literally no information about the accident or the victim. No record. Neither is there any record of a funeral, in fact, what happened to the body is also unknown. I am told there were three witnesses to the accident who were in a four-by-four. One was Signora Fairbright, the second an Englishman who now visits her from time to time. The local police didn't get a chance to interview them, not even the carabiniere who had been accompanying them, since within minutes, an order came through from Rome for them to stand down."

"Who was the third?"

"A young woman who had been staying with them the previous evening at the Villa Incantata di Chiana, an exclusive agriturismo south of Castiglion Fiorentino. There had been an incident the day before at Signora Fairbright's villa, but the record for that is also missing."

"Is there a description of the young woman? What was her name?"

"The carabiniere said she was around thirty; she had dark hair, and she was pretty and slim. As for her name, I have checked as far as I dare, but there is no record of it."

"Nationality?"

"As I said, the officer accompanying them only had a chance to speak briefly to her. He said she was Italian and he also thinks from her attitude that she might have been a police officer."

"If he was accompanying them, why didn't he see the accident?"

"He was in a police vehicle and leading the way. I think he was well ahead of them; he was rather vague about it."

Rosselli gave a derisive snort. "Idiot."

He ended the call. In spite of the incompetence of the police driver, this was useful information. Assuming the mysterious young woman was Ginevra Mancini, it confirmed that Fairbright knew her, and if she knew her, they might still be in touch. He needed access to the villa, but given the stories of high-tech security, attempting a break-in was too risky. He would have to try another way, and for this he would have to base himself in the area.

Rather than use a hotel in Castiglion Fiorentino, where the staff might be too local for where he intended to cast his net, Rosselli chose an anonymous commercial hotel twenty minutes away on the outskirts of Arezzo where he would be just another faceless client. His utterly placid pug Goccia was trained to sit quietly beside him for hours on end. He often used her when, heavily disguised, he was observing and collecting information. She was a distraction. People would remember her rather than him, and anyway, who would suspect anything about a quiet, elderly man enjoying his coffee and listening to music while petting his beloved dog?

In Bar Fulvia, Rosselli adjusted the beige fedora that was part of his disguise, pulling it more tightly over the wig of leonine grey hair as he listened patiently to Connie and Henry's conversation. They had yet to mention the elusive Ginevra Mancini, but Rosselli was convinced they were all linked.

The couple appeared to be about to leave when Connie leaned towards Henry, her voice dropping to an almost conspiratorial level.

"Sweetheart, when did you say you last spoke to Jennifer?" I was wondering how she's settling in after the shock of her boss having a heart attack."

Henry's reply was equally muted "Let's see, it was, er, Tuesday of last week. I was on location on the coast south of LA and I caught her in my lunch break. With the time difference, it was about 9 pm in England and she had just got home from work. She was tired and we didn't talk for long. She seems to have dealt with it. She's incredibly busy, as ever."

"Her work never stops, does it?" replied Connie, "Look how much she had to do with the gallery case, for the Met and for Rome."

Rosselli's hand had now frozen on Goccia's neck as he struggled to pick up the conversation. The pug turned her head and nuzzled at his fingers, demanding that he continue with the stroking.

"And on top of that," continued Henry, "there was Freneton's death. But fortunately, Massimo stepped in and, as if by magic, it all went away."

"Friends in high places," mouthed Connie, with a flick of her eyebrows.

"After two attempts on my daughter's life, they are the kind of connections she deserves," added Henry.

Connie nodded. "Yes. Jennifer can't always rely on you riding in like the cavalry, especially when you spend most of your time six thousand miles from her."

"I'm far happier now she's back in Nottingham and she has Derek watching her back on a daily basis."

He took her hand. "Come on, there are things to do before I leave. Let's get back."

Connie looked up coyly at him and Henry grinned.

"I meant around the house, but they shouldn't take too long."

As Connie and Henry waved goodbye to Mario, the bar owner, Rosselli sat reviewing the valuable intelligence he had gained in the past few minutes along with everything else he'd learned over the previous four days. Cambroni's associate, Maria, had been right, Ginevra Mancini was English, and not only that, she was also this man's daughter. Her real name was Jennifer and she was a police officer who worked in Nottingham in the UK.

He had checked out the Englishman as a matter of course since the man had been with Fairbright and Mancini when the Fritchley woman was killed. He was the actor Henry Silk, and although Rosselli didn't recall any mention online of a daughter, this was progress! From the rest of the conversation, the daughter didn't appear to be married, so presumably she would be Jennifer Silk, assuming Silk was the actor's real name.

And there was another name. What was it? Yes, Freneton. Who

was Freneton? The woman who died was called Fritchley, not Freneton. Like Fritchley, it sounded an unusual name. Another one to add to his search list.

He ruffled the fur on Goccia's neck and she stretched in enjoyment. "Come on, little lady, we have some more work to do before we can be one hundred percent sure we have the right woman."

Chapter Eleven

Rosselli trawled every search engine, bulletin board and online gossip site he could think of, but he could find no mention anywhere of Henry Silk having a daughter. There was some scandal earlier in the actor's career, a bad-boy image that had haunted him and hindered his progress in the acting world for more than two decades, but no daughter. He had hoped for a photograph of the two of them together, but, interestingly, there was nothing. The actor must have worked hard at keeping the information quiet.

After exhausting the search for Henry and his daughter, Rosselli shifted his focus to the name Freneton. Here his search was more successful and with a little thought he was able to make sense of the information.

Olivia Freneton had been a rogue British police superintendent. A serial killer wanted for several murders in England, she had fled the country after the attempted murder of a young female detective. From the conversation between Connie and Henry, that detective must have been Jennifer.

After the attempt on Jennifer's life, the killing spree had continued in England with at least two more murders and two attempted murders, one of the latter aimed at a black police officer called Derek Thyme. Was this the Derek Henry Silk had mentioned? But then Freneton had disappeared again and, given the confidence with which the police had announced that the public would have nothing more to fear from her, the perceived wisdom in the press was that she must be dead.

Rosselli flicked around the articles and decided that Freneton and Fritchley must have been the same person, with the woman taking on the latter identity in an attempt to steal from and perhaps kill Connie Fairbright. And Henry had stopped it. Interesting, thought Rosselli. *No wonder they are all such a tightly knit group.*

Satisfied the pieces were falling into place, Rosselli turned his attention to Jennifer. It was more than his reputation was worth to kill the wrong person; it would be sloppy and shoddy, and Cosimo Graziano Rosselli was neither. He was an assassin, not a murderer. His killings were tidy and painless business arrangements that took advantage of his exceptional skills to ensure the targets did not suffer. They were not random affairs of the heart or mindless acts of cruelty. He despised people who killed out of anger, frustration or antisocial tendencies as much as the next upright citizen, and he certainly did not consider himself or his work anywhere close to such behaviour. The only reason he might even think of killing anyone who wasn't one of his professional targets would be if his freedom or his life were threatened. And in that respect, he considered himself no different from anyone else.

It was, therefore, crucial to him to have a photograph of the woman whom he now thought of as Jennifer Silk, a photograph he could show Ettore Cambroni for confirmation. Once again, a search online proved fruitless. There were plenty of Jennifer Silks, but none fitted the bill for all manner of reasons.

Given the relationship between Henry and Connie — and that was something else that had been kept quiet, with no mention anywhere of any connection between the pair, not even in the grimiest gutters of the movie world gossip sites — and the fact that Connie herself was clearly close to Henry's daughter, Rosselli reasoned there would probably be photographs of Jennifer around Connie's villa. The problem was how to gain access to them. He had been told the villa was impregnable. Was that really the case? He needed to know, and if it were, he needed to know how the staffing worked. Were the staff imported foreigners whom the Fairbright woman shipped in and out in the luxury of her private jet, or did she use carefully screened locals? A period of quiet observation was required, something at which Rosselli excelled.

Before first light the following morning, Rosselli was driving alone through the Val di Chio in the direction of Connie's villa, having reluctantly left Goccia behind in his hotel room. He was intending to work his way through the undergrowth of the forest near the villa, and although Goccia was highly trained and well behaved, he couldn't risk a single whimper or whine from her at the wrong moment. If dogs were used as part of the villa's security, they would definitely respond by barking if they detected Goccia's presence. He had left the pug in front of the cartoon channel, something she seemed to enjoy. He hated to think of her being bored.

Rosselli drove up the steep incline at the end of the valley, turning off at an unsurfaced track beyond the turnoff to Villa Brillante. A hundred metres along the track, out of sight of the main road, he tucked his ageing Panda in amongst the trees. If anyone were to come across it, they would assume it belonged to someone local searching for mushrooms in the woods.

Rosselli himself looked twenty years younger and altogether different from the elderly man who had been sitting in Bar Fulvia. This Rosselli was closer to the real thing; a man in his early forties with close-cropped dark hair speckled with a little grey, most of it hidden by a peaked cap; a slim and fit man but otherwise unremarkable. Average in height, Rosselli wasn't handsome or ugly, he had the forgettable features of a faceless commuter, someone who was seldom given a second glance. This was Rosselli's strength and he used it to the full. His physical presence was no more memorable than his shadow, hence his nickname in his exclusive world where anonymity was everything.

Dressed in loose fatigues that were the common garb for local countrymen, Rosselli slipped into the woods and made his way towards Villa Brillante. His goal was to observe the road leading directly to the villa, his assumption being that if the staff were local, they would likely be transported to work daily. This would happen early in the day.

His assumption soon proved correct. He hadn't been in place among the trees for more than ten minutes when he heard the gentle whoop of a siren announcing the opening of automatic gates. A moment later, a black four-by-four appeared. Empty, apart from the driver Rosselli had seen waiting in the car outside Bar Fulvia over the previous four days, the car sped off along the road, the rumble of its diesel engine soon lost in the trees.

Twenty minutes later, he heard the car returning as it climbed the steep main road from the valley floor, appearing moments later on the track heading back towards the villa. As far as he could make out, there were now three more people besides the driver: a man in the front passenger seat talking animatedly to no one in particular, and two women in the back. Rosselli had no interest in the man, but the two women had potential. If they were ferried in daily like this, they must be household staff. Cleaners probably, who would have access to the various rooms in the house and would know of any family photographs on display. The challenge now was to win one of them over.

He settled back in his hiding place, leaning against a tree, prepared for a long wait until one or both of the women were returned to wherever they lived.

At five in the evening, the four-by-four once again left the villa carrying the same three passengers. Rosselli made no attempt to rush back through the woods to follow them, since he wanted to repeat his observations over a couple more days to be sure of the household routine. Right now, he needed to get back to Goccia.

After two more days of observation, Rosselli was satisfied that the arrival and departure times of the two women followed a predictable enough schedule; one more day would confirm it. But instead of sitting in his hiding place getting bored, he decided to scout the perimeter wall of Villa Brillante to examine the sophistication of its security.

It didn't take him long to appreciate just how much effort had been put into securing the villa. Impregnable had been no over-statement; the security was state-of-the-art. As well as concealed cameras on the wall itself, there were others carefully placed in the trees up to fifty metres beyond the wall. Having detected the first of these, Rosselli quickly retreated deeper into the woods and resorted to using a pair of binoculars to survey the area. After two hours of making slow progress, while he was confident he had escaped detection, he saw there was no point in continuing all around the wall. The coverage was expertly applied with no sign of any weak spots. He had examined less than a tenth of the distance, but continuing with the rest would only increase the risk of making a mistake and being discovered, which was unacceptable.

After returning to his car, he drove two kilometres along the main road and stopped. The long-suffering Goccia, whom he had brought with him that day, needed a well-deserved walk. He had decided that any more days of cartoons and the otherwise placid pug would become stir-crazy.

Shortly before five in the afternoon, Rosselli was back in a thicket of trees overlooking the point where the road from the villa met the main road. Goccia sat placidly with him. At five, the four-by-four appeared with its cargo of three and headed down into the Val di Chio. Once the car had disappeared, Rosselli walked to a vantage point he had located that gave him a view along the valley as far as Castiglion Fiorentino, eight kilometres away. From there he watched the progress of the car through the valley until it disap-peared close to the town.

"Change of scenery tomorrow, little lady," he said, looking down at the pug. "We'll park in the valley near the town and follow them from there."

Goccia wagged her tail.

Chapter Twelve

The following afternoon, disguised again as the elderly man from Bar Fulvia and with Goccia keeping him company, Rosselli followed the four-by-four to where the women were dropped off in a residential area below the old town. Both lived in modern two-storey apartment buildings, but in different streets.

Rosselli parked his Panda, put the leash on Goccia and they ambled off together to take a closer look at the two women's homes.

It took only a few minutes to rule out the first woman, the elder of the two. As Rosselli dawdled opposite the building where the woman lived, she appeared at the top of the steps leading up to her first-floor apartment, and bellowed at two children playing in the street. After initially ignoring her, the children, a boy of about ten and his younger sister, reluctantly dragged themselves away from their friends and sulked their way back to where their mother was now standing at the top of the steps, arms folded in menace. The girl complained in a whining voice, but it was the boy who was cuffed around the head as he passed his mother.

Rosselli looked down at Goccia and whispered, "I don't think so, do you, my sweet?"

The pug registered her agreement by turning her back on the objectionable human spectacle, preferring to examine a hedge she suddenly found fascinating. Rosselli bent to pick her up, deciding to try the other woman. Just as he turned to walk away, a screech of tyres from the end of the street caught his attention. He had no reason to suspect the activity was anything to do with him, but in his world there was always the need for vigilance. He braced himself, ready to run.

The car raced down the street and pulled to a halt in a cloud of dust outside the house Rosselli had been watching. A large man in his thirties jumped out and slammed the door with far more force than necessary. Unshaven for several days and wearing a stained singlet that had once been white over a pair of greasy jeans, the man strode towards the steps.

"Irena!" he yelled, his tones slurred and full of threat. When there was no answer, he bellowed his wife's name again.

Rosselli watched in fascination as the man continued shouting while he climbed the steps. On reaching the apartment, the man grabbed the door handle, flung open the door and disappeared inside. The sound of raised voices immediately followed, after which a loud slap cracked like a bolt of electricity as one of the occupants of the apartment was hit.

Eager to leave the scene of domestic violence behind him, Rosselli gave Goccia's leash a gentle tweak and walked off in the direction of the second woman's apartment. On entering the street where she lived, he stayed on the far side of the road from the apartment, keeping the front door in his peripheral vision as he talked quietly to Goccia. He was a few steps past the path to the door when the door opened and the woman appeared. Her head was turned back as if she were talking to someone inside the apartment, giving Rosselli a chance to look at her. She had changed into jeans and a loose top and her hair was hanging loose. In her early twenties and therefore far less likely to have a brood of objectionable children following her, she was immediately of more interest to Rosselli.

As if confirming Rosselli's thoughts about her family situation, the woman called out to someone inside. He couldn't catch what she was saying, but it wasn't being said in anger, and it finished with the word 'Mamma'.

Rosselli bent to fuss with Goccia while he waited to see which way the woman went, his mind in overdrive as he considered his options. He needed to get back to his car to remove his old-man disguise before finding an excuse to talk to the young woman.

The woman turned in Rosselli's direction and her eyes immediately fell on Goccia. She tilted her head and smiled as she made to walk towards the elderly man and his dog.

This was not how Rosselli wanted things to pan out. About to walk away, he heard a ring tone and in the corner of his eye he saw the woman stop to pull her phone from a pocket in her jeans.

"Ciao, Irena," she said, "Did you forget—"

She stopped, her face horror struck as she was interrupted by her friend.

She turned in the opposite direction. "Are you injured, amore? Wait, I'll be right there." Still holding the phone to her ear and issuing more instructions, she ran off along the road.

Rosselli turned the other way and hurried back to his car. Once inside, he stowed Goccia in her basket on the back seat where she quickly settled, seeming to understand that for now, she had played her part. Rosselli opened the glove compartment and removed a bag of tissue and a bottle of solvent with one hand as he pulled off the leonine wig with the other. Checking himself in the mirror, he quickly removed the subtle make-up on his face, ripped the scarf from his neck and slipped out of his chino trousers. Less than a minute later, a man of around forty in jeans stepped from the car pulling on a thin, stylish pullover. He pulled open the rear door and Goccia looked up hopefully, but Rosselli said, "Sorry, my angel, you'll have to stay here. I won't be long." He lowered the window a few centimetres so the pug would have some air before locking the car with the key fob as he ran down the road.

He was sure the young woman was heading to her workmate's apartment, and that would mean trouble. Another thirty seconds confirmed his suspicions. As he rounded the corner of the woman Irena's street, he saw that a crowd of about ten people had formed at the bottom of the steps to her apartment. And the younger woman, who only minutes ago had been about to coo and fawn over Goccia, was marching up the steps, her features set in determination.

"Irena!" she shouted. "Are you all right? Answer me!"

"Help me, Sonia!" called a voice from inside the apartment. "He has gone crazy!"

Another loud smack of hand on face sounded, followed by a scream. A moment later, the apartment door crashed open and Irena's husband appeared, his face red with anger and his mouth contorted into a vicious sneer.

"Stay away, bitch! This is nothing to do with you. Take another step and I'll throw you down these stairs."

But even though she had seen this brute's temper many times, Sonia was not intimidated.

"If you don't stop, I'll call the police," she shouted, the spittle from her mouth spraying onto the man as she reached the top step.

He laughed in disdain. "You think that frightens me? The ispettore and me are great friends. He knows the only way to treat a wife who disobeys is to beat her."

He stood back to give himself room and raised his right arm, ready to strike Sonia. But still she stood her ground. After pausing for a second, the man launched himself at her, pushing her hard. Sonia screamed in fright but instead of falling backwards into space, she found herself caught in two strong arms, whisked around and sat on a stair.

Rosselli had seen what was about to happen and bounded to reach the steps, flying up them just as the man lashed out. Once he was sure that Sonia wasn't about to tumble any farther, Rosselli stood up to face the man. He sidestepped a totally predictable punch and in what appeared to be a whirl of limbs, the man spun around, his right arm twisted up his back in Rosselli's firm grip, and was forced into the apartment. Rosselli kicked the door closed behind him, gave the man's arm a sharp twist before pushing him into the living room where Irena and her children were cowering in a corner.

In another blur of movement, the man found himself facing Rosselli, but only for the briefest of moments. A sharp jab to his body was perfectly aimed and the man doubled up in agony, falling to the floor clutching his abdomen as he gasped for air. Rosselli took aim and kicked the man hard in the groin, first once, then again, after which he grabbed him by his filthy vest and dragged him to a half-sitting position. He put his free hand under the man's jaw, his index finger and thumb digging hard and painfully into the points where the man's jawbone articulated with his skull.

"Listen to me, you slob. You have one chance. Do not even think this is as bad as it can get. I can cause you more pain than you can possibly imagine. Do you understand?"

He tightened his grip. The man grimaced, a strangled gurgle coming from deep in his throat.

"S…Si," he slurred.

"Good, because from now on I shall be watching you, and when I'm not around, others will be watching you. If I ever hear of you laying a finger on your wife or your kids or anyone at all, I shall rip your heart out and feed it to the pigs."

He let go of the man's jaw, letting him fall forward. As he did, he grabbed the man's chest with both hands and gripped tightly, digging his fingers deep into the man's ribs as if he were about to tear him apart.

He let his eyes pierce deeply into the man's, watching the fear consume him. Abruptly, he pushed the shivering wreck away and stood up.

"Apologise to your wife."

The man turned his head to him in incomprehension, as if he had no idea what an apology was.

Rosselli took a step back and kicked the man in the mouth. "I said apologise," he growled, his voice low and menacing.

Clutching his mouth to contain the blood now flowing freely from it, the man rolled over towards his wife.

"I… I… Irena," he slurred through damaged lips and broken teeth. "I am s…sorry. I will never hurt you again, I swear to God, on my mother's grave. I—"

"Enough!" barked Rosselli. He turned to Irena who was still cowering in the corner of the room, her arms protectively clasping her children to her.

"Signora," he said, his tone now softer. "If this pig ever lays a hand on you in anger again, you will tell me. Your friend Sonia will know how to contact me." He smiled in reassurance. "Don't worry, you are safe. He has had his only chance."

Gulping back her tears, Irena found her voice. "Thank you, thank you—"

But Rosselli had already left the room.

After closing the front door behind him, he bent down to check on Sonia.

"Are you all right, signorina?" he asked, lightly touching her shoulder.

She turned her head and looked up at him, her eyes questioning.

"Irena?"

"She is fine, and from now on her husband will be as meek as a lamb."

He took her hand. "Come," he said, "Let me buy you a coffee, or perhaps a brandy."

He smiled at the shock in her eyes. Girls like Sonia didn't drink brandy.

"Maybe a corretto," she said.

She stood and Rosselli turned to face the crowd still waiting at the bottom of the steps.

"Signore e signori, the show is over. Please go back to your homes."

Chapter Thirteen

After introducing himself as Gianpietro Tebaldi, an art dealer from Rome, Rosselli let Sonia guide him to a bar just inside the medieval walls of the town. On the way there, when he casually mentioned he had been trying to find Villa Brillante, Sonia readily told him she worked there.

Seated in the cafe, Rosselli continued with the charm.

"I cannot believe my good fortune in bumping into you," he enthused, looking into the myopic eyes peering back at him through the thick lenses of Sonia's cheap spectacles. "I was completely lost. I've been up and down so many white roads, tracks and mule paths that I was beginning to think Villa Brillante didn't exist anymore, that my friend Connie had given me the wrong instructions. She can easily do that, you know. She's a wonderful person, but she has absolutely no sense of direction."

Sonia brushed her poorly cut hair over her ears. She was desperately aware that it needed a wash after her hot day cleaning the terrace tiles at the villa.

"She's not actually at the villa at the moment," she told him. "She left last night with Signor Silk. I think they've gone back to America."

Sonia was right. When Connie learned that Henry was filming at a studio outside LA near to one of her many properties, she had gone with him on a whim, delighted by the rare opportunity to see him after his daily schedule. As far as Rosselli was concerned, the news couldn't have been better, but he couldn't let Sonia know that.

"I can't believe I missed them," he continued, pushing his fingers against his forehead head in apparent dismay. "Henry's such an amazing actor. Have you seen any of his films?"

Sonia shook her head. She didn't like foreign movies; she preferred Italian comedies, especially those featuring her home town's local hero, Roberto Benigni.

"Aren't you amazed at how serendipitous this all is?" enthused Rosselli. "I mean, of all the people I could have rescued from their friend's violent husband, I choose the one person who works at one of my oldest friend's villa in the countryside."

Sonia's laugh was edged with nervousness. She didn't know what serendipitous meant, but if this clever man thought it was amazing, she would accept it.

Rosselli sat back and let a triumphant grin form on his face.

"You know, Connie being away gives me the perfect opportunity to set up a little trick I've been planning for ages. She loves the games I play on her. Always has."

He smiled to keep the encouragement going. "I was going to make a copy of one of her photos with my phone and then play around with it on Photoshop. Do you like doing that, Sonia?"

Sonia pulled a face, hoping it would hide her lack of understanding. "I'm not much good with computers."

Rosselli laughed. "I can't believe that. You play with your phone, don't you?"

She nodded.

"Well, it's the same, only better. I must show you sometime."

"Where did you meet the signora?" she asked. The suddenness of the question surprised him, but he was up to the innocent challenge.

"Let me see, it must have been about twenty years ago when she came on a trip to Italy with her late husband. He was always occupied with his business affairs, but Connie loves art and even back then she had plans to start a collection."

He smiled wistfully, giving the impression of fond memories.

"I had just set up my first gallery, in Rome. She came in one day and we immediately took to each other, as friends, of course." He paused and laughed. "She quickly told me she was married. I think she was worried about the reputation of young Italian men with foreigners."

Sonia blushed, adding, "Not just foreigners."

Rosselli's knowing smile was designed to confirm his interest in her.

"Anyway," he continued, "I sold her some paintings, modern pieces that were not really what she was looking for, but she liked them for the boldness of their colour and brush strokes. I remember she said she found them refreshing. Yes, that was the word she used."

He repeated it in English, and although it meant nothing to Sonia, she was suitably impressed by what she saw as his worldliness. She had never had a conversation with anyone as knowledgeable as this man before.

"How are you feeling, Sonia?" asked Rosselli, reaching out to touch her arm, an expression of concern on his face. "Would you like another corretto? I think it would do you good. That was an intense few moments. Fortunately, I've done some training in martial arts. It's very useful in situations like that."

"I don't think I should, Gianpietro," she said, enjoying addressing him by his name. "I'm not used to alcohol."

"Of course. Perhaps another coffee then, without anything in it. I certainly feel as if I could use one."

She hesitated. "I should be getting back to Mamma. She worries if I'm gone for too long, but … well, I'm sure another few minutes won't hurt. Thank you, I'd love another coffee."

Two minutes later he was back with coffees, glasses of water and a selection of pastries.

"These look too delicious to ignore, don't you agree? The owner tells me they are fresh from the oven. Please, try one. Or more, if you like." He laughed, encouraging her.

He paused to let her bite into one of the pastries before continuing.

"I was thinking, while I was getting the coffee," he said, allowing a little hesitancy into his voice. "With Connie being away,

I can't just turn up at the villa unannounced. She told me in an email that she has a whole new security team since my last visit, and, of course, they won't know me. It would be embarrassing for me to be turned away and embarrassing for them when Connie found out."

He looked up to make sure he had her attention.

"I was wondering, Sonia. Are you working tomorrow? At the villa, I mean."

"Yes," enthused Sonia through a mouthful of pastry.

Rosselli quietly swallowed his disgust: table manners and etiquette were paramount to him.

"Excellent!" He leaned forward conspiratorially. "I was wondering if you'd like to help me with my little scheme."

"How can I do that?"

"Oh, it's very simple. The last time I was at the villa was just after the restoration was finished. I don't think you were working there then; I'd remember if you had been." He smiled, letting his eyes capture hers.

"No," she said, soaking up the flattery, "I started working there about six weeks after Signora Fairbright moved in."

Rosselli nodded. "That explains it."

He leaned closer. "I remember seeing several photographs of Connie around the place," — he was ad libbing wildly and hoping he had got it right — "on her own and with Henry Silk." He paused, wanting to draw the information from Sonia. "I'll bet there are some new ones since then, too, aren't there?"

Sonia frowned, thinking about the photographs.

"A couple," she said. "There's one of Signor Silk with his daughter, I don't know if you saw that."

"His daughter? No, I don't remember any of his daughter. But one of her with Henry would be perfect. That would add so much to what I'm planning for Connie."

"How can I help?" asked Sonia, excited now by the prospect of being part of this man's scheme. Rosselli wanted to kiss her.

"Simple. You have a smart phone, don't you?"

She reached into her pocket and pulled out an ageing iPhone.

"I love that model! I used to have one, but it was stolen," said

Rosselli, drawing her in further. "What you could do for me, Sonia, is take some shots on your phone of some of the photos at the villa. One with Connie and Henry together and the one of Henry with his daughter. Could you do that, take the photos on your phone?"

She nodded her agreement.

"Perfect! But since I'd like what I'm doing with them to be a complete surprise, it would be better if you didn't tell Irena or anyone else at the villa. Just take the shots when there's no one around and we can meet up again and transfer them to my phone."

"How do we do that?"

"I'll show you tomorrow. It couldn't be easier."

Sonia thought through the instructions.

"I can do it while Irena's cleaning the kitchen. The photos are in the bedroom, you see."

Rosselli sat back and beamed. "That would be absolutely wonderful, Sonia. I shall be forever in your debt. And once Connie sees what I've put together, so will she. As for Henry's daughter, she'll think it's hilarious."

"I can't wait to see it," said Sonia. "You will show me, won't you? Once you've finished."

"Of course, Sonia, of course. But again, we must keep it our little secret."

He reached over and squeezed her hand. "I can see that this is going to be the start of a very special friendship. I can't believe how lucky I am to have bumped into you. And please tell Irena that I'm a man of my word when you see her. She'll understand."

Chapter Fourteen

Soon after seven the following evening, the two met again at the same bar. In the interim, confident that after he had collected the photographs from Sonia he would be finished in the area, Rosselli had driven back to Rome to leave Goccia in his apartment with his partner Giorgio, the only other human being he trusted with his secrets.

He returned the Panda to an ancient lock-up garage in a back street before walking three streets to a larger lock-up where he housed a Toyota 4x4 and a steel-grey two-door BMW saloon, the latter a car that far more suited the image that Sonia would have of him than the ageing Panda.

Rosselli was early and when Sonia walked into the bar, he hardly recognised her. She had attempted a chic, sophisticated look: figure-hugging black trousers and a loose white silk blouse with a high cutaway collar. The blouse was open to just above her breasts, now far more in evidence than the previous evening, thanks to the help of an uplifting bra. A necklace of red beads completed the ensemble, but what surprised Rosselli more was not only her hair, which was now clean, sleek and falling lightly onto her shoulders, but also the absence of spectacles. Her face looked totally different.

He wasn't convinced the contact lenses Sonia was wearing helped her plain looks, but the girl was clearly pulling out all the stops.

"Sonia!" he said, standing and reaching out to take both her hands in his. "You look sensational!"

He leaned forward to air-kiss both cheeks. "You should talk to Henry Silk about being in one of his movies. No, not just one; all his movies! You should star alongside him. A home-grown Italian bombshell. You would take Hollywood by storm."

"I don't think I would do very well in Hollywood," she replied, blushing, "I don't speak any English, and they say that American English is even harder because it's full of slang."

Rosselli shrugged his shoulders dismissively. "They have language coaches, voice-overs, all sorts of tricks. Once they're done, you would sound like the perfect Italian film star, purring her English to the delight of the audience."

Sonia's laugh revealed her discoloured teeth. Rosselli averted his eyes.

"Tell me about your day. Was it successful?"

Resting her elbows on the table, she leaned her chin onto her hands and tilted her head coyly, a slight smile on her face. "Maybe," she said, with what she hoped was a teasing tone to her voice.

Rosselli fought hard to quell his impatience.

"I can't wait to see the shots. Are they good? I've been thinking about them all day and I've got several great ideas. I know Connie will love it when she sees what I've done."

Sonia sat back and reached for her small handbag. But before she opened it, she caught Rosselli's eyes again.

"Did you mention something about dinner?" she said, trying to sound sophisticated.

Rosselli wanted to snatch her bag and run, but instead he wagged a finger at her.

"You have pre-empted me, Sonia. I assumed, no, that's wrong of me, I *hoped* we should be having dinner together, but I was going to rely on you to recommend a restaurant. I am, after all, a stranger to these parts. It doesn't have to be in Castiglion

Fiorentino. I've heard that Cortona has some excellent restaurants, or Arezzo, perhaps. What do you think?"

Sonia wrinkled her brow, appearing to think of a restaurant, but really she was imagining walking through the streets of Arezzo, the nearest large city, arm in arm with this man, or even hand in hand.

"There are several in Arezzo, so I've heard. I haven't actually been to any. Perhaps we could look online for a recommendation."

"Excellent idea," Rosselli enthused. He had already done it, just to be sure. "Actually, now you mention it, I remember someone telling me there's a famous one in the Piazza Grande, up in the old town. I think it's called the Golden Lance. Have you heard of it?"

Sonia nodded enthusiastically and Rosselli felt himself weakening. After all, he needed to eat and this guileless woman had, he hoped, got him the information he wanted. Perhaps he should confirm that first.

"Why don't we sort out the photographs and then we can head off?" he suggested.

"Oh yes," giggled Sonia, "I almost forgot."

She opened her bag, removed her phone and touched the photos icon. She had copied three photos, but only one showing Henry Silk with a young woman whom Rosselli had to assume was Jennifer.

"These are perfect, Sonia, well done! And that's a lovely shot of Henry's daughter, don't you think? I couldn't have asked for anything better. Now, let's just airdrop them to my phone and we're done."

He swiped the screen of her phone, hit a couple of icons and in a moment, his phone pinged.

"There," he said, "as simple as that. Excellent! Well, that's the business sorted for the evening; I can't thank you enough. I'm going to have such fun playing with these. I can't wait for Connie to see the results."

He returned the phone to Sonia and held out his hand. "Shall we? My car is just outside the walls."

• • •

As the evening light over the Piazza Grande faded into deep cobalt, their dinner under the portico lived up to the reviews Rosselli had read online. For Sonia, every moment was magical, and when Rosselli showed interest in her collection of Tyrollean cuckoo clocks, she decided to let this man do as he pleased with her. She would go with him to wherever he chose.

For Rosselli, Sonia's body language made it all too obvious what she wanted, which was precisely what he didn't want. The thought of disappearing to a hotel room with her, or even a fumble in his car in a quiet spot in a nearby wood, filled him with horror. Sonia or any woman, it made no difference; the idea was simply abhorrent.

However, he had met many other Sonias over the years while gathering information during the preparative phases of countless assignments, although few had been as guileless, and he had a tried-and-tested escape plan. A second phone in his pocket, an older design with keys, was programmed to send a single word text when he pressed a sequence of three keys. Within five minutes, he would receive a phone call on his smartphone from Giorgio posing as his brother insisting he return to Rome immediately. Their mother had been taken ill and he must drop everything and come at once.

Rosselli played the part well. They were strolling back through the Piazza del Duomo on the way to the Pietri car park north of the city walls. Rosselli had one arm around Sonia who was leaning into his body. She had drunk two glasses of wine, far more than she was used to, and was a little unsteady on her feet. With his free hand, Rosselli felt inside his jacket pocket and pressed the appropriate buttons on the old phone. As they approached his car, the shrill of his ringtone broke the spell of the comfortable silence between them.

"I think I'll ignore that," he said. "I'll turn it off so that we aren't disturbed again."

He pulled his smartphone out of his pocket and made to switch it off. But Sonia stopped him. "What if it's important?"

Rosselli laughed. "At ten thirty on a Wednesday night? I doubt it."

He paused for effect before shrugging his shoulders "OK, if you think I should."

His dismissive glance at the screen was immediately followed by a theatrical double take. "It's … it's my brother," he said, frowning. "Sorry, Sonia, I'd better take it. He never calls me this late. In fact he hardly ever calls me at all."

The rest of the theatre played out according to plan; Sonia was far too concerned about Gianpetro's mother to worry about the fragments of her shattered dreams now evaporating into the night. There would be other nights, she was sure. She even suggested she took a taxi home rather than delay the poor man, but he wouldn't hear of it, and thirty minutes later Rosselli duly dropped her off outside her apartment with a brief kiss and a promise to get in touch as soon as he could.

The next day, a huge bunch of flowers was delivered to Sonia's apartment together with a note of apology. The following week, a card arrived with the good news that his mother was showing signs of recovery along with the bad news that he had been called urgently to a sale in New York by a client he couldn't afford to refuse. Chocolates and another brief note that told Sonia nothing appeared a week later but after that, she heard no more. She didn't worry, even though she had overlooked taking Gianpietro's phone number or his address in Rome. Connie Fairbright knew Gianpietro Tebaldi and since they were old friends, he would probably arrive one day at the villa and surprise her.

Chapter Fifteen

Cosimo Graziano Rosselli's final meeting with Ettore Cambroni in the neglected back-street building craving the mercy of a demolition order was brief and to the point.

As before, Ettore was given no opportunity to see Rosselli's face. Not that the ruined art forger was interested; he had worked with the mob for long enough to know ignorance was the best policy.

Once again, he was made to wait, a common enough tactic to put him on edge, and as before, when he finally spoke, Rosselli's voice cut through the darkness of the room with the clinical precision of a surgeon's scalpel.

"In the folder in front of you is a photograph."

There it was again, an echo in the tone, no more, but still enough for Ettore to hear the underlying cadences of a Sicilian.

He had seen the folder as soon as he sat down on the upright chair, but he hadn't dared to open it. He assumed it represented a test, a measure of his patience, and he wasn't going there, but in the wait before Rosselli spoke, Ettore's eyes kept drifting back to it.

"Look at the woman in the photograph inside and tell me if she is the subject of this contract." Rosselli knew it was. How could it not be? But he needed to hear it from his client.

Ettore leaned forward and pulled the folder closer, staring at the cover for a few seconds before slowly opening it. And there she was. Ginevra Mancini. Not just looking back at him, but laughing, as if to mock him and his gullibility. His fingers closed into a ball around the edge of the folder, bending and creasing it as his grip tightened. The room around him ceased to exist as his whole consciousness focussed on the image of Jennifer. He hardly even registered the man standing next to her in the photograph.

"Well?" came the same bark, slicing through the room's silence, the very air molecules forced apart by its authority.

Ettore didn't answer immediately, his voice paralysed with tension.

Finally, as his eyes narrowed in hatred, he confirmed what Rosselli had come to hear.

"It's her. *That* is Ginevra Mancini. This time you got it right." His mouth twisted into a vicious snarl. "I could kill her with my bare hands."

A derisive snort came from the darkness on the other side of the table. "I very much doubt it, Signor Cambroni. The woman is a British police officer. She will have been given extensive unarmed combat training; you wouldn't stand a chance against her."

Rosselli paused to let his client absorb what he had said, before adding, "which is why you have me."

Ettore could sense the supercilious smile on Rosselli's face as he peered into the darkness, even though he couldn't see it.

As with the end of their first two meetings, a silence of finality fell on the room, but again, Ettore didn't dare to challenge it until given permission. After ten minutes, the same clunk he had heard before sounded and the lights in the room flooded him with too much brightness.

The assassin had gone, leaving one of the doors on the far wall standing ajar. Ettore looked down at the folder open on the desk, Ginevra's face still taunting him. He stood and made to turn, but before he did, his eyes fell one last time on the photo. He had no desire to take the folder and its poisonous contents. The snarl returned and he spat with explosive force at the face. As he turned and walked away, a grim caricature of a smile distorted his lips. The die was cast.

Chapter Sixteen

With the exception of Switzerland, which required an extra layer of careful planning, Rosselli preferred to work in continental Europe. The reason was simple: with open borders, he could drive everywhere and take his weapons with him.

Not that he could afford complacency since there was always the possibility of a random border check, especially when re-entering Italy in an Italian-registered car. The trick was in the choice of vehicle. Nothing ostentatious, just smart enough to be outside the border officers' radar. But even small risks were to be avoided. If he were caught in possession of his weapons, his life would unravel and he would spend the rest of it in prison. This was why he had customised the two vehicles he used on assignments outside Italy with concealed compartments in their boots to carry the guns and knives that were his stock-in-trade, and behind their dashboards for a selection of passports and other documents. He had never been stopped, but if he were, his secret weapon was Goccia. The combination of the cute pug batting her eyelids and Rosselli disguised as an ageing professorial type minimised the chances of his car being subjected to detailed scrutiny.

Crossing the channel to England added further complications. Rosselli needed a selection of weapons and being more than cautious, he was loath to involve a third party. To his way of thinking, if more than one person knew a secret, it was no longer a secret. It would be relatively easy through mob contacts to obtain the guns and knives he would need to use if arranging an 'accident' became unworkable, but he didn't know them, these British thugs, didn't know whom he could trust, didn't know who had built-in prejudice to foreigners and might therefore be persuaded to loosen their tongues.

Rosselli kept both vehicles in a secure back-street lock-up in Rome's working-class Testaccio district. He kept his weapons in the same lock-up, but in a concealed climate-controlled vault built into the cement floor.

Having confirmed Jennifer's identity, Rosselli began to flesh out his preliminary plans for her assassination. There was much to do even before he reached England, but he had done it many times; it was simply a question of following his own well-constructed protocols.

He chose the larger of his customised cars, the five-year-old Toyota 4x4, for transporting his equipment to England, his plan being to take the most direct route through the Italian and French motorway systems. Traffic cameras would record his vehicle, but that was of no consequence since once in France, he would change the vehicle's genuine Italian plates for fake ones. Once in England, he would store the Toyota in a double-size garage behind a parade of ageing shops in Caterham, south of London, a lock-up bought for hard cash many years before. For his assignment, he would use one of his false identities to rent a right-hand drive, UK-registered car.

Before leaving for England, Rosselli gave himself a month to prepare. He was obsessive about physical fitness, his daily routine a punishing round of weights and exercises. But in the lead-up to an assignment, he redoubled his efforts to ensure he was in optimal condition. His timing and responses must be as perfect as humanly possible. And to assist him in this, his adored and trusted partner Giorgio monitored and encouraged him every inch of the way.

The pair would spend time at a spa on the coast south of Rome where their privacy was guaranteed and where Giorgio would supervise Rosselli's training. They both knew that Rosselli's job entailed high risk, that the chances of either getting caught or being killed could not be taken lightly, shrugged off as if he were some two-dimensional villain in a spy movie.

Giorgio was no assassin; he could no more take another person's life than take his own. Both were anathema to him. It had therefore surprised him to find that he had no problem with Rosselli's chosen career. Since the start of their relationship seven years before, he had relished his role as Rosselli's behind-the-scenes support, his sounding board for creating new and innovative ways of dispatching Rosselli's targets as humanely as possible, since neither of them enjoyed the thought of the targets suffering. Giorgio was the one exception to Rosselli's views on secrets; with Giorgio, he discussed almost everything.

After a particularly gruelling workout two weeks into their stay, the pair had showered and were sitting together on the generous balcony of their spa suite enjoying breakfast. Rosselli looked up from where he was spreading lavender honey on a piece of soft pastry he had pulled from a cornetto. "Is something wrong, amore? You seem distracted this morning."

Giorgio sat forward and laid a hand on Rosselli's arm. "Only the usual, Cosimo. It's the way I always feel when you're going away for a job. I know I can't come with you, and in that respect, I'm insanely jealous of Goccia who, I notice, is maintaining an aloof superiority in my presence at the moment."

Giorgio smiled and reached out his other arm towards Goccia, who was stretched out on the tiles to his left. At the mention of her name, she raised her head, her eyes flicking from one of her adoring owners to the other.

"You're a wicked little strumpet, Goccia; you know you are and you revel in it, don't you?"

The pug rolled onto her back, her eyes now directing Giorgio to rub her belly.

Both men laughed. "Too sweet," said Rosselli.

He took Giorgio's hand. "I know how you feel, amore, I hate

being away too. But if we want to maintain this exotic lifestyle, I have to use the talents God has given me. And it's not as if my targets are good people. The world is a far better place without them."

"I think that's part of it, Cosimo. From the file you've assembled on this English policewoman, she was only doing her job. There's nothing to say that she's intrinsically a bad person."

Rosselli nodded. "Yes, that bothered me too when I was given the assignment. But I have to regard her as an adversary. After all, she wouldn't think twice about arresting me and locking me up for the rest of my life, given the opportunity. And if that happened, my clients would be forced to look elsewhere for someone to tidy their lives for them."

His whole upper body joined his arms in an emphatic shrug. "I'm the best, amore, and more to the point, I am humane. I care about my targets. When I separate their bodies from their souls, I can almost always guarantee they will feel nothing. I am completely different from others in my profession, most of whom are emotionally challenged automatons. Many of them actually enjoy inflicting pain." He closed his eyes as he shuddered distaste. "*So* unprofessional."

He leaned forward, both hands now flat on the table. "You see, amore, this Jennifer Silk is a thoroughly capable officer, it's true. But in the execution of her work, she upset the equilibrium of my clients. The Cambronis weren't bad people; they were just crooks. No one was hurt by their fraudulent schemes. After all, their targets were rich and the rich can afford to see a little of their wealth fall by the wayside. But they have been hurt. I could see the pain in Ettore Cambroni's eyes, the suffering he has borne to see his father dying in a dreadful prison. I can't imagine that this Jennifer Silk cares one jot about that, which makes her no different from the automatons I mentioned. She knows the risks. She should consider herself lucky that I, Cosimo Graziano Rosselli, will be the one to catapult her to heaven. In my hands, she won't feel a thing. It will be instant; one moment she will be alive, the next her soul will be on its way while her body crumples to a lifeless shell."

Giorgio's smile was tinged with uncertainty.

"I know all that, Cosimo, amore mio, and I agree that you are probably the most conscientious and kind assassin in history. I know you will be merciful and dispatch her with compassion. What worries me is that she is so good at her job. If she should get a single notion she is being targeted, not only would entire squadrons of British police officers be mobilised to hunt you down, she would be setting one trap after another for you herself."

Rosselli sat back in his chair. "I think you worry too much. You must remember that she has no idea she has been targeted, and neither will she suspect an old man with a dog. Goccia and I have a number of cards to play, not the least of which is the princess herself. Such a beautiful lady by my side is bound to distract."

Giorgio nodded. "You're right, of course, and you are the professional; I am only an enlightened amateur, thanks to all your briefings over the years. The problem with these overseas assignments is the unknown. Normally, we weigh up everything together, but we can't in this case since you have so much still to establish: where she lives, whom she lives with, where she works, what the best method is for her. I know you have done this many times entirely on your own, and you have always been successful. But I'm not sure you have ever been up against a person such as this. And she's a woman too."

Rosselli laughed and wagged a finger at Giorgio. "That's a rather sexist remark. I'm sure that feminists would object if they thought they weren't entitled to equal status as assassins' targets."

Giorgio giggled involuntarily, as he tended to when teased, a trait that Rosselli found endearing but one that also reminded him that Giorgio's limited control over his emotions would make him a useless assassin.

"Look," continued Rosselli, "just because I'll be in one country and you in another doesn't mean we can't confer. I have a totally secure line through a series of proxies. The conversation itself will be encrypted and the source will bounce around the world at an incredible rate. Our discussions will be impossible to monitor or trace. I've put the same system on the phone you'll use back in the apartment, so every day I can bring you up to date with what I've found and what I'm planning, and you can add your much-appreciated counsel to the discussion. Work for you?"

Giorgio nodded enthusiastically. "It will give me great peace of mind, amore. I shall be living the assignment with you."

"Well, in that case, it's time we stopped worrying and relaxed in this marvellous place. We have two more weeks; we should make the most of it."

But then Goccia ate something that disagreed with her, resulting in several anxious visits to a nearby vet. And no sooner had she recovered and returned home than Giorgio contracted a serious chest infection. Their planned month became five weeks, six and then seven, and it wasn't until almost eight weeks after his final meeting with Ettore Cambroni that Rosselli drove away from the couple's apartment in Rome. Goccia, excited and perky in the rear seat, couldn't understand why her two masters were so emotional.

Chapter Seventeen

Rosselli's drive through France to Calais and the Eurotunnel was quieter than he expected, given it was late August and still the holiday season. He far preferred the thirty-five-minute tunnel journey to any ferry crossing, remaining in the privacy of his car with a dozing Goccia being infinitely more civilised than having to mix with hordes of families on some ferry's public deck. Once he had presented Goccia and her papers to the pet reception at the Calais terminal, the two of them were essentially invisible.

The drive up to Caterham was equally uneventful, roadworks on the M20 and heavy traffic on the M25 notwithstanding, and by late afternoon, he had checked into an Ibis hotel only half a mile from his lock-up garage. Not trusting the outdoor car park attached to the hotel, once he had taken Goccia for a short walk, he drove straight to the lock-up.

Sealed behind the locked garage door, Rosselli spent an hour dismantling the floor of the Toyota's boot to gain access to the secret compartments. After this, he removed a panel at the rear of the glove box to retrieve several hidden passports. After stowing everything inside a large fireproof vault buried in the garage floor, Rosselli reassembled the Toyota's interior, set the alarms and traps that would be activated if someone broke in, and returned to the hotel.

Relaxed now that his weaponry was no longer at risk of theft, he called up the encrypted app on his iPad that gave him CCTV views of the lock-up's interior as well as links to all alarms and confirmed the same app was fully operational on his phone. Slipping the phone into his jacket pocket, he looked across to Goccia. He knew she was itching to check out the myriad new and exotic smells from countless local dogs and to leave notice announcing her arrival.

"Let's explore, shall we, little lady?"

Goccia bounced in anticipation as Rosselli attached her lead to her collar.

The walk was punctuated by endless stops and starts as Goccia navigated her way through a paradise of odours. But just as she could hardly contain her enthusiasm when she set out, once she was sated, she followed her usual pattern of sitting, snorting and turning her eyes to Rosselli's.

"Basta, little one? Enough?" he said. Goccia agreed by thumping her tail on the ground. "OK, let's go back and get something delicious to eat and drink."

The something delicious was spirited out of a cool box in Rosselli's overnight bag: doggie pasta for Goccia and a gourmet mixture of the finest Italian cheeses, prosciutto, bresaola, salumi and plum tomatoes Rosselli had chosen for himself on the day he left Rome. There was only enough for a few days, after which he would have to resort to the gastric assault of British food, but for now, to celebrate their successful arrival, he would indulge himself with the best.

As for the wine, he had six bottles of his favourite Sicilian red in a chilled carrying case that kept them at precisely 18°C. At this stage of the assignment, he could enjoy a celebratory glass or two, but once he began to close in on his target, his days and nights would be entirely alcohol-free.

The following day, accompanied as always by Goccia, Rosselli walked the mile to the car rental agency where he had pre-booked an innocuous Ford saloon in the name of Martin Smithson, a name he had used on a number of occasions and for which he had a genuine UK driving licence and a credit card from a UK high-street bank. It had required a little ingenuity to set up the bank account and licence some fifteen years before, but once in the system, it had been a simple matter to maintain them. If no flags were raised, nothing was ever checked.

Once back at the lock-up, he changed the rental's number plates for a pair of fake ones and swept around the outside of the car with a device designed to detect the presence of an embedded GPS transmitter. He didn't expect to find one; he had carefully chosen the smaller rental company because it had not yet switched to tracking its cars by GPS, but he liked to be sure. Company policy could change at any time and websites were not always kept up to date.

It was late afternoon by the time he finished, and he chose to spend another night in the hotel before heading up to Nottingham for the more difficult part of the assignment: finding the woman he thought of as Jennifer Silk.

Although Rosselli had been to England many times, he had never been to Nottingham. However, in recent years, he had taken advantage of the opportunities available online for becoming intimately acquainted with a town or city before ever setting foot in it. The method was foolproof. While still in Rome, he spent many hours studying street maps of Nottingham and working his way around every street on Google Earth's Street View until he knew the city better than a taxi driver. It was an approach he had found invaluable on many occasions, since having correlated a map of a town with its Street View images, when he arrived, it would be as if he had lived there all his life, the buildings, streets and intersections all comfortably familiar.

To Rosselli's amusement, on the afternoon of his arrival in Nottingham, he was standing in the city's Market Square dressed in his usual elderly gentleman disguise with Goccia at his heel when a bewildered tourist approached him with a map and asked him the way to the Castle.

"It's that way, my friend," answered Rosselli without hesitation as he pointed the man in the right direction.

The system worked.

He was aware from his search of the online newspapers that Olivia Freneton had worked for a squad of the Nottingham police called the Serious Crime Formation. Jennifer had worked for the same team and as a starting point, Rosselli had to assume she had returned there. Another search gave him the address of the building where the SCF HQ was situated. Walking up past the Theatre Royal to the streets behind, he quickly located the old four-storey building that had once been a police station. He was closing in.

While confident of being able to identify his target should she exit the building, he could hardly hang around waiting for that to happen. And besides, more information on her and her squad's activities might give him some creative inspiration for an imaginative ending to her life. He looked down at Goccia.

"Another little walk, principessa, then we'll settle ourselves in the nearest pub and see what transpires."

Goccia wagged her tail in approval.

Two hours later, the lounge bar of the Horse and Hounds pub was slowly filling with its normal Friday evening regulars, many of whom were detectives from the nearby SCF HQ. It was now several weeks since Hugh Gregson's funeral and the initial shock of his sudden death had passed. Life had drifted back to a strained normality as Len Crawford tried to keep things on track as acting superintendent. That he was uncomfortable in the role was clear from the constant pained expression that had settled like a monsoon cloud over his features; he couldn't wait for the new detective superintendent to be appointed. The problem was that if anything was happening on that front, the DCS was saying nothing.

First to arrive at the pub of the SCF team were Neil Bottomley and Dave Coulson, one of the DCs. Although Rosselli had never seen either of them before, as soon as they came through the door, every nuance of their bearing spelled cop to him. He doubted they would give him more than a passing glance, but if they were any good, they should have at least registered his presence. He repositioned his iPod so that its microphone would target their conversation, separating it from the general background rumble of chatter and laughter. He saw their eyes occasionally scanning the room while they practised the art of quiet, inconsequential conversation. As two local men relaxing after a long week, their accents shifted up a gear to a level that Rosselli found harder to follow. However, they had, so far, only talked about football and more importantly, he was sure their eyes passed over him with no interest whatsoever.

After five minutes, two more detectives joined them and although the conversation became noisier with banter about the relative merits of Forest and County, nothing work-related crept into it. This continued for a further ten minutes with none of the detectives now giving Rosselli a second glance. He had blended into the furniture and was essentially invisible. Goccia dozed on a chair beside him, content with the occasional reassuring ruffle of her head from Rosselli's fingers. When a tall, fit-looking black guy walked in and made for the group, Rosselli immediately focussed his attention on him. Was this the Derek he had read about in the reports on Freneton, the one also mentioned by Henry Silk?

"Justin, my boy," boomed Neil Bottomley, "once again you live up to your moniker, and guess what? It's your round."

Derek cast a disparaging look at what remained in Bottomley's glass. "Pushing the boat out tonight are we, sarge? Sure you can drive to Southwell on all that ginger beer without stopping for a leak every hundred metres?"

Bottomley pulled a rueful face. "At three weeks from giving all this up, I don't want to risk my pension by having some wet-behind-the-ears young bobby stop me and wave a breathalyser at me, do I?"

Derek motioned to the barmaid to fill the glasses. She smiled at him. "Usual for you, Derek?"

"Yes, please, Nancy, gotta rehydrate before the training session."

"Worried that Jennifer will have the edge on your sprints around The Park, laddie?" said Bottomley, smirking at him.

"You're joking, sarge," scoffed Derek, "I could be three sheets to the wind and I'd still beat her."

"Doesn't do to steal the limelight from one of your senior officers, DC Thyme," added one of the other detectives. "Isn't that right, DS Bottomley?"

Neil Bottomley looked suspiciously at his ginger beer and nodded in mock seriousness. "Aye, laddie, you're right. Both DS Cotton and I expect full respect at all times, you know that. My advice to you, young Thyme, is to let her win if you know what's good for you."

Rosselli sighed silently in relief. He hadn't understood the joke when Neil Bottomley called Derek by the nickname of 'Justin', and had thought that maybe he had the wrong man. But now, the subsequent banter had confirmed his original thoughts and added more information: the black detective was DC Derek Thyme. Rosselli was now so focussed on processing the intense flow of intelligence that he didn't notice another figure approach the group, half hidden by the swelling crowd, until he heard her voice.

"He doesn't have to let me win; it comes naturally to me," announced Jennifer as she emerged into Rosselli's full view. Turning to Derek, Jennifer continued. "Come on, it's time for your usual thrashing."

Derek stood to attention. "If you say so, ma'am. Are we going for a run as well?"

The detectives winced as one at Jennifer's withering look.

As she made to go, the sudden movement caught Goccia's attention. In an unusual response, the pug pricked up her ears and barked. Jennifer turned to look; in the few seconds she'd been in the bar, she hadn't registered the presence of the dog or its owner. She smiled and took a step towards Rosselli.

"What a cutie," she said, offering the dog the back of her hand. Goccia jumped up, her tail becoming a propeller as her eyes fixed on Jennifer's.

"May I?" said Jennifer, glancing at Rosselli.

Rosselli forced a smile. "Of course." He would have preferred to have kept his distance.

Jennifer reached out to rub Goccia's neck. "Very pretty. What's her name?"

"Goccia," said Rosselli, one hand adjusting his tinted spectacles. " Her name is Goccia."

"Interesting handle for such a little bundle," said Jennifer, as something pinged quietly in the deep recesses of her mind.

"It's just a name," said Rosselli, "but she seems to like it."

He dropped his iPod into his pocket and picked up the dog. "Come, Goccia, time for your stroll."

"Gotcha?" called someone from the group of detectives as Rosselli walked past them. "Police dog, is she?"

Jennifer waited for the man to leave, assessing him as he disappeared into the crowd.

"It's Italian," she said, turning to the group. "It means a drop or droplet."

She touched Derek's sleeve. "Come on, let's get home and hit the tarmac."

She hurried out of the pub, hoping to see which way the man had gone, but there was no sign of him. He had vanished.

Chapter Eighteen

Rosselli felt elated and angry in equal proportions. His stake-out in the pub had provided him with two important pieces of information. Firstly, his target's name wasn't Jennifer Silk after all; it was Jennifer Cotton. He didn't understand why that would be the case when her father was Henry Silk. Unless of course the girl had been married and carried her husband's name, as was the custom in the UK, a custom he found rather bizarre. Certainly, if she had been married, it was all over since she was clearly attached to the black detective. He shrugged as he hurried away from the pub with Goccia. It was inconsequential detail; the girl's personal life wasn't his problem.

The second snippet of information was that Cotton and Thyme appeared to live in or near a residential area called The Park. Rosselli had come across the area when he was researching maps of the city, drawn to it because it was a private estate close to the city centre into which the Google Street View cameras had only been allowed to record two tiny grassed areas. There were no street-level details of the houses or roads to be found. The area stood out like a black hole in the long-distance satellite shots that showed the Street View grid of the city, but given the high quality of the overhead shots now available, much of the detail of the individual houses was still visible from above. Once he had discovered where Jennifer Cotton lived, he could make plans and supplement them with walks around the area during the daytime when the detective wouldn't be there to spot him.

For this was the essence of his anger; he had been rather too physically close to his target and while, thankfully, he had been disguised, she had heard him speak. He knew his English accent was perfect, but would someone with Jennifer Cotton's finely tuned bilingual ear detect any Italian in his vowels? He had used Goccia as a distraction and it had slightly backfired on him since using her in the future would only draw attention to him. He hoped the UK TV cartoon channels were as good as the Italian ones; he might need them.

Back in his hotel room, he removed his disguise and relaxed on the bed. After calling Giorgio for his daily update, he opened his laptop and worked his way through a UK electoral register site. For a small fee, he quickly discovered Jennifer Cotton's full address in a flat that was part of a house on Lincoln Circus. The name puzzled him until he discovered from a map that the circus was a large, grassed roundabout near The Park's upper end. He noted from the data that Derek Thyme was not listed as living at the same address. Another ten minutes on the register site and he had Thyme's details as the owner of a flat in the Nottingham suburb of Beeston. He didn't know if this information would be valuable or not, but he stored it away just in case.

Shortly after ten the following morning, after apologising to Goccia for having to leave her in the hotel room, Rosselli made his way to The Park to examine Jennifer Cotton's house. His appearance bore no relation to the distinguished elderly man who had been sitting in the pub the previous evening with his dog. Dressed from head to toe in black lycra with black running shoes to match, he ran The Park's main roads in an elegant stride for over an hour, and, while he touched on many of the roads and junctions, the one he focussed on was Lincoln Circus. While apparently checking his performance on an app on his phone, he stopped to take a series of shots: the entrance gate, the imposing seven-foot wall around the property, bell-pushes and what he could see of the house from the road through trees that partly blocked his view. As he did, the gate in the wall opened and a middle-aged woman walked out and strode off in the direction of the city. By sheer good luck, he had his phone to his face as he play-acted a short-sighted study of the screen while in reality recording the view through the gate.

Later, he would combine the information with that from the bell-pushes to find that there were four flats in the house, two on each floor, Jennifer's occupying half of the upper floor. And she was the owner. This was an apartment far costlier than a police detective constable or sergeant could afford; she must have had help from her film-star father.

The other useful information from his photographic recce were details of the many security cameras on the house exterior. They were top-of-the range models, again indicating there was money behind DS Cotton. Lucky girl, thought Rosselli. Until now, that is.

The presence and quality of the security cameras indicated to Rosselli that any attempt at breaking into Cotton's flat would be foolhardy. It would be next to impossible to achieve it and remain unseen. No, she would have to meet her demise elsewhere. Perhaps it would involve her car. Once Rosselli had the details, he could work on a plan to follow her and maybe arrange an accident of some sort. It was only a notion at that point; Jennifer Cotton's departure from this life was still a work in progress.

Part Four

TRISHA MCVIE

Chapter Nineteen

Jennifer was about to head out for lunch the following Monday when her mobile pinged. She glanced at the screen and smiled.

"Trish! Hi. I've been meaning to call you."

"Yeah, I know how it is. Out of sight and so on."

"Not true and you know it," protested Jennifer. "Actually, I got a call from Sofie over the weekend and she said the two of you had had a fun night on the tiles."

"Yeah, she's got hidden depths that girl and even though she seems to be infected with the same fitness fanaticism, she's a better drinker than you."

She paused before continuing in a far softer voice. "Listen, are you somewhere quiet where you can react to some earth-shattering news with gusto, or do you think you can contain yourself in front of your colleagues?"

Jennifer glanced around the squad room. "Most of them have gone for lunch, and the two that are left are more or less out of earshot, if I keep my voice down. Come on, shatter away. Don't tell you've found Mr Right and he's proposed?"

"That wouldn't be earth-shattering, it would be galaxy-bursting. No, nothing new on that front, well, not really."

"So, what is it? Don't keep me dangling."

"I've been studying my crystal ball and I have a prediction for you."

"A prediction? What do you mean?"

"I predict that tomorrow morning, if not before, but I don't think it will be before, no—"

"Trish, you're waffling."

"Sorry. I predict that tomorrow morning, DCS Hawkins will make an announcement to the gathered ranks of your illustrious team."

Jennifer's eyes widened. "You mean you've heard who's going to—"

"Don't say it!" interrupted Trisha. "Remember, if there are ears in your room, they'll be trying to tune in."

"Well, you say it then."

"Hawkins will announce who your new D Super is going to be."

"And you have some insight into that?"

"I do, yes."

"And?"

"Ready for this?"

"Stop teasing … oh my God, you don't mean … Wait! Don't say another word. I need to shift."

Jennifer jumped up from her desk, hurried into the corridor and along to the stairs where she knew she wouldn't be overheard. But just to be sure, when she carried on talking, it was in an excited whisper.

"It's not you?"

"Why shouldn't it be?"

"You mean it is?"

"Yes, DS Cotton, I'm going to be your new guv."

"Madonna e tutti i santi!"

"What?"

"You're kidding me, right? I thought things were really clicking where you are."

"They are, but there's still something about it that's not right. And anyway, when Hawkins phoned and—"

"He phoned?"

"Yes, to suggest I might like to think about it."

"When was that?"

"About a week ago."

"And?"

"I thought about it, and then I talked it over with my boss. He wasn't over happy about the idea but although I don't actually like him a lot, he's a genuine enough guy who thinks about other people as well as himself. He said he thought it would be a good career move, reminded me that Hawkins has about three years before retirement, so if it all works out …"

"Gosh, DCS."

"Let's not jump ahead of ourselves. The important thing is that in spite of its recent trials and tribulations, your team has a pretty good reputation, so being part of it at a command level can be no bad thing. I mean, for all his gruffness, Hawkins is highly thought of. Rumour has it that he's turned down further promotion a number of times because he's so dedicated to what he's doing now. Sees it as a fitting end to a distinguished career."

"I don't know what to say."

"How about 'congratulations'?"

"Sorry, yes, of course. I'm thrilled for you, and working with you, or rather for you, will be brilliant. It's just that …"

"I know, you're worried about dynamics. We'll have to work that out. Probably have to keep our piss-ups to your place or mine once I have one, rather than the streets of Nottingham."

"It wasn't the piss-ups I was thinking about, it was the office. Working together. That'll be something new."

"We'll sort it, Jennifer, don't worry. I think we know each other well enough to strike the right balance."

"What does, er, what's his name? I keep forgetting."

"Steven."

"Yes. What does Steven think? He can't be over-impressed you'll be moving out."

"I haven't told him yet."

"What!"

"To be honest, I think it's run its course. He's a selfish bugger, which of course I am too, but if there ever was a spark, it's pretty much gone. When I tell him, there'll be a monumental row and I'm not ready for it. He was away in the States all last week, gets back tonight. I won't broach it until he's got over the jet lag, but I suspect I shall arrive unencumbered."

"When do you start?"

"Fairly soon, as it happens. Hawkins, being the impatient sweetheart you know and love, of course wants it to be yesterday. And as it turns out, he has almost got what he wants. I'm at a good point case-wise to hand over without dropping some poor sod in it, so I'll be able to report for duty in a week or two. But in the meantime, once he's announced it tomorrow, Hawkins wants me to pop up to be introduced to everyone. You and Derek are the only ones I've ever met, apart from Hugh Gregson, of course, and I was as devastated as everyone else to hear the news. He was such a good bloke and a great cop. It'll be a challenge to step into his shoes."

"I'm sure they'll fit you better than they are temporarily fitting Len Crawford. I know I'm not supposed to say this, but you're not my boss yet so I will. He's really floundering."

"I'm not surprised. I've been told he's a lifelong lieutenant, not a leader. Of course, I haven't actually met him, so perhaps I shouldn't pass judgement."

"His heart's in the right place, but he'll be happy to have an immediate senior officer to make the important decisions."

"OK," said Trisha, laughing loudly. "That seems to have everyone sorted and in their place."

"Which day are you here?"

"I'm driving up tomorrow evening for the meet and greet on Wednesday morning. I'll stay over until about Thursday lunchtime, but I've got to be back for a meeting here late Thursday afternoon with some prat of a politician. I shall be happy to trample all over his pomposity now I know that I won't be dealing with him again."

"Attagirl. Do you want to stay at my place, the spare room's always ready and waiting?"

"Thanks, but Hawkins wants to keep it formal. He's booked me into a hotel for a couple of nights. Somewhere near the SCF."

Jennifer laughed. "Probably the Old Nottingham. It's right outside The Park. Watch out for the ghost of your predecessor, Olivia Freneton. That's where she spun her web around Henry. It all began there."

"Oh," said Trisha, with an exaggerated shudder. "I didn't know that. I wonder if she still stalks the corridors."

"If you hear anything weird, let me know and I'll get an exorcist in."

"Thanks for that, Jennifer. Makes me feel much better. I probably won't sleep Tuesday night now."

"I'll pop round with a bottle of something red, if you like."

"Thanks, but I'll be fairly late arriving. Maybe we can get together on Wednesday evening."

"Righty-ho. Hey, this is great news, Trish. It's already growing on me. By the way, remember that there's a big storm blasting its way in from the Atlantic tomorrow. Take care on the road; the M1 can be a pig in bad weather. Oh yes, come off the M1 at junction twenty-five. It's the best way into town for your hotel."

"I'll do my best, but it'll depend on the mood of my satnav. We have a bit of a love-hate relationship and it's dedicated its electronic existence to showing me the scenic routes of England. However, with my sense of direction, I've little option but to rely on it."

Chapter Twenty

DC Gus Brooke was working late. He had to; he'd been letting things slip for far too long. Since Gregson died, he'd found that Crawford was a less forgiving boss, too insecure to be flexible, and the new DS, Jennifer Cotton, expected everything by yesterday. The problem was she had the ear of the DCS and the heart of one of the team of DCs, if not all of them. Brooke felt hemmed in by his own inefficiency, unable to do things the way he preferred. The casual way.

And to make matters worse, they'd been told yesterday that Gregson's replacement was another woman, Detective Superintendent Trisha McVie. High flying, hard-hitting and hard-nosed if you crossed her, according to a number of ex-mates in the West Mids who had contacts in the Manchester Force. Brooke had never met her, but her reputation preceded her and she was arriving tomorrow to meet the team. With a number of high-profile cases on the books, she was going to be looking for any shortcomings; it was what all new bosses did to show how bloody clever they were. And Gus's shortcomings had been gaining traction lately, branching out into uncharted territory where they hadn't previously ventured.

Which was why he was working late. Trying to get back on track.

Another flash of lightning filled the Nottingham skyline with fleeting electric daylight, the angry sonic shock of battered air molecules following almost immediately as the storm raged over-head. Gus looked up at the sheets of rain blurring the windows. The forecast reckoned there would be no let-up for several hours and he not only needed his sleep to be fresh for the team's nine o'clock summons, but he was also starving. He had missed lunch in an effort to gain momentum in the voyage of discovery through his files, only to be thwarted by Cotton mid-afternoon with an instruc-tion to drive up to the suburb of Arnold to get more information from a reluctant witness. A valuable two hours down the drain in a down-at-heel dump trying to coax the memory of some old dear about what she might or might not have seen. The woman was far too nervy ever to be a reliable witness; Cotton should have under-stood that and not wasted his time.

He glanced at his watch: nine o'clock. Bugger it, he'd had enough. With Mo away at a sculptors' retreat she was supervising in the depths of Croatia for over a week now and not returning for another week, Gus was fed up with looking after himself, fed up with the lack of company, fed up with living two miles from the nearest village in some ancient cottage Mo had insisted they buy because its 'uninhibited authenticity' gave her inspiration; just bloody fed up. Sod the files, he'd have to try his usual charm offen-sive in the morning and hope for the best. Perhaps McVie would be so keen to impress that she wouldn't notice the little things, the important details that were the lifeblood of any investigation.

Whatever. He shut down his computer, grabbed his jacket and headed for the top floor of the car park, sprinting for his car in a brief slackening of the rain's intensity while the clouds regrouped to maximise the impact of their next barrage.

With the wipers on full, Gus could just about see the road ahead as he gingerly made his way towards Trent Bridge, after which he took a minor road heading south of Nottingham towards the forgettable village of Rappington.

Originally one of the rural feeder roads leading to the M1, its inadequacies as a conduit for busy traffic had been forgotten with the creation of a new road through farmland that bypassed Rappington. The village had been left in peace with no further thought about and certainly no funding earmarked for straightening out a slew of tight bends on both sides of the village. Gus assumed the inadequate roads followed ancient cart tracks, but why even cart tracks would be quite so eccentric in their traverse of the countryside was beyond him.

After Rappington, there were two almost ninety degree bends separated by a hundred metres of teasingly straight road guaranteed to fool the unwary into speeding up too much. Gus knew the road well enough to treat it with respect: he had slowed for the first bend and was maintaining a careful twenty miles an hour as he approached the second.

With much of their light reflected back at the car from the wall of rain ahead of him, Gus's headlights were doing a poor job of showing him the way. As he peered through the windscreen, he became aware of another pair of headlights approaching fast from the opposite direction and he instinctively slowed some more. He was rewarded by the spectacle of a red Volkswagen Golf executing a tight anticlockwise spin as it careered across the corner in a whirlwind of spray and sparks as a wheel rim and the road made reluctant acquaintance. The car rocked wildly on its suspension as the driver fought to regain control before shuddering to a jarring halt two feet short of a huge oak tree, an immovable object that would have inflicted terminal damage on the Golf's bodywork should the two have collided. But they didn't and the Golf remained intact but listing over a rear nearside wheel bearing the shredded remains of a deformed and useless tyre.

Gus brought his car to a halt a few feet from the Golf, left his headlights picking out the car in stark relief and switched on his emergency hazard lights. As he jumped out of the car, he remembered there was an umbrella on the back seat, but one blast from the swirling wind told him not to waste his time. He was soaked to the skin in seconds and no umbrella was going to help.

Leaning into the wind, his head down, he hurried as far as the driver's door and rapped on the glass. Peering closer, he could make out a woman staring ahead while still clutching the steering wheel. He rapped on the glass again and the woman turned her head, her eyes seeking his through the waterfall drowning the window.

"Are you all right?" he yelled, but his voice made little headway against the force of the storm.

The door opened, forcing Gus to take a step backwards. The woman got out, halting briefly as Gus shouted at her. "Better to stay inside; you'll be soaked in seconds out here."

The woman looked down at her clothing. "Too late for that, I think."

She took a deep breath. "That was a bit close. I wasn't going particularly fast, but that corner came out of nowhere and at the same time, something weird happened to the steering."

"Looks like you got a puncture at the wrong moment," shouted Gus, pointing at the rear wheel. "If you hit the brakes on the corner, chances are that you'd lose control."

He bent down to assess the damage. "The tyre and wheel are both wrecked," he said, as he stood up again. "The tyre was probably running almost flat for a few hundred metres until it gave up on the corner. Have you got a spare?"

He looked into the woman's eyes, making a rapid assessment. Good looking, late thirties, laughter lines around the eyes. He glanced at her hands. No wedding ring.

The woman turned and opened the Golf's tailgate, bending under it to get some shelter. Gus leaned in next to her and the noise of the storm lessened enough for them to stop shouting.

"Under there, last time I looked," said the woman, pointing to the boot floor covering.

"Jack? Wheel brace?"

The woman lifted up the floor panel. "Here, next to the wheel."

As Gus reached forward to release the jack, the woman touched his arm. "I can't ask you to do that, not in this weather."

He snorted a short laugh. "I'm hardly going to stand and watch. And I couldn't get any wetter if I walked back into Rappington and jumped into the village pond."

"Well, if you insist. It's really very good of you."

"Shouldn't take long," said Gus, letting his eyes close slightly as he smiled at her. He knew from experience it was a winning look, and he was already making plans.

The woman held out her hand. "Emma Carrington," she said, smiling back at him, a suggestion of interest in her eyes ticking another box on Gus's mental assessment sheet.

"Martin," he said, taking her hand and holding it for slightly longer than necessary. "Mart. Mart Burton."

"Please to meet you, Mart. Your timing was perfect."

The spell was broken by another clap of thunder.

"Better get a move on," said Gus. "The wind's picking up now. Don't want to add chill factor to being soaking wet."

He bent to loosen the wheel nuts before locating the jack beneath a bracing point forward of the rear wheel, noticing out of the corner of his eye that rather than taking shelter under the tailgate as he had suggested, the woman was standing immediately behind him, seemingly oblivious of the rain.

Trisha McVie's drive up to Nottingham had been a pig from the moment she drove out of the underground car park into the foulest storm she could remember.

The day had actually started well. Some case review meetings at the Yard followed by a light lunch with her boss and the assistant commissioner. She didn't like either of them much, but they liked her, and that was all that mattered. She was on their radar as a future star and if the occasional lunch was all that was needed to keep the flame burning, she was prepared to go with it. They both had speech defects which entertained her when she lapsed into bored silence while they swapped self-congratulatory snippets, speech defects she would enjoy mimicking at a later date on a boozy night with Jennifer.

In the late afternoon, she had treated herself to an adventurous new hair style and colour to match. Ash blonde. She'd experimented with streaks of the colour before, but this time she'd taken it a stage further, combining it with a shorter, layered look. A change of style for a new city full of new opportunities. Jennifer would be surprised but positive, as she always was; she was that sort of woman.

As the miserable drive out of London worsened with the fading light and the storm showing no sign of abating, Trisha's mood darkened. She had hoped to drive up on a bright September evening, the sun disappearing somewhere to her left as she headed north, a warm glow across the fields. Instead, it was slate grey fading to black, the spray from the trucks and massive lorries relentless, like driving through one car wash after another.

To make the drive even more uncomfortable, her partner of six months, Steven, persisted in continuing with a series of acrimonious phone calls that had started the previous evening.

When Steven had called the night before with the news that he had been held up on his trip to the States, Trisha had finally told him about her new job. An hour of apoplexy later, her response had oscillated between indignant rebuttal of his anger and regret that surprised her: it hadn't occurred to her that she might actually have feelings for the man. Steven had finally slammed the phone down on her after calling her a shallow, unfeeling and heartless fucking bitch who wouldn't recognise honest commitment if it slapped her around her arrogant head.

The second part had stung. She had been in meaningful relationships before, plenty of them. It was just that ultimately they weren't right.

Later, when it was time to get up in New York, he'd called again, and he was clearly hung over. She told him she couldn't talk until later when she would be in the car, forgetting that the weather would require all her concentration. She hoped he might have work to do but as she passed Luton, the phone buzzed again.

"Christ, Steven, give me a break. Do you realise what the weather's like here? It's like the end of the bloody world, swirling oceans of rain crashing down on all sides, headlights picking out weird shapes and massive trucks trying to kill me. I really don't have time to carry on from where we stopped last night."

"Well, bloody make time! I thought you people went on advanced driving courses. You are supposed to be experts."

"Even if I had been on one of those courses, which I haven't, I'd still need to concentrate. Shit! Get out of the way, wanker! Bloody lorries, they should be banned in this weather."

"Listen, Trish." Steven was trying a different, more humble tack. "I've been thinking. If you're serious about this transfer to Nottingham—"

"Which I am. I'm on my way there now," interrupted Trisha.

"Right. Well, as I said, I've been thinking. I could, at a stretch, get a transfer to somewhere around there."

Trish snorted her derision. "How could you possibly do that? You're more or less the boss. You work in head office. You said yourself the Midlands office was a waste of space."

"Yeah, well, perhaps I was overstating it. With a good shake up, the sort that I could give it, it could perk up considerably."

"I'm not going to tell you how to run your life, Steven, but if you think that moving to the Midlands will change the downward spiral we're in, you're mistaken."

"What downward spiral? Two weeks ago you were saying how great everything was."

"I was pissed. Merlot-coloured glasses. Right now, I'm just pissed off. I've nearly had three accidents since you called. Are you deliberately trying to kill me?"

"Stop bloody exaggerating, Trish. You're such a fucking drama queen."

"Bollocks!" screamed Trisha, as another wall of water hit her car. "That was too close! What did you just call me?"

"I said—"

"I don't bloody care!" She hit the end call button on her remote and snarled though the windscreen. "Stupid man."

With no let-up in the storm, and the endless heavy traffic, it was almost two hours before Trisha pulled into Watford Gap services on the M1 for a much-needed coffee. She snatched her phone from the hands-free cradle, stuffed it into her handbag and ran for shelter. As she burst through the doors into the steamy, stale air of the entrance to the coffee outlets, fast-food chains and mini-supermarkets selling little of nutritional value, she glared menacingly at three smokers taking surreptitious drags in the shelter of the entrance rather than go outside where they were supposed to be. She was about to lecture them when her phone rang again.

"Bugger it, Steven, don't you ever give up?"

"Sounds quieter. Has the rain stopped?"

"What? No, of course it hasn't. It's never going to stop. I'm just taking a caffeine break."

"Then you can talk."

"No, I can't, or at least I don't want to. I've had it up to here. Don't you get that?"

"No, Trish, I don't. I thought we had something."

"We did. It was called lust. But *lust* doesn't always *last*, Steven, and ours got *lost*."

"I suppose you think that's clever. You rolled it out so smoothly that it must be a line you've used before."

"Oh, for God's sake! Look I'm getting a coffee and then I'm off. I really don't want to talk."

"But—"

The phone went dead as Trisha closed the call. She stared at the screen for a few seconds, sighed and switched the device off. It was contrary to protocol, but it was the only way she'd keep her sanity for the last part of the journey, especially since the rain appeared to be getting heavier, if that were even possible.

When she got back into the car clutching her coffee, she tossed the phone into a well on the dashboard, switched on the engine and glanced dismissively at her satnav.

"OK, Dolores, let's see if I can find my way out of this bloody maze and back on the sodding motorway without your help."

Dolores, the soft Irish voice Trish had chosen for the device, purred back at her. "After fifty yards, turn right, then keep right, then ta—"

"Are you bloody listening, Dolores?" screamed Trisha. "I said I can do it! Just shut it and save your voice until we get back on the motorway."

Dolores said nothing further as she waited patiently for Trisha to find her way to the slip road.

Forty-five minutes later, there was less traffic, but the response of those drivers still heading northwards was to speed up in total disregard of the hazardous conditions.

When Dolores burst into life, she gave Trish a start. "In two miles, take the exit."

Trish frowned. "Really? Are you sure?" She glanced at an approaching overhead sign to see the next exit was number twenty-four. "I'm sure Jennifer said twenty-five, Dolores. Has the rain affected your contacts?"

"Take the exit."

"OK, you know best. I certainly don't fancy trying to navigate this place without your help."

She looked at the time-left-on-journey read-out and it seemed about right. "Let's do it, Dolly," she said.

Leaving the roundabout after crossing over the motorway, Trisha noticed the signs to Nottingham took her onto a new-looking dual carriageway. She winked at the satnav. "Soon be there."

But Dolores had other thoughts. Not half a mile down the road, she surprised Trisha by telling her to take the next road on the left.

"You're joking, Dolores, aren't you?" said Trisha, peering at the satnav screen and then at a signpost. Rappington 4. "Never heard of it," she grumbled. "But I must bow to your superior knowledge, Dol; perhaps you know a shortcut."

She turned left as instructed and almost immediately hit a huge puddle of water that had gathered in a depression in the tarmac. "Hope you can swim, Dolly girl," she said, peering through the windscreen as she tried to distinguish road from ditch.

Normally Trisha would have kept half an eye on the satnav screen and seen the approaching tight bends. But on this occasion, with the rain beating on the windscreen, she was too focussed on trying to see anything at all and it wasn't until she was almost on the first bend and driving too fast that she made out several large trees directly ahead where previously there had only been road. She hit the brakes and the car took on a life of its own.

The tyre had finished its slow deflation two miles back, but with the speed at which Trisha was driving, along with suspension that was too clever by half, it wasn't until she braked hard that the car dipped alarmingly and its rear left wheel rim connected with the tarmac. It was all Trisha could do to stop the car from bouncing off the road and by the time it eventually shuddered to a halt perilously close to a massive tree, she was white with fear, her hands shaking as they gripped the steering wheel.

Using the name Emma Carrington was second nature to her. It was what she always did when she met someone in a social situation that was unlikely to call on her role as a police officer. She had learned from rather too many examples that using her real name was dodgy if her job became known; it was too much information for someone to have on her, especially after a one-night stand. And if she made her job known immediately, it was more often than not a total turn-off. She could read it in the eyes; too many people had too much to hide.

Nearly writing off your car and having a passing knight in shining armour change your wheel for you was hardly a social situation, but you never knew what might transpire. She certainly saw no reason to announce to Mart Burton that she was a detective superintendent of police. She had a well-rehearsed alternative life story she had used successfully on a number of occasions; she would stick to that.

Gus Brooke wound down the jack and the red Golf settled comfortably on its spare tyre. He looked at it and pulled a face. It needed some air but it would get her safely enough to where she was going, assuming that wasn't too far away. For similar reasons to Trisha McVie, Gus seldom used his real name or mentioned his job when he met someone new who had no reason to know the truth.

Telling a woman he might casually try it on with when Mo was away that he was a cop was an almost guaranteed bucket of cold water. There were far too many women on one recreational drug or another who would become shit-scared in the presence of the law. Best they had no notion of who he was or what he did.

Trisha watched as Gus hauled the wrecked wheel into the well in the boot of her Golf and put the cover back in position. With water running in competing rivulets down his face and his clothing sodden, he was a mess. He looked down at his grimy hands and filthy suit trousers and laughed. "Glad I don't spend much on my suits."

"I'll buy you a replacement set of clothes; it's the least I can do," said Trisha.

Gus shook his head. "Not a problem. This old suit has been through worse than this. Look, it's getting a bit chilly and this rain is showing no sign of stopping. I don't know how far you have to go, but you're as wet as I am. We should both get out of our clothes before we turn into candidates for A&E. My little cottage is less than a mile from here; you will have passed it but in this weather you wouldn't have seen it. I've got plenty of hot water and fluffy towels. A hot cup of something wouldn't go amiss either, or something stronger if you'd prefer. You're probably still feeling shaken up after that near miss; I know I would be."

He paused before catching her eyes. "You'd be most welcome."

"You really are Sir Galahad," said Trisha, laughing. "It's a kind offer, but I should be getting along. I've still got quite a way to go."

"All the more reason for accepting my offer," said Gus. "If you drive far like that, you'll end up with pneumonia."

Trisha made a show of considering it further before tilting her head in apparent capitulation.

"A hot shower right now is certainly rather appealing," she said. "OK, thank you, Mart. You're very kind."

Chapter Twenty-One

Trisha was impressed by what Gus had called his 'little cottage'. It was far larger than she'd imagined and renovated in a modern, country style that was both minimalist and practical without losing its charm.

Gus showed her to a bedroom on the ground floor, one of four, he told her. "I prefer the bathroom in there to the others. The water pressure is a bit better and I'm rather proud of the quirky solution I dreamed up to fit everything in. In fact, I was so pleased with myself that I repeated the design in the bathroom of the master bedroom, even though it wasn't absolutely necessary."

"I'm intrigued," she said, tossing her handbag and overnight bag onto the bed.

"I'm going to bung my stuff in the washer on a quick cycle," continued Gus, moving towards the door. "Put yours in too, if you like. It'll all be ready in an hour."

"That would be great," enthused Trisha. "These jeans are the only casual clothes I brought with me; the rest is work stuff for the next two days. Can't stand wearing it after hours. While I'm at it, I'll chuck in the top, jumper and undies too, if I may; they're all sodden."

"Sure," said Gus. "Toss them all in the hallway and I'll take them through to the utility room once I've had my shower."

. . .

Trish closed the bedroom door and continued her quiet inspection. She was convinced that much of what she was seeing had a female influence, a female with a strong designer instinct. It was the colours, textures and fabrics, along with some big, bold paintings, all swirling colour, heavy on oil. If Mart Burton wasn't an interior designer or an artist, and there was something about him that said he wasn't, he'd either employed a professional, which would be costly, or had a wife with her finger on the decoration pulse.

Not wanting to drip on the bedroom carpet more than necessary, she made straight for the bathroom and peeled off her clothes. There were two fluffy white bathrobes folded neatly and stacked alongside several bath towels on raw wooden shelving next to the double washbasin. She ran a hand over their pristine folds; she was already looking forward to snuggling up in one while she waited for her clothes to finish drying.

But what caught her eye more than the free-standing bathtub and the large shower with its tropical-rainforest shower head, were two steps leading up to a raised dog-leg in the bathroom floor beyond the bath where the loo and bidet were placed. This was clearly the design feature Mart was so proud of. Gives sitting on the throne a whole new meaning, she thought, smiling to herself.

Wanting to give herself plenty of time to luxuriate in a steaming shower, she slipped on a bathrobe and gathered her clothes together, intending to leave them outside the bedroom door as instructed. But when she opened the door to the hallway and heard a shower running elsewhere in the house, she continued on as far as the kitchen and left the clothes on a chair.

On her way back through the bedroom, she stopped as she caught sight of her handbag on the bed next to her overnight bag. The handbag contained everything that identified her: credit cards, driving licence and, in particular, her warrant card. The last thing she wanted was for Mart to snoop through her bag while she was in the shower and discover her true identity; discovering she was a senior police officer might spoil a potentially fun evening. However, the solution was simple: obsessive about tidiness, she had packed the overnight bag with her accustomed pristine neatness, and with a few deft changes of order to its contents, the handbag was stowed away towards the bottom, next to the clothes she intended to wear the next day.

For the next fifteen minutes, she enjoyed the comfort of the scalding hot water as she washed away the memories of her crappy drive up, the filthy storm, the puncture and near write-off of the car. Added to those, she took particular enjoyment in washing away memories of bloody Steven Hawthorn, whom she'd now decided was her ex.

As she dismissed him from her mind and her life, she remembered that she'd left her phone in the car, switched off after that final pathetic call with him whining away. She should retrieve it and turn it back on; she'd have any of her junior officers' guts strung on a line for being out of contact for anything more than a brief, justifiable period. No doubt Mart would have an umbrella; she'd fetch the phone once her clothes were ready.

"Ah, there you are, Emma," said Gus, turning towards her from where he was opening a bottle of red wine in the open-plan kitchen. "I thought maybe you'd drowned in the bath."

Trisha smiled at him. He looked relaxed and sure of himself in a pair of slate-grey lounge pants and a loose, pale-grey cotton top. His hair was slicked back, still wet from the shower.

"I was drowning all right, but not in the bath. I was drowning in the luxury of winding down in that lovely shower. And this bathrobe is magical; it has a warm glow all of its own. I also dug a hairdryer out of a cupboard in the bathroom in an attempt to breathe life back into my hair. I paid a fortune to have it done only this afternoon; I could have asked dear Julian to give me a drowned-rat punk look there and then. It would have cost far less."

Gus laughed. "Looks pretty good to me."

"Mmm," conceded Trisha, with a nod, "it did fall perfectly into place as it dried, so I suppose he knew what he was doing."

Gus held up the bottle of red wine. "I'm having a glass of this, if you'd care to join me. Alternatively, the kettle's just boiled.

There's a selection of various packets of things that claim to be tea, including good old-fashioned builder's, or there's coffee if you'd prefer. And if you still want warming up, there's hot chocolate as well."

He smiled, his arm still extended upwards with the wine bottle.

Trisha sighed her indecision. "The wine is certainly tempting after everything that's happened today, but I'm not sure how far I still have to drive, and in this weather, I'll still need my wits about me as well as staying on the right side of the law. It's something I'm very strict with myself about."

"Staying on the right side of the law or not drinking and driving?" said Gus, raising an amused eyebrow.

Trisha pushed her lips together in a smile. "Both. But particularly drinking and driving. I keep whole fleets of taxis in business in London."

Gus unscrewed the bottle cap. "It's your choice, Emma. But if you do want to have a drink, you're perfectly welcome to stay the night. As you've seen, the bed along there in the downstairs guest room is all made up. As are the others, in fact."

Trish stretched and yawned. "Sorry," she said, patting her mouth. "I must say the thought of not going out again tonight is certainly appealing."

She paused before adding, "Thank you, it's a most generous offer."

Gus took a second wine glass out of a wall cupboard next to him and held it up. "So, that's a yes?"

"It's a yes," smiled Trisha in agreement. "Do you mind if I pull a chair up by the log burner? I love the glass front; I can see that winters here wouldn't be so bad."

"Only moved in last spring, so it's hard to say. But, yes, that's the general idea." He handed her wine to her and drew a second chair closer to the stove for himself, "Tell me, what brings you to this part of the world on a filthy September night?"

Trisha took a breath, ready with her tale. "I'm an art dealer," she said, "for a rather exclusive little gallery in Mayfair. Our clients expect the personal touch, so I'm often out and about giving them notice of work coming our way that might interest them. It's a pain when it could all be done by email, but you'd be surprised how much difference it makes."

"Rubbing shoulders with the rich and famous, eh? Another world, I should imagine."

Trisha laughed. "Sometimes, yes, but most of the time it's the rich and self-absorbed. I'm seeing someone tomorrow at their home in The Park in Nottingham," — she quietly thanked Jennifer for living there, otherwise she wouldn't have had a clue about the better quality districts in the city — "and after that I'm off out into the sticks somewhere. Can't remember the name, but I've got it all written down."

She paused and took a large pull on her wine. "Mmm, that's delicious. Cabernet?"

"Cabernet-Merlot blend."

"What's with the throne in the bathroom," she asked. "I must admit, it looks good, but is it necessary?"

Gus laughed. "It is, actually, yes. On the other side of the wall behind the shower is a stairway to the cellar and a void that was just begging to be filled. So with a little wall rejigging, I created the raised floor over part of the void and a cupboard as well. Wouldn't have had nearly so much room in the bathroom without putting the loo and bidet there. As I said earlier, I liked the look of it so much that I repeated the design in the master bathroom."

Trisha nodded. "Clever stuff. Is that what you do? Cottage refurbishment?"

"No, not at all. I'm in software. I work for a computer company writing various types of business programs. My company opened a new East Mids office last year and gave me the job of getting it up and running."

"Sounds interesting," she lied as she ran her eyes over him while he stared into his glass. She had never seen anyone less like a software engineer in her life.

Gus shrugged dismissively. "It has its moments. And it keeps the wolf from the door."

He drained his glass and stood up. "Are you hungry? I know I am. I've got some great curried chicken left from last night. I normally make enough for two or three nights rather than start from scratch every time, and there's loads of salad, nuts and cheese."

Trisha nodded. "Yes, I'm starving. That all sounds wonderful."

She stood and followed Gus to the kitchen area. "What can I do?"

"Top up the wine?" suggested Gus, nodding towards the bottle. "And there are plates in there," — a nod towards a lower cupboard — "and cutlery in the drawer in front of you."

"Where are we eating?" asked Trisha, pulling a pair of plates from the cupboard.

"Here, at the counter?" he suggested. "It's warmer than in the dining room."

Trisha set two places.

"Will the washing be ready yet? Not that I was thinking of dressing for dinner, if that's all right."

"If you're comfortable, it's fine by me." He held up a wooden spoon. "Do you want to taste this curry sauce? See if it's okay?"

She walked over to the cooker and stood close to him. She could smell plenty of spice, but it was from his deodorant or cologne, rather than the food. Whatever it was, the effect was more than pleasing. She wondered if he would notice the Chanel No. 19 she'd found in the bathroom cabinet and sprayed liberally. It was her favourite, but she hadn't used it since that arse Steven had accidentally knocked her bottle off a shelf and watched it smash on the bathroom floor. She'd been livid and there'd been another monumental row. And the bugger hadn't even replaced it.

Gus held the spoon out for her, more or less forcing her to place her hand on his to draw the spoon into her mouth.

"Wow!" she said, nodding her head in approval. "That's delicious. Is it Mary Berry or an old family recipe?"

Gus half-closed his eyes mysteriously. "It was a secret my grandmother taught me."

"Was she Indian?"

"Not as far as I know. She was from Bournemouth."

"Then I reckon she had a secret admirer in a local restaurant."

Realising she still had her hand on his, she pulled the spoon towards her again for a second taste.

"Magic," she said, finally dropping her hand.

"Perhaps I'd better check the washing. If it's ready, is there somewhere I can hang it up to air?"

"On a night like this, probably better to chuck it all into the tumble dryer. Twenty minutes should do it. Could you bring in another bottle of this red as well? There's a pantry beyond the washer with a large rack in it."

Trisha came back a few minutes later carrying two bottles of wine, a mischievous glint in her eye.

When Gus saw them, he smiled inwardly to himself. The evening was turning out well.

"Seeing how that bottle is more or less empty," said Trisha, "I thought that two … well, you know."

"Excellent thought," said Gus, as he emptied the remains of the first bottle into her glass and took the two she was carrying from her. "Shall we eat?"

Half-an-hour later, they had finished the food and the second bottle of wine. Trisha's head was beginning to spin, but she still felt as much in control as she needed to be. She was surprised how relaxed she felt in this man's company. He was at least ten years younger than her and more than a little arrogant with his opinions and self-satisfied stories, none of which she believed. She didn't care; she knew exactly where the evening was going and she was looking forward to it, in spite of a nagging feeling that she should get at least a little sleep so she didn't look too washed out in front of DCS Hawkins and the SCF team in the morning. However, experience told her that just a little sleep would be more than suffi-cient. And in spite of a degree of over-confidence, which was prob-ably an act, she was enjoying Mart Burton's company. He was amusing, and it was interesting to follow his line of seduction.

"When is it, Emma?" he said, surprising her as his voice inter-rupted her thoughts.

"Er, sorry," said Trisha. She had drifted slightly deeper into the heady lake of red wine and lost the last half minute or so of conversation.

Gus smiled at her. "I was talking about performance."

He paused, letting the suggestive tone register. "On the track or in the gym, I mean," he said, his smile indicating that the track and gym weren't remotely connected to what he meant. "And you mentioned the half-marathon you are training for."

"Did I? Oh, yes."

Bugger, she must have that slip. Bloody race. Now she'd transferred to Nottingham, Jennifer would probably get all keen about it once again.

"It's not until the spring," she ad libbed. "Plenty of time for training."

As she emptied the contents of her glass, she remembered what he'd been telling her.

"Do you really run every morning?"

"Yes, like I said, there's a network of waterways around here, irrigation channels and so on. Several of them have paths alongside that make great running tracks, and they're flat, for the most part."

Gus removed the top of the third bottle. "A top-up?" he said.

"I will if you will," she said, suppressing a boozy giggle and holding up her glass.

The glasses generously filled, Gus put the bottle down and leaned towards Trisha, raising his glass. "Cheers, Emma," he said, as she responded by leaning in his direction and clinking his glass. "Here's to the storm."

As if in direct response, a flash in the sky outside was followed immediately by a deafening crash of thunder. They both laughed.

"Long may it last," said Trisha.

Then, suddenly, they were kissing.

"Wait," said Trisha, pulling back. He looked at her, briefly puzzled until he saw she was taking his wine glass and putting it out of harm's way next to where somehow she had already placed hers.

"Better," she said, and both arms were around his neck and the kissing became deeper and stronger, while very quickly hands were moving, exploring, stroking, and her bathrobe fell from her shoulders.

"Is it as warm in your bedroom?" she murmured.

"Oh, yes. Deliciously so."

"Then let's go there. I need to be horizontal."

Chapter Twenty-Two

At six the following morning, the relentless drumming in Gus's head that had been dragging him into a reluctant semi-consciousness was temporarily swamped by the insistent shrill of his bedside alarm.

"Fuck it," he mumbled as a practised arm swung towards the alarm and silenced it. But the drumming continued and was getting louder.

"Aargh!" he growled as his hand reached for his neck and tried to squeeze the pain into submission. His eyes opened slowly, grateful for the weak light from a sky still full of cloud after the previous night's storm. His first thought was a simple fact: he couldn't possibly go for his morning run. His second was a question: why was he in this state? Gradually, the events of the night before filtered into his mind, and in spite of the drumming, he smiled and flipped onto his side.

The other half of the bed was empty, although there was a depression in the pillow next to his.

Bathroom, he thought.

He sat up. He was naked, which confirmed he'd had company. He tried to focus on the room. In an untidy heap near the door was the bathrobe that … what was her name? Emily? Emma? Yes, Emma … that Emma had been wearing when he half-carried her to the bedroom. He smiled, remembering how the bubble of concern he'd had over her falling asleep once they lay on the bed had burst as she immediately rolled on top of him and began hungrily removing his clothes.

Taking a deep breath, he rotated his shoulders and stretched his neck, twisting and rolling his head to ease the drumming. Better. He checked the time. What had she said? She had a nine o'clock in Nottingham? It was only a half-hour drive, so perhaps …

He stood and pulled on his own bathrobe, steadied himself and walked over to the bathroom to knock on the closed door.

"Emma?"

Nothing. Perhaps not wanting to disturb him, she had gone to use one of the other bathrooms. Then he remembered that all her clothes had been through the wash and left in the drier. She was probably downstairs, unless she'd buggered off. It had happened before.

He pulled the curtain back. It had finally stopped raining, and, yes, there was her red Golf behind his car. Just as well they didn't have neighbours. He smirked at the thought; it was one of the advantages of living where they did when Mo was away.

After checking the other two upstairs bathrooms, Gus went down to the kitchen, but there was no sign of Emma. He flicked on the kettle before walking along the corridor to the downstairs guest room.

"Emma? Good morning. Are you there? Would you like some tea?"

No response.

In the bedroom, he saw Emma's overnight bag was on the bed and the bathroom door slightly ajar.

"Emma? Everything all right?"

He knocked on the door and slowly pushed it open. "Emma?"

But the bathroom was empty, just the remains of her activities evident from the night before where she'd showered and tidied herself up. Herself, he thought, but not the bathroom. Still, there was plenty of time for that.

Returning to the kitchen, he picked up an empty wine bottle from the surface of the island unit and tossed it in the pedal bin as he walked to the half-open utility room door. He peered into the room. Emma wasn't there. Puzzled now, Gus strode over to the washer and drier and pulled open their doors. The washer was empty but in the drier were what looked like all the things he'd washed along with Emma's.

He pulled out the tangled heap of clothes and separated them into his and hers. Jeans, top, cotton jumper, panties and bra. Everything she'd been wearing, as far as he knew. The jacket she'd grabbed from her car while he'd been changing the wheel had, he thought, been tossed onto a peg as they came into the cottage, her wet shoes kicked off nearby.

Frowning now, he went back into the kitchen and looked over to the outside door. Emma's jacket was on the peg, a small puddle of water still on the floor beneath it. He had meant to give the jacket a shake and hang it up, but he'd forgotten, as had Emma, who, he now realised, had been far more interested in cleaning herself up, getting warm and dragging him to bed. A memory of their energetic romp flashed across his mind. She was quite something; definitely someone to keep in touch with.

If he could find out where she was.

Seeing her jacket reminded him that with her clothes still in the drier and the bathrobe she'd been wearing on his bedroom floor, she had nothing to wear. Perhaps she'd dressed in whatever she had in her overnight bag. Dressed for her meeting, that must be it. So, where was she? Had she gone for a walk?

He checked the kitchen door, only to find it locked and the key hanging up in its normal place on a hook near the coats. He ran through the hallway to the sitting room where the old main door to the house was situated, the one they seldom used. The lock was a Yale and its button was down, as usual. She couldn't have gone out that way.

On the way back to the kitchen, he went into the downstairs guest room and unzipped Emma's overnight bag. Apart from a space where she'd pulled out a washbag, everything else was neatly folded and looked undisturbed. It seemed extremely unlikely that she'd removed anything from it. Which must mean that she was still somewhere in the house and either naked or wrapped in a towel she'd grabbed from somewhere.

He smiled as the solution occurred to him: she'd got up, gone to the master bathroom for a pee and dozed off. She would certainly have been blurry. After their first half hour in bed, they had paused to get yet another bottle of wine, and although she'd been almost legless, she'd still demanded more and more from him once they were back between the sheets.

Chapter Twenty-Three

Several hours earlier, Trisha had been forced awake by her bladder. She had somehow remembered to drink two large glasses of water. She didn't know exactly when, but she thought it was probably before she and the man now snoring next to her had staggered up the stairs and set about each other in a ridiculous drunken passion.

She half fell out of the bed, self-conscious without any clothes and wanting to wrap herself in the bedsheet. But she couldn't, it would disturb … what was his name? Mark? Martin? No, Mart. In fact, she doubted his name was Mart any more than hers was Emma Carrington. So what? She needed to pee.

She staggered around the end of the bed, forcing her legs to work. Christ! How much had they had to drink? But through the blur of her memory was a feeling that whatever followed had been fun. Her arms, legs and thighs were certainly aching and her face felt raw. Why didn't men shave these days? As she passed a chest of drawers, she reached out to steady herself, but her hand fell onto something soft and leathery that slipped on the polished wooden surface rather than resisting. Her hand went with it and, already unbalanced, she fell, thumping one knee against the drawers.

"Shit!" she cried, and immediately threw a hand over her mouth, hoping she hadn't woken up Mart-or-whatever-he-was-called. Sitting on the floor, her eyes trying to focus in the gloom, she saw the leathery object that had caused her fall. A wallet. A wallet! She'd have a look inside, ever the nosy copper.

Snatching the wallet from the carpet, she opened it to peer at the contents. It looked like the usual collection of bank cards, driving licence and membership cards. She couldn't tell; it was too dark and the spinning room wasn't helping.

Keeping hold of the wallet, she groped for the edge of the chest of drawers and pulled herself first to her knees and, after a breather, to her feet.

She tried to stand upright, but the urge to pee was too strong. Stooping slightly, she hobbled towards the bathroom, pushed open the door and went in, closing the door behind her.

"Hmm," she slurred, as she leaned against the door. "That was a mistake. Can't see a bloody thing. Shit! The sodding light switch is outside."

Her arms not fully in control, she was waving haphazardly at the wall behind her looking for the door handle when an array of soft lighting filled the space to her left. She turned her blurred eyes towards the lights. Controlled by a sensor near the door, they were mounted beneath a row of wall cupboards above a pair of round, plain-glass washbasins set in a slab of white marble. She frowned at the marble slab. At first glance, it seemed to be hanging in space. The improbability of it distracted her and, grabbing the rim of one of the washbasins, she sank to her knees to look underneath.

"Ah," she mumbled, "concealed brackets. Very swish."

She tried to sit back on her heels, but her balance still wasn't working and she slipped sideways, her head banging against the marble sheet.

"Shit!" she slurred as she dropped the wallet and lifted a hand to rub her head. She looked up, vaguely aware of a large shower cubicle to her right. Her head wobbled and her eyes fell again on the wallet.

"OK, Mr Burton. Let's see who you really are."

This time there was enough light to read the cards. She pulled out a credit card. Fergus J Brooke. She frowned. Why did that name ring a bell? Next among the cards was his driving licence, which gave the same name and an address in

Rappington, Notts. She'd seen a sign to Rappington the previous evening and Mart-now-known-to-be-Fergus had mentioned the name too. But why was the name Brooke so familiar?

She glanced at the other cards. They all had the same information. She opened the wallet's main section to see that next to a number of ten- and twenty-pound notes were several business cards. She pulled one out and held it up.

But before she even got as far as the name, her stomach was turning somersaults of anguish. There, in dark blue on the card's pale blue background, was a crest. A police crest. Nottinghamshire Constabulary. She clenched her teeth, a wave of panic threatening to drown her. No! Please, God. No!

But no amount of pleading to any deity would ever change what was printed on the card.

Fergus J Brooke
Detective Constable
Serious Crime Formation

She stared at the name, the awful reality of her predicament setting her pulse racing. She had screwed one of her junior officers before he even officially became one. Did that make it better? Of course it didn't, you stupid, stupid bitch. You simply didn't do this, not if you wanted to maintain some semblance of self-respect. Or integrity. Or authority. Or your job.

Brooke. Now she remembered. Jennifer had talked about him. Cocky bugger, she'd said, known as Gus, a bit of a player. Well, he was certainly that. Wait — hadn't Jennifer also said he was married? Yes, she had. Definitely.

Trisha tried hard to focus her thoughts, but the red wine was still sloshing through her system, confusing her brain. She couldn't think straight as a thousand fragmented thoughts whirled in her head.

"Hang on," she said, slurring no less than before, "suppose the wallet isn't Mart's. Perhaps he found it, or nicked it. That would be good."

Eagerly she snatched at the driving licence and held it up to look at the photo. Bugger. It was him. Burton was Brooke.

She threw the wallet angrily across the floor. It would have to be Plan B. Blackmail. Brooke was married. How much was his marriage worth? She looked around, still trying to focus. This place was pretty well set up and would have cost far more than a DC's salary could run to. His wife must have a good job; perhaps all this had been done with her money. He wouldn't want to give that up.

She'd wake him up, shake some consciousness into him and read him the riot act. She was his boss now, for Christ's sake. They'd work something out; it was in both their interests.

But more than anything, right now she really did need to pee.

She reached up to the edge of the marble and hauled herself to her feet, the room swirling around her again. She opened her eyes as wide as she could, stretching the muscles, willing them to focus and her head to calm down. She took a breath followed by a tentative step. The loo was mounted on a raised part of the floor like the one in the downstairs bathroom, the design feature Mart had been so proud of. But this one seemed higher.

After her first step, she felt more confident and leaning forward to let the marble slab take her weight through her arms, she took a second. Expecting her foot to find the tiled floor, she was surprised to find it was soft. But she was committed and her weight continued to apply pressure onto whatever she'd trodden on. The wallet slipped backwards, taking Trish's foot with it. She stumbled, and with no more marble slab to grab, she fell heavily forward, her face crashing into the edge of the bath, all but breaking her nose.

She slid to the floor, letting out a yelp rather than a scream, one hand attempting to support her in a twisted sitting position while the other grasped her nose. The hand on her nose filled with blood.

"Bugger! No!" she whimpered. "This can't be happening."

She looked around through a blur of tears and blood, the dizziness still playing tennis with her head making her see double. She was aware of towels on a shelf near her face. She grabbed one and wadded it onto her nose, yelping again at the pain.

Ahead of her was the raised floor with the bidet and loo. The loo. If she didn't get there now, she'd be peeing all over the floor.

She flopped over onto her knees and grabbed the edge of the bath. Panting, she reached out for the steps, climbing them on her hands and knees like a toddler learning to walk. Once she was on the raised floor, she grasped the rim of the bidet and dragged herself to a standing position, reaching out for the tiled wall in an attempt to steady herself. Still wobbling, but confident now she could take the final step to reach the loo, she let go of the wall and, forgetting the damage to her nose, took a deep breath. A wave of pain shot through her head and the room began to spin faster than before.

Confused and needing to balance, she swung her foot behind her, but there was nothing for it to find except space; she was too close to the steps.

The raised part of the floor was almost two feet above the main bathroom floor, unnecessarily high, its inherent danger never once occurring to Gus Brooke. He thought it looked cool and there was, after all, plenty of wall to hold on to. Two extra feet meant the top of Trisha's head was now over seven feet from the main bathroom floor and as she tumbled backwards from the edge of the raised floor, by the time her skull crashed into the five-centimetre-high lip of the shower tray, the speed of her fall was enough for the impact to be fatal.

She didn't cry out. After the dull thud of bone on tile, her body collapsed almost silently across the bathroom floor, the blood from the new injury mixing on the tiles with the blood still oozing from her nose.

Chapter Twenty-Four

"Emma?"

Gus knocked again on the bathroom door.

"Emma. Are you asleep in there?" He tried to inject some light-
ness into his voice, amusement to counter the inevitable embarrassment she would feel knowing she'd crashed out on the bathroom
floor. Curled up next to the loo, perhaps, or in the bath. Whatever.
They'd be laughing about it over coffee in half an hour or so. Or
perhaps giggling about it in bed.

He put his ear to the door. "Emma, I'm coming in. Is
that OK?"

Nothing, not a peep. The wine had certainly knocked her
for six.

He reached out for the handle but stopped as a thought crossed
his mind. If Emma was lying naked, spreadeagled across the floor,
she'd be more than embarrassed to think he might have been
getting an eyeful. If was different when they were in bed, different
rules. This was the cold light of day. Well, dawn.

There were towels on the shelves, but grabbing one of those
might be too late if she roused as he entered the room. He looked
around and saw the bathrobe on the bedroom floor, the one she'd
been wearing the previous evening and looked so sexy in. He
smiled at the memory.

He hurried across the room and picked up the bathrobe. He

could either throw over her or hold it up so she could slip into it. That would add to the chivalrous image she'd had of him when he'd rescued her in the storm.

"Emma! I'm coming in now. Ready?"

Taking the silence as acceptance, he pushed open the door and all but collapsed in shock. There was blood everywhere. A huge pool on the floor around and beyond Emma's head and spatter all over the bath and walls near her body.

Her body!

Christ! No!

Throwing the bathrobe behind him, he stepped forward, mindful not to tread in the blood, his police training for procedure at crime scenes automatically kicking in.

One look at Emma's face confirmed his thoughts, but he still felt her neck for a pulse. There was nothing. She was dead.

But how? What had happened? How come he hadn't heard anything?

He looked again at her face and saw the large wound to her nose. It was split and a bruise had spread under her eyes. That meant something, but he couldn't remember what.

What the fuck was he going to do! This couldn't be happening; it had to be a dream.

He clasped his hands together as he fought the involuntary shaking that had taken over his body. She was dead. In his house. After a night of sex.

His heart was beating so rapidly, he could hear the blood pounding through his ears. At the same time he was gulping air, almost hyperventilating in fear.

One of Emma's arms was stretched out in his direction, her fingers seeming to point at him, begging for help. He took her hand. It was cold and stiff. He tried to bend her arm but it resisted. Had rigor mortis already set in? He tried to move it again and found he was tilting the body by simply lifting her hand, her arm acting as a lever. He let go of the arm. From the little about pathology he knew, he was sure the stiffness meant she'd been dead for several hours.

What time was it now? The alarm had gone at six; it couldn't be more than six thirty. She must have gone out to the loo and fallen. How long ago? What time had they finally flopped to an exhausted halt in bed and collapsed into sleep? It must have been at least one.

None of that mattered. What mattered was what the hell was he going to do? He had the naked body of a woman in his bathroom, a woman he'd shared his bed with who was now dead. He had no idea who she was; she was just someone who … Bugger! Her car was outside. This might be a rural back road these days, but there was always traffic going past in the daytime, people from Rappington heading for the M1. It was the quickest route for them; they would see the red Golf. Maybe someone who knew him, or worse, knew Mo, would see it and tell her. That couldn't happen; he had to get rid of the car.

But what about the body? Think, Brooke, think!

He couldn't report the accident for the simple reason that his wife would get to hear about it. He was a police officer, for Christ's sake, it would be the end of his career as well as the end of his marriage.

As he stared in anger at Trisha's body, anger at the predicament she'd dumped him in, the implications of the injuries to her face hit him. She had what looked like a broken nose. Some clever lawyer, or even his bosses, might think they'd had a fight, that he'd smashed her in the face, broken her nose, knocked her down and beaten her head against the shower tray. That would be murder and difficult to talk his way out of. His DNA would be all over her. It would be his word against theirs, since Emma couldn't support his tale, couldn't tell them that he'd slept through the whole thing.

Panicking now about what he was going to do, he jumped to his feet and ran into the bedroom. What the hell was the time? 6:40. Right. Then he remembered. The new guv. What was her name? Yes, Trisha McVie. The new guv was arriving at the SCF that morning for a nine o'clock meeting. Didn't Emma say she had a nine o'clock? In The Park? That wasn't going to happen, but his meeting was, and he had to be there.

Thank God Mo was away. No, thank no one. If she hadn't been away, this wouldn't have happened.

Priorities, man, priorities. Think like a cop.

OK, number one, the body wasn't going anywhere. If he turned off the heating in the bathroom, the decay would slow down. Mustn't open the window though, the flies would be in. No one was coming into the house. Mercifully he had put his foot down with Mo about a cleaning lady. They couldn't afford it, he said. He knew they could, but it would cramp his style. So the body wasn't a priority, but the car was. Right, number two, the car. What was he going to do with it?

He looked up as he heard a car go by. It still wasn't fully daylight, and with the remnants of the storm still filling the sky, it was darker than normal. He had to drive the car somewhere, dump it and return to the cottage. How would he do that? Walk? Run? His bike! The car was a Golf, a hatchback. If he folded the rear seats down he could just about get his bike in the back. After dumping the car, he could cycle home.

But he couldn't just dump it on the road; it would be found and maybe someone would link its description to one they had seen outside his cottage.

Then he remembered the factory.

One of the first cases Gus Brooke had been involved in on moving to the SCF had been staking out a derelict industrial premises on the Nottingham side of Rappington. Located half a mile off the old Rappington road on a lane that went nowhere, the site had originally been an ambitious factory project built in the 1960s for small manufacturing businesses to pool resources they could otherwise not afford, a project that failed spectacularly at the first hint of a recession. The buildings and plot were sold to a repackaging business that used it until the mid-90s when alternative technology in more convenient locations forced its closure. Now largely derelict, for the past twenty-five years, the site had been left to decay, ignored by its owners as an inconvenience they would rather forget. However, the original name of the project, 'the factory', was still just visible in faded all-lower-case lettering over the main entrance, and the name had stuck.

During the past year, there had been rumours of the factory being used as a drug den, or possibly as a lab for drug manufacture, while other rumours had squatters or vagrants living there. There had even been talk of it being used as a location for making porn movies.

The SCF had staked it out for several weeks, monitoring all vehicles along the Rappington road, taking numbers, looking for frequent visits of people who had no right being there. They had also scoured the place for signs of any activity, but ultimately they found nothing. Eventually, other cases had come up, more important ones and the budget for the surveillance was pulled.

But the outcome was that Gus knew the factory well, knew that the main gateway appeared to be locked up with padlocks and secure fencing, but wasn't. It was a façade. It was easy to pull the gates open, if you knew how, easy to drive in and disappear into a central yard that was hidden from the road. Even better, the rear of the factory site bordered one of the nearby network of irrigation channels, one with a path running alongside it, and he knew of a well-disguised break in the fence where he could get through with his bike.

He checked the time again. 6:50. Working backwards, the meeting at the SCF was at nine; it took him twenty-five minutes from cottage to office; so he should aim to be leaving by 8:30 tops, earlier if possible to allow for any snarl-ups in the traffic.

It would take no more than ten minutes to get to the factory and dump the car. He could take a couple of the pathway routes to cycle home, perhaps being spotted by other fitness regulars who would support his story, should he need it, that he was out doing nothing unusual on the day that Emma Carrington disappeared.

He just about had time to do it if he left in the next fifteen minutes.

Where were her car keys? Jacket. They were probably there. He'd take the jacket and shoes and dump them with the car. What about the overnight bag? Surely it would be better to dump it in the car just in case the car was found. The assumption would be made that she'd been abducted with her car, driven to the factory, and taken somewhere else. Yes, better to lose the bag with the car.

A cold realisation hit him. Suppose, just for a second, that for some reason he came under suspicion. Ridiculous. Why should he?

But suppose. What had he touched? The bag when he peered inside it. He'd wipe around it, the jacket and shoes, too. From now on he'd wear disposable gloves. What about the car? He needed to wipe around the boot area along with the tools and wheel nuts. What else? He couldn't remember touching anything else and he didn't have much time.

Snapping into gear, Gus pulled open his wardrobe, grabbed his cycling kit and ran downstairs. After dropping the kit in the kitchen, he ran out to his car where he kept a bag of scene-of-crime coveralls, gloves and overshoes in the boot. He was going to have to put them all on to drive the Golf and trust his luck that he wasn't seen. He picked up the scene bag, returned indoors and quickly dressed in the cycling kit followed by the scene gear. Looking now as if he were ready to attend a crime scene, he hurried back to the Golf and lowered the rear seats. But before fetching his bike from the garage, he lifted the boot floor covering and wiped the damaged wheel, the jack and the brace. After putting the cover back in place, he wiped its handle. Worried about grease and oil from his bike, he fetched a large bin bag from the kitchen which he spread over the Golf's rear floor. It didn't cover it completely, but it would have to do. The bike stowed, he bent to wipe the nuts of the nearside rear wheel. It was overkill, he knew, given the heavy rain that had continued to wash them, but little details were important. Finally, he made one more trip into the house for Emma's overnight bag along with her jacket and shoes. As he picked up the bag, something nagged at him. Had Emma had a handbag? And where was her washbag? Bathroom. He ran there, eyes searching. Got it. She appeared to have put all her cosmetic stuff back in it, and anyway, if he found something else later, he'd dump it. He carefully unzipped the overnight bag and put the washbag back in place, spotting the top of a handbag as he did. Emma must have stuffed it in there. But something was still nagging at him. Something that might spoil his plans. What was it? Something that might prevent … of course! The factory gates. He hadn't been back there since the operation finished. What if the owners had finally followed the police advice and fitted a proper padlock? That would certainly screw him.

He ran back into the garage to fetch a pair of bolt croppers and added them to a backpack he'd stowed in the rear of the Golf to carry the scene-of-crime coveralls when he cycled back home after dumping the car. Slamming the tailgate shut, he exhaled in relief. Bases all covered.

Keeping a wary eye out for traffic, he was grateful for once that Rappington was a backwater with little going on and with most of its houses set back off the road. He couldn't believe his luck when he reached the turnoff to the factory site without seeing another vehicle.

In the end, since there was still no padlock securing the chain on the gate, the bolt croppers weren't needed. He was quickly inside the site with the gates closed behind him. He drove the Golf into the centre of the yard where the ground was concrete with little surface debris. He didn't want to leave a trail even though his sports shoes were covered with booties. He was relieved to see that in spite of the overall poor condition of the buildings, the drainage in the open yard was good and the previous night's weather hadn't created any problems.

It was at this point he noticed the mobile phone sitting in the cup holder on the dashboard. He froze. It must be Emma's; why hadn't he seen it before? A sick, sinking feeling of impotence threatened to overwhelm him. The phone would be happily sending messages back to the service provider announcing where it was and where it had been. This was, after all, the age of Big Brother. Even smashing the phone now or taking it somewhere else wouldn't affect that record. It would tell whoever investigated Emma's disappearance that it had been outside his house the entire night. This damn little device would be his nemesis and there was nothing he could do about it. In fact, what he was doing now, hiding the car and thinking about how he might dump Emma's body was only making things worse in the light of the story the phone would tell. Shit.

He reached for the phone and pressed the home button. Nothing. He pressed it again. Still nothing. A glimmer of hope lit up in his mind. The phone was either turned off or it had run out of juice. He had to know which it was since if it was flat he could still be in trouble, depending on when that happened, but if Emma had switched it off, the chances were she did it before the puncture. Why would she do that? Maybe worried about calls distracting her when she was concentrating hard on driving in the storm.

He dug around in the various receptacles in and under the dashboard, looking for a paperclip or something similar with which he could release the phone's SIM tray, but he found nothing of any use. Dammit, he kept the one that had come with his phone on his normal key ring along with his car and house keys, but he had left that key ring back at the cottage, grabbing only a single key for the kitchen door from a hook as he left. He checked Trisha's key ring, but again, there was nothing.

"She must have something I can use, for Christ's sake," he whined in frustration.

His eyes made a frantic scan of the dashboard. The glove compartment! He pressed the button on the front and the compartment burst open to reveal a jumble of maps, manuals and a plastic document pouch stuffed to the brim with papers. And yes! Several were stapled together.

Tearing at the corner of one sheaf of insurance bumph, he removed a staple, straightened it out and pushed it into the tiny hole in the side of the phone. After removing the SIM card, he closed the tray and took a deep breath. "Please," he begged as he pressed the button on the phone's top edge to switch it on. After two heart-stopping seconds, the screen lit up as the phone went through its boot routines, the battery condition quickly showing in the top right corner. When it registered eighty-six per cent, Gus knew he was OK. It had been switched off which meant that when the phone was near the cottage, no information was being transmitted.

"Magic," he muttered through clenched teeth, his faith in his luck restored. He slipped both the SIM card and phone in his coverall pocket. "You two are going straight in the nearest stream."

The phone crisis over, Gus removed his bike from the Golf, put the seats back in place and stowed the bin bag in his backpack. He threw Emma's jacket onto the front passenger seat, shoes in the footwell and the overnight bag in the boot. The keys he left in the ignition. If some chancer came along and stole the car, all the better. They'd have some explaining to do if they were caught.

He picked up the bike, not wanting to leave any tyre tread marks, and carried it to the spot on the site perimeter where he could pull the fence apart. Within ten minutes of arriving at the factory, he was cycling along the pathway rather faster than normal and although feeling dreadfully hung over, he was relieved to have completed the first part of the cleanup.

Arriving back at the cottage at 7:45 gave Gus time for a much-needed shower in one of the spare bathrooms. By ten minutes past eight he was in his car, trying to put thoughts of how he was going to deal with the dead body in his bathroom out of his head as he drove into Nottingham to meet Detective Superintendent Trisha McVie.

Part Five

GUS BROOKE

Chapter Twenty-Five

Gus Brooke was the last of the SCF team of detectives to arrive in the main operations office, the rest having left nothing to chance on their new boss's unofficial first morning. Even though Trisha McVie's introduction wasn't scheduled until nine, no one wanted to be caught out by an unexpected early arrival.

Jennifer followed Gus with her eyes as he laboured his way across the room to his desk. She was surprised: he looked dreadful, as if he'd had no sleep, and he was making eye contact with no one. She continued to watch him as he switched on his computer, but after keying in his password, he simply stared at the monitor, his eyes not moving.

Trying to think positively, rather than assume he'd had a late, boozy night, she thought maybe he was sickening for something and had made an effort to come in, not wanting to make a bad impression.

She caught Derek's eye and nodded towards Gus. Derek glanced in his direction and turned immediately back to Jennifer, pulling a face. Jennifer frowned at him, signalling with an insistent nod to talk to Gus.

Raising his eyebrows to heaven, Derek turned.

"Morning Gus. Are yer right, mate?"

For a moment, Gus appeared not to have heard him, but then he nodded, his eyes still fixed on his screen. "Fine."

Derek persisted. "It's just that your eyes look like two piss holes in the snow. Heavy night?"

He grinned knowingly, trying to encourage a response.

"Couldn't sleep, is all," grunted Gus.

Derek straightened in his chair and looked over to Jennifer, shrugging as he silently mouthed, 'Wanker'.

Jennifer shook her head, suppressing a giggle.

The usual quiet buzz of conversation was missing as the team waited, knowing the DCS would also be waiting. He had sent Len Crawford to the Old Nottingham to pick up Trisha McVie and those who had a view into the corridor expected to see the pair of them pass in the direction of Hawkins' office at any moment.

Jennifer picked up her mobile, wondering if Trisha had left a message in response to the several calls she had made to her, some the previous evening and more that morning. On each occasion Trisha's number had been unobtainable, which was more than strange given Trisha's insistence on keeping communication channels open at all times. She called the number again with the same result.

As she put the phone back down on her desk, the door at the end of the room opened and Hawkins' secretary, Maureen, looked in.

"DS Cotton," she called. "Mr Hawkins would like a word."

Jennifer got up and followed the mousey fifty-year-old into the corridor, her senses on alert. Maureen almost never called her anything but Jennifer. Hawkins must have barked at her.

"Morning, sir," she said, as breezily as she could when she saw the storm cloud on Hawkins' face. She waited, standing in front of his desk.

Hawkins was staring at his mobile as if it were some kind of alien object, the lines on his forehead knotted in a frown.

"You heard from Superintendent McVie at all, DS Cotton?" he growled.

"No, sir, I haven't. I've been trying but—"

"Crawford just called from her hotel. They said she hasn't checked in."

"Hasn't checked—"

"Don't stand there repeating what I've just said, Cotton."

"Sorry, sir. It's just that I'm rather shocked. It's not like her."

"I should hope not. Not an auspicious start. When was the last time you spoke to her?"

"Monday, sir."

"Before I announced it?"

"Yes, sir."

"And I assume she told you. About the transfer, I mean."

"Er, yes, sir, she did. In strictest confidence, of course. She was very excited about it."

"Hmm." The grunt spoke volumes about Hawkins' disapproval. But Hawkins also knew that it wasn't Jennifer's fault she had been told.

"And she said she was coming up here yesterday?"

"Late afternoon, sir, yes. Of course, the weather was foul, but if she'd been delayed, she would have called."

"What kind of car does she drive?"

"A Golf, a red one. It's not new but it's perfectly roadworthy. And Tr … Superintendent McVie's an excellent driver."

"You don't know the registration number, by any chance, do you?"

Jennifer shook her head. "Sorry, sir, I don't."

"Maureen's calling the Yard now to find out. Just thought you might. Once I've got it, we'll get onto traffic to see what accidents there were."

"From the news I heard on the radio this morning coming in, sir, the M1 remained remarkably incident-free. There were no reports of anything major."

"Would she have definitely come that way?"

"From where she lives, yes, it's the obvious route. And we discussed it a bit on the phone. I told her to take junction twenty-five."

There was a tap on the door and Maureen put her head round.

"I have the registration number, Mr Hawkins."

"Thank you, Maureen. Pass it to DS Cotton. Jennifer, follow it up, will you? Get on to Traffic Control from here to London and find out if McVie's car was involved in anything. Anything at all."

"What shall I tell the team, sir?"

"Tell them there's been a delay."

All heads in the squad room looked up as Jennifer came through the door. Apart from one.

"Where's Gus?" asked Jennifer, addressing no one in particular. It was Derek who answered.

"Gone to the bathroom. Said he wasn't feeling well."

"From his colour, I should say that's the understatement of the year," said Jennifer. "OK, everyone, this morning's meet and greet has been, er, delayed. Detective Superintendent McVie didn't arrive at her hotel last night and her phone's giving an unobtain-able signal. Has been since last night. I know that 'cause I've been trying to call her. I'm about to chase up traffic in case she's been involved in an accident, and Terry," — she caught the eye of one of the younger DCs, Terry Purchase — "get in touch with the tech people. Find out when her phone was last on and where she was."

She grabbed a pad from the nearest desk and scribbled on it. "Here's her number."

The answer from Traffic came back quickly. There had been no accidents nor any other incidents involving Trisha McVie's car.

Jennifer had just put the receiver back on her desk phone after receiving the report when Gus Brooke rushed back into the room. He stopped at the door, a look of confusion on his face.

"Sorry, er, sarge," he called to Jennifer. "I didn't think I'd been very long. I haven't missed the meeting, have I?"

"No, Gus, you haven't. It's been postponed. And if I were you, I'd sit down before I fell down."

"Sorry, yes, I will. It's just a headache. I've taken some parac-etamol. I'll be fine."

Jennifer gave him a Hawkins-like 'hmm'.

A phone rang and Terry Purchase answered it. He scribbled on a pad as he nodded rapidly.

"Thanks, mate," he said, and put the phone down.

"Well?" said Jennifer.

DC Purchase stared at the pad and blew out his cheeks.

"Bit odd, sarge. They've traced the phone. It was switched off at 19:48 yesterday evening at Watford Gap services."

"That's it?" said Jennifer. "Nothing else since?"

"No, sarge, nothing."

"Right, call the control room at Watford Gap and get them to look in the car park, see if her car is there. Perhaps she's been taken ill and is in the car as we speak. Although I can't imagine why she'd turn off her phone."

In fact, she had a good idea why, but she wasn't about to share Trisha's personal life, not at this moment. Steven. Trisha had predicted he'd be difficult about her move. Perhaps they'd been rowing about it, him on the phone from the States, her in the car driving in foul weather. If Trisha hadn't been feeling well, the only way to shut him up would be to switch off the phone.

"Tell them to make it snappy, Terry. She might need medical assistance."

Gus had been listening to the conversation with only half an ear. He knew he looked terrible but it wasn't the remains of the headache that was weighing him down, draining his colour. Insistent visions of his blood-soaked bathroom with the body of Emma Carrington lying in the middle of it kept flashing across his mind. A body that was still there, stiff and cold, a body he needed to deal with. It wasn't the fact she had died there; that wasn't his fault. It was the consequences that kept squeezing his guts, twisting and tearing at them, the awful sequence of events he had now set in motion and from which there was no turning back. If he came clean now, there would likely be a murder charge, and even if there weren't, he would lose his job, his wife and his house. Actually, her house. Mo had bought it and it was in her name. That was one of the problems. He would walk away with nothing. *If* he managed to walk away.

He took a deep breath and tried to focus. He leaned across to the next desk.

"What's going on, Jeff?" he said to the DC who was tapping on his keyboard.

"The new super's gone AWOL. Disappeared."

"What? When?"

"Didn't turn up at her hotel last night and Terry's just found out that her phone was switched off early evening at Watford Gap services."

A deep, funereal alarm tolled in Gus's head.

"Watford Gap?" he repeated. "What was she doing there?"

"Driving up from London. Her car's gone missing too, unless Traffic find it in the car park. Can't see that happening though."

"Missing?" Gus felt as if his head was going to explode.

"Yeah, sounds like it. It hasn't been in an accident."

Although he was terrified of the answer, Gus had to ask the question.

"What … what type of car is it?"

The DC stopped typing and turned his head towards Gus.

"I heard the sarge talking to traffic about it. It's a Golf," he said, "a red Golf."

It took all that was left of Gus's self-control not to bend over and beat his head on his desk until he collapsed unconscious.

His problem, enormous and fraught with danger for him though it was, had just got a million times worse. Waves of nausea tore through him as he said the words to himself in his head. The body in his bathroom wasn't Emma Carrington, Emma Carrington didn't exist, not in his life, anyway. The body in his bathroom, the fatally injured, bloodstained and naked body, was that of his new boss, Trisha McVie. He had seduced and screwed his new boss, and then she had died in his bathroom from terrible injuries. He had dumped her car and he was now planning to dump her body. The boss. The boss who would now never be the boss. The detective superintendent. A senior police officer. She had died from unnatural causes in his cottage and he was intending to throw her away like so much trash.

"Gus." His name coalesced from the whirl of thoughts blocking him from the reality of the office around him. "DC Brooke!" It was Jennifer's voice. He looked up; she was holding the handset of her phone.

"Are you up to speed with what's going on or are you still daydreaming?"

"No. Yes. I'm fine, sarge. Sorry."

"Good, because I want you to do something."

"Yes, sarge."

"I want you to contact the traffic control rooms for the M1 from Watford Gap north to … let's say junction 30. That's way beyond Nottingham so we'll see what that turns up. We'll stick to the M1 for the moment. I want them to run all the CCTV from yesterday evening for any sighting of Superintendent McVie's car. I want to know where it went and what time it went there."

Chapter Twenty-Six

While the SCF team waited for the M1 traffic control to come back with results from the traffic cameras, details of Trisha McVie's car were also circulated to all the East Midlands forces to report any sightings.

The first results back were from Watford Gap services where the red Golf was recorded entering the service area on the north-bound side at 19:35 and leaving at 19:51.

Jennifer stared at the figures on the printout Gus Brooke handed her.

"Any record of her in the car park?"

Brooke shook his head. "Not so far, sarge. I'll get back to them."

"So," mused Jennifer, "she arrives there at 19:35 and presumably drives into the car park. Maybe she visits the loo and gets a cup of coffee. At that stage her phone is still switched on and—"

"She was on the phone almost until it was turned off, sarge," called out DC Purchase.

"How long was the call?"

"That last one was three minutes and six seconds."

"Do we know who it was from?"

"It was a WhatsApp call, sarge. It'll take a little longer to find out who the other party was."

"Pound to a penny it was her current partner calling from the

US," said Jennifer. "They probably had a row and she switched off the phone. OK, Doug, get back to Traffic at Watford Gap. We need to know whether she bought petrol there between 19:35 and 19:51 last night. It's a narrow window, so the petrol station should be able to find the record. See if there's any CCTV and get them to speak to whoever was on duty. Find out if she was alone."

Twenty minutes later, Gus Brooke was pretending to search through the road maps of the area, but in reality, his mind was elsewhere. The shrill of his phone snapped him back to life. Jennifer watched him as he listened and wrote on a piece of paper. Ringing off, he said nothing, much to Jennifer's frustration.

"Well!" she yelled at him.

His eyes slowly lifted to hers, but to Jennifer they didn't seem to be focussed.

"DC Brooke?" she called.

"Er, yes, sorry, sarge, I was working out the times in my head," he lied. "That was Traffic again. They have a record of the Golf leaving the M1 at junction twenty-four at 21:16."

"Do they know which way it went?"

"No, but it was in the right-hand lane on the slip road, so she was probably going round the roundabout to head towards Nottingham on the new road."

"I wonder why she chose that route," said Jennifer, puzzled. "I told her to take number twenty-five."

Derek looked across from his monitor. "If she was using a satnav, it would probably bring her off at twenty-four if she just programmed in Nottingham," he said. "It's a shorter distance, especially with the new road."

Jennifer nodded. "She would have been using her satnav for sure; she's got no sense of direction. Perhaps in the rain and the dark she decided to just let it take her the way it chose. Bloody things."

Another two hours passed while they waited for any further sightings, but there were none. Then a call from the Watford Gap

Traffic Unit informed them there was no record of a Golf with McVie's registration number filling up with petrol.

Jennifer was drumming her fingers on her desk, frustrated and wanting instant answers. More than anything she was increasingly worried that something had happened to Trisha.

"Gus," she called. "Get onto City and see what's keeping them. Given that she was heading for the Old Nottingham, we know the route her satnav would have taken her, don't we? There must be some further record of her car."

"Shall I drive out to the roundabout at junction twenty-four and get my satnav to guide me to the hotel?" suggested Derek. "Just in case there's a possible alternative route and the car's in a ditch somewhere."

Jennifer glared at him, not wanting to hear that possibility. But she saw it made sense.

"OK, Derek. Good idea. Take Coulson with you."

As Derek walked back to his desk to fetch his jacket, the phone on Doug Coulson's desk rang. He picked it up and listened, his eyes widening in disbelief.

"Sarge," he called. "There's a possible sighting."

"What do you mean, 'possible'?" snapped Jennifer. "Surely it's positive or it isn't. They have the registration number, don't they?"

Coulson was shaking his head. "No, I doubt they do. That was a report from the traffic helicopter patrol. There was an accident this morning between junctions twenty-four and twenty-five, nothing to do with the super's car, and the helicopter's been patrolling the motorway, checking conditions. On their way back to base, they flew over a disused industrial site near Rappington called the factory. You wouldn't know the case, sarge, but a few months ago, we were keeping eyes on the place following reports of it possibly being used as a drug manufacturing centre, or even a location for making porn films. It didn't come to anything and the DCS closed the operation down. Traffic were briefed at the time to check the place out from the air for any activity whenever they passed by. Anyway, they took that route this morning and called in to say they'd spotted a car parked in the middle of an open space at the factory that they are sure wasn't there yesterday and wondered if we were still interested."

He paused, unnerved by Jennifer's obvious agitation at his long-winded explanation.

"And?" said Jennifer.

"The car's red and could be a Golf."

Before Coulson had time to say any more, Jennifer was on her feet and heading for the door.

"Brooke," she called. "You come with me. DC Thyme, forget the satnav thing and follow me with DC Coulson in your car. And someone call uniform, get the nearest patrol car to check the report. But tell them to do it from a distance, only close enough to see the registration number. Tell them not to touch anything and to keep an eye out for tyre prints."

"Jen," said Derek, quietly.

"What?" she snapped.

Derek tilted his head towards the DCI's office.

"Shit," muttered Jennifer and swerved towards the other door. "I'll brief the bosses; see if they want to come. Gus, I'll catch you up downstairs."

Their blue lights flashing and sirens whooping, the two cars sped along the dual carriageway taking them south of the city. Five minutes into the journey, Jennifer's phone rang. It was Terry Purchase.

"Sarge. Just had confirmation from a uniform patrol who were in the Rappington area. The Golf's registration matches Superintendent McVie's car. They followed your instructions, but one PC moved in close to check if there's anyone in the car. As far as he can see, it's empty."

"OK, tell them we'll be there in …" She paused and turned to Gus Brooke, expecting him to tell her the answer, but his eyes were fixed on the road.

"DC Brooke!" she shouted, rather more loudly than she intended.

His head shot round towards her, his expression radiating incomprehension.

"How long?" demanded Jennifer.

"Sarge?" asked Gus, still not understanding.

"For Christ's sake, man. How long until we get to the factory?"

Gus looked along the road, as if seeing it for the first time.

"Er, um, another five to ten minutes, sarge."

"Terry," said Jennifer into her phone. "We'll be there in five." She ended the call.

"Step on it," she growled to Brooke.

The police patrol car was waiting in the lane outside the factory gates. One of the uniformed PCs was in the car talking on the radio; the other hovered near the gates. Jennifer was out of the passenger door of Gus Brooke's car almost before it stopped, hurrying towards the PC.

"DS Cotton," she called out, holding up her warrant card. "Are you the one who approached the car?"

"Yes, sarge. PC Stone. I did as you said and touched nothing. But I was concerned there might be someone injured—"

"Of course," interrupted Jennifer. "Good work. Were the gates like this? Ajar?"

She pointed to the entrance to the site behind the PC.

"No, sarge, they were closed with a chain across and they looked secure, but there was no padlock. I took photos on my phone before moving the chain and then opened the gates enough to get through."

"Good," repeated Jennifer. She turned to Derek who had arrived next to her.

"Derek. Shoe covers and gloves for now—" She stopped as she saw he was holding up several packages, a smug smile creasing the corners of his mouth.

"Right," she continued, ignoring him, "let's get those on. We'll go in but keep an eye out for any tyre marks. If the car's been dumped here, whoever did it must have had access to other transport. This place is remote. So we could be dealing with two people and another car."

She turned to the PC. "Was there any sign of anything out here? Any tyre marks?"

PC Stone shook his head. "There's a big puddle just inside the gates and what looks like one set of marks leading from it towards the factory buildings. But nothing else. I kept well clear, just in case."

"OK," said Jennifer, "we'll take a look."

She turned to Derek and Doug Coulson and frowned. "Where's Brooke?"

They all looked back towards the road. Gus Brooke was still in the driver's seat of his car.

Jennifer's scowl had PC Stone taking a step to one side, just in case he was in the firing line.

"Doug," snarled Jennifer. "Ask DC Brooke if he'd be good enough to join us. And make sure he's got the covers on his shoes and is wearing gloves. Derek, let's go."

The factory comprised four connected two-storey buildings arranged in a rectangle around a central open yard large enough for lorries to turn once they had loaded or unloaded at one of the many bays facing onto the space. Access to the enclosed area was through a wide passage in the centre of the building facing onto the concrete road that led from the gates. The passage was about five metres high, with the building's upper floor crossing it. Two metal sliding doors designed to add extra security to the central area were wide open.

"Those doors were open like that when we were watching this place," said Derek, as they walked towards them. "From what I remember, the yard inside is concrete and in better nick than the buildings. Probably not much chance of tyre prints, given the ones from the gates stopped soon after the puddle."

They hurried through the passage and into the yard where they immediately saw the red Golf parked in the centre.

Jennifer stopped, her heart racing with worry as she tried to maintain an objective, professional approach. She shuddered as she looked at the car, trying to work out how it had approached from the passage.

"Looks as if it drove through, turned to the left and stopped," she said. "Let's walk towards it from the side so there's less chance of disturbing anything."

They bent down to look along the concrete surface of the yard, but apart from the loose stones, scattered debris and leaves, nothing appeared to have been disturbed.

As they made their way closer to the car, Jennifer felt her stomach tighten in anticipation. She had become increasingly anxious about Trisha with every new piece of information. She could think of no innocent explanation for why her friend's car should be parked in this yard; it made no sense.

Derek was equally tense as he peered through the windows.

"There's no sign of her, Jen. There's a jacket on the front passenger seat, and some shoes on the floor, but that's about it. Shall I try one of the doors?"

Jennifer nodded and waited.

"It's unlocked," announced Derek as he opened a rear door. "She's not in here, but I need to open the tailgate door to be sure."

He walked to the rear of the car and pulled up the door, shaking his head as he looked inside.

"There's an overnight bag in here, but that's it," he said, "I think I should look in the front, check for …" Reluctant to say what they were both thinking, his sentence petered out.

Jennifer nodded. "Yes. Signs of disturbance. Blood. Anything."

She looked back as she heard footsteps.

"DC Brooke!" she yelled, taking Derek by surprise. She waved her arms to stop Gus Brooke in his tracks and pointed towards Doug Coulson, who had worked out the best approach route to the car. "Follow DC Coulson. *Don't* continue straight towards us, you could disturb tracks on the ground."

She glared at him before turning back to Derek.

"Christ!" she muttered, "That idiot seems to have completely lost the plot. He's not normally this incompetent."

Derek shook his head. "No, he isn't. That must be some hangover."

After checking the car, Jennifer called the SCF to inform Crawford and Hawkins of progress and to arrange for a forensic team to examine it in situ before transporting it back to the laboratory. The laboratory contracted to undertake most of the SCF's forensic work, Forefront Forensics, was located on the Nottingham ring road no more than fifteen minutes' drive away.

However, with the thought that Trisha might be lying injured either in the factory buildings or nearby, Jennifer wasn't prepared to delay the search while she waited for forensics. She instructed Derek to team up with Gus Brooke — "I'm sick of the sight of him today. Just keep kicking him, Derek, you're the lead officer for the pair of you, don't let him drift off to wherever he keeps going in his head. He needs to focus." — while she paired with Doug Coulson.

They hadn't got too far in their search when the forensic teams arrived. Jennifer immediately requested extra pairs of hands to assist them. As she saw it, every second could count and finding Trisha now rather than later could make the difference between life and death. Another fifteen minutes into the search, four vans carrying uniformed police officers arrived at the gates. Hawkins also didn't want to take chances with Trisha's life and as soon as he had heard that Trisha wasn't in the car, he had commandeered thirty officers to join the search in the factory buildings themselves and the land comprising the factory site, and then for half a mile outside the fence perimeter.

Jennifer's phone pinged. It was Hawkins.

"Who's arrived so far?"

"Forensics and uniforms, sir."

"Right. DCI Crawford mentioned a jacket on the front seat of the car. Can we assume it's McVie's?"

"Definitely, sir. I've been with her on a number of occasions when she's worn it. The shoes are hers, too."

"Good. Then I'll get a dog team out. I've also been looking at the map. There are several streams and irrigation channels in that

area, and the Trent isn't far away. There's what looks like an irrigation channel to the rear of the site, with a footpath running alongside it. I'm getting divers in to search all the waterways. There are
also a few wooded areas, one quite near the factory site, and farmland. I've contacted the force helicopter services and they are going
to search the area with a thermal imaging camera. Anything they
spot will be immediately followed up by one of the search teams on
the ground. We have to cover all the possibilities, Jennifer."

"Yes, sir," said Jennifer, her words catching as she spoke.

Hawkins heard her falter. "We'll find her, lass. There'll be some
sensible explanation for this. I have a good feeling about it."

I don't, thought Jennifer, not for one moment.

Chapter Twenty-Seven

Since arriving in Nottingham, Cosimo Graziano Rosselli had been slowly gathering valuable information about his target, Jennifer Cotton. Over the past few days he had discovered that she drove a Mediterranean Blue BMW 1 Series Sports Hatch, another confirmation that she had more than a detective sergeant's pay supporting her. She was obsessed with fitness, taking every opportunity to run or cycle around the smart residential area where she lived. Normally she would be joined by her boyfriend, the tall and powerfully built black police officer, Derek Thyme, who worked with her. Rosselli had spotted the buzz between them when he first saw them in the Horse and Hounds pub. Thyme appeared to be one of those athletes who could cruise with effortless ease for hours running or on a bike at a pace that most people would regard as punishing. Rosselli himself was no slouch when it came to fitness, but he had to admit that Derek Thyme had a distinct edge.

Thyme's car, which he parked in the street outside Jennifer's apartment, was a quirky scarlet Mini Cooper that he clearly loved in spite of the challenge of folding his tall frame into it.

Rosselli had watched and listened when Derek locked it in the street. The locking beep sounded ominous and a scan using a pair of binoculars revealed the telltale dark blip in the upper door frame of a tiny webcam. In Rosselli's estimation, it was probably one of several. The car was clearly protected with a sophisticated alarm system and anyone foolish enough to try to break into it would be recorded in the act. Although breaking into cars was one of Rosselli's many skills, he knew which ones to avoid and Thyme's was such a car. Since Jennifer's car was normally garaged, he hadn't had the opportunity to scrutinise it, but he was sure her security system would be equally sophisticated. Tampering with either car was out of the question.

Jennifer and Derek normally left for work at about the same time every morning, but in the days Rosselli had been watching, they went in separate cars. Rosselli followed them in his inconspicuous rental to the multi-storey car park next to the SCF HQ. Over a few days, Rosselli learned the identities of many of the other police officers in the SCF, together with several of the more senior civilian staff. He also made a note of the cars they drove and the registration numbers. He was always cautious, never parking in the same place in the car park and never staying there for too long. There was a good alternative of on-street parking nearby that gave him a view of the SCF building, parking that conveniently was not covered by any of the otherwise abundant CCTV cameras in the city.

From the lack of any obvious urgent activity, Rosselli assumed that much of the work of the SCF was conducted in front of computers. This left him wondering if he would be forced to resort to a straightforward shooting; he was only prepared to spend so much time on the assignment, even though right now he was enjoying himself.

On the Wednesday morning, a week after his arrival in Nottingham, Rosselli was parked in the street near the SCF building when Derek Thyme's Mini screeched onto the street, a magnetic blue light attached to its roof flashing with authority. Was this what he had been waiting for?

On the rear seat in her basket, Goccia looked up with a questioning whine.

Rosselli reached over and rubbed her head. "It's all right, little lady, after all these days of dozing in the car, we might be getting some action. But you'll have to be quiet."

He watched the car roar up the street and was about to follow when he saw Jennifer run from the SCF building entrance towards the exit from the car park. Seconds later, a rather scruffy dark-blue Ford driven by one of the detectives Rosselli recognised from his earlier surveillance squealed to a halt beside Jennifer. She jumped in and the car accelerated away in the same direction as Thyme's car, a blue light also flashing on its roof.

Rosselli started his car, U-turned in the street and followed them, their blue flashing lights beacons that allowed him to keep his distance.

With half an eye on the car's large satnav screen, Rosselli followed the two cars south of Nottingham towards the village of Rappington. About half a mile short of the village, the cars turned right onto a lane that led towards some distant woods. Somewhat closer than the woods were flashing police vehicle lights that appeared to be stationary. Whatever the urgency, Jennifer Cotton's destination was clearly somewhere along the lane.

Rosselli drove past the end of the lane and continued towards Rappington until there was a convenient place to pull over and consult Google Maps. The satellite view showed him that the police must have stopped outside a fenced area containing what looked like a series of buildings. On zooming in, he could see it was an industrial premises, but in poor condition, derelict probably if several holes in the roof were anything to go by. There were four buildings surrounding a central yard, while wasteland extended beyond on three sides and a small wood bordered the side closest to the main road. On the opposite side from the lane, a narrow waterway bordered the plot about a hundred metres from the buildings, a footpath running alongside it.

As Rosselli continued to study the waterway features, he was suddenly distracted by the high-pitched whine of another patrol car heading past him at high speed towards the lane. Deciding it would be unwise to remain in an exposed position for too long, he slipped the car into gear and drove on into Rappington where he parked outside a village shop. After locking the car, he followed his phone map and made his way to where a stream flowed past the rear of the village.

He was casually dressed in jeans and a light jacket over a

checked shirt. A large baseball cap concealed much of his head and with his sunglasses, a small backpack, strong walking boots and a stout walking stick, he gave the impression of a man out for a pleasant day's walk with his dog.

But the façade stopped there. Cosimo Graziano Rosselli went about his surveillance in deadly earnest. Something important had happened at the derelict industrial site and he wanted to know what.

He could only walk the footpath so many times before he was noticed. Initially, all the activity was hidden behind the tired walls of the buildings, but within half an hour several more vehicles arrived and Rosselli saw groups of uniformed police officers searching the scrub at either end of the site.

However, with their attention focussed on the ground as they looked for signs of flattening or disturbance of the grass, weeds and bramble, a solitary walker striding away from them along the footpath was of no interest.

Beyond the industrial plot, the waterway turned to the left while the land on Rosselli's right rose gently through a field towards a small wood. From there, concealed by bushes, he used binoculars to observe the activities in and around the site, watching closely as squads of uniformed police officers, plain-clothes officers and people wearing scene-of-crime coveralls meticulously combed the area for whatever it was they were looking for.

After about three hours, a low-loader arrived and disappeared into the heart of the buildings. Twenty minutes later, it left carrying a red, five-door Volkswagen Golf. Rosselli pulled a compact, 60x magnification telescope from his backpack and focussed it on the car's registration number. An hour later, the squads of searchers began spreading beyond the site's perimeter, among them officers with dogs. Rosselli decided he should go. Rather than retrace his steps back across the field, where he would be seen by any of the searchers who happened to look up, he turned into the woods and found a different path back to the waterway. Since none of the searchers would have seen him earlier that morning, he decided he could risk returning along the footpath to Rappington, especially as the police dogs seemed to have gone the other way. A team of police divers with their support crews were occupied in the water, but no one paid any attention to Rosselli as he walked briskly by.

Returning to Rappington, Rosselli decided to wait until at least the late afternoon to check on developments, but he didn't want to risk being too close to all the activity too often. A pub in the village advertised snacks and lunches, so he settled down there with a sandwich, a pot of tea and a bottle of sparkling water, using his time to search the Internet on his phone. Goccia dozed on the floor beside him.

After logging on via a series of secure VPN proxies, he accessed a site that would give him registration details of all UK cars. When he entered the number of the red Golf, he was rewarded with the registered owner's name: Patricia Claire McVie, with a home address in London.

With the street address, Rosselli quickly established that McVie was the sole occupant of the listed premises, her age given as thirty-nine.

He sat back in his chair, tapping his teeth with his pencil. "Who are you, Patricia Claire McVie?" he whispered quietly to himself.

Still operating through the same proxies, Rosselli searched for McVie's name using various spelling and diminutives of the given names. And when he tried Trisha McVie, he came up trumps. A series of newspaper articles over the last eight years recorded several high-profile case investigations led by a Trisha McVie in various ranks from Inspector to Chief Inspector and then Superintendent. In the latest article, dated a year ago, her age was given as thirty-eight.

So, Trisha McVie, he thought, as he stared at his phone screen, you are a police officer and your people have found your car abandoned in a disused industrial site, but you, clearly, aren't there. From all the activity, you must be missing. Was this anything to do with last night's storm? Did you get lost? And if so, where are you now?

Before continuing his research, he ordered more tea and a slice of cake, both of which he considered safe enough in this culinary desert of a country.

As he bit into the cake, he flipped back through the newspaper articles. The more recent ones referred to cases in London while for earlier ones, the cases were in Manchester. So what was she doing in Nottingham?

Shortly after seven o'clock, Rosselli made his way back to his car, wondering whether to risk another stroll in the evening light along the footpath. He could go a short distance, see if the divers were still there, and if they were, turn back and try another approach.

He was about to head off when he heard a vehicle approaching quite fast, given it was driving through a village. He looked up and saw a scruffy dark-blue Ford that was definitely exceeding the speed limit. He checked the number plate and immediately recognised it. The car belonged to one of the SCF detectives, the one that had brought Jennifer Cotton to the area that morning. Definitely worth following, especially as the detective was now on his own and, in the split second Rosselli saw him as the car passed, had the appearance of someone facing execution.

Rosselli jumped into his car, quickly settled Goccia and followed the blue Ford. About a mile from the village, the car slowed and the driver pulled onto an area of compacted mud near a farm gateway. Rosselli slowed as he drove past, stealing a look. He was surprised to see the detective leaning forward with his arms wrapped round himself as he banged his head on the steering wheel.

Has a body been found? thought Rosselli. Is he one of those wimpish types who faints at the sight of blood or a body? Or does his behaviour indicate something more significant? He pulled up at the next opportunity and waited as he watched the Ford in his rear-view mirror.

After several minutes, the dark-blue Ford pulled away from the side of the road and made its way past him. Rosselli gave it a distance of about two hundred metres before he started to follow. He didn't have to go far. About half a mile farther on, the car slowed and turned into the short drive of a large cottage. Rosselli drove straight past with hardly a glance, but in his mirror he saw the driver's door open and the occupant stagger towards a door at the side of the house.

Rosselli stopped, turned and drove slowly past the house, making a note of the number. It would be the work of only a few minutes to find this man's name.

Chapter Twenty-Eight

As the daylight faded on Wednesday evening, the huge squad of men and women who had gathered to search for Trisha McVie had found nothing to indicate she had been at the Rappington factory site, and neither was there any sign of her in the woods and farmland beyond. DCS Hawkins had dug deep into his own resources and those of neighbouring forces, all of whom had willingly sent extra officers and their own divers to speed up the search of the waterways, units from Leicestershire, Lincolnshire, Derbyshire and South Yorkshire. The police were missing one of their own and nothing was too much trouble.

By nine o'clock, most of the SCF team had returned to the office, reluctant to call it a day but hampered by the darkness. The divers were still searching since most of their work underwater was in darkness even in the daytime, but as their perimeter widened, the chances of Trisha McVie's body being in any of the local waterways diminished.

Only two of the SCF team of DCs were missing: Joe Barnes, whose wife had gone into labour that afternoon, had been sent off to the hospital by Jennifer, and Gus Brooke, who at about seven in the evening had pleaded that the bug that was messing with him still had the upper hand. Jennifer reluctantly sent him home with a lack of sympathy she immediately felt rather guilty about.

"Get a good night's sleep, DC Brooke. You look like an extra from The Walking Dead."

Jennifer was about to insist that everyone went home when Len Crawford marched into the operations office to summon them all to the incident room for a briefing from the DCS.

"Right, listen up, everyone."

Pete Hawkins was standing in front of a situation board that contained little information apart from a photograph of Trisha McVie and a large-scale map of the Rappington area.

"I've just spoken to the lab and there's nothing inside the factory to indicate that Superintendent McVie has ever been there. This is not exactly news since most of you here were involved in the search. She's not there, and unless trace evidence from the lab shows different, she's never been there at all. That's the end of it.

"There is also nothing, zilch, from the area outside the factory buildings or beyond the site, there's nothing in the waterways and the thermal imaging search with the helicopter produced nothing of value.

"But that's one thing. The most puzzling part of this inquiry so far is that the lab has found evidence of only one car driving into the site, the red Golf. There were good tracks from the Golf leading from the gates towards the factory buildings, but nothing else. So we're now assuming that whoever dumped the car must have left on foot, closed the gates and either walked away, which seems unlikely, or was picked up in the lane by an accomplice in another vehicle. There were no fingerprints on the gate, by the way.

"Unfortunately, there are no traffic cameras in the nearby village of Rappington and neither are there any at either end of the Rappington road. So it's possible to leave that site unrecorded, head either towards Nottingham or towards the new Rappington bypass and the M1, and merge into the general traffic. We've looked at the footage showing the Golf leaving the motorway last night and there's nothing to indicate another vehicle at that stage.

And from what can be seen and from the statements of the staff at Watford Gap services, Superintendent McVie was alone.

"So whatever happened to her happened after she left the M1 at 21:16 and 10:32 this morning when the traffic helicopter spotted her car at the factory.

"We've also contacted a Mr Steven Hawthorn who has been in America for the last week or so and is still there. Superintendent McVie is currently in a relationship with Mr Hawthorn and he admits that last night they had several heated telephone conversations while Superintendent McVie was driving up the M1 in the storm. Mr Hawthorn also said that at the end of the last conversation, which we know was while Superintendent McVie was at Watford Gap services, he was cut off. The time on his phone, he tells us, coincides with the time at which Superintendent McVie's phone was switched off. Presumably she'd had enough and didn't want to be distracted anymore.

"Another unexplained fact is that Superintendent McVie's overnight bag was in her car, along with her jacket and shoes, which were slightly damp. Inside her bag, as well as clothes that we think she would have planned to wear today and tomorrow, was a cosmetic bag and a small handbag containing her warrant card, credit cards, cash and other cards. Nothing appears to be missing and the overnight bag doesn't appear to have been rifled through. However, the lab is still checking it."

He paused and looked around the room. "Any questions so far?"

Neil Bottomley raised a hand and immediately began to speak.

"Do we know what she was wearing last night, sir? Either from the CCTV or witnesses at the motorway services?"

"Yes, Neil, I was coming to that. Watford Gap have come up with a CCTV recording that briefly shows her entering the shopping area at 19:38. There's also one that is less clear, but appears to show her leaving several minutes later carrying what looks like a coffee. Both recordings show she was dressed casually in jeans and what appears to be the coat found in her car over a loose jumper. Her shoes are definitely shoes rather than trainers, they have low heels and appear to agree with the shoes found in her car."

He looked around again. "Anything else?"

"Where do we go from here, sir?" asked Jennifer.

"There's a number of things in hand, even though at this moment we are dealing with a missing person. This is not, as yet, a kidnapping or a murder enquiry. But from the information we have, and DS Cotton has given a statement of her recent conversations with Superintendent McVie, as have several of her colleagues in the Met, there is nothing to indicate that she has gone AWOL, flipped, done a bunk or anything of that nature. She has shown no abnormal behaviour and has given every sign that she was looking forward to joining us at the SCF.

"So, what's next? Firstly, although I think we've covered the factory and the area immediately around it, I'm organising a different team of uniforms to search again tomorrow. Just in case. But after that, I'll be calling off any further searches at the site and the surrounding area. By tomorrow evening, it will have been more than thoroughly combed, thanks to all the extra hands generously provided by neighbouring forces and I'm already convinced there's nothing. It would be a waste of resources to continue there. The owners have been contacted and they will be installing a new padlock on the gates so that vehicular access at least is prevented once we hand over the site tomorrow evening, assuming nothing has been found. They are not interested in increasing other security, so it's still possible for someone to climb over the fence, but frankly, I'm not convinced the car being there has much to do with wherever Superintendent McVie is now.

"But what the lab is looking at tomorrow, along with help from us, is to narrow down where the car went. It's a bit of a long shot since we know she didn't buy fuel on the motorway. From what DS Cotton has told us, it is Superintendent McVie's habit not to fill her car every time she buys petrol, rather she just buys twenty or thirty quid's worth at a time. From her credit card records, it looks as if the last time she bought petrol was three days ago. Of course she could have bought some since then and paid cash, which doesn't help. However, by measuring how much is left in the Golf's tank and looking at average consumption figures, they are going to see what they can do. I don't wish to appear negative, but it looks like a non-starter to me in that we'll end up with a huge possible circle of where the car might have gone before it was dumped.

"There's another point about the car that forensics found which in my opinion could be more significant. The spare in the boot is in a mess, with severe damage to both the wheel itself and the tyre. And the damage is fresh. They reckon that the tyre probably had a slow puncture and overheated as it ran close to flat. The lab says that from the condition of the wheel, the rim must have come into forceful contact with the road surface. This is more likely to have happened if Superintendent McVie hit the brakes hard at some point, especially on a corner, when the car would lean heavily on the wheel with the flat tyre. When this occurred there's a strong chance the driver would lose control of the car.

All the CCTV footage of the car on and leaving the M1 show no sign that the car is behaving oddly, so it looks as if the incident with the flat occurred after Superintendent McVie left the motorway. The lab people will be making a search of the road from the motorway to the factory in Rappington for any damage to the road surface. In addition, there is going to be a press release tomorrow morning calling for any eye witnesses who might have seen the car stopped by the roadside in the Rappington area last night. It will be repeated tomorrow evening unless there's any progress. As you know, it was a filthy night. Maybe someone stopped to help her. We don't know, but we'll have pictures of the car and of Trisha McVie.

"Frustratingly, the present nearside rear tyre now on the car, which was the spare, is quite worn, which means it presumably must have been one of the car's regular tyres in the past. So even if we find that the puncture or whatever it was happened in the Rappington area, the condition of the car's tyres tell us nothing about how far or where the car went after the change of wheel and the car being dumped at the factory. We can't assume that just because the two might be close that the car didn't go elsewhere in the hours in between. Which is why CCTV footage will have to be searched from a potentially wide area.

"Now, once we release this, the press are going to be all over us, local and national. It's not every day that a senior police officer disappears off the face of the earth. There will be speculation of all kinds and I've no doubt all of you will be contacted in one way or another. What I want is for all enquiries, and I can't emphasise that strongly enough, *all* enquiries, to be referred to DCI Crawford. I don't want statements from anyone else and I don't want to read about information from anonymous sources. Are we all clear about that?"

A rumble of agreement rolled around the room.

"Good. DS Cotton, I'm aware that DCs Barnes and Brooke are not here tonight. Will you please make sure everything I've just said gets to them first thing tomorrow?"

"Yes, sir, I will."

Hawkins drew in a deep breath. "OK, all of you. Go home, get a good night's sleep and come in refreshed tomorrow. Unless there's some kind of national emergency, from now on until we find Superintendent McVie, this enquiry takes precedence over everything."

Chapter Twenty-Nine

Gus Brooke was less than half a mile from his cottage when a fit of uncontrollable shaking racked his body. Gasping for air, he hit the brakes and pulled the car to a halt.

He wrapped his arms around himself, his fists clenching and unclenching, his jaw set as he leaned forward and banged his head rhythmically on the steering wheel. His heart was beating so hard he felt it was about to burst through his chest and desert him in disgust.

Slowly, as he regained control of his limbs, with his teeth grinding and his fists in a ball, he began to calm, his breathing returning closer to normal.

He couldn't believe his bad luck. The old Rappington factory site should have been perfect; no one *ever* went there. He was stupid to have left the car in the middle of the yard; he should have left it in one of the loading bays where the police officer in the helicopter wouldn't have been able to see it. *Helicopter*? It hadn't even occurred to him that a police helicopter would fly over the place. But it had and he had to live with it.

He knew he had behaved like an idiot in front of his team. They weren't the easiest of colleagues at the best of times, but today …

An image of DS Cotton flashed into his mind. She had made no attempt to hide how pissed off she was with him. If ever the finger of suspicion were pointed at him, they would remember how he'd been. But why should it? There had been nothing so far.

But he had to get rid of the body and all traces of it from his cottage.

He clenched his jaw as he tried to combat another fit of shaking that was rocking his frame.

How was he going to do it? His eyes flickered from side to side as he thought through what he needed to do in the house.

At least, he thought, her body is in the bathroom. All tiles and easy to hose down. Mercifully, they didn't have those stupid fluffy mats in front of the loo and bath.

He looked up through the windscreen. He had stopped shaking and felt calmer. With another deep breath, he slipped the car into gear and drove the remaining distance to the cottage, parking the car as close to the kitchen door as he could.

Evidence, he thought, as he staggered into the cottage. Forensic evidence. Evidence to link McVie with him and the cottage. Fingerprints, body fluids, DNA, fibres. He shook his head; the list was endless and the chances of him removing everything horribly remote. But he had to try. Had to clean up the body, clean up the bathroom and the rest of the cottage, and once that was done, get rid of the body.

How the hell was he going to do that? He thought, briefly, of cutting it up and dumping bits of it in rubbish bins across a wide area. But firstly that would take too much time and secondly he didn't think he had the stomach to cut a body into small pieces. He hated postmortems, even from a safe distance; the very thought of getting hands-on revolted him.

No, he had to think of somewhere to dump it, somewhere it wouldn't be found for a long time.

Burying it seemed an obvious choice, but where? If he dug a big hole in the garden, Mo would ask questions. She was far too keen on her garden not to notice.

Shit, he thought, first things first. I've got to deal with the mess in the bathroom. After that, I'll worry about what to do with the body.

The first thing he saw when he walked into the bedroom was

the crumpled mess of bedsheets from the previous night. He snatched them from the bed, together with the pillowcases and the mattress protector.

"Fuck it, there'll be body fluids everywhere," he spat through clenched teeth. "Plus traces of whatever perfume she was wearing. Mo's got a sense of smell like a bloodhound; all women have. Gotta get some fresh air into the place."

He knew that taking the bedding down to the utility room and loading up the washer was a delaying tactic, a few extra minutes before facing up to what was waiting in the bathroom. But the washing needed to be done; he might as well get it going. He would put it through three cycles, just to be sure.

Back in the bedroom, he eyed the mattress. There was nothing to be seen, no stains, but just in case, he would turn it. Mo wouldn't suspect anything since they turned it regularly. And if there were a forensic examination, there was a good chance they wouldn't think of spraying their damn reagents on the underside. Wasn't there?

He pushed open the bathroom door and stood in the entrance, steeling himself to look at the scene of sheer horror in front of him. The blood had mainly dried, although closer to the body it still looked wet. OK, first things first. The body. Need to get it into the bath. No, that wouldn't work; there was no hand shower. It would be better to drag it into the large shower cubicle where in addition to the tropical shower head, there was a detachable shower head with a long hose.

He took a step into the room and stopped. However he cleaned up the body, he was going to get wet and bloodstained himself. Better not to be wearing anything either. And he would need detergents, disinfectant and a scrubbing brush. He ran a hand through his hair. There was so much to do. At least he had plenty of time.

A trip to the utility room armed him with the cleaning materials he thought he would need. He stripped off as far as his boxers and stopped. Although, given what he was about to do, it made sense to strip off completely, he couldn't. It just seemed too weird. He would bin the boxers along with McVie's clothes, the ones he had washed and dried last night, but not in the same place. There was an array of bins he knew of behind a parade of shops in

Beeston, totally anonymous. He'd use those for the superintendent's clothes, all bagged in black bin liners, and some other bins near the road in Lenton for his boxers. A simple detour on the way into the SCF in the morning and he'd be rid of them.

He slipped on a pair of yellow household gloves he'd picked up in the kitchen. Better to minimise direct contact, he thought, even though he would be hosing everything down a million times. And now, finally, he was ready to move the body.

The amount of rigor mortis still present surprised him as he pulled Trisha McVie's stiff and unbending body into the shower. Her face was a mess, with congealed blood plastering hair to her face and a thick mat of blood-soaked hair around the wound to her skull. He remembered from somewhere that cold water was better for removing bloodstains, so he grabbed the hand shower, knelt down and turned on the cold water.

Over the next twenty minutes, Gus scrupulously hosed, soaped and scrubbed the entire surface of Trisha McVie's body, hands, fingernails, hair, everything, including working liquid soap into her vagina and flushing it with water until he felt sure that none of his body fluids remained. He had worn a fresh condom each time they'd had sex, but he needed to be certain. Then he remembered her mouth. She'd been uninhibited in the exploration of his body; there could be fluids there. He forced her jaws open, the tight muscles still stiff with rigor, and soaped and flushed inside.

Finally, she was clean and he had hosed all visible blood down the drain. He would return to the shower for another session of cleaning once he had removed her. But for now, her body was still stiff and unyielding. He wondered if a soaking with hot water would speed up the end of the rigor process; he knew it only lasted so long. He still had to clean the edge of the bath, the walls and the main part of the floor, which again he would do with cold water. While he did that, he could leave scalding hot water running over the body in the hope it would become more flexible. Worth a try.

It was only when he turned his attention to the large pool of blood on the bathroom floor and bent over to flush the blood towards the floor drain that he thought to look under the sink unit. And there on the floor, lying by the wall where it had scooted after

Trisha stood on it, was his calfskin wallet, large bloodstains soaked into its soft absorbent surface.

"Shit!" he yelled, dropping the shower head and reaching for the wallet. It had been a Christmas present from Mo, one she'd picked up in Italy on a trip there for one of her classes. It wasn't something he could pop into town and replace.

"Buggering bollocks!" he shouted in frustration. "Why is that here?" Then he remembered. Distracted by the approaching storm, he had forgotten to take it with him the previous morning when he went to work. Normally it would be with his warrant card and SCF office pass, ID that he'd quietly tossed in a kitchen drawer before peeling off his sodden suit to avoid Emma discovering he was a police officer. In his eagerness to move the evening forward, the absence of his wallet had escaped his attention.

As he opened the wallet to see the extent of the damage, wondering if in any way it was recoverable, his eyes fell on something farther along the wall under the sink unit. His business card, with his name, rank and posting. Had Trisha McVie discovered who he was? Was she about to confront him when she had the most God-awful accident? He shook his head. Whatever she had learned, it was of no importance now; she was dead.

He took the wallet and card, also bloodstained, into the bedroom and laid them on the bathrobe that was still lying in a crumpled heap next to the bathroom door where he had thrown it. He would deal with them later; for now he had to complete the cleanup of the bathroom.

After twenty minutes, every surface in the bathroom appeared to be spotlessly clean with no visible sign of any blood. Gus knew from various forensic briefings there could still be residues, traces lurking in the grouting, a minute drop he had overlooked that once sprayed with the reagent Luminol would shine like a beacon. He shrugged. It would have to do for now. Once he had moved the body, disposed of it, he could clean the bathroom again and again over the next few days. Mo wasn't due back yet. He had time.

He turned off the shower and let the water drain away from

around Trisha McVie's body. Somehow, washed clean of blood, the wound to her nose and the frozen look of horror on her face seemed even worse than before. He averted his eyes and bent to lift her arm. Although there was more movement now, there was still considerable resistance. It would need more time before he could wrap the body in the old white bath towels he remembered had been stored in the garage for tearing into rags. In the meantime, he must clean and tidy up the downstairs bathroom, gather together the clothes he'd washed the night before, wipe down all the kitchen surfaces, locate every dish, glass, knife and fork they had touched and stack them in the dishwasher for a double run. What else was there? Wine bottles. Christ! How many had there been? He would soap and rinse the outsides to remove any prints and dump them in a recycling bin somewhere the next time he went out.

By eleven that evening, he had ticked off all the items he could think of on his mental list. The kitchen and utility area were pristine, as was the downstairs bathroom, while in the master bedroom, there were clean sheets on the bed. The sheets from the previous night had just completed their third wash and were tumbling in the drier. He looked longingly at the chairs by the wood-burning stove, but he knew if he sat down, he'd be asleep in seconds, and there was still the body to be moved. He wanted it out of the bathroom and hidden somewhere. If it was sufficiently flexible, he could wrap the body in the old towels and store it at the back of the garage until he had decided where to dump it. As yet, there was no visible decay and he would take the precaution of wrapping the head in a plastic bag, tying it securely at the neck to prevent the wounds from transmitting their inviting signals to blowflies. Tomorrow, he would buy some large bin liners and securely wrap the body. Even with those, he wanted to dispose of it within the next two days before there was any serious deterioration.

Carrying the towels from the garage, he returned to the master bathroom and tested Trisha McVie's arms. There was definitely more movement and with a little extra force he persuaded them to lie alongside her torso. Soon, he had the body stretched out on the largest of the towels, ready for wrapping. But before that, he fetched a bin bag from the kitchen and wrapped Trisha's head to isolate the wounds. After wrapping another layer of towels around the body, he bent to lift her. She was heavier than he expected, but he was strong and since the body appeared to become more flexible with every passing minute, he decided to sling her over his shoulder in a fireman's lift.

Once the body was out of the house and hidden in the garage, a sense of relief swept across Gus, one he knew was premature but for which he still felt grateful. Returning to the master bathroom, he felt he should clean it once again, but he was almost asleep on his feet and he had to be presentable the following morning or DC Cotton, and possibly the bosses, would ask more questions. Returning to the master bedroom to strip off the fresh shorts and T-shirt he had put on after his extended session in the bathroom, he noticed again his wallet lying on the bathrobe.

He sighed. "Always one more thing."

After removing the banknotes and cards, he filled the washbasin with cold water, added some soap and submerged the wallet in the water, holding it down with a large tube of toothpaste. "Maybe I'll be lucky," he said, finally stripping off his clothes and braving the shower he'd spent so long cleaning before collapsing on the bed for some much-needed sleep.

Chapter Thirty

After watching Gus Brooke stagger into his cottage, Rosselli found a lay-by next to a stand of trees half a mile along the road, parked and picked up his phone. Scrolling through the electoral records for the area, he discovered that the occupants of the cottage were listed as Fergus John Brooke and Maureen Hazel Brooke. A further search and Google rewarded him with details of Mo Brooke's career as a sculptor and instructor, and, with a little digging and the putting together of two and two, Rosselli learned she was currently in Croatia with a class.

So Detective Brooke was home alone. Why should that make him so downcast? Was he missing his wife? Rosselli pulled a face. He didn't look the type.

A soft whine from Goccia reminded him that she needed a stroll. As he clipped her lead onto her collar, he contemplated his progress. He felt as if a play were unfolding before him, a mise en scène to which he was an audience of one. But, as the acts proceeded, he could see opportunities in the developing plot for audience participation; the spectator could become a player.

He leaned over to stroke Goccia's neck.

"I know you fancy sniffing your way through those woods, little lady, but do you think you can keep nice and quiet? I'd like to find out a little more about this young detective. I have a feeling that it could be the disappearance of the police superintendent that's making him depressed. Is it a coincidence that her car was found so close to his house? Shall we see what he's up to?"

Goccia wagged her tail with enthusiasm.

"I knew you'd see it my way, cara. I'll tell you what, I'll make a deal. If when we get to the detective's house we find there's no sign of anything going on, we'll go straight back to the hotel and get a good night's sleep."

By eight o'clock, having hiked with Goccia in the fading light through the wood behind the lay-by and across several fields, Rosselli had established himself in Brookes' garden in the cover of a large plum tree and an ageing garden shed, about twelve metres from the cottage. With no neighbours to worry about, he was confident he could hear and observe any activity in the house without drawing attention to himself, as long as Goccia remained quiet, and that was something at which she excelled.

Having made Goccia comfortable, Rosselli took out a pair of powerful binoculars that had an option of night vision when needed, although for now there was more than enough light coming from the various cottage windows. Not being overlooked, it wasn't Gus Brooke's habit to close any curtains or blinds.

Rosselli was intrigued by the constant activity. He could hear a washing machine rumbling away in a utility room located in a single-storey projection of the house into the garden, and Brooke seemed to be spending an inordinate amount of time going backwards and forwards from one room to the next.

For a long time, he could hear the shower running in an upstairs bathroom, running for so long that whatever the detective was doing, it was far more than simply taking a shower. At one point, when the shower was still running, Rosselli caught a glimpse of a haunted-looking Brooke carrying more clothing or bedding through the kitchen towards the utility room. At first sight, he appeared to be naked, but then Rosselli noticed the waistband of a pair of boxer shorts. However, what caught his attention more was that the man was wearing a pair of bright yellow kitchen gloves.

Brooke only remained briefly in the utility room, after which

Rosselli saw him heading back upstairs. About ten minutes later, there was a loud cry of 'Shit!' from the area of the upstairs bathroom, followed quickly by what sounded like 'Buggering bollocks!'

Goccia's head shot round and Rosselli immediately bent to comfort her.

"It's nothing, little one," he whispered, "just an angry man. Go back to your dreams."

A short while later, Brooke spent a considerable length of time in a downstairs bathroom, but unfortunately for Rosselli, the window was closed and although the light was on, he could only see shadows of movement through the frosted glass.

After Brooke had spent more time in the kitchen gathering and washing crockery, Rosselli's patience was finally rewarded when the detective appeared at the kitchen door, now wearing a T-shirt in addition to the boxers. The yellow rubber gloves were still on his hands. Brooke hurried to the side door of the garage, pulled it open and went inside. Rosselli heard a faint click, after which light flooded through the open door. A few minutes later, he emerged carrying a pile of limp white towels.

When Brooke disappeared back into the house, Rosselli bent down to whisper to Goccia. "I think we are reaching the climax of this particular act, tesoro. We won't have long to wait now."

His intuition proved correct. After no more than fifteen minutes, Brooke appeared again at the kitchen door, this time carrying a heavy load wrapped in white towels that was draped over one shoulder. To Rosselli's practised eye, the heavy load could only be one thing.

He heard Brooke moving things in the garage for a while, after which the garage light went out and the detective returned to the house.

Rosselli was stunned to see that he hadn't even locked the garage door behind him.

When he heard an upstairs shower start running, Rosselli slung the small pack he'd brought with him over his shoulder, picked up Goccia and made his way back across the fields to where he'd left his car. After placing the pug in her basket on the rear seat, he whispered to her. "I've just one more thing to do, tesoro, then we'll head home." Goccia settled obediently.

By the time Rosselli returned to the cottage, the place was in darkness and he felt confident that Brooke would already be in a deep sleep.

Making no noise, he slipped on a pair of latex gloves, opened the garage door and shone a pencil torch around inside. Towards the rear but about a foot from the wall, he saw a stack of plastic garden chairs and a pair of folded garden loungers standing on their sides. Looking behind the garden furniture, he could see that lying on the floor was the load that Brooke had carried in a short while before.

After donning a head torch, Rosselli used his phone to record how everything was arranged before systematically and silently removing the items blocking his way to the body. Having recorded how the towels were wrapped around the head, he removed them along with the plastic bag beneath them.

"Superintendent Trisha McVie, I presume," he whispered quietly as he shone the light onto the face. He could see from the damage to the nose that it couldn't be a fatal injury, so he felt carefully around the back of the head, carefully separating the damp hair. "Ah, there we are," he said, as he found the large wound to Trisha's skull. "Did you have a fight, or was it all one horrible mistake? Whatever it was, your Detective Brooke has got himself into a terrible mess, one that we can take good advantage of, I think."

He took several shots of Trisha's face, after which he tilted the body forward and recorded the injury to the back of the head, before lying her down again. It was then that he noticed the stud earrings in Trisha's ears. He smiled as an idea formed in his mind. "One of these might add even more value in my dealings with Detective Constable Brooke." He removed the earring from the right ear and slipped it into his pocket.

"Now," he said, "we need something in the shot to show that the body was here in this garage."

He looked around. Under a workbench, he noticed a pile of box files. Opening the first one, he struck gold. It was full of old photographs. He selected one of Gus Brooke on his own, a head-and-shoulders portrait of him smiling and relaxed, and another showing Brooke with a woman whom Rosselli recognised from the pictures he'd seen online as Brooke's wife Mo. This one had a handwritten message on it.

To Gus, all my love, Mo.

"So you're Gus, are you, Detective Constable Fergus Brooke," said Rosselli, smiling. "That's worth knowing."

He placed the photographs one on either side of Trisha McVie's head and recorded another image on his phone.

"Gotcha!" he smiled. "The police officer in the pub was right; it's a good name."

Ten minutes later the photographs were back in the box file, the file under the workbench, and the bag and towels wrapping McVie's head and body completely reassembled. As he worked, Rosselli compared everything with the photos he'd taken earlier on his phone to ensure the final arrangement of everything looked identical to how he had found it. Two more minutes and there was no indication that anything had moved in the garage; it was exactly as Gus Brooke had left it.

Rosselli stood in the shadows outside the garage, careful to avoid a full moon whose intense light kept teasing from behind the scudding clouds, remnants of the weather front that had brought the previous night's powerful storm. Gus Brooke was providing him with excellent material for the perfect scenario to achieve his goal: the removal of Jennifer Cotton from this earth without anyone suspecting her death was anything other than an unfortunate accident; killed in the line of duty.

He wondered where Detective Brooke was planning to dispose of the body. Would he use the abandoned industrial premises? It had clearly been his immediate choice for dumping the car. However, there was no need to speculate; the detective would let him know in due course, although he wouldn't realise it.

Rosselli fished in his backpack and removed a tiny transmitting device. He switched it on and attached it to the underside of the rear of Brooke's car, the powerful magnet in its casing guaranteed to hold it in place. The battery in the device would last for about ten days, more than enough for the job in hand, and if it wasn't, he would replace it. He took his phone from his pocket, called up an app and activated the device. Every time Brooke's car moved he would be alerted.

"Time to go home, tesoro," said Rosselli, as he climbed back into his car ten minutes later. Curled up in her basket, Goccia subconsciously registered his presence with a slight flick of her tail, but at this stage of the evening, she was only interested in sleep.

Chapter Thirty-One

Early the following morning, Gus Brooke's mind began nudging his subconscious with image after image of Trisha McVie sitting astride him on his bed, grinding rhythmically as she leaned over him, blood from her massively distorted nose dripping onto his face.

Tossing his head from side to side in an effort to avoid the blood, he reached up to push her away, but as he grabbed her face, half her head came away in his hands as water from a powerful jet hit her body from behind and bounced onto a mobile of glass ornaments above the bed, setting them spinning and crashing into a screeching cacophony of smashing glass that slowly transformed into an insistent beeping.

Thrusting the image away from him, Gus sat up in bed with a gasp, his face and body covered in sweat. But the beeping didn't stop. His alarm. Shit. It would be still set for 6:00 and the last thing he was capable of right now was a run or a bike ride.

As the images in his head crumbled into fragments and disappeared, Gus looked around the bedroom in the grey early morning light, relieved to see the walls and fittings weren't dripping blood and a mutilated Trisha McVie wasn't still writhing in his bed.

The events of the last thirty hours began to clarify in his memory and he closed his eyes, willing it to be a crazy nightmare. But it wasn't. Trisha McVie's body was wrapped in old towels in the back of his garage and needed to be dealt with. Other things also needed attention, like her clothing, his clothing and his wallet. And sheets needed ironing to Mo's exacting standards. He shook his head, trying to clear it, but all he achieved was to make himself dizzy. Which was when he remembered he hadn't eaten for over twenty-four hours. His last meal was the one he'd eaten with Trisha the night before last. There hadn't been much of a chance yesterday, and even when someone had thrust a sandwich at him at lunchtime, he'd refused it, worried that if he ate it he would throw it back up.

The first thing he saw as he turned on the bedside light was the bathrobe still lying by the bathroom door, the bathrobe that Trisha had worn and which might still bear evidence of her on it: hairs, or traces of her perfume. How had he missed it? Slipping on a pair of boxers he grabbed from a drawer, he picked up the robe, took it downstairs to the utility room and tossed it in the washer, after which he set about making himself some breakfast.

Half an hour later, at 6:45, he heard his phone ringing. He pounded up the stairs to where he'd left it in the bedroom. It might be Mo; she often rang at unreasonable hours, almost as if she were trying to catch him out.

But it wasn't Mo.

"Morning, sarge," he mumbled when he saw the name on the screen, angered at Jennifer Cotton calling so early.

"Good morning, DC Brooke," she replied. "Apologies for calling at the crack of dawn, but I seem to remember you saying that you're normally up with the lark for your morning exercise."

"Yes, just got back," he lied.

"Good, so you're obviously feeling better."

"I am, sarge, yes. Sorry about yesterday. It must have been something I ate. I've never felt so weird. I really wasn't at the match."

"You can say that again. Anyway, we all have bad days. I thought I'd catch you before you head into work to give you a heads-up on how things were left last night. The DCS suggested I call both you and Barnes, although I don't think we'll be seeing Joe today given he was up half the night while his new son was coaxed into the world."

Gus grunted. Children held little appeal for him.

For the next few minutes, Jennifer filled him in on progress.

"So we're not going back there?"

"No point, although the boss is sending in another team today, just to be a hundred and ten percent sure. Every inch of the place has already been searched. It helped that a number of you knew it well from the operation there a few months ago. The site will almost definitely be released this afternoon, once the second search is over, after which the owners have promised they will secure the gates with a padlock and chain.

"Most of the SCF team will spend their day searching through traffic cams from the nearby area, and once we have the info from the lab, we might be able to confine the search to a more definite radius. Hopefully this morning's press release will throw up something as well, but to be honest, we're clutching at straws at the moment."

"OK, sarge, thanks for that," said Gus. "I'll be in shortly, as soon as I've had a shower."

He closed the call, staring at the screen. Jennifer Cotton had unknowingly given him an idea. With the search of the factory over, it would now return to its previous obscurity; a decaying shell that no one was interested in redeveloping. It would probably remain unvisited for years, and even if the current owners did call in, they would hardly be conducting a detailed scrutiny of every last inch. What better place to dump Trisha McVie's body than somewhere in the factory buildings, somewhere well hidden? It was a pity the chain across the gates was going to be padlocked, but it might be possible to cut the padlock with his bolt croppers and replace it with another. He had some suitable padlocks in his garage. The owners would just think there'd been a cock-up over the keys. And if that way in failed, there was always the break in the fence by the footpath which, as far as he knew, no one apart from him knew about. It would mean manhandling McVie's body along the footpath from the nearest place he could drive the car, and it would have to be done in the dead of night, but none of that posed much of a problem.

He picked up his cup of coffee and tilted it towards his phone.

"Thanks, Detective Sergeant oh-so-super-smart-much-favoured-Jennifer-fucking-Cotton, I think you've given me a way out."

Chapter Thirty-Two

Almost three hours later, Cosimo Graziano Rosselli was sitting in his hotel room after breakfast scrolling through the TV channels for local news. He was impressed: so far, there had been no reports about the disappearance of Trisha McVie; the police must be keeping a tight lid on it.

"It would not be like this at home, Goccia," he said to the pug curled up on the bed next to him. "In Rome there are far too many police officers linked up with local journalists; someone would have tipped off the pack. A senior police officer victim of a kidnapping or murder? They would be baying for more while making up every possible scenario under the sun and selling them all as real. Giorgio will be stunned when I tell him."

Goccia continued to watch the screen without comment, hoping perhaps for the cartoons rather than a succession of boring humans droning on excitedly about nothing.

Finally, at 9:30, a local news report for the East Midlands came on. It led with an appeal from Nottingham City and County Serious Crime Formation who were urgently seeking information on the whereabouts of Patricia Claire McVie, also known as Trisha or Trish McVie, a thirty-nine-year-old detective superintendent of police last seen at the Watford Gap services on the M1 between 19:35 and 19:51 on Tuesday evening. Detective Superintendent McVie was alone and driving a red 5-door VW Golf which traffic cameras recorded leaving the M1 at junction twenty-four at 21:16 and heading in the direction of Nottingham. From there, she could have followed the new dual carriageway directly towards Nottingham or she could have branched off and taken the older road through the village of Rappington. It was thought that her vehicle might have broken down or had a puncture, or that she might have stopped to help another motorist. Anyone who saw a red Golf by the side of the road in the area mentioned at or around nine thirty on Tuesday evening, either alone or with another vehicle, was urged to contact the police on the number given on the screen. The image switched from a stock library shot of a red VW Golf to a head-and-shoulders shot of Trisha McVie as the announcer gave a description of her height, hair colouring and build.

Rosselli stood and walked closer to the television screen.

"There she is, Goccia," he said, his eyes carefully scrutinising Trisha McVie's features. "My research was accurate, which of course we knew. Perhaps I should call the number and tell them to look in Mr Brooke's garage. But that would hardly help my cause. Letting Mr Brooke continue with his plans promises to be far more productive."

He felt in a trouser pocket and retrieved the earring he'd taken from Trisha's body the previous evening and held it up. "Well, well, principessa, look at that. I have one of the earrings shown in the photograph. She must have worn them regularly. It might prove very useful as our plan develops. We'd better keep it in a secure place, somewhere better than a hotel safe whose lock can be opened in seconds."

He walked over to a small rigid suitcase on a chair by the window. A heavy-duty tungsten-steel chain ran through its substantial metal handle and around a water pipe serving a radiator, preventing the possibility of casual theft by any of the hotel staff. He whirled the six wheels of a combination dial to their correct position and turned a high-security key in a central lock. After popping open the case, he slipped the earring into a pouch in the lining of the lid.

"Allora, my little beauty," he said, rubbing Goccia's head.

"Now we must be patient while we wait for our Detective Brooke to make his next move. I suspect it will be sooner rather than later; he won't want to keep the superintendent's body in his garage for long, will he?"

Goccia looked up at him expectantly.

Rosselli smiled. "You are right, tesoro, it's time I took you for a walk."

Chapter Thirty-Three

Detective Sergeant Neil Bottomley sat back in his office chair, his arms folded over his large belly, a deep frown furrowing his normally crease-free forehead.

"No wrinkles on a balloon, lad," was his normal retort to anyone who mentioned the absence of lines on his ageing face.

But today the lines were clearly visible; there would be no such retort. Neil was unhappy that his long and devoted service as a detective was about to end with the disappearance of a senior officer before she'd even had a chance to start work. His jaw worked as he ruminated over the run of disasters that had blighted the SCF more or less since its inception: Rob McPherson, murdered by his own boss, the insane Olivia Freneton. Mike Hurst, also killed by Freneton. Then there were Freneton's attempts on the lives of Derek Thyme and Jennifer Cotton, together with her two attempts on his own life, the second one also involving his wife.

And even though Freneton was dead, the bad luck had continued. Hugh Gregson had dropped dead from a heart attack, and now there was this. And while Trisha McVie's disappearance wasn't yet classified as a crime, all Neil Bottomley's intuition was telling him she was also dead. He didn't know how or why, but the more he thought about it, the more he was convinced, and it didn't sit comfortably with him.

He mused over the evidence accumulated so far. They had

McVie's car, her belongings, her cards, money and warrant card. Nothing appeared to have been stolen. And following the TV appeal for witnesses, they now had a little more.

Within an hour of the previous morning's appeal, two men living in the Rappington area had called to say they had been driving towards Rappington from the M1 motorway on Tuesday evening during the storm. They both said they had seen two cars stopped on a tight bend a mile or so before Rappington, one of them red, the other ... they weren't sure. Something dark. According to one of the witnesses, one of the cars might have been jacked up; the red one, he thought. But as to the drivers of the two cars, neither witness could say anything; one hadn't even seen them. It had been pelting with rain; it was pitch dark apart from the headlights and both men were more concerned with safely negotiating the bend than paying attention to details at the roadside. The witnesses had now been interviewed and their formal statements taken, but the only extra information that had been coaxed out of their memories was that at least one of the cars had its hazard lights flashing.

The witnesses' cars had now been identified on the traffic camera footage at junction twenty-four and the timings correlated. One car left the motorway exactly five minutes after Trisha McVie's red Golf, the other after eight minutes and twenty-five seconds. It all fitted together. They knew from forensics that Trisha McVie must have had a puncture; now it appeared that someone had stopped to help her. Was that person significant? It had to be assumed he or she was, but with the barest of information about the person's car — it was probably a black or dark-blue saloon or small hatchback, but the make, model, size and condition were unknown — they would have to hope there would be more witnesses.

DCI Len Crawford had earlier sent Jennifer Cotton and Doug Coulson to the location on the Rappington road where the witnesses had seen the two cars. Two vehicle accident experts from Forefront Forensics were waiting for them.

"We've found a good tyre print in the mud beyond the road," explained Colin Maitland, the more senior of the pair. "I've sent an image of it back to the lab and they've already confirmed that it matches the make of tyres on the red Golf. We'll be confirming later that it's actually from the Golf. There's also a mark that's consistent with the base of a jack. I've taken a soil sample for comparison with the mud I remember was on the base of the jack in the Golf."

"So this is pretty definitely the spot where Detective Superintendent McVie stopped," said Jennifer, her eyes roaming the area as she tried to get a feel for it. "Any indication of tyre marks from the other car?"

Maitland shook his head. "Nothing. He must have stopped on the road. But there's more to explain why Superintendent McVie stopped in the first place. You'll remember from our preliminary report that the nearside rear wheel on the Golf appeared to be the spare, that it had been changed and the onboard wheel and tyre both had fresh damage, the tyre pretty much shredded. Well, there's a gouge mark in the road surface here," — he pointed to the road near where they were standing — "together with deposits of rubber. It looks as if the tyre either punctured or was extremely under-inflated. She must have hit the brakes hard as she approached the bend, causing the vehicle to dip towards the flat or nearly flat tyre. At that point, the wheel rim would have come into contact with the road and there's a good chance she would have lost control of the vehicle."

Jennifer pointed at the large oak tree beyond the corner.

"Could've driven straight into that," she said. "Pity she didn't, really. The whole incident might have played out rather differently."

"Maybe," agreed Maitland. "I'd say the gouging here is consistent with what I've just explained. We'll be comparing residues on the edge of the wheel with the debris on the road surface, of course, to confirm this gouge is from the Golf's wheel."

Doug Coulson was walking farther along the road looking for anything else that might have been missed when Jennifer called out to him.

"Doug, didn't the witnesses say that one of the reasons they couldn't say much about the other car was because its headlights were aimed towards them, lighting the Golf to help whoever was changing the wheel?"

"That's right, sarge. They said all they could see were the lights, which stopped them getting a look at the car itself."

Jennifer nodded and pointed ahead of her.

"Wouldn't that indicate the other car was stopped here on the left side of the road, the side heading away from Nottingham and towards the motorway? The super's car was here, pointing towards the tree," — she paused and moved near to the corner where the gouge marks were — "which means the other car was here, its lights aimed at the side of the Golf."

"Meaning it's likely the other car had originally been travelling towards the motorway," said Coulson.

"Precisely," said Jennifer. "He'd come from Nottingham. And if for whatever reason the super decided to follow him after the wheel was changed, she would have had to turn her car around to do it."

Jennifer called the DCI immediately with the new information, but Crawford pointed out that it didn't prove McVie's car had driven off with the other car back towards the motorway.

"Doesn't make a lot of sense, Cotton. Why would she do that?"

"I don't know, guv. Maybe the driver of the other car lives in the area and offered her the opportunity to dry out. They would have been soaked to the skin, after all."

"Possibly, Cotton, but she wasn't exactly far from where she was going. I don't see why she'd turn round and head off in the opposite direction."

Jennifer wanted to tell Crawford to start thinking laterally, but she knew she couldn't. Instead she quietly ground her teeth. As far as she was concerned, they had an important new lead and here was Crawford pouring cold water on it.

The DCI had, however, passed on Jennifer's thoughts to Neil Bottomley and it was this scenario he was now considering.

His eyes wandered around the office where several detectives and civilian staff were concentrating on their monitors. When they fell on Gus Brooke, they stopped, something nagging in his head. Then he remembered.

"Brooke," he called.

"Sarge?" said Gus, alarmed by the unusually stern note in Bottomley's voice.

"Don't you live somewhere in the Rappington area?"

Gus had been waiting for someone to remember this and was ready with his story.

"I do, sarge, yes. About a mile and a half beyond the village."

"You mean on the M1 side of the village?"

"Yes, sarge."

"Don't suppose you saw anything odd on the road on Tuesday night?"

"Unfortunately not, sarge, especially since I left the office around nine and normally I would have been passing through the village about the time the witnesses say the Golf was there."

"Normally?"

"Yes, I normally go that way home since it's quicker, but the weather was so dreadful on Tuesday night I decided to avoid the sharp bends on either side of Rappington where I might've ended up in a ditch. Instead, I took the new road, doubling back to the cottage from where the Rappington road meets it closer to the M1."

"Hmm," grunted Bottomley. "And you didn't see anything?"

"No, sarge, nothing."

Gus Brooke knew he was taking a risk. Another witness might come forward and claim he saw his car in or near Rappington, or worse, next to the red Golf on the bend. But he thought that unlikely. He could only remember two cars passing while he was changing the wheel. On both occasions his back was to them while he concentrated on what he was doing and the heavy rain would have blurred everything for the drivers. Added to that, he knew there were no traffic cameras on the Rappington road or at either end of it.

Reassured, he took a silent but confident deep breath. There would be nothing to contradict his story.

Chapter Thirty-Four

As soon as she closed the door to her apartment after arriving home on Friday evening with Derek, Jennifer turned to him and burst into tears.

Saying nothing, Derek wrapped his strong arms around her, stroking her hair as she sobbed into his shoulder.

"I don't know if I can carry on with this, Derek, putting on a façade of professionalism when my heart is breaking. I know the worst has happened, I can feel it. There's no other explanation. She's dead, Derek. Everything points to it. I know it, I don't understand it and I hate it."

"Yeah, Jen, I know," whispered Derek. He had felt the same ever since the reports from the witnesses seeing Trisha's car on the Rappington road on Tuesday evening had arrived.

"I just don't get it. It all seems so calculated. Dumping the car where it could have gone undetected for months. What kind of person would do that?"

Jennifer straightened. Her emotions were in tatters but her brain was still working. "That's a good point. It *was* calculated, but they messed up."

"Messed up?"

"Yes, whoever drove the car into the factory site was under stress, wanting to dump it and run, get away with their accomplice before they were spotted. I think the thought process was that the car wouldn't be found, which would have been true if it had been hidden more carefully, in one of the loading bays, for example, where it wouldn't have been visible from the air. If they'd done that, we'd have almost nothing to go on except a few useless sightings on traffic cameras."

Arms around each other, they walked into the sitting room and flopped onto a sofa.

"Glass of wine?" asked Derek.

Jennifer shook her head. "In a bit. I just want you to hold me for now. Stay close." Her bottom lip quivered as she buried her head in his chest. "God, it's horrible. Poor Trisha. We've got to find her, Derek. Got to."

"And find the bastards responsible for whatever's happened," added Derek.

Jennifer pulled a tissue from a box on the coffee table in front of them and blew her nose. "You know, in spite of how daft it sounds, I'm not happy with the accomplice idea, not happy with more than one person being involved."

"You think whoever dumped the car just walked away? Bit risky, don't you think?"

"No, I don't. The Rappington road is hardly busy. The car must have been dumped during the night or very early in the morning, so the chances of someone passing are small enough. And the area is surrounded by fields and footpaths. Perhaps whoever dumped it went that way."

"That would have to mean that it's someone local, surely."

"Maybe, but it's not that far into Nottingham. The Trent's pretty close and once across it, there are footpaths all the way to Beeston and beyond. Wouldn't take long."

"Yes, but remember the car the witnesses saw was facing the other way, as if it were heading away from Nottingham. You're the one who spotted that. And anyway, to do what you just said, you'd have to cross the river and the nearest bridge is on Clifton Boulevard. It's the only bridge for miles, unless they swam across."

Jennifer sat up. "Let's look at what we know. We know Trisha left the M1 at junction twenty-four. The traffic cams indicated she was alone in her car and there were no other cars following her. A few minutes later, she gets a puncture and almost loses control of her car on a tight bend. She's shocked by that, shaken up. Don't forget there's a horrible storm as well. Then someone sees her car at an odd angle and stops—"

"Or he saw the incident and stopped," suggested Derek.

"Yes, possibly. Anyway, he offers to help and changes her wheel. Has the lab come up with anything in the way of fingerprints or DNA from the Golf?"

"Nothing yet, no."

"So what happens next? They are both soaked to the skin, drowned rats—"

"And if he does live locally," cut in Derek, "he might have tried the old come-back-to-my-place routine. Would Trisha fall for that?"

Jennifer sighed. "Depends how young and good looking he was; it *is* Trisha we're talking about. But even so, it's a huge jump from 'come back to mine', even if said with intent, to killing someone, which must have happened otherwise why would it be necessary to dump her car?"

Derek leaned forward on the sofa, his hand pulling at his face. "Why did he dump the car and not the body?"

"Perhaps moving the body was difficult for some reason."

"So why the car?"

"Too visible? Maybe it was outside his house and he wanted to get rid of it before anyone saw it there. Perhaps he has nosy neighbours."

"Did Crawford say anything about house-to-house in the area? After all, the appeal for witnesses focussed on the Rappington road. There are several villages apart from Rappington that aren't far away. If our man lives in one of those, perhaps a neighbour saw something."

Jennifer frowned. "Crawford announced it this afternoon. Oh, it must have been while you were out seeing the witness in that old Mapperley case Crawford won't let go of. I forgot to tell you when you got back: we're starting house-to-house tomorrow."

"Well, at least it will feel as if we're doing something, even though house-to-house can be an exercise in frustration. And

Saturday morning will be a good time to start; more people at home."

"Yes, and in the meantime, if Trisha is dead and still in someone's house, they have the problem of what they are going to do with her body. God! I can't believe I'm saying that. Not about Trish."

"No," agreed Derek. "It's unreal. Did Crawford say how he's going to organise the house-to-house?"

"He's given it to Neil, who said he thinks the best approach will be to start where Trisha was last seen alive, i.e. on the Rappington road, and work out from there. Visit every house, farm, small business, everything."

Derek looked round from where he was still leaning forward. "You know whose house will be one of the first to be visited, don't you?"

Jennifer frowned. "No, I don't."

"Gus Brooke's. He and his wife Mo have a place just along the road towards the M1 from where Trisha's car was last seen."

"That's right, they do. I'd forgotten that. Pity he chose to drive a different way home on Tuesday evening. He can't have seen anything or he would have said. I wonder if Mo saw anything. Perhaps she was looking out of the window at the storm as Trisha's car passed by, following another car."

Derek was shaking his head. "No chance. Gus told me she's away lecturing somewhere in Europe."

Jennifer stared across the room. "So Gus is on his own, is he? I wonder why he was in such a bad way on Wednesday."

Chapter Thirty-Five

Gus Brooke's mind was in increasing conflict, his thought processes a maze of indecision. He had to get rid of Trisha McVie's body, remove it from his house before either Mo returned from her trip or the finger of suspicion pointed in his direction and his house was searched.

Was that likely to happen? It shouldn't; he was simply one of the police officers involved in the case. Like all his colleagues, apart from Jennifer Cotton and the DCS, he had no known connection to the missing woman. But he had behaved like a prat on Wednesday, his nerve failing him on a number of occasions, and he hadn't been much better the next day. And worse, there was a team of civilian officers assigned by Crawford working with the forensic lab on establishing possible alternatives for where the Golf could have gone before ending up at the derelict factory. Gus's cottage would be one of the possibilities, maybe the best possibility. How likely were they to treat it as a strange coincidence and dismiss it? He didn't know; he could only hope for the best.

But what he did know was that the body had to go and the only place he could think of was the factory. It ticked all the boxes even with the possibility it might be searched again sometime in the future, regardless of what the DCS had said. There wasn't much he could do about that; he would have to take a chance because he didn't have time to research anywhere else.

. . .

Excusing himself on the grounds that he was still feeling slightly odd, he left the SCF offices shortly before seven on Friday evening and headed home. But before arriving at the cottage and facing up to moving the body, he needed to confirm there was no longer a police presence at the Rappington factory, even though Crawford had said it had been handed back the previous evening.

He passed no cars on the Rappington road and the lane to the factory was deserted as he made his way along it. After stopping his car in front of the gates, he got out and walked closer to inspect the new padlock. He almost laughed out loud. The lock was hardly worthy of the name, the type of rubbish sold for suitcases that could be levered open with a screwdriver. The ones in his garage he could use as a replacement were far superior; he'd be able to drive all the way in.

It was seven thirty and the light was starting to fade. No one else would visit the site today and probably not over the weekend. Indeed, having fitted their long-overdue padlock, the factory owners were unlikely to have any pressing need to revisit the site at all.

He smiled to himself, a sense of relief lifting his spirits. He hadn't been looking forward to carrying McVie's body from his car along the footpath to the spot where he could get through the fence. It was quite a distance and even though he had planned to do it at around four in the morning, there was still a danger of being seen. Fitness fanatics were a weird bunch; some thought nothing of pacing the highways and byways at all times of the day or night. The flat, straight footpaths alongside the irrigation channels were a particular favourite.

Instead, he could now open the gates, drive through them and, after closing them, continue into the yard where he had dumped the Golf, his car out of sight of the lane while he hid the body. The road surfaces in the site were all concrete and after three days with no more rain, they were dry. With all the activity from police vehicles, any tyre prints from his car would disappear into the jumble of tracks already present.

. . .

By the time he returned to his cottage, Gus had made his plans. He would set his alarm for four in the morning and drive the body to the factory. He had found the perfect spot to hide the body when he was with the team searching the decaying buildings: one of a number of large metal bins at the rear of the upper floor open platform. He had looked inside two of them and found that both contained a jumble of heavy-duty ropes, most of them old and greasy. They would be ideal for covering the body.

The whole process shouldn't take too long and with luck he would be back at the cottage by five, well before the residents of Rappington surfaced for their Saturday morning.

In the meantime, since he had to wait for darkness to fall before he could carry the body to the car, he decided to revisit everywhere Trisha McVie had been in the cottage, look at everything she might have touched, everywhere her blood might have splashed. He had done it once and been meticulous, but he had also been dog-tired and in shock over the whole incident. He was cooler now, more focussed, less likely to overlook small details. And anyway, it would do no harm to wash down both bathrooms again and check above and beneath every surface.

And sure enough, when he was down on his hands and knees with a torch examining the underside of the marble shelf supporting the hand basins in the master bathroom, he noticed a tiny spot of what appeared to be blood on the chrome surface of the drainpipe from the basin. Or was it rust? It shouldn't be, the fittings had cost a fortune, but either way, you couldn't be too careful. He swabbed the entire area with disinfectant, rubbing and polishing the surfaces until he was satisfied they were clean of any contamination.

His wallet was still soaking in one of the washbasins. Gus picked it out of the water and peered at its water-stained surface. The blood seemed to have gone, but he suspected the watermarks would always be there. He was reluctant to throw the wallet away and he tried to convince himself that the marks added to its appearance, a random pattern of dark and light leather. He would tell Mo he had dropped it in the garden in the rain where it soaked in the mud for several hours before he found it. It would be a way of underlining how much he valued it and hopefully appease her anger at it being spoiled.

He sighed, realising that he was deflecting his thoughts from the main task now that darkness had fallen. Trisha McVie's body.

On arriving home, he had reversed his car into the short drive alongside the cottage, taking it as close to the garage side door and the kitchen door as he could. Now, it was time. After pulling on a pair of latex gloves, he left the cottage through the kitchen door, lifted up the car's tailgate and switched off the interior light. With the kitchen lights also off and the kitchen door closed, the car was in darkness. Taking two bin liners from a pack he had bought on the way home, he spread them across the boot space.

Once inside the garage, he closed the door and turned on the light. He was immediately relieved to smell nothing more than the ordinary garage smells: his precautions had worked. He pulled the garden furniture out of the way and bent to pick up the body. When he had placed it there on Wednesday evening, the rigor mortis was still apparent, but now it seemed more flexible, yielding to his grip. It would make carrying it and stowing it in the car that much easier.

Five minutes later, the body was in the car, the white towels wrapping it covered with another black plastic sheet, and the items in the garage back in their normal places.

Now all he had to do was wait until four the following morning. And in the meantime, although he had never felt less like eating, he would force something simple down while avoiding the temptation of a glass of wine or a beer, and try to get some sleep.

Visions of Trisha McVie again haunted Gus's night, the pulse of his alarm morphing into a dream where her body was rolling around his car and rocking it so alarmingly he was afraid it would overturn. He sat up in bed with a jolt, the silence of the cottage a welcome relief.

Dressed from head to toe in plain black lycra and wearing

another pair of latex gloves, Gus made his way to his car and set off. He glanced at his watch. Eight minutes past four.

As he approached the lane leading to the factory, he switched off his lights and pulled to a halt. There was nothing on the road but he wanted his eyes to adjust to the moonlight before driving along the lane without his headlights on.

The bolt croppers made short work of the padlock and the chain was quickly removed. Once through the gates, Gus closed them behind him — he would secure them with the new padlock when he left — and drove into the entrance to the yard, stopping his car just before the end of the passage.

Leaning into the boot, he lifted Trisha McVie's body, thought briefly about tossing it over his shoulder but then decided carrying it would be easier. He hurried across the yard to the main door. Inside, the darkness was complete as Gus stumbled in the direction of the steps. "Shit!" he muttered. "I need the head torch."

He tried to balance Trish's body on one knee while he fumbled in his jacket for the torch but it was too difficult and he was forced to put her down.

Panting with the effort of carrying the body up the stairs, Gus laid it on the ground in front of one of the storage bins at the rear of the platform area. He lifted the storage bin lid and peered inside. There was enough room to place the body on the ropes and cover it with more ropes from another bin. But after placing the body in the bin, he paused and stared down at the white towels wrapping it. They might have evidence on them from the garage or the car; they should be removed. What about the plastic bag covering the head? Could there be traces on that to connect the bag with the garage, the cottage or Gus himself? His own lycra clothing was less of a problem; it probably didn't shed fibres. It would be sensible to bundle the towels and plastic bag in a bin bag and dump them in a communal rubbish bin in another village. But against all that, he didn't want to see the body again, didn't want to have those lifeless eyes staring in his direction, didn't want to desecrate the body further by leaving it naked in this alien place.

After a few more moments of indecision, he made up his mind. Regardless of his feelings about the body, the towels had to go, as did the plastic bag covering the head. The effort of pulling on the ends of the towels rolled the body and as they came away, the body ended up exactly as he didn't want it: face up.

Doing his best to avoid looking at Trish's half-open eyes, he lifted ropes from the adjacent bin. It proved harder than he had imagined. They were heavy with many protruding sharp fibres that quickly shredded his gloves, forcing him to return to his car to put on several pairs of new ones.

Twenty minutes later, Gus stood back to admire his handiwork. Trisha's body was now entirely covered by the ropes filling the remaining space in the metal bin. He closed the lid and for good measure, pulled a few more ropes from another bin on top of the lid, partly covering it.

After gathering up the towels and plastic, he took one last glance around before hurrying for the stairs. Twelve minutes later, he stepped from his car outside the cottage and quietly shut the driver's door. It was four minutes past five; he had completed everything in less than an hour.

Standing in a steaming shower, Gus felt as if the last vestiges of his encounter with Trisha McVie were flushing away with the soapy water. Strangely, he felt little regret for what had happened to her even though he had no reason to wish her dead. It had been an accident, no more, and he could not be held responsible. He was no more guilty of murder or manslaughter than anyone else, although the law would doubtless see it otherwise.

All his actions following McVie's death were acts of self-preservation, totally justifiable in the scheme of things. What use would it serve anyone for him to be locked up in prison, his life destroyed? Prison was for criminals, a place for penance and rehabilitation, a deterrent for others not to commit the same crimes. No deterrent was going to prevent accidents; they happened.

It was a pity that McVie's body couldn't be given the respect of a decent burial, but such a thing was out of his hands. Her body would now rest nestled among the ropes for many years and probably be reduced to a pile of bones by the time it was discovered.

The most important thing was that there was nothing to connect him or his car or cottage with her or her car. He had covered it all. He could now stand back and watch while his colleagues continued to simmer in their frustration, something that would continue for a few weeks until more pressing issues took over and the McVie case was put on a back burner until it became just another cold case.

Fully refreshed, Gus dressed and made himself a fry-up and a mug of strong coffee for breakfast. While he was tucking in, he flipped open his laptop to find an email from Mo. She had tried to call him but couldn't get an answer. He frowned. Why not? He retrieved his phone from his jacket and found out why: he had let the battery run down to nothing. Bugger it; he'd be in trouble with everyone from Cotton upwards if they had been trying to call him. He reached over and plugged the phone into a cable dangling from a socket near the outside door and returned his attention to the email. Mo was coming home early, arriving on Wednesday. She was pissed off that she'd missed the weekend, but she hoped they could make up for it next weekend.

He smiled. We can certainly do that, he thought. Time I turned over a new leaf and stopped succumbing to temptation. It had been a close call, too close, not something he wanted to repeat. It had been the thought of losing Mo and all that came with her that had driven him to dealing with Trisha McVie in the way he had. It was time to draw a line under it, become a good boy and a better cop.

Chapter Thirty-Six

When Gus Brooke had left the SCF offices shortly before seven on Friday evening, prior to dumping Trisha McVie's body, Rosselli was in his hotel room performing the daily ritual of cleaning his Glock 30 handgun and his long-range sniper rifle. He looked up as his phone sounded an alert: Detective Constable Brooke's car was on the move.

Before carefully wrapping the weapons and returning them to the safety of his high-security metal case, he quickly checked the car's location. It was heading out of Nottingham towards Rappington; Brooke was going home.

The weapons stowed, Rosselli idly stroking Goccia's head as he sat watching the moving blue dot on the screen. When it turned into the lane leading to the factory, he smiled.

"It looks as if he is still interested in the derelict industrial site, little one. Look, his car has stopped outside."

Less than a minute later, when the blue dot started to move again, Rosselli nodded. "Interesting. I wonder what he's up to. But whatever he was doing, he now appears to be heading for his house. I think it's time for another walk through the fields and woods. If tonight is the night he intends to dump the body, I want to be there to see him load it into the car."

. . .

It was almost dark by the time Rosselli arrived at his spot in the Brookes' garden, Goccia obediently and silently waiting at his side. The cottage was ablaze with light, but none of it reached him; he could watch and wait undetected.

From the activity in the cottage it appeared that Brooke was cleaning the same upstairs bathroom he had already devoted hours to. Although Rosselli applauded the diligence, he felt it was borne out of fear rather than cold common sense: Brooke was terrified of missing something that might later incriminate him.

Soon after nine thirty, the kitchen door opened and Brooke emerged dressed entirely in black. After releasing the tailgate of his car, which he had reversed into position to ensure it was close to both the garage and kitchen doors, he hurried to the garage.

Rosselli turned to Goccia and put his fingers to his lips. She obliged by hunkering down and resting her chin on her front paws.

After some muffled scraping sounds from inside the garage, Brooke appeared at the garage door, carrying the wrapped body in his arms. He paused, listening for any noises from the road. Hearing nothing, he continued on to the car and carefully placed the body in the boot.

Leaving the car's tailgate up, Brooke hurried back to the garage to fetch two large bin liners which he draped over the white towels wrapping the body. Once he had finished in the car, he returned again to the garage where Rosselli heard him tidying the interior. It didn't take long and soon Brooke was back indoors, the car, garage and garden left in silence and darkness.

Half-an-hour later, all the lights in the house went out. When Brooke didn't emerge, Rosselli assumed he had gone to bed. Dumping the body in the early hours of the morning would make more sense than doing it now when there might be witnesses to his movements. Nevertheless, he patiently waited fifteen more minutes before emerging from his hiding place. With Goccia padding along beside him, he walked silently towards the detective's car and gently clicked the tailgate release. He lifted the door and pulled the bin liners to one side. There wasn't much light, but it didn't matter.

Rosselli had an app on his phone that accumulated dozens of exposures in poor light and made a half-reasonable job of rendering an image. However, it did involve holding the phone still, which he achieved by pushing it against the padded roof above the body before hitting the shutter release. Four attempts later he had some acceptable shots. He would have preferred flash, but he didn't want to risk anything that might draw Brooke's attention to his presence, and anyway, the shots were only an insurance against possible resistance from the principal player in his plot.

After carefully putting the bin liners back in place over the body, he decided that rather than make his way back across the fields and through the woods in total darkness, he would risk walking with Goccia along the road to the track where he had left his car.

Settling the pug in her basket on the rear seat, he removed her lead and fed her one of the small nibbles she loved. "Well done, tesoro, you were so quiet, an angel. We can go back to our hotel now. When the misguided detective heads off in the darkness to dump the superintendent's body, the little bug on his car will tell us exactly where he has gone, and since he went there earlier this evening, I think we know where that will be. We can visit in our own time to make further preparations."

A ping from his phone awoke Rosselli at 4:08 on Saturday morning, alerting him that Gus Brooke's car was moving once again. He sat up in bed and switched on the bedside light, but a suspicious growl from Goccia, who sensed the unexpected activity had nothing to do with her being taken for a walk, saw him quickly turn it off again.

"Go back to sleep, principessa, I'll take you out later."

From the comfort of his bed, Rosselli watched the blue flashing marker on the map move from Brooke's cottage, pass through Rappington and take the lane towards the factory. There was a pause while Brooke opened the gates, after which the marker moved inside the factory perimeter, paused again, and then moved towards the enclosed yard. When it stopped short of entering the yard, Rosselli nodded his approval.

"Hidden from the lane; our young detective is learning," he whispered quietly, not wanting to disturb Goccia again.

If the bug on the car remained stationary for more than ten minutes, the app was programmed to ping with the next movement, which it duly did nearly fifty minutes later once Brooke had hidden Trisha McVie's body and began driving back to the cottage.

Rosselli had been dozing, knowing he could rely on the app, but he was instantly alert as he watched the progress of the car back to the cottage.

"Fifty-six minutes, Goccia," he said, but not loudly enough to wake his sleeping pug. "Efficient, but given Detective Brooke is an amateur, rather too efficient. I suspect he will have made a few mistakes. We'll see when the coast is clear."

Chapter Thirty-Seven

The house-to-house enquiries on Saturday morning produced no information of any relevance. No sightings of the Golf the previous Tuesday evening, no one acting suspiciously, no one who saw Trisha McVie. Nothing. A frustrated Len Crawford sought the DCS's approval for widening the radius of the search into Saturday afternoon, but still there was nothing.

The choice of the derelict factory to dump the car puzzled Jennifer. It couldn't be random; whoever made that choice must have known it was deserted and not well secured. As well as her routine questions, she also asked what people knew about the factory, whether they had heard anything about any activity up there.

"It was interesting," she told Derek later that afternoon when they met back at the SCF HQ. "The older residents in Rappington, the more well-to-do ones who have lived there for donkey's years, couldn't say a good word about the place. Some of them remembered it being built in a boom in the early sixties, moaned about it bringing heavy lorries through the village destroying their peace and quiet and lowering the tone of the place."

Derek pulled a face. "I wasn't aware it had a tone to lower. It's a real non-entity of a village. Nothing pretty about it even with the pond near the church."

"P'raps it was better back then," said Jennifer.

She grinned knowingly at him. "You know, you should have bent their ears when you were looking into the place earlier this year, they might have saved you some time. None of them knew of any activity there, no cars at strange times, no vehicles at all, in fact. Several of them walk their dogs around there but they all took the chains on the gates at face value, assumed they were actually doing something and not just window dressing. You missed out on good intelligence from their neighbourhood watch."

"Possibly, but I think Crawford reckoned the locals might have been involved, didn't want to frighten them off."

"Most of the oldies I spoke to were hardly likely to have been involved in drug manufacture, and I don't think porn would be good for their collective blood pressure."

Derek laughed. "Good point. I agree with you, though, I think the chances are that it's someone local. Have you talked to Gus? I mean, he's lived there for a few months, he must have had some conversations in the local pub, got to know a few people."

"I haven't, no, but I will. I must admit that I still find it strange that he didn't say anything about living nearby when the Golf was found."

"P'raps he assumed everyone knew."

The shrill of Derek's desk phone interrupted their conversation.

"DC Thyme. Oh, hi, mate, how're you doing? I haven't seen you at the track for a while. Everything OK?"

"Everything's fine with me, Derek, yeah." replied Leroy Crosby, a forensic scientist from Forefront Forensics whom Derek knew from their shared passion for athletics. "But me kid's been sick and with the missus about to pop with number two, I haven't had time,"

"Probably haven't had permission, either, I should guess," joked Derek.

"Tell me about it."

"Anyway, what can I do for you, mate?" said Derek. "Don't you know it's Saturday afternoon?"

"The service is twenty-four/seven here at Forefront Forensics," said Leroy, singing out the advertising slogan in a theatrical voice. "Actually, the hours are all over the place for me at the mo. I was off half of yesterday owing to a false alarm from Minnie. But I did have time to put something on for an overnight analysis that I thought looked interesting. That's why I'm calling."

"Really?"

"Yeah. Well, I was wondering. Was Trisha McVie a cyclist?"

"A cyclist? Don't think so. Hang on, Jen's here. I'll ask."

Derek put the handset into his shoulder and turned to Jennifer.

"It's Leroy from the lab. He wants to know if Trish was a cyclist."

Jennifer shook her head. "No, not unless she was keeping it from me."

Derek spoke back into the phone. "Jen says no."

"But perhaps she owns a bike?" suggested Leroy.

"Own a bike?" said Derek to Jennifer.

"No."

"No, mate, she didn't. What's this about?"

"Well," said Leroy, "when I examined the Golf interior yesterday, I found a trace of oil on the edge of the tailgate, right next to the door trim, just left of centre. It was missed during the first examination, but when I used a laser light, I spotted it.

"As I said, I was called away in the afternoon, but I left a sample to be analysed overnight on the GC/MS and the results are interesting."

"Enlighten me," said Derek, his eagerness sounding in his voice.

"It's a complex mixture," explained Leroy. "Dozens of components and it's contaminated as well. But from the various databases I've looked at, I'd say it's pretty definitely a high-grade lube oil, the kind a dedicated cyclist would use on the chain of a road bike or a mountain bike."

Derek frowned. "How would it get in the car?"

He looked up to see Jennifer issuing silent questions to him, impatient to hear what Leroy had to say. He held up his hand to stop her and turned his attention back to the scientist.

"Probably from lifting a bike either in or out of the car," continued Leroy. "Depending on the car, it's not always easy to do without part of the bike touching something. Especially at the end of a ride when you're knackered. You must have done it."

"In *my* car!" said an incredulous Derek. "It would be easier to fit my Mini into my bike than my bike into my Mini."

"Right," replied Leroy, laughing, "but you know what I mean. That stuff sticks like dag to a sheep, as an Australian ex-girlfriend of mine used to say. Mind you, this was a tiny amount. I reckon the boot must have had something spread over it to protect it. What I've found must have missed the cover, or maybe a pedal was contaminated with it from the chain or front cogs and touched the rim of the well as the bike was lifted in or out."

"So you obviously think it's significant."

"If there's no other explanation, yes, it could be."

"Thanks, Leroy, that's bloody brilliant."

He put the phone down and explained to Jennifer what Leroy had found.

"I'm ninety-nine per cent sure about Trish not having a bike," she said. "But we can confirm it easily enough. A team from her old squad is going to her place in London this afternoon. Probably there now. I'll call them, get them to double-check about a bike."

She tapped some numbers on her phone.

"You know what this means, Derek?" she said, as she waited to be connected.

"Yeah, of course. It means that whoever dumped her took a bike with him as well so he could get home."

"Which is good and bad news … hang on." She spoke into the phone and explained what she wanted to know. The answer came back immediately.

"OK," continued Jennifer as she closed the call. "Confirmed; Trish didn't have a bike."

"Why is it good news and bad news?"

"Think about it. It's good news because it narrows the search to a cyclist, probably one with a quality bike. It's also good news because it means there's only one person involved, which certainly makes sense."

"And bad news?"

"It's bad news because it widens the search area enormously. We might not be dealing with someone from around Rappington at all; they just needed to know about the factory. They could have come from, I don't know, up to twenty miles away. Maybe more."

Chapter Thirty-Eight

After Gus Brooke had dumped Trisha McVie's body, Rosselli continued to monitor the detective's car throughout the day. He needed to know where the police were occupying themselves before he felt he could safely visit the factory and begin his preparations.

It quickly became obvious that Brooke and many other detectives were conducting house-to-house enquiries, starting close to Rappington and working outwards. The large search group was criss-crossing the area and although they didn't move back to the factory site, Rosselli felt they were too close for comfort. He would wait at least another day.

On checking his app on Sunday morning, Rosselli was surprised to see Brooke's car in Beeston, a suburb of Nottingham on the other side of the River Trent from Rappington. A quick trip to spy out activity confirmed what he thought: the search had been expanded to cover other areas. Something must have happened to persuade the police to look farther afield and, more importantly, they obviously still had no suspicions about Detective Constable Brooke.

With the police now occupied elsewhere, Rosselli drove to the factory and found it deserted. The gates were secured with a padlock that would have only taken him seconds to open. However, it would be too risky to drive his car into the site but neither could he leave it outside in full view of anyone who happened by. He would have to leave his car in the village and return to the site using the same path alongside the irrigation channel that he had taken the previous Wednesday, when the area had been alive with police activity.

After parking his car in Rappington village in the small space hidden from the main road behind the village church, Rosselli clipped Goccia's lead to her collar and the pair set off. For Goccia, the walk was even more exciting than before since a number of police dogs had taken the same route and left their delicious scent behind. As she nuzzled her way along the grass bordering the wire mesh fence that defined the limit of the factory site, she pulled harder against the lead, as if she wanted to tunnel under the fence. She stopped and gave a low whine.

"What is it, my little bloodhound? What have you found?" asked Rosselli as his attention fell on the fence. "Oh, Goccia, you clever girl. Where would I be without you? You've found us a way in."

He bent over and carefully separated the mesh at the same spot Gus Brooke had used after he dumped the Golf. It was well interwoven, giving the appearance of being one continuous stretch of mesh, but it gave easily to his fingers. Seconds later Rosselli and Goccia were inside the fence and Rosselli was closing the breach.

"Come, cara," he said, glancing up and down the path, "we're a little exposed here; there might be other strollers and their dogs."

He hurried towards the factory buildings, skirting them until he reached the far side and the internal road that led from the main gates through the large vehicular access passage to the central yard. Looking up before he walked into the passage, he saw the faded sign.

"The factory?" he read. "Couldn't the owners have thought of something more imaginative to call it?"

Staying in the shadows, he continued through the passage to the yard and then on to a pair of double doors that served as the main entrance.

For the next three hours, Rosselli made a meticulous examination of the derelict buildings, assessing them from his own point of view as a possible place of execution for Jennifer Cotton, and also to find where Gus Brooke had hidden Trisha McVie's body.

For the execution, after considering several possibilities, he decided that a large, open area on the upper floor of the rear building would be ideal. The area had once been a reception and dispatch area for consignments of goods in small crates. These would have been hoisted from the ground floor loading bay below and transferred to a pulley system running on girder rails rigged ten feet from the floor. It was the hoists and rails that attracted Rosselli's attention along with the rusted and compromised safety rails designed to prevent anyone falling from the edge of the area and tumbling five metres into the loading bay.

He stood back, taking in the whole area while a sequence of events played out in his mind. He could visualise the action and it made perfect sense, but which players apart from his target would be present was still based on certain assumptions and the consequences of actions that hadn't yet taken place. As the days passed, the detail would change, even though the overall outcome would be the same. There was no urgency; he had the time and the patience. For now, he was still merely an observer waiting for the main actors to commit themselves further.

Satisfied with his provisional plans for Jennifer Cotton, Rosselli turned his thoughts to Trisha McVie. He had kept her body in mind as he examined the factory, checking and eliminating various locations where a body could be hidden.

Then, as his eyes roamed the open area above the loading bay, he noticed a number of large storage bins arranged along the rear wall. Clusters of heavy-duty ropes were scattered on the floor, and one bin had some lying across its lid. As Rosselli walked over to the bins, he could see that the dust and grime on the floor showed signs of disturbance: cleaner patches alongside some of the ropes that appeared to be fresh. He shrugged. Perhaps they were the result of disturbance during the police search. Nevertheless, the bins were worth investigating, and it was as he looked closer at the jumble of heavy ropes that he saw residues of shredded plastic tangled up with them.

He bent to examine them. "Latex, from protective gloves,

Goccia. The sort that the police would wear at crime scenes. But surely the officers who searched here last Wednesday wouldn't have been so careless."

He paused, smiling. "But perhaps our detective was, if his mind was distracted while dumping the body. If these residues are from him, he might as well have left his address and phone number along with a signed confession."

He looked up at the bin with the ropes lying across its lid. Why would one bin be like that?

"I think we might have found what we're looking for, little lady."

After recording the scene as he had found it, Rosselli opened his backpack to retrieve a pair of heavy-duty industrial gloves and began pulling the ropes from the lid.

On lifting the lid, he saw that the bin was almost full of more rope, and again, the telltale shreds of plastic adhering to the rope's rough surfaces. Sure now that he'd found the body, he recorded the arrangement of rope on his phone and carefully began removing it from the bin.

As the ropes were removed, first a hand was exposed, and then a foot. Several minutes later, Trisha McVie's entire body lay before him, spread across the packed rope beneath her.

He already had a record of her face and the injuries to her head from when he first discovered the body in Brooke's garage. He took a few more shots including several showing the whole body in situ.

Apart from the damage to Trisha's nose, Rosselli could see no other injuries to the front of the body. He carefully rolled her sufficiently to examine the rear of her torso before rolling her body back its original position.

He looked over to where Goccia was sitting watching him and shook his head.

"You know, principessa, the only injuries are to her head and nose; there are no other marks on this body. No defence bruising on her arms or scuffing to her knuckles. Nothing. I have a feeling there was no fight involved here, but an unfortunate accident. So sad for a young woman to lose her life that way and end up here, tossed in a dirty bin to rot. But her loss is our gain. She has given us a great opportunity to complete our mission of ending the life of another young lady who clearly does deserve to die and placing the blame squarely on Detective Brooke's shoulders."

Goccia's tail thumped the floor in apparent agreement; she always enjoyed her master's little lectures.

Ten minutes later, using the shots he had taken on his phone as reference, Rosselli had finished putting the ropes back in place on the body, closed the lid and replaced the ropes on top.

When Brooke returned here, which the detective probably imagined he would never do, he would see nothing out of place and yet have everything to panic about.

***

Despite the ropes and the heavy-lifting work, Rosselli approved of the location Gus Brooke had chosen to hide the body. The lid closed tightly onto the bin, effectively sealing it from the outside environment. He assumed the blow flies would have had a limited opportunity to lay their eggs on the body, depending on where she had been in the cottage for several hours and how sealed that location was. And from the body's condition, he worked out that Brooke must have washed it thoroughly before wrapping it in the towels, towels that Brooke must have removed for disposal along with the plastic bag that had encased her head. Anyone turning up here over the next few days wouldn't be assaulted by the stench of a rotting corpse or swarms of buzzing, hungry flies.

Rosselli now turned his attention to the system of overhead rails onto which hoists with attached hooks had once been secured for hauling boxes of cargo.

He looked around the scattered debris in the cargo area until he located a number of old and rusting hoists. He examined each one with a critical eye and found them perfectly acceptable for his purposes.

The rails were more than three metres above the cargo area floor, and in order to reach them, Rosselli dragged an old table from a dark corner of the area along with some metal-framed chairs. After positioning the table beneath the rails and a chair on the table, he climbed up to run his hand along each of them, checking their condition. They were all rusty, several substantially, but not irretrievably. For now, he chose the smoothest. Grabbing the hook dangling beneath it, he pulled its wheels along the rail and back again several times.

"Progress, Goccia," he said, catching the pug's eye as she responded with more tail thumping. "A few hours' work with some abrasive paper, grease and lubricating oil and we'll have these operating as smoothly as they did on the day they were installed. But before we do that, we need to be sure we have eyes on the place so we are warned of anyone visiting the site. And the eyes will be useful during the final act of our drama."

During his examination of the factory, Rosselli had located a small storeroom away from the main platformed cargo area, its door unlocked and the simple lever-operated handle working. It would make the perfect spot for hiding the essential materials he needed for his operation in the factory.

After finishing his trials with the hoists, he called Goccia. "Come, little one, let's go; there are things to do. And the first is to change hotels to somewhere far closer to this so-called factory. Then tomorrow morning, we'll make a few purchases before coming back here to complete our preparations."

Chapter Thirty-Nine

On Sunday evening, after a tiring and ultimately fruitless day pounding the streets in and around Nottingham along with a large squad of their colleagues, Jennifer and Derek returned to the flat in The Park frustrated and dejected.

Jennifer peered without interest into the fridge for dinner inspiration.

"This whole exercise is pointless, Derek. There's nothing to be gained from widening the search this far. The farther we get from Rappington, the more red Golfs there are and the more false leads. We're missing something and I'm convinced it's got to do with the factory."

Derek peered over her shoulder and on seeing the sad state of the fridge, made a decision.

"Pizza," he said. "I'm phoning for some."

"That'll be the third time this week. We've got to have something healthier."

"Indian?"

"OK, as long as I don't have to make any decisions. My brain is bursting."

As Derek pulled the menu of a nearby Indian restaurant from behind a fridge magnet, Jennifer's phone beeped.

"It's Henry," said Jennifer. "I must talk to him. He doesn't know about Trish and he'll be gutted. He's very fond of her."

She shuffled into the sitting room and flopped on a sofa, calling up Henry's FaceTime contact details as she did.

Henry responded almost immediately with his normal cheery greeting, but one look at Jennifer's face on his screen sounded alarm bells.

"Jennifer, whatever's happened?"

Jennifer took a deep breath, but couldn't hold it together and burst into tears. Hearing her from the kitchen, Derek ditched the call he was making to the restaurant and ran in, taking Jennifer's phone from her.

"Hi, Henry," he said, peering at the screen. "Got some difficult news."

For the next few minutes, with Jennifer curled up against him, Derek explained what had happened and where they had got in the search for Trisha.

"That's tragic," said Henry. "I don't know what to say. It's horrible. Have you got no leads on what might have happened?"

"None," sobbed Jennifer. "She's just evaporated. It's ridiculous."

"Look," said Henry. "I've just arrived in Perugia and the car is taking me to the villa. Do you want me to pick up Connie and fly over? Perhaps there's something we can do to help?"

"Thanks, Henry," said Derek. "But we've got dozens of people who do this for a living racking their brains. No offence."

"None taken. It's just, you know, she was, is, a friend. And you don't know for sure that she's dead, you know. There could be other explanations, surely."

"Well, she could be being held somewhere against her will. We just don't know, there's nothing to go on except the dumping of the car."

"This factory sounds odd," said Henry. "Why do you think the car was dumped there? Who knew about the place?"

"Any number of people," said Derek. "It's been derelict for years. I think the last company moved out in 1994."

"But isn't it secured?"

"No, the chain across it wasn't doing anything."

"Who knew that?"

Derek paused to think, but before he could answer, Jennifer took the phone from him and spoke to the screen. "The owners will have known, and anyone passing who happened to examine the chains, which seems an unlikely thing to do. And significantly, there has been no vandalism at the site for about twenty-five years. It's out in the middle of nowhere, after all. A bit far for the town lads unless they have transport. And anyway, there's nothing worth stealing there. There was talk some months ago that it might be being used in connection with organised crime, which is why the SCF undertook surveillance for a while. But it turned out to be rumour, nothing more."

"So you can add the police to your list of people who knew about the chain," said Henry.

"You're not suggesting a police officer is involved, surely?" said Jennifer, rather more sternly than she meant.

"Not at all," replied Henry, feeling slightly rebuked. "Just completing the list. Surely you have to consider everything and everybody."

"But no one in the police here knew Trisha," said Jennifer, still objecting forcefully. "None of them has any reason to hurt her."

"Perhaps it was an accident," countered Henry. "Maybe something happened to Trish that put someone in a difficult position."

Jennifer still wasn't convinced. "But it's only the car that's been dumped there. Why dump the body in a different place. The factory couldn't have been searched more thoroughly, believe me."

"I do. But perhaps that should give you hope. Suppose there isn't a body; maybe she's still alive and being held."

"So why draw attention to themselves by dumping the car there?"

"From what you say, it wasn't meant to be found. Could whoever's involved have taken Trisha there after the search?"

"Unlikely," said Derek. "The gates have been locked up with a padlock for the first time in years. The owners put one on as soon as the final team moved out on Thursday afternoon."

"Any other ways in?"

"Don't think so, and anyway, if you're talking about dumping a body or forcibly taking someone there, if you don't go in through the gates, there would have to be a hole in the fence. And you'd have to carry the body there on foot."

"The fence was looked at," added Jennifer. "Gus Brooke walked the perimeter and checked it. It was about the only useful thing he did do. I was happy to have him out of the way for half an hour."

"Not the best of your plods, then," said Henry.

"Oh, he's OK. He was having a bad day. I think he was sick. Certainly looked it."

"Hmm," mused Henry.

"What?" said Jennifer, challenging again. "You don't even know him."

Henry laughed. "I wasn't thinking about your Gus Brooke. I was thinking about perspective. You know that Trisha stopped by the roadside near Rappington and her wheel was changed by some Sir Galahad. This person then whisked her away, overcame her and whatever happened, felt the need to dump her car only four miles from where she'd stopped with a problem. Firstly, it's all very local, and secondly, it's Trisha we're talking about here. She's a cop, like you guys. She can look after herself. She's trained to be suspicious. If some oik, even if he was big and beefy, looked like he was about to try something, she wouldn't give in easily. I suspect he would be damaged."

"Interesting thought," agreed Jennifer. "And it would be good to think whoever is behind this has been hurt. But suppose she went willingly and something happened that was out of her control. Suppose she was slipped a Mickey, for instance."

"Why?" said Henry. "That's normally for rape, not murder."

"Could've gone wrong," suggested Derek.

"Sure, but I still think that makes it local. Look, the car's just climbing the hill to the villa and the reception's rubbish from about here until I get onto the villa's wi-fi. I need to tell Connie. She'll be shocked. She only met Trisha once, I think, but she liked her a lot. I'll call you back shortly."

"Actually, Henry," said Jennifer, "I'm knackered and heading for my bed as soon as we've eaten something. I need to be fresh tomorrow. Along with most of the team, I'll be trawling through hundreds of traffic cam records from a wide area around the city from last Tuesday night to when Trisha's Golf was discovered. There's a possibility that wherever she went after the wheel was fixed was actually some distance from Rappington. We can't afford not to do it just in case there's a sighting of her following someone for whatever reason. It's work that requires a good deal of concentration, but at least I won't be pounding the streets like today."

"OK, Jennifer. Let's talk tomorrow or the next day. And try to stay positive. Trisha's a resourceful lady; she might be hanging in there somewhere."

"We can only hope," replied Jennifer, but something in her heart told her otherwise.

Chapter Forty

The following afternoon, Rosselli returned to the factory site with Goccia, his backpack laden with a number of purchases he had made in the back streets of a Nottingham suburb earlier that morning.

Setting his backpack on a table, he removed three identical boxes containing battery-powered CCTV cameras, each of which would last up to three months on one charge. The storeroom had little in it apart from the table and more metal-framed chairs. Rosselli had resigned himself to balancing on one of the chairs until he noticed a serviceable wooden ladder in a dark recess in the corner. "Perfect!" he exclaimed to Goccia.

He had decided to set up three cameras through which he could monitor activity via an app on his phone. All three required care in their placement; discovery would spell disaster.

He placed the first camera on the wall outside a window high on the upper floor, its lens pointing towards the main gates and the concrete road leading from them towards the factory buildings. Triggered by movement, the highly sensitive camera could beam him information day and night, alerting him with images of any activity in that area. The other two cameras were to monitor activity closer to where he'd found Trisha McVie; one giving him a wide view of the cargo area while the other focussed on the metal bin containing her body.

Once all three cameras were in place, tested and operating perfectly, he removed a fourth camera from his bag he had brought along as a spare. Something about his surveillance had been nagging him, but until his eyes fell on the spare camera, it had eluded him.

He smiled and winked at Goccia. "Your discovery, my little one, my inspiration. The break in the fence you found. What if I'm not the only person who knows about that? Suppose our Detective Brooke decides to use that way. It would be a pity not to know in advance, don't you think?"

Goccia kept her counsel.

With the fourth camera in place, Rosselli was satisfied he had sufficient surveillance of the factory site for his remote monitoring. It would also warn him of any intrusion that afternoon while he undertook the maintenance and installation work on the rails and hoists, work that might take several hours. The last thing he needed was an unexpected interruption. The cameras and the alerts they would generate would give him sufficient time to hide away and watch whoever was intruding until they left. He hoped for their sake some random intruder didn't discover McVie's body. In that unfortunate circumstance he would have no choice but to add the intruder's body to the storage bin.

To Rosselli's pleasant surprise, the servicing of the rails and trolleys he intended to use, along with the installation of some extra features, all went better than he had anticipated. Just two hours after starting work on the first rail, he had completed and tested everything.

As well as cleaning, greasing and oiling the pulleys and rails he needed as part of his plan, Rosselli needed a little more information before he could implement his final strategy. And for this he was planning a spot of house-breaking.

He checked the weather forecast and was pleased to find the UK living up to its reputation for overcast and wet days. The entire week ahead was going to be dull, with particularly heavy rain the following day, Tuesday, weather that meant that anyone driving past the Brookes' cottage would be concentrating hard on the road if they happened to pass him as he walked the half mile from his parked car.

Over breakfast in his room at the hotel on Tuesday morning, Rosselli was alerted by a ping from his phone as the app monitoring Brooke's car announced the vehicle was moving. He watched the pulsing blue circle on the screen show the car leave the cottage and head towards Nottingham where Brooke parked as normal at the car park next to the SCF offices. The only risk for Rosselli now was whether Brooke's wife was going to return from her overseas trip. He called up her social media account and discovered she was finishing up that very afternoon and returning the following day, flights permitting. There was no time to lose.

After parking his car in what had become his usual spot along a lane and out of sight from the Rappington road, Rosselli settled Goccia in her basket.

"I'm sorry, tesoro, I don't want to risk you leaving muddy paw prints in Detective Brooke's cottage, and if it happens that I need to leave in a hurry, I don't want to be worrying about you."

He rubbed the wrinkles of skin on her neck, tossed her a few of her favourite nibbles and closed the door, leaving the rear passenger windows open a fraction to give her some fresh air.

Rosselli knew from his previous visits to the cottage that there were no CCTV cameras silently watching the outside, and nor was there a box high on one wall announcing the presence of a security system. But a hidden internal alarm was another matter. The last thing he wanted was to alert Brooke by triggering something that would talk to the detective's phone, or worse, silently alert a security company.

Fortunately, the windows at the rear of the house were completely hidden from the road, giving Rosselli the opportunity to scrutinise them carefully for the telltale signs of alarm fittings.

There were none and to his complete surprise, as he made his way along the windows he found a small upper window in the downstairs bathroom was open. He couldn't believe his luck: this man was a police officer and he had left his house open! Either the detective's mind was a total mess or he was obsessed with ventilating the cottage after McVie's body had lain there for more than twenty-four hours.

Rosselli chose not to break in through the downstairs bathroom. He was wet and the chances of leaving traces of mud before he could get his boots off were high. But the open window gave him the confidence that even if there were an alarm system, it wasn't set.

The locks on the kitchen door gave every appearance of being sophisticated, but it was an illusion. Rosselli defeated them in seconds and slipped into the kitchen, laying a plastic bag on the doormat onto which he placed his boots while he made a rapid assessment of the room. An alarm control panel would by necessity be within easy reach of the outside door. None was visible and there was nothing in any of the nearby cupboards. In addition, a scan of the door itself showed no signs of any alarm contacts. The potential danger passed; Rosselli was in with more than enough time to achieve his goals.

He slipped off his jacket and hung it near the door, not something he would normally do when breaking into a building, but the jacket was wet and he wanted to avoid the possibility of leaving any water stains.

The focus of Rosselli's break-in was Brooke's computer. Rosselli needed various phone numbers and those on the detective's phone would almost certainly be duplicated on his home computer.

With no sign of a computer in the kitchen, he continued his search in the other downstairs rooms. One large space was clearly Mo Brooke's workshop. Messy and dusty from her work as a sculptor, it held no attraction for Rosselli. Even with its double-door entry system and powerful extraction fans, designed to prevent dust getting into the rest of the cottage, it would be more or less impossible to enter it without picking up traces of dust and leaving any number of prints and impressions. He was relieved to see no sign of a computer and he quickly closed the door. On the opposite side of the corridor from the studio was a small dining room that would seat no more than six people, and from the state of the table top, the room appeared to double as an office. Centrally placed among the scattered papers and files was an Apple laptop computer, its screen open but black. Bingo!

Before touching the computer, Rosselli approached it from the side and gently squeezed a tiny ball of plastic putty onto the camera lens from a small tube he kept in the pouch containing his array of lock picks. He knew there was a lot of exaggerated hype about how cameras in apparently sleeping computers could spy on surroundings, but given it wasn't entirely science fiction, he didn't want to take any chances.

And before hitting any keys, he needed to turn off the Internet connection, again in case Brooke had an app alerting him to any unauthorised activity on his computer. Since the modem wasn't in the dining room, Rosselli returned to the kitchen, but it wasn't there either. Finally, he moved onto the sitting room beyond the dining room where he saw a smart TV. Behind that, among a tangle of cables, announcing its presence with a set of pulsing lights, was the modem. He removed the power cable and returned to the dining room.

A tap on the spacebar of the laptop's keyboard brought up a screen with a photograph of Brooke and his wife standing by what Rosselli assumed was one of Mo's creations. It was a distorted but recognisable bronze of a barn owl in flight. Impressive, he thought. Perhaps when this little adventure is over, I'll peruse Mrs B's catalogue.

Distracted by the barn owl, it was a few moments before Rosselli registered the significance of the sharp image: the computer wasn't asking for a password. He shook his head once more at the folly of the detective.

Moving his latex-gloved fingers over the trackpad, Rosselli brought up the contacts list. It was extensive and he quickly noted down the numbers against Jennifer Cotton's name, Derek Thyme's, Neil Bottomley's, and, for good measure, Mo Brooke's. But Gus Brooke's own number wasn't listed. However it wasn't difficult to find. He clicked on FaceTime, accessed Preferences and there it was listed under '*You can be reached for FaceTime at:*' along with three email addresses that might also be useful.

Rosselli smiled. "Thank you, young detective, I think I have everything I need to turn your life into a living nightmare. But before I leave, I would like to see how well you cleaned up the scene of your superintendent's death. Have you been as thorough as you thought?"

He waited until the computer returned to sleep mode, stepped to one side and carefully removed the plastic putty, after which he rubbed over the lens with a lint-free cloth to remove any residue of oil remaining from the putty.

As he returned to the hallway from reconnecting the modem in the sitting room, he remembered the activity of the previous Friday evening when Gus Brooke was frantically removing what he hoped would be all traces of Trisha McVie's presence in the cottage. Much time had been spent in the downstairs bathroom. He looked at the doors and opened one between the dining room and the sitting room: a guest bedroom and leading from it, an en-suite bathroom.

He raised his eyebrows in appreciation as he surveyed the bedroom. It was as pristine as a five-star hotel room following a makeover from housekeeping. Everything was perfectly in place with no indication that anyone had been in it. Was the bathroom the same? He pushed open the door, looked in and smiled. If he hadn't witnessed the attention paid to the room when it was being cleaned, he could have been fooled into thinking that it hadn't been used for some time. Everything was perfect; too perfect. Bath towels, robes and hand towels were all neatly folded and stacked on shelves by the handbasin; the shower, bath, toilet and bidet spotless; the mirror above the washbasin gleaming. Pulling on the mirror revealed a cupboard behind it equipped with neat rows of creams, lotions, razors, toothbrushes in their wrappers, a slightly used tube of toothpaste and a hairbrush. He picked up the brush to examine it closely, noting several either grey or blonde hairs trapped in its bristles. He frowned. The desktop image on Brooke's computer showed a dark-haired Mo Brooke, but ... He pulled out his phone and called up the photos of Trisha McVie's body.

"Ash blonde," he said, "and from the look of the roots, a recent treatment. Oh dear, Detective Brooke, your wife won't be pleased to find those."

He carefully placed the brush back where he'd found it and picked up the next item on the shelf, a bottle of Chanel No.19 perfume still in its packet, although the cellophane had been removed. Touching just the edges of the flap, Rosselli opened the box and slid out the bottle, taking care not to touch the spray release cap. He reasoned that since she had used the hairbrush and possibly a drier that was also in the cupboard, the superintendent might well have used the perfume. Given Brooke's failing with the hairbrush, there was a good chance that McVie's fingerprints and therefore her DNA were on the cap and the spray release itself. He returned the bottle to its packet and placed it back on the shelf.

Rosselli's next stop was the master bedroom and bathroom. In contrast to the downstairs guest bedroom and bathroom, and the two others he'd glanced at upstairs, the master bedroom showed obvious signs of use. Untidy male use, thought Rosselli as he took in the unmade bed, the pile of unwashed laundry on the floor and a damp towel strewn across a chair.

The bathroom was the same, although on close examination of the tiled surfaces, Rosselli noted their pristine cleanliness. There wasn't a smear or deposit of dust anywhere, not even in the most inaccessible corners. But Rosselli was no amateur; he knew exactly where to look. Unlike, it seemed, Detective Constable Brooke.

He stood back and tried to imagine how a fall could have happened in this room, one severe enough to have ended Trisha McVie's life, and the more he thought about it, given the injuries, the more he was convinced it had been an accident. She must have damaged her nose first, maybe on the bath rim if she fell. If she were the worse for wear after a boozy night, such a fall could easily happen. Perhaps she felt dizzy after damaging her nose and fell backwards from the raised platform housing the toilet and bidet, striking her head on the shower tray. There must have been a lot of blood, given the severity of the injuries. Since there was no hand shower in the bath, Brooke's better option would have been to wash the body down in the shower where there was a detachable hose as part of the shower fitting in the shower cubicle.

So he probably scrubbed her clean here, thought Rosselli, as he knelt down by the shower. He peered at the drain cover. It showed no sign of having been recently removed; there were still the slightest of telltale residues around the chrome fitting. If Brooke hadn't removed the drain cover, there would very likely be an accumulated mat of hair clinging to the pipe beneath it that could include some of the superintendent's hair. Ash blonde. Once the forensic teams examined this bathroom, and Rosselli intended to make sure they did, they wouldn't miss something as obvious as the drain. It was a prime source of evidence.

Satisfied with the outcome of his visit to the cottage, Rosselli locked up and made his way back to the car where Goccia was ready and waiting, having heard his footfall long before any human would have done.

His preparative work complete, all he had to do now was sit back and wait while the police continued with their fruitless searching, their lack of results merely increasing their frustration and worry, while with every passing day, the confidence of Detective Brooke that his plan had worked would increase.

And then, when it was least expected, Rosselli would begin his end game.

Chapter Forty-One

Two days after Rosselli had completed his arrangements at the derelict factory, Gus Brooke was sitting at his desk in the SCF main squad room trawling through one of the hundreds of traffic camera videos from the night of Trisha McVie's disappearance.

He wasn't alone. The entire SCF team of detectives and civilian support had spent the past four days examining every frame from every camera in a ten-mile radius of Rappington for Trisha McVie's car. Since the search area included stretches of the M1 motorway, the whole of the city of Nottingham, the town of Loughborough and part of the city of Derby together with other towns with significant populations, the number of cameras was huge.

Jennifer had concluded that their lack of success meant either their search radius was too small, which seemed ridiculous given how large it had become, or more realistically, Trisha had only travelled a short distance from where her car was last witnessed having its wheel changed by the roadside to wherever she had been separated from her car and belongings, somewhere that wasn't covered by any traffic cameras. Which meant a location in or near Rappington.

House-to-house had proved useless and a trawl through criminal records against the names of people registered as living in any of the houses had only produced fruitless leads that were soon dismissed.

They were missing something, Jennifer could feel it, something crucial, something that should be blindingly obvious but instead was frustratingly elusive.

The Met had come to the party again after their initial trawl through all Trisha's computer files, emails, texts and other phone messages had come to nothing the day after she went missing, her life exposed. They were nothing if not efficient; Jennifer was impressed. Trisha's old squad, the squad she was still officially part of, had gone out on the streets to question everyone they could find with whom she'd had dealings during her time in London. Every suspect, every criminal who had done time and been released, every slime bag she'd questioned and given a hard time to, every informer she'd cultivated. They had looked at her private life, which had raised a few eyebrows, interviewed Jennifer and others for what they knew about present and past relationships, anyone dumped and bearing a grudge. But there was nothing. While the life of Trisha McVie had been colourful and peppered with several dubious lovers, there was no one who would have resorted to the lengths that would have been necessary to stage the events of the Tuesday evening when she disappeared.

Equally, her professional life was full of nothing but merit and praise from her fellow officers, even those who had been on the sharp end of her tongue on numerous occasions. She was respected, admired and regarded as exemplary.

Jennifer's despondency increased with every negative result added to the whiteboard in the incident room. No one disappeared off the radar like this except in horrible circumstances, circumstances that she didn't want to think about. Macabre scenarios of Trisha at the mercy of some madman haunted her every waking moment, while her nights were restless and tormented. Yet no matter how bad these were, they were preferable to the alternative of Trisha's body lying discarded somewhere, perhaps so well hidden it would never be found.

· · ·

The lack of progress was wearing down everyone in the SCF, the gloom of their efforts pressing on them an ever-burgeoning cloud of despair. Conversations were brief; there was no banter, just endless frustration. Every time anyone's phone rang or pinged with a message, ears pricked up around the room and eyes focussed on the recipient for an indication of something, a crumb, anything.

Gus Brooke's phone had pinged two hours previously and he had immediately noticed the hush that descended around him, and the need for clarification when he muttered, "shit," under his breath.

"What?" said Derek. "What is it?"

Gus looked up. "Er, nothing. It's nothing. It's from Mo. She was supposed to be coming back yesterday from the course she's been giving but it was extended until tomorrow and now it's been extended again. She's thoroughly pissed off but there's nothing she can do about it. She's in place and so it makes far more economic sense for her to stay where she is than fly someone else out to replace her. I think the company she's contracted to works on a shoestring."

Gus had lost the interest of most of those around him with the first 'nothing' but Derek had continued to stare at him so he'd felt obliged to explain. It helped; it was the closest he'd had to a conversation for a while, even if it was a monologue.

"Bugger, huh?" commented Derek. "More dinners for one?"

"Yeah," grunted Gus.

And now his phone had pinged again, a different sound from an email, this was a message and this time it gained less attention. Which was just as well given the explosive nature of the contents.

Gus picked up his phone. The message was an image with no text. At first it meant nothing, an image taken at night in poor light that made it difficult to interpret. But as he stared at it, frowning, he slowly understood what he was looking at and the blood drained from his face.

When his phone pinged a second time, he nearly dropped it in shock. He scrolled to the text, his hand shaking.

Have I got your attention, Gus?

He reached for the bottle of water that was sitting on one side of his desk: his mouth had gone so dry he could hardly swallow. He scrolled back to the image. It was a shot taken in the boot of his car. The tailgate must have been raised and whoever took the shot had leaned into the car. There was no doubt about it, someone must have been watching when he put Trisha McVie's body in the back of his car.

He quickly turned off the screen and looked nervously around, but only Derek Thyme seemed to be looking at him. Gus looked up, a weak smile on his face as he tried to speak.

"Just Mo again," he said, shrugging his shoulders. "She's confirming what she said earlier. Don't know why she needed to repeat it all; except to make it worse. Apparently it could be even longer than a few days."

"Tough being in demand," said Derek, his voice flat. He was trying not to show the uncomfortable feeling he had that Gus Brooke was lying. He'd watched the detective's face as he read the messages, and from his reaction he would say the content was far more significant than Mo announcing a further delay in her return, something more like the end of the world.

Returning his attention to his phone, Gus switched the screen back on, hit the reply button and began to type.

Who is this? What do you want?

There was no reply.

As he stared at the screen, Gus thought about how strong the reaction had been in the room to any messages, his included. Particularly his? Or was he being paranoid? But there could be more such messages, almost definitely would be, and he didn't want them announced to the world. He called up settings and switched the phone to vibrate only for all incoming texts, emails, WhatsApp messages, and for good measure, Facebook and Twitter, although he hardly ever used them.

Getting back to concentrating on the CCTV recordings was now even more impossible than before. Before he had just been play-acting, knowing there was nothing to be found; now he could hardly even focus on his monitor. Who the hell had been watching him? And how much did they know? Was it going to be about blackmail or worse? Did they intend to tear him to pieces emotionally before reporting him?

He tried to make sense of the time frame. They must have been in the garden watching the house. Why? The house was in the middle of nowhere. Had somebody he hadn't noticed been passing, a dog walker, perhaps, seen him carrying the body from the garage to the car and put two and two together? That would make it a local person. But there weren't any local people. His nearest neighbour was half a mile along the road or about the same across the fields at the back of the house. Perhaps that was it. He'd never got on with the farmer whose fields backed onto his cottage. Awkward bugger who treated the land the cottage was on like his own.

Gus had once threatened to arrest him, which hadn't gone down well. Perhaps the bastard had been spying on him and struck lucky. Well, he wasn't going to let some cocky farmer spoil his life.

As he sat at his desk chewing his bottom lip while plotting the farmer's demise, he saw his phone's screen light up again with another incoming message.

He glanced nervously around the room, moving just his eyes, not wanting to attract attention. When he dropped his eyes to the phone, it was all he could do not to scream. There in front of him was a close-up shot of Trisha McVie's face, the wound to her nose visible in vivid detail, her eyes half-closed in death as they had been when he'd first seen her body. He hadn't wanted to touch them to shut them completely.

He closed the screen before any prying eyes had a chance to see it, returning his gaze to the monitor as he tried desperately to work out where the shot had been taken. There was something behind her head. A sack or bag of something. It was at the rear of the garage where he'd taken the body after ... after wrapping it up in the towels. Whoever took the shot must have gone into the garage, removed the bag and towels from round the head and photographed it. But he must have wrapped it all up again because when Gus had gone to move the body two nights later, nothing had been out of place.

Two nights later!

Whoever it was had been there when Gus had first taken the

body from the cottage to the garage and again when he carried it to his car. Does that mean he knows where the body is? Had he followed him to the factory?

What had the person been doing at his house on the Wednesday night when he was cleaning up the body and the bathroom along with everywhere else McVie had been? Why had he been watching and waiting? Waiting for him to do something with the body? But who on the Wednesday evening even knew that Trisha McVie was missing? Only the police after the damn car had been found. The search teams. Christ, there were dozens of officers, police and civilian, involved. It could be any one of them.

Was it someone in the SCF? It made the most sense. These were the people who knew him, the people who had been less than welcoming. Did one of them bear a grudge? Whose toes had he trodden on?

He looked around the room, watching for anyone who might be looking at their phone. He'd send a reply, see if anyone's phone pinged.

There had been no further message with the second image, just the stark horror of McVie's dead features.

He picked up his phone, called up messages and began to type.

Who the fuck are you, you bastard?

As he hit send, his eyes flashed around the room, but no one moved, no one picked up their phone. He glanced at his screen. Against the message the word 'delivered' appeared and almost immediately a reply arrived.

Now, now, Gus, that's not very nice. Would you like to see some more images? I have lots.

No one in the office had been typing on his phone, which ruled them all out, didn't it? Who was missing? He did a head count. Everyone was there. Even Joe Barnes had come back to work, eager to prove his worth. The only people in the SCF not in his view were … the senior officers. Surely not, it couldn't possibly be. There was only Crawford and Hawkins, and he doubted that either of them was even capable of taking a photo on a phone, especially in the dark.

Shit! Who could it be?

Gus checked the time, wondering how early he could reasonably make an excuse and leave. He wasn't sure he could stay at his desk for much longer. He could feel his heart racing as the fear of what might happen next consumed him. If the person was sending messages to him, they could just as easily send some to others in the room. Was he about to be dropped in it?

Fighting to maintain an outward appearance of calm, he forced his eyes onto his monitor and the useless traffic cam videos. At least he didn't have to try to spot McVie's number plate; he knew it wouldn't be showing up.

His hands were opening and closing involuntarily as he chewed on a lip, his eyes scanning the room as much as the screen. No one seemed to be watching him, but it wasn't always easy to tell. At least his back was against a wall; there was no one behind him.

The screen on his phone jumped to life again with another message. This time there was no photo.

Did you notice anything odd in the photo, Gus? Anything missing? Compare it with the press photo, see what you think. Could be a bit of a problem.

Dropping his hands below desktop level, Gus scrolled again to the image of Trisha McVie's lifeless head and let his eyes search it for detail. Missing?

Then he saw it. She was only wearing one earring, in her left ear. Had the one that had presumably once been in her right ear been missing when he was with her, or after, when she was lying dead in his cottage? He didn't know. He looked across the room to the whiteboard with the case details, the scribbled notes and the few photos, including the photo of Trisha that had been released to the press. It was too far away for him to see clearly.

After slipping his phone into his pocket, he stood and stretched, working his neck and shoulders. He saw Derek watching him.

"Got to take a break," said Gus, his voice little more than a hoarse croak. "I'm going goggle-eyed." Without pausing for any response, he made his way towards the door, deliberately taking a longer route than necessary so he could pass close to the whiteboard. He saw what he needed to see immediately: the photo released to the press showed McVie wearing two earrings of the same design as the one shown in the image of her lying dead in his garage.

He had the answer to his tormentor's question, but he had to continue the charade. He hurried to the washroom where he threw some water onto his face and stared at his reflection in the mirror, his grip on the edge of the washbasin leaving his knuckles white with tension. He searched his face for answers. What did this person want? What were they going to do?

When his phone vibrated in his pocket, he spun around to lean against the washbasin, grabbed the phone and called up the message.

Worked it out, Gus? Of course you have. Not difficult, was it? The question is, where is the missing earring? Did it drop off in your house and roll somewhere? Is it under your pillow? Surely not, even you aren't that careless. Mo won't be pleased when she finds it, will she? It'll be one more thing she'll find that you've missed. No, you definitely won't be her favourite person. Happy hunting, Gus.

He nearly smashed the phone against the sink in anger. Instead, he hit reply.

WHAT DO YOU WANT?

The answer was a smiley emoji, a glib face.

Gus was still staring at the image when the washroom door flew open. It was Doug Coulson. "All right, mate? You're looking a bit edgy. Know how you feel, this bloody case is a pig and my head is pickled staring at them videos."

"Yeah," said Gus, "they've been getting to me too. That and thoughts about what might have happened to the super."

"Too right. It'll be good to get away early for a change."

"Early?"

"Yeah, the DCS just told everyone to bugger off home. Said we all needed a break. Said to come back tomorrow refreshed and raring to go. I'm heading over the road for a couple of pints and then the missus is picking me up. Fancy a quick one?"

"Thanks, but I'll give it a miss. With Mo being away, I need to get on top of my mess before it gets out of hand. She's a stickler for tidiness."

Chapter Forty-Two

Cosimo Graziano Rosselli reached behind the driver's seat of his car to where Goccia sat in her basket and squeezed the loose skin on her head.

"That seems to have caught our young detective's attention, principessa. Let's go back to the hotel for a while and let him build up a head of steam."

He removed the SIM card from the phone and with a flick of index finger against thumb, launched it into the undergrowth next to where he was parked in a quiet lane a few miles north of Nottingham.

"Not much chance of the foolish boy trying to search for the card signal, little one, not in his state of mind," he said, to an enthusiastic response of tail thumping. "But we can't take chances. We must allow for every contingency, and one of those is that he puts up his hands. If that were to happen, we'd have every phone expert on the police force trying to trace us."

He smiled as he tossed Goccia a biscuit before turning to start the car. "We have a good stock of anonymous SIM cards; we can afford to be wasteful."

A ping from his regular phone alerted him to Gus Brooke's car leaving the car park and heading in the direction of Rappington.

"So early? I wonder what excuse he gave. Whatever it was, we'll have some food before we move onto the next stage."

. . .

Back in his hotel room, Rosselli removed his Glock pistol from the reinforced metal case and went through the daily routine of disassembling and cleaning it. The Glock was now his weapon of choice for the scenario he had planned in the factory premises, although only as a back-up if his main plan was compromised. Satisfied it was in perfect working order, he reassembled it, wrapped it in its lint-free cloth and stowed it in his rucksack along with the silencer.

After giving Goccia her supper and taking his own in his room, he checked the time.

"Mmm," he said, looking down at his beloved pug. "It's been three hours since our detective returned home. I should imagine by now the place has been turned upside down, wouldn't you, tesoro?"

Goccia looked up from her food, her eyes catching his. She sensed what was coming next and didn't like it.

"Little one," he said, as he gently stroked her head, "I hate doing this, as you know, but this evening I must leave you here. If my plans go awry and I have to move fast, I don't want to risk your welfare. I should hate anything to happen to you. Let's find you a nice cartoon channel, shall we?"

Goccia settled in her basket in front of the television, resigned to her master's decision.

Although he hurried home as fast as he dare in the early evening traffic, Gus Brooke decided he would still make time to check on the padlock on the factory gates. He had deliberately left the chain and padlock oriented in a particular way that anyone removing it to enter the site would be unlikely to replicate when they left.

Satisfied it hadn't been touched, he ran back to his car and drove the last few miles home.

Before starting the search in the cottage, Gus wanted to find out where his tormentor had been hiding outside. He stood near to where his car had been parked when he moved Trisha McVie's body and let his eyes roam the outside of the garage and the garden, remembering that it had been dark when the man was watching.

As his eyes searched the area, the name Olivia Freneton jumped into his mind, someone still often mentioned in the SCF. She had been well before Gus's time, but he knew the case and knew she was dead. But thoughts of Freneton made him wonder if he was wrong in assuming his tormentor was a man? It was a natural assumption, but could it be a woman? Another Freneton? He hoped not. She had been a ruthless bitch with no qualms about killing anyone. There was no way his own natural charms would work on someone like that.

The garden shed caught his eye and thoughts of Freneton evaporated. With a mature plum tree next to it giving extra shade to an already naturally shady part of the garden, anyone watching could remain hidden but still have a clear view of the rear of the house along with activity to and from the garage.

He walked over to the area to take a closer look. There were hints of shoe prints but nothing substantial, while on the other side of the fence, a grassy bank that was part of a public right-of-way footpath bordering the farmer's field appeared undisturbed.

Next he looked in the garage at the spot where he had initially stored Trisha's body. He had moved much of the garden furniture in the garage himself when creating the space for the body; the intruder must have moved some too but he had put it back in place, and after that, Gus had moved things again to access the body. It was all too difficult and staring at the spot wasn't going to help. He would just have to wait for the next text bombshell and hope he would be alone when it arrived.

Once in the kitchen, he tossed his keys on the worktop and stood by the cooker, trying to recreate in his mind the sequence of events on that wretched Tuesday evening. Assuming McVie had been wearing both earrings and that she hadn't lost one earlier, how likely was it that one would just fall out? Extremely unlikely, in his opinion. That's what the butterfly back of an earring was designed to do: to prevent the post from coming loose.

So assuming it wasn't damaged, how would it come loose? He

thought about it and decided the most likely possibility was when McVie undressed in the guest bedroom. The earring could have become caught up in her clothing or dislodged when she was drying her hair. The other possibility would be when she had the accident in the upstairs bathroom. Could the impact of the head on the shower tray have loosened it sufficiently for it to fall out? Either way, the two bedrooms and bathrooms were the most likely places, not the kitchen, not the car. No, definitely not McVie's car: the forensic team would have found it.

Two hours later, Gus had searched every inch of the master bedroom and the one downstairs, moved furniture, lifted rugs, examined and felt down curtains, everywhere. There was nothing. He had moved his search into both bathrooms where the opportunities for a rogue earring to become hidden or lodged in something were far more limited and the result was the same. Was the tormentor having a laugh? He wished he had been more observant. He had no recollection of Trisha McVie, or Emma as he'd known her, even wearing earrings. Earrings hadn't exactly been the focus of his attention, anymore than they had been McVie's.

He returned downstairs and slumped in one of the two easy chairs he and Mo kept in the kitchen, somewhere comfortable to sit while one or the other of them was busy preparing food, cooking or washing up.

Picking up his phone, he clicked on the images sent that afternoon and studied them again. This person had been all but breathing over his shoulder. Why hadn't he noticed? God, there was so much he hadn't noticed.

He still had no idea who the person could be, although he was pretty convinced he knew what they wanted. Money. Well, for that, they would have to come to him, and when they did, he would confront them, overcome them and get rid of them, whoever they were. He was fit, tall and strong. Not an easy opponent. He knew how to fight. There was no option. There was room in the metal bin for another body; the person could join Trisha McVie and they could rot together.

. . .

He needed a drink, a scotch. His nerves had been to hell and back again since the first text arrived; he deserved some consolation. All he could do now was wait and hope that when the person contacted him again, he wasn't with his colleagues.

As he stood to walk over to the drinks cupboard, he was surprised to see the kitchen clock showing 8:56. When he'd arrived home, it had been daylight; now, night had fallen. Outside, with no street lights, it was completely dark, just as it had been when he moved Trisha McVie's body, when the person who had burst into his awareness that afternoon had been standing in the shadows outside. Watching. Waiting.

And worse, recording incriminating images on his phone, images that would without doubt send Gus Brooke to prison should they ever surface.

He retrieved a prized bottle of fifteen-year-old single malt from the cupboard and poured himself a generous measure. He stared at the amber liquid, looking for some solace, some reassurance, wishing he could turn the clock back ten days and block the whole episode out of his life.

He raised the glass to his lips but before it reached them, a sharp rap on the kitchen door froze him in his tracks.

Chapter Forty-Three

Gus Brooke put the untouched glass of single malt on the countertop and walked over to the kitchen door, an incredulous frown on his face. Surely it couldn't be his tormentor. Would the man be so stupid? Whoever it was, he would be no match for a fit six-foot-two police officer who excelled in unarmed combat. As he reached for the door handle, he remembered the outside light and flicked the switch to turn it on. The sudden light would give him an advantage, perhaps briefly dazzling whoever was standing on the other side of the door.

He pulled open the door with a confident tug and took a slight step back, poised to spring as his eyes surveyed the area covered by the pool of light. There was no one there.

He leaned forward, peering into the darkness. Had he imagined the knock?

"Hello?" he called.

"Good evening, Detective Constable Brooke," said a voice from the darkness. "I doubt you were expecting me."

A figure stepped forward out of the shadows, but remained well out of reach. He was about four inches shorter than Gus and dressed entirely in black: tight leggings, a lightweight padded jacket, a ski mask covering most of his face, a thin glove on the one hand Gus could see, the left, and the straps of a backpack over his shoulders. From his stance, he looked fit and well toned, not someone to mess with.

"The element of surprise is always an advantage," said the man. "You thought I would continue to send you messages and more of the many images I have of your unfortunate superintendent, didn't you?"

He paused, his eyes piercing into Gus's eyes. "We can talk about them in a moment, but first, I should apologise for wasting your time searching for this."

His left hand swung forward as he tossed something small and light towards Gus. Gus's automatic reaction was to catch it.

"You bastard," said Gus, glancing at the earring. "You had it all the time. Did you take it off her?"

"No, Detective Brooke, I did not," lied Rosselli. "I found it when I inspected your cottage after you cleaned up. You overlooked a number of important things, you see, one of them being the earring."

"No way!" said Gus, shaking his head. "I would have seen it."

"You have too much faith in your own abilities, detective. You should be careful; it could get you into trouble. However, the important thing is that you have the earring now. What will you do with it? Put it back in the poor lady's ear? Or perhaps you can keep it as a trophy."

Gus's body tensed at the taunt. Everything was telling him to rush this man and overpower him, ruin his stupid scheme, whatever it was. But something about the man's confidence stopped him, plus he couldn't see what was in the man's right hand.

"What do you want?" he snapped.

"Good question, Gus. You don't mind if I call you Gus, do you? What do I want? Well, first I'd like to come in. It's not the warmest of evenings and we have much to discuss. I'm sure you'd agree it would be better done inside."

Gus stared at him in disbelief. "You expect me to invite you in?"

"Well, it's not as if I haven't seen your place before, Gus. I'm pretty familiar with it, really."

"Jesus!" muttered Gus. He stood aside, making room for Rosselli to pass.

Rosselli laughed. "No, no, that wouldn't do, now, would it? You back into the kitchen so that you can keep an eye on me, and of course, I can do the same with you as I follow. And please, Gus, keep your distance. I don't want you coming within six feet of me."

As Gus moved slowly backwards, Rosselli sighed. "I'm not convinced you understand me. Perhaps I should show you what I have in my other hand."

He brought his right arm forward and held up the Glock with the silencer attached.

"Had much firearms training, Gus? It's an excellent weapon. And with my level of accuracy, you'd be dead before the sound wave from the discharge reached you; you'd die not hearing or feeling a thing."

He smiled. "Reassuring, don't you think?"

Gus backed away from him, his eyes flicking from the gun to the man's face.

Rosselli followed him in and pushed the door shut behind him. He looked around and gestured towards one of the two easy chairs near the wood-burning stove. It was the perfect spot; far harder to get out of in a hurry without signalling your intention well in advance. Brooke was much less likely to try to rush him from there.

As Gus sat down, Rosselli pulled one of the two bar stools away from the island unit to give himself room to manoeuvre should he need it. He lay the Glock on the countertop, sat on the stool and turned to Gus.

"Well, my young detective," he said, as he pulled back the ski mask to reveal his face, "you have got yourself in a mess, haven't you?" His smile was all sympathy, but Gus simply glared at him. He felt utterly outwitted.

"Am I right in assuming that it was all some dreadful accident?" continued Rosselli. "You had a fun night in the sack, but your superintendent slipped and had a fatal fall in the bathroom? That's certainly how it looked from her injuries. May I assume also there was quite a bit of alcohol involved?"

Gus glared, resenting the accuracy of what he was hearing. "Yes," he muttered, "to all of it."

Rosselli nodded. "Tell me, Gus, I'm intrigued. Do all young and junior police officers like you end up in bed with their seniors? It seems a strange way to run a police force."

Gus's eyes flashed angrily for a moment but then his face sagged and he sighed heavily. "How the hell was I to know she was my senior officer? I'd never seen her before. Her car skidded to a halt in front of me with a puncture and I stopped to help her out. We were both soaked from the filthy weather so she came back here. We both willingly took advantage of the situation and clearly we'd both been there before since we lied to each other about our names, meaning neither of us knew who the other was. Fucking hilarious, when you think about it, except for the way it turned out."

Rosselli nodded. "I can appreciate your predicament and you might have got away with it, depending on how observant your wife is." He paused, his expression now full of regret. "Actually, I doubt you would have got away with it; there's still too much evidence in this cottage I think your wife will pick up on. But of course that wouldn't necessarily lead to the discovery of the superintendent's body; it might simply mean your wife kicks you out. The body could easily have remained where you put it for years. It's a good spot."

"Could have?" said Gus. "Does that mean you're going to report me?"

Rosselli shook his head, his face registering his utter distaste at such a notion.

"No, no, of course not. I wouldn't dream of—"

"As long as I pay you a hefty amount of money?" interrupted Gus, his tone sarcastic.

Rosselli reply was dismissive. "Money? No, Gus, it's not your money I want."

"Then what *do* you want?"

Rosselli gave a slight shrug, as if the answer should be all too obvious. "Your assistance. A guarantee of your help."

"You want my help?" Gus's mouth wrinkled in scorn. "Why

should I help you? You've screwed up my plan. Without you sticking your nose in, Trisha McVie might never have been found."

Rosselli's smile was condescending. "You are forgetting your wife. She will definitely be suspicious, and once your friends in the police have spoken to her, they will put two and two together. I'm sure it's only because you are one of their colleagues that they are blind to what should have been blazingly obvious. But they'll get there, and when they do, you'll be in trouble."

"So what have I got to lose?" said Gus, shifting his body and legs as subtly as he could to prepare himself to spring at the man.

But Rosselli had read him. A slight smile still on his face, he fixed a hypnotic stare into Gus's eyes and suddenly, with no warning, the gun was in his hand and pointing at Gus.

"I'm ahead of you, my young friend, so I think you should relax."

Gus sat back in the chair, raising his arms in a gesture of submission.

"That was fast," he said.

"Practice makes perfect," replied Rosselli. He replaced the gun on the countertop without taking his eyes off Gus.

"What I don't understand," said Gus, "apart from the fact that I don't appear to have much choice, is if I help you, what do I get out of it? It sounds like you're going to watch me just dig a big hole for myself."

"That's a good point, Gus. You are right to expect something in return for helping me. Let me see. Yes, I could help you move the body somewhere it definitely will never be found. I'd recommend cutting it up into small pieces and distributing them in rubbish bins over a wide area."

Gus shuddered. "I'm not sure I could do that."

"Happy to oblige, Gus, don't you worry," said Rosselli, enjoying himself with the lie.

"What about this cottage?" said Gus.

"What about it?"

"You said I'd missed some evidence, something that might incriminate me if my wife found it."

"You strike a hard bargain," continued Rosselli with amusement, "but, yes, I can help you with that as well. However, let's not get ahead of ourselves. First things first. We need to establish the rules of the game."

"Rules?"

"Yes, Gus, rules. You see, you are a police officer, and that means from my perspective you are inherently untrustworthy. I cannot rely on you and so I must be sure of what you will and won't do. And what you won't do is try to double-cross me."

He paused and his face darkened. "Ever."

He studied Gus's eyes. "I can see defiance, Gus. That's not good. You're thinking that you'll appear to agree with me to appease me but then quietly let me down. It's a natural enough reaction."

"Fine," spat Gus. "Whatever you say. Come on, enlighten me. Tell me your plan."

Rosselli shook his head. "You have a poor attitude, Gus. Remember, I'm the only person who can rescue you from yourself. Now, let me tell you one or two things to sharpen up your thinking.

"Firstly, I should let you know that I am not working alone. I have a partner who watches from afar to check on my well-being. I report to this person every twelve hours with a coded message that informs him I am in no trouble. But, as professionals, our protocols allow for contingencies. It could be, for some reason, that I can't send the message exactly on time, so we allow for a little slippage. However, if after another twelve hours, he has still not received a signal, his instructions as of this evening are to kill you."

While he was telling the truth about the conversations with Giorgio, the death threat to Gus was fiction.

Gus blanched; the man's cold, clinical delivery was more than unnerving.

"So you see," continued Rosselli, "if I were to be separated from my means of communication because, say, I had been apprehended or arrested, my partner would seek you out and execute you. You'd be surprised how quickly it would happen and I can assure you that you certainly wouldn't see it coming."

He paused to let Gus process the information before continuing.

"But, that's not all. You see, you might think you could try to outwit my partner. It's a possibility I have to allow for and so in the unlikely eventuality that you did, I have made copies of everything I have on you: the photographs of the poor superintendent, a detailed account of your actions, a list of the evidence that is still here and in the factory to support the account, many other photos of you at the factory all of which are terribly incriminating, in fact a complete dossier of your actions with the superintendent and compelling evidence to support it. You wouldn't have a leg to stand on. As a police officer who had behaved so badly, an example would be made of you. You would go to prison for a long time. And where will these copies be sent? Well, if my partner isn't around to stop it, they will automatically go to your superiors, and just in case they decide they are not going to take action, copies will also go to the press. I should add that we're not just talking about the present. If I help you by disposing of the unfortunate superintendent's body, I shall, of course, record that and all the details will be added to the dossier."

He paused, his face now serious, his eyes cold. "So, detective, I think you get the picture. Am I right?"

Gus was crushed. He had been offered no room to manoeuvre.

"What is it you want me to do?" he said, his voice hardly audible.

Rosselli smiled. "Right now, Gus, nothing. Nothing at all. I simply need to know that should I need something from you, I can rely on you providing it."

Gus shook his head. "I still don'—"

"Don't get it, Gus?" snapped Rosselli, as if reprimanding a naughty child. "Come on, surely even in your confused state you should understand. You're a police officer. I and the people I work for might need your assistance someday, somewhere, to help something … go away, shall we say?"

"Are you talking about organised crime?" said Gus, the light dawning, "because if you are—"

"What? If I am what?" interrupted Rosselli. "What will you do? Come clean and be willing to throw away your future and your freedom? I don't think so."

Gus stared at Rosselli in horror at the thought of what he'd got himself into, not realising for one moment that Rosselli was making it all up.

"What are you?" said Gus, as he thought through the conversation. "A fixer for the head honcho of a drugs ring or something? Someone who seeks out suckers like me and effectively blackmails them into working for them?"

Rosselli smiled. "Fixer," he said. "I like the sound of that, and yes, detective, it's not far from the truth, although you make it sound rather melodramatic."

In reality, about a million miles from the truth, he thought to himself.

"So," said Rosselli, standing and picking up the Glock, "let's not waste any more of your time. I think we've covered everything. I fully intend to keep my side of the bargain. I'll be in touch soon about the removal and permanent disposal of the superintendent's body and about cleaning up this place so your wife doesn't throw you out. We have plenty of time before she returns home."

He turned and walked to the kitchen door. Opening it, he looked back. "And Gus, don't think about following me or doing anything stupid. I have eyes on you, I'll know what you're doing almost before you've done it. Just relax and wait for my call. It seems to me we have a mutually beneficial partnership, don't you think?"

The door slammed, leaving Gus staring at its bland, painted surface, wondering what had just happened and whether his life would ever be the same again.

Part Six

JENNIFER COTTON

Chapter Forty-Four

Sonia Landi was worried. It had been two months since Gianpietro Tebaldi had magically appeared in her life, charmed her with his sophistication and cast a seductive spell on her; two months since the most wonderful dinner under the stars in the Piazza Grande; two months since the phone call that ruined it all.

She thought endlessly about Gianpietro's poor mother and the selfless way Gianpietro had abandoned his plans for them that evening to rush to his mamma like the dutiful son he was. And she still fantasised about a huge bed in a luxurious hotel room or a love nest somewhere in the hills. He had left her with the gentlest of kisses, followed by flowers the next day and later by chocolates and notes of reassurance about his mother's recovery.

So why had she heard nothing more? Why had Gianpietro not called or written?

What if he were, with his impeccable manners, shielding her from some terrible news about his mother? Had the poor lady recovered or had she, perhaps, succumbed to whatever illness had struck her down? Was Gianpietro too grief-stricken to contact Sonia, bearing the weight of his sorrow alone?

Sonia had spent long hours anguishing over these possibilities, convincing herself that she, and only she, was the one to help Gianpietro through his misery. If only he could understand she was there for him, waiting to help him, ready to lift him out of his despair and move onwards in their new life together.

She had to make contact; it was the only way, even if it risked spoiling the surprise he had in store for the signora. Surely his little scheme had been forgotten in the all-consuming tragedy that had overtaken him, so really there was nothing to spoil. Perhaps the signora, his old and dear friend, didn't know about his mother's illness, perhaps this was another example of Gianpietro's sensitivity towards those close to him, not wanting to burden them with his pain.

Sonia's daily routine included dusting and tidying the master bedroom of Villa Brillante, the room where the three silver-framed photographs she had copied with her phone for Gianpietro were displayed. And every day she spent more and more time staring at the photographs as her level of concern over Gianpietro increased.

After noticing Sonia's time performing her bedroom chores was getting longer and longer, Connie watched her over several days before eventually attempting to raise the subject.

"Is something the matter, Sonia?" she said, as she walked silently into the bedroom. The maid was standing motionless in front of the photographs and the question took her by surprise.

"Signora!" she gasped, snapping out of her reverie in embarrassment.

"You don't seem yourself," said Connie. "You keep staring at those photographs."

Sonia was having trouble working out Connie's Italian, the words, heavily accented with American vowels, were difficult to follow, especially to an ear normally tuned to the local Castiglion Fiorentino dialect.

"I am sorry, signora, I don't understand."

Connie tried again, speaking slowly and simply, remembering her unconventional Italian tutor Alessandro Rossi's instructions back in Rome. "*If you can't say it one way, you must find another. Think, Connie, think about the message you are trying to get across and reduce it to its simplest components.*"

"Tell me what it is about the photographs that you like so much. I think the one of Signor Silk with his daughter is very good, don't you? It captures such a feeling of joy in both of them."

Sonia frowned at her. She had to seize the opportunity but she wasn't sure the signora would understand.

"When you were away in Usa, signora," she began, the words spilling out in a rush, "I met your friend, Signor Gianpietro Tebaldi."

She paused, waiting, hoping the look of confusion on Connie's face would turn into one of comprehension. It didn't help that Sonia spoke fast in dialect and instead of sounding the individual letters of 'USA', she pronounced it in the Italian way as 'oo-sah'. In the flurry of other words, Connie didn't even recognise that her country had been mentioned.

Connie sighed, irritated that once again the nuances of the language were eluding her. The other cleaner, Irena, was easier to understand and had often acted as interpreter when Connie was trying to get something across to Sonia. At that moment, Irena was elsewhere in the villa, but Henry, who never seemed to have any trouble talking to either woman, was conveniently seated outside on the bedroom's large balcony, sipping coffee and catching up with the world news on his phone.

"A moment, Sonia, let me fetch Signor Silk."

She left the maid standing awkwardly by the bed and walked over to the balcony doors.

"Henry, could I interrupt you for a moment?"

"For as many moments as you like," grinned Henry, holding out his arms.

She raised her eyes. "You actors are all the same. Incorrigible."

"And that's based on your experiences with how many?"

"Henry!"

He blew her a kiss. "What can I do for you, m'lady."

"It's Sonia, the maid. She seems distressed. But her accent is so strong I can't make much sense of what she's saying. Would you mind talking to her?"

"My pleasure," said Henry. He dropped his phone on the table and stood up, his expression turning serious. "You know, I keep thinking about Trisha. It's so worrying; I wish there was something we could do. It's been about ten days now since she disappeared; nearly a week since Jennifer called with the news. I wonder what progress they are making."

"Jennifer will be in touch as soon as she has some news," said Connie. "Let's just hope it's good news."

She took his hand and led him into the bedroom.

"Ciao, Sonia," said Henry. "Tutto bene?"

Sonia's eyes drifted up from the spot on the floor she'd been focussing on. Apart from Gianpietro, Henry Silk was the most handsome and intelligent man she'd ever met. And he was a film star. She always felt a strong flutter of nerves in his presence.

She took a deep breath and launched into a whirlwind of dialect. Henry immediately put up his hands and grinned at her. "Lentamente, Sonia. *Slowly*. Please, allow for me being a stupid foreigner."

Sonia bit her bottom lip and smiled coyly.

"I apologise, signore. I'll start again." She paused to gather her thoughts, but they still emerged as a torrent once she started speaking.

"When you and the signora were in America a couple of months ago, I met one of the signora's close friends near to where I live. He was lost and happened to be in the street. And he was so brave. He faced up to Irena's brute of a husband, taught him a lesson and the pig has been a lamb ever since. Irena can't believe the change in him. He hasn't hit her once and he's actually helping her around the house. You'd never—"

"The signora's friend?" interrupted Henry as gently as he could.

"Sorry, signore, yes. He told me he'd been looking for the villa but couldn't remember the way since it was some time since he'd been here. He was amazed to find that I worked here. He was such a gentleman; we hit it off straight away. After he'd, er, helped Irena with her husband, I took him to a bar in the town and we had a long chat. Then the following evening he took me out to dinner in Arezzo."

"How nice for you, Sonia. So what's the problem?"

"The problem is that he was called away at the end of the evening, just … er yes." She paused, blushing.

"His mother had been taken ill and he needed to get back to Rome. He sent me flowers and chocolates afterwards, but then he was called away to America and I haven't heard from him since. I'm really worried about his mother and whether he's being driven crazy with grief. But I have no address or number for him. I was wondering if the signora would mind contacting him for me."

Henry repeated the gist of what Sonia had said to Connie, adding quietly that it sounded like a con.

"Did she give a name?" asked Connie.

"What's his name, Sonia? The signora has many friends, especially in Rome."

"Sorry, signore, of course she does. I apologise for being a bother. His name is Gianpietro Tebaldi. He's an art dealer the signora has been friends with for about twenty years, I think he said."

She stopped, a nervous smile of anticipation on her lips as she waited for Connie to react with pleasure to the name.

"Mean anything to you?" said Henry after repeating the name to Connie.

Connie frowned. "Never heard of him. I think I know just about every reputable art dealer in Rome, and a few that aren't so reputable. But that name means nothing."

Henry turned to Sonia. "Gianpietro Tebaldi? I heard it correctly?"

"Yes, signore." Sonia's face was still fixed with a nervous smile.

Alarmed that a stranger with knowledge of Connie and Villa Brillante appeared to be propositioning one of the staff for information, Henry needed to find out more.

He tried to sound as reassuring as possible, not wanting the girl to run from the room in tears.

"Maybe he uses a different name professionally, Sonia. Dealers sometimes do that when they are rubbing shoulders with rich people if their deals are confidential."

Sonia nodded, her face now serious as she swallowed the story. "Yes. I know he has some very important clients."

"Exactly," said Henry.

Connie touched his arm. "Ask her why she's so interested in the photos, the ones over there on the drawers."

"Sonia, the signora tells me you like to look at the photographs over there. Any particular reason for that? Apart from the fact that I'm in most of them."

He grinned mischievously and winked at her.

Sonia giggled, thrilled to be having a real conversation with the famous Henry Silk. She couldn't wait to tell her mamma how the actor had been teasing her.

She looked down, still uncertain about spoiling Gianpietro's little game.

"It was meant to be a surprise, signore. Gianpietro said that he'd been planning to play a trick on the signora for some time and that she'd find it very funny."

"What kind of trick?"

"I don't know, exactly. It was to do with photographs and changing them on the computer. I didn't really understand what he was saying; I don't know much about computers. He said he wanted to get a photograph of the signora, and perhaps one of you and the young signorina—"

"Jennifer?" interrupted Henry, all trace of levity now absence from his voice. "Did he know her name?"

"I … I don't know, signore. He didn't say her name. He asked if there were any new photographs from the last time he'd been here and I told him there was one of you, signore, with … your daughter." Her voice trailed away as she realised she might have made a mistake.

She pouted, needing to justify her actions. "He said he would make something on the computer and give it to the signora as a surprise," she said, her tone defensive. "He said it would be very funny."

Henry frowned. "Make something on the computer?" he repeated. "He would need copies to do that. Did he ask you to do anything, Sonia?"

Sonia was no longer certain about Henry's tone. How badly had she screwed up?

Connie picked up on her change in expression and touched Henry's arm. "Gently, sweetheart," she said, quietly.

"Er, yes, he did," continued Sonia. "He told me he remembered that the last time he was here in the villa, he had seen some of the photographs and that those and the new one of you with the signorina were just the ones he needed for his trick. He showed me how to make copies of them on my phone."

"And did you do that?"

Sonia nodded, diverting her eyes, fully aware now that she had done something wrong.

Henry walked over to the drawers and beckoned for her to follow.

"Which ones did you copy, Sonia? Could you show me, please?"

She pointed. "There were three, signore."

"Do you know what he did with them?"

"He did something to put them on his phone, said they were exactly what he was looking for."

"Sonia, the signora isn't sure she knows which of her friends this man is. Could you describe him for me?"

Sonia looked blankly at him.

"OK," said Henry. "Was he as tall as I am? Taller? Shorter? How old was he?"

"A bit shorter, signore, and he was, I think, about forty."

"Was he fat, thin? What was his hair like?"

"He was slim, signore, and very strong. He had short black hair, slightly wavy."

"Good looking? Roman nose or a hooked one from the south."

"He looked like a Roman, but not the aristocratic type. His features were … gentle. Kind and considerate."

Henry turned to Connie. "Are you getting the gist of this?"

Connie nodded. "What do you think he was after?"

"Doesn't sound like he was casing the joint," replied Henry, pulling a face. "You know, planning a burglary or something."

"Good luck with that," said Connie, dismissively.

"Exactly. No, I think he was after a photo of Jennifer. This is worrying. I wonder if it's anything to do with the Cambronis and Jennifer's time in the gallery."

Connie's eyes widened. "Retribution? That's a bit of a leap, don't you think? Perhaps he was a journalist who's got a sniff of some information and is trying to follow it up. What better way than to befriend someone on the staff. After all, he didn't seem to know about Jennifer until this gullible girl told him, and he possibly didn't even know her name. I think he was a journalist."

"You're probably right," sighed Henry, "but I think we should try to get more on him."

He turned back to Sonia but before he could continue, he was interrupted by a quiet cough from the direction of the door from the corridor. They looked around and saw Irena standing there.

"Excuse me, signora," she said, looking flustered. "I was looking for Sonia. There's something I need her to do. Is everything all right?" As Sonia's immediate boss, she took Connie and Henry's welfare and Sonia's behaviour as her personal responsibility.

Henry asked Irena about Gianpietro Tebaldi and the incident with her husband.

"He was amazing, signore, like something in a film. When he came into my apartment, he was more or less dragging Carlo, then he spun him round ever so fast and kicked him, but I couldn't follow his arms and legs moving. They were just a blur."

"Could you describe him, Irena?" asked Connie. She had followed this part of the conversation since Irena had the ability to keep it in standard Italian with no dialect.

"I could, signora, yes, but I think I can do better than that. With all the noise and threats from Carlo, the usual bunch of nosy neighbours came out to watch and comment. Some had phones and they later told me that when Gianpietro came out of the apartment to look after Sonia, they took some pictures of him as he told them to go home."

"Excellent," said Henry. "I think with those photographs the signora will be able to identify which of her friends it is. Irena, do

you think if we went now to where you live, some of your neighbours would be there, the ones who took the photos?"

"Definitely, signore. I know for certain that Paola Bonavventura
will be at home. She has five children, all small, and her mother
lives in the south. She has no time to go out to work."

"Ok, let's go. Coming Connie?"

Connie shook her head and diverted her eyes towards Sonia,
who was looking disconsolate.

"I think I'd better struggle on with this one. She's been conned
and needs to be let down gently. It needs a woman's touch."

An hour after Henry Silk left Villa Brillante with Irena, he was
back and running up the villa's main stairs to where Connie was
now sitting with a morose Sonia on the bedroom balcony.

"Did you get them?" asked Connie, looking up.

Henry nodded. "Yes. Transferred them to my phone. Irena was
in her element, like she was accompanying royalty. But before we
got there, I reminded her of our agreement of keeping quiet about
both of us and of how generously she was paid as part of that
agreement."

"Well done. Our privacy is so important. Anyway, what do we
do now? I know I won't recognise the man in the photos you have,
which will shatter our young maid's dreams. I've been preparing
her for the possibility, but she's still clinging on to her hopes."

Henry shrugged. "No idea. Your call. Me, I'd tell her. No point
in delaying it. The man was after something, he used her, got what
he wanted and then buggered off."

"Yes, the tactic of using an ailing mother was clearly all
prepared. I wonder why. Our friend here was obviously ready to let
him have his evil way. I wonder why he backed off."

Henry pulled another sceptical face. "Perhaps he has certain
standards. She's no oil painting."

"Henry!"

"Well, she's not. I don't know. Perhaps he's gay. Anyway, take a
look at the photos, then it's up to you what you tell her."

He pulled his phone from his pocket and called up the images he'd obtained from three of Irena's neighbours.

"They'll take some playing with on the computer since he's quite far away, but a couple are full face. Should be enough to work on."

Connie kept her face expressionless while she scrutinised the images.

"Never seen him before," she said, as she handed the phone back to Henry. She puckered her lips. "OK, off you go and play on the computer. I'll fetch the Kleenex."

Two hours later, Connie had given both Sonia and Irena the rest of the day off. Irena, older and wiser, insisted to Connie that she'd had her doubts about Tebaldi in spite of how he'd improved her life for her. She also told Connie she certainly wasn't going to tell anyone of developments, particularly her husband. She wanted him to remain in fear for the rest of his miserable life.

Just to be sure of her ground, Connie had called some of her art dealer contacts in Rome and floated the name of Gianpietro Tebaldi. No one had heard of him. One of her closer contacts had gone further by checking in a catalogue of dealers nationwide, with the same result. If the name was real, he wasn't in the art business.

After sending the maids on their way, Connie sought out Henry in the downstairs office. He looked up as she opened the door and patted the seat next to him.

"Perfect timing, sweetheart. The facial details have come up better than I thought. Come take a look."

They both sat in front of the large, high-resolution monitor staring at the screen.

"You know," said Henry, "there's something about that face. I can't put my finger on it, but it's ringing all sorts of bells."

"Same here," agreed Connie. "Do you think he's a serious threat?"

"Hard to say. But I think it's worth following up on the journalist angle. I'll call my agent. He has more journalist contacts than you could shake a stick at, including several in this country. If there's a hack called Gianpietro Tebaldi, he'll be able to find him."

"And if there is, what do we do?"

"Talk to him; find out what he knows and what he's up to. I'm sure we can come to a mutually beneficial arrangement, as they say."

"Sounds dodgy to me."

"Exactly," said Henry, with a knowing smile.

Chapter Forty-Five

The week following Jennifer's call to Henry in Tuscany seemed endless. She and the rest of the team had spent hundreds of hours searching traffic camera videos from an area far greater than was initially considered necessary, but the chief constable had ordered that nothing was to be overlooked and if that meant extending the search to an extreme level, so be it.

After a long Sunday in the SCF squad room, Jennifer and Derek once again returned home bleary-eyed and frustrated carrying yet another take-away, the thought of preparing food too much for either of them. Derek grabbed two glasses and poured them both a generous measure of red wine.

"That should help me sleep," said Jennifer eyeing the volume of wine. "I didn't know you could get almost an entire bottle into two tulip glasses."

"Deceptively large," said Derek. "Anyway, I think we need something to take our minds off traffic videos."

Jennifer nodded. "Yes, I never want to look at one again; they're driving me crazy."

"Me too," agreed Derek, "but unless they want to extend the search to cover the whole country, at least we've finished with all the videos that have been sent in. Maybe tomorrow we can get on with something else, although what exactly, I don't know."

"Which is why, with all my accumulated overtime, I plumped

for taking tomorrow off," said Jennifer. "Rather than stare at the big board in frustration, I want to devote some time alone to think everything through, away from the noise and interruptions of the office."

Derek took a large slurp of wine and looked at her over the top of his glass. "You're not telling me the whole story, DS Cotton. I know you, something's on your mind that doesn't sit happily and you want to tease it to death."

Jennifer clinked his glass with hers. "I must be more transparent than I thought."

"Only to me," said Derek. "Come on, kiddo, spill the beans."

Jennifer adjusted her position on the kitchen bar stool and stretched.

"It's nothing new, not really, it's just that, well, voicing it sounds almost like a betrayal, a suspicion for which there aren't any grounds, so it's no more than a hunch, I suppose."

Derek took her hand in his. "Cut the waffle and get to the point, before the wine fuddles my head."

Jennifer studied her glass, avoiding his eyes. "It's Gus Brooke."

"What about him?"

"He's the one person who hasn't been looked at."

"What's to look at? Just because he lives near to where Trisha was last seen doesn't make him a suspect. He's given a statement to the Met guys; he didn't go that way home. He saw nothing."

"But we only have his word for it. There's nothing to back it up."

"What are you saying, Jen? Do you think he's involved?"

"No … I don't know. Look, let's play 'What if?' Just us, informally, not a conversation we could have in the office."

"O … kaaay," said Derek, not sounding convinced.

Jennifer took a deep breath. "I've already said I think the traffic cams are a waste of time, that it all happened much closer to home. Henry echoed those thoughts immediately when we discussed the case with him. And I've been tossing his doubts over in my head. We've interviewed and looked at the background of everyone in and around Rappington. Everyone, that is, apart from Gus. An assumption that he's telling the truth has been made from the get-go. Because he's a cop and because his background is known. It's all there on file."

"Are you thinking about his Romeo reputation?"

"Yes and no. I mean, it's a factor, sure. But the important thing is that while everyone else in his neighbourhood has been scrutinised in detail and eliminated from consideration, Gus has simply been taken at face value. He's a cop. End of story. Well, suppose it's not like that. Suppose he is involved."

"It's a big suppose, Jen."

"Is it? Why? Why shouldn't he be considered? Let's think about it for a moment. Suppose he's lying about the route he took home and he actually went the way he says he always goes. He said he didn't go that way because of the weather. But surely that's rubbish. He's a good driver, for Christ's sake. It was stormy, yes, but it wasn't a hurricane; there weren't huge chunks of debris flying around. Why would he choose to go a longer way? The trouble is that because it was a filthy night, no one is likely to have seen his car if he drove through Rappington village, so there's little chance of finding someone to refute his story."

"And no traffic cams," said Derek, taking another drink. "Do you want some nibbles, or shall I warm up this take-away?"

"Nibbles, if you must. I want to concentrate. This is what I meant about not wanting to do this in the office."

"Sorry."

Jennifer caught his eye and leaned over to kiss him. "No, *I'm* sorry. I know I get a bit intense."

"Really? Can't say I've noticed."

"Prat," she said, punching him on the arm. "Right. Let's suppose for a moment it was Gus who stopped to help Trisha. We know the other car was pointing in the right direction, I mean away from Nottingham, and we know it was a dark colour. It must have been nothing special or one of those two witnesses might have noticed. And you can't get much more forgettable or invisible than Gus's crappy dark-blue Ford."

"True," conceded Derek.

"Right, he stops, maybe witnesses the car dancing in circles on that corner, and he offers to help. Changes her wheel for her. After that, they are both soaked and he suggests going back to his place."

"Jen. We've been through all this the other night. We discussed this."

"Not with respect to Gus, we didn't. In fact we assumed it wasn't him. He wasn't given any thought."

"OK, carry on."

"So they go back to Gus's cottage. You've been there; what's it like? Could she park in his drive or would she have to park on the road?"

Derek pursed his lips as he thought about it.

"I've only been there once and I parked on the road. But, yes, I think there would be room for two cars on his drive."

"And if she parked right behind him, anyone driving past and concentrating on the road in the storm probably wouldn't see the car," said Jennifer.

"Sure. They are hardly likely to be taking note of cars in drive-ways," added Derek. "Why should they?"

"Exactly," agreed Jennifer, nodding. "OK, they go in and … is there more than one bathroom?"

"Yes, several, as I remember. There's one downstairs and more upstairs. I used the one downstairs. It's got some daft arrangement with the loo. The floor's on two levels and it's on the higher one."

"How odd. Anyway, she has a shower and … wait a minute. I was going to say changed her clothes. But the bag in her car hadn't been touched. Everything was neatly folded. If anything had been taken out, it was the wash bag, which was at the top, and that had been put back."

"What are you saying?"

"They were both wet and probably mucky, Perhaps Gus bunged their clothes in the washing machine while Trish had a shower. Perhaps she dressed in a towel or bathrobe while waiting from them to dry.

"While they are waiting, he pours them both a drink, which Trish would only have accepted if she were staying. She's totally rigid about drinking and driving: she won't do it."

Derek nodded. "And one drink leads to another. And another,

and … OK, so they end up in the sack. That's a long way from ending up dead or kidnapped."

"What if something went horribly wrong?" said Jennifer. "Is Gus into kinky stuff? Trisha has never mentioned it, but who knows? Maybe he tried it on, she resisted and they had a fight. Perhaps he strangled her by mistake."

"Or even deliberately if he lost his rag. He's a big lad and would have the edge on Trisha even in unarmed combat, especially if she'd had too much to drink."

"Does he lose his rag?" Jennifer wasn't convinced.

"Not really, although he can be quite intimidating with suspects at times."

"Have you noticed any bruising on him?"

Derek shook his head. "No, but I've only seen his face and hands."

Jennifer picked up her wine glass and stared at it for inspiration. "Anyway, whatever happened, if Gus suddenly found himself up shit creek with a dead body on his hands, what would he do?"

She paused and turned to Derek. "What would you do? Your wife's away and you know if she finds out, she'd throw you out. Would you risk coming clean?"

"Probably not. But disposing of her body and her car? You know, he was totally out of it the following morning. We all thought he was hungover. What if it was more than that? What if he was carrying the guilt of what had happened and what he was planning to do?"

"If he was, it's amazing he was functioning at all."

"Do you think they knew who each other was? I mean, she was coming up here to be his boss."

Jennifer shook her head. "As far as Trish is concerned, I'd say definitely not. She's done this before; gone on one-nighters with complete strangers, I mean. I've told her how risky it could be if they found out she's a senior police officer, but she's pretty driven when she's in the mood. I don't know about Gus."

"I doubt he'd announce he's a cop," said Derek, "but if he told her his name, wouldn't she recognise it from the staff list she'd been sent?"

"Only if he told her his full name, which I doubt he would. And Trish certainly wouldn't give hers. She once told me she has an alter ego called Emma something; maybe Gus does the same if he regularly plays the field."

Derek frowned as he tried to visualise the sequence of events. "If what you're suggesting actually happened, they would have lied to each other about their identities, and perhaps in the panic of the moment, Gus didn't go through her bag."

"Yes," agreed Jennifer. "But the first thing he'd need to get rid of would be her car. She might well be dead somewhere in the cottage, but the car's outside. He can't risk anyone local seeing it; they might know Mo, and tongues can wag."

"And," exclaimed Derek, "he was involved in the stake-outs and surveillance of the factory from when he first came up here; he knew the place was abandoned. Perfect for hiding the car. Perhaps he even had thoughts of putting the body there too, sometime later."

"But it all went wrong," said Jennifer. "The car was spotted and the place searched."

Derek's eyes opened wide. "Twice, by two separate teams. No stone unturned and all that. And once it was over we released the place. What better place to hide a body than somewhere that's already been searched and written off?"

"Surely that would be full of problems," replied Jennifer, "not the least of which is that unlike when the car was dumped, when there was no padlock on the gates, the owners have now put a new lock in place. He'd have to find another way in. And the fence is the one thing about that place that seems to be reasonably strong as well as high."

Derek shrugged, "He's a big strong lad; he could carry a body slung over his shoulder some distance, but you're right, there would have to be another way in."

"It would have to be done in the dead of night," continued Jennifer. "I know Rappington's sleepy now with the by-pass, but it's not that sleepy. But, you know, you've got a point, and now I think about it, it doesn't necessarily have anything to do with Gus."

"What do you mean?"

"We've just discussed a detailed scenario involving Gus being off the radar as a suspect. Suppose there's someone else local, someone we've interviewed and rejected but who has something in their past we don't know about. Someone who has a knowledge of the layout and conditions in factory. As you said, what better place to hide a body when the place has already been searched."

"Can't see it flying with Crawford," said Derek, "or with Hawkins, no matter how much he thinks you're a genius. You know how they are, both old school. And you could never float the idea with Gus being centre stage in your cast of suspects."

Jennifer took a sip of her wine as she studied a spot on the wall.

"I'm off tomorrow. Suppose I—"

"No, Jen. Absolutely not. You can't go looking round the factory again. It's been handed back. We'd need a warrant. And I don't think Hawkins would take your ifs, buts and maybes as plausible grounds. You mustn't go in there."

Jennifer was shaking her head. "I was actually thinking of Gus's place. What I thought was that I might pop along there while he's at work. Get a feel for it. You can keep an eye on him and let me know if you think he's about to go home. And don't worry, I won't break in; I just want to snoop a bit. After that, I'll check the padlock on the gates, which, as a responsible police officer passing by the place and knowing its history, is a reasonable thing to do, and then I might take a wander around the perimeter, have a look at the fence. All perfectly above board, and after all, it was Gus who did that on the day the car was found. Perhaps he conveniently forgot to mention any break he discovered. If I find one, it could be enough to persuade Crawford to search the place again. Showing someone could have had continuous access to the place since our search ought to be good enough grounds for us going in again."

Derek grunted unhappily. "I don't like it Jen, and I don't trust you not to hop over the fence. You mustn't, not on your own. And I can't keep tabs on Gus, I'm in court all day, don't you remember?"

"Bugger, I'd forgotten that. But anyway, if Gus is at work, he'd have no reason to return home. I'll make it quick, as I will at the factory. As I said, I'm not planning to go in. One step at a time."

"But suppose your other suggestion is correct."

"What suggestion?"

"That it's not Gus but someone else local. He could be loitering about and if he sees you snooping around, things could get nasty."

"Firstly, I don't think either of us seriously thinks someone else from the area is involved, and secondly, if on the off chance you're right, if the whole thing was an accident, then he's probably not going to be a mean-hearted killer, just some poor sod who got unlucky. So I think I'd be more than a match if it came to fisticuffs. And anyway, I guarantee I can outrun him."

"Well, just make sure your phone's fully charged in case you need to summon help."

Chapter Forty-Six

The following morning, Jennifer attempted to distract herself with a number of household chores, waiting for Derek to call with the information that Gus Brooke was at his desk.

"What's everyone doing this morning?" she asked.

Derek smiled as he heard the impatience in Jennifer's voice.

"The guv has put four of the DCs back on other cases that needed some urgent attention and he's given three of us, our friend included, the job of reviewing everything we've got so far, including the results from the forensic lab, although apart from the oil, there were no surprises there. That's what I'll be doing as and when I get back from court."

"I'd forgotten about the oil. That's something else we overlooked last night. Gus is a keen cyclist with some classy gear, according to him. He's bound to use a high-tech chain lube. I think I might just take a sample if I come across his bike."

"It wouldn't be admissible."

"No, but if it happened to match, it could be formally taken at a later date. Right, I'm off in a mo'. Buzz me if anything changes."

"Take it easy, kiddo."

"That's no way to address your senior officer."

"What do you suggest? Kidd'am?"

. . .

It was a bright morning and before leaving her flat, Jennifer dressed in lycra leggings and top with a pair of running shoes. She had decided that once she had finished snooping around Gus's cottage and the factory, she would mix business with pleasure by going for a run along the footpaths and tracks that interlaced the waterways and irrigation channels near Rappington.

As she approached the new dual carriageway leading from Nottingham to junction twenty-four on the M1 motorway, she reset the trip odometer on her car's dashboard to zero, set her stopwatch and took the road to where the Rappington road rejoined it after Rappington village. She turned right and followed the old road back as far as the Brookes' cottage. After making a note of the odometer reading and time taken, she reset the odometer and stop-watch and continued along the Rappington road to where it met the dual carriageway at the Nottingham end. Her measurements told her the way to the Brookes' cottage via the new road was two kilometres farther despite it being a straighter road, and the time taken a minute and a half longer. For someone in Gus Brooke's position wanting to get home on a stormy night, the old road through the village offered the better option. His story made no sense.

Jennifer turned her car round at the junction and headed back towards Rappington. As she passed the lane leading to the factory, she glanced along it, but could see no sign of any activity.

After Rappington, she continued on past the Brookes' cottage where, as expected, there were no cars parked: Gus Brooke's car was at the SCF car park in Nottingham while his wife's was presumably at an airport car park awaiting her return. Jennifer decided to look for a spot to leave her car where it wouldn't be visible near the house. About five hundred metres along was the same track Rosselli had used. She drove a short way down it, locked the car and jogged back to the main road.

Once she reached the cottage, Jennifer stopped, running on the spot, making a show of consulting her watch like an obsessive jogger while she glanced up and down the road. Seeing no one, she ran down the path to the side of the cottage and was soon hidden from view from anyone passing on the road.

Looking up, now she was at close quarters, she wasn't sure that 'cottage' accurately described the substantial house. It had originally been three or even four cottages, she couldn't tell, and clearly money had been spent on it.

The solid wooden kitchen door was opposite a side door to the garage and visible from the road. But there was a window nearby that looked into the kitchen. She had to risk it; she needed to get a feel for the house. She wanted to imagine Trish there, think of where she would sit and what she would do. She peered through the window and could see the kitchen extended into a sitting area with two easy chairs near a wood-burning stove. In the kitchen area itself was a large island unit with two barstools. Would Trisha have sat in the easy chairs? She doubted it; Trish was more of a bar stool person.

The kitchen was impeccably tidy, too tidy for the average man whose wife was away. Gus Brooke gave no indication from the clutter on his desk at the SCF that he was obsessively tidy by nature, so the attention paid to this space must have been no accident. Then Jennifer remembered that his wife's return had been delayed a couple of times. Perhaps he was keeping it tidy in case she turned up unexpectedly.

She checked the other downstairs windows, but all were locked and there was nothing to be seen. Frustrated, she hunted around, searching under plant pots and loose paving stones for a spare key. But Gus Brooke wasn't that lax.

Turning to the garage, she decided that if it happened to be unlocked, there was nothing to lose by having a snoop. She turned the handle to the side door and pulled. It opened and she slipped inside.

With no room to house a car, the garage was no different from many: a home for garden furniture and a resting place for household things no longer needed but not yet moved to a tip or put in a car boot sale. There were also many boxes of various sizes that appeared to contain materials for Mo's work as a sculptor, but on the whole, it was orderly enough.

On individual stands near the main garage doors were two bikes, both expensive, both Cannondale; one a road bike, the other a mountain bike. Jennifer bent to examine the chains. They were relatively clean, the road bike's more than the mountain bike's, but there was enough residue of oil on them to smear onto a surface such as the opening on a car tailgate if they happened to touch them while being stowed in the car. She was considering taking samples when she looked up at a shelf above the bikes and saw that among the bottles stored there was a plastic container of chain lube oil, the brand an expensive one. "No need for samples from the chain," she said, triumphantly, "I'll copy the label onto my phone for the lab to follow up."

Aware that the bikes might well be sent for a full forensic examination if Gus Brooke became a suspect, she moved away, not wanting to contaminate them.

Returning to the garden, Jennifer noticed a small, old-looking shed next to a large plum tree a dozen metres from the house. She walked along the stone path to the shed and on trying the door, she was surprised to find it unlocked.

"For a cop, you have little idea about security, Gus," she muttered under her breath as she pulled open the door.

Inside, the space was almost entirely full of garden tools: spades, a rake, a fork, an axe and a sledgehammer, all leaning against an electric lawnmower. Empty plastic and clay flower pots were stacked on shelves along with an assortment of plastic bags, ties, string, seed packets and seedling containers.

"Just your average garden stuff," said Jennifer, closing the door and taking a last look around the garden.

She returned to the corner of the house, listened for any traffic noise and jogged back to her car.

Once seated back behind the wheel, she called Derek.

"Didn't expect you to reply," she said, when her call was answered immediately.

"Still waiting for my turn. You know what it's like; I could wait all day just to be told I'm not wanted."

"Well, at least I can talk to you now. The cottage was frustrating; I want to get in for a snoop around."

"You mean you resisted the temptation?"

"All locked up. But I could see the kitchen through a window. It was pristine, ridiculously so. Like a showroom; absolutely nothing out of place. Weird for someone whose wife's been away for a while."

"Being OCD isn't a crime, you know."

"Except he isn't."

"Perhaps his wife has him well trained."

"Perhaps I need to talk to her, find out what her secret is."

"Think how boring your life would be."

"My vote is with boring. Do you know when his wife is coming back? Perhaps it's all in her honour."

"Another week, according to Gus. Seems a bit early to start turning the straw."

"OK," said Jennifer, "I'm off to the factory site to have a look at the fence."

There was a grunt of disapproval from Derek. "Stay alert and if there's anything odd or suspicious, call for back-up. *Don't* go in there alone, OK."

"Message received et cetera."

Ten minutes later, Jennifer pulled to a halt by the factory gates and got out.

She stared through the chain-link fence at the decaying buildings. Their stillness in the slight breeze was in stark contrast to the urgency of the day the SCF team had descended en masse to locate Trisha's car and begin searching the site for any sign of the detective herself.

She felt drawn to the building, as if it were calling her in to search again, telling her that thoughts of it being the perfect hiding place for a body or there being a cell in which to imprison someone were highly relevant. It was several minutes before she realised she was standing right next to the fence, her hands raised above her head, grasping the links. She had no idea how long she had stood there, but finally she tore her eyes away from the building and focussed on the chain and padlock securing the gates.

"Not exactly high-tech," she said, lifting the padlock in her gloved hand and looking closely at the keyway. "But better than nothing, and given there's nothing inside worth the effort of breaking in, it's probably good enough. But hey, maybe there's another way in."

She started to walk, slowly following the fence in an anticlockwise direction as she meticulously searched for any breaks in the links. After fifteen minutes, she was on the far side of the site where the fence ran alongside the narrow pathway bordering the irrigation channel. Halfway along she saw that the chain-link wasn't as clear, as if some of the mesh was overlapping. She bent forward to examine it more closely. On pulling gently at the diamond-shaped mesh, she found she could easily and quickly create an opening large enough to pass through. The break in the fence was well disguised, but a few scuff marks on the ground beneath the fence convinced her that someone had been through here recently. Had Gus missed it, in his distracted mental state, or had he deliberately not mentioned it?

Remembering her conversation with Derek, she stood and looked around, her eyes following the path in both directions. She was relieved to see it was deserted. The local dogs must have already had their morning walks.

Would a break in the fence be enough to convince Crawford and Hawkins that a second search of the factory was justified? She didn't know. She decided to continue her examination of the entire fence perimeter; if there were other places where it was broken, they would strengthen her case.

She continued along the footpath in the direction of Rappington village as far as a small stand of silver birch that marked the limit of the site. Here she turned left and since there was no path, she picked her way along through roots and undergrowth as she followed the fence back towards the lane that led to the main gates.

Halfway along this section of the fence, she found a second break, this one smaller and even better disguised than the first. From the look of the links, it hadn't been disturbed for some time. Hidden by the stand of silver birch, its existence had probably been long forgotten by whoever made it.

Fifteen minutes after finding the second break, she was back at her car. She had found no more damage to the fence.

She leaned against the driver's door, staring at the factory, her mind in conflict. On one hand, she should follow procedure, inform her bosses and if they agreed, wait for back-up. *If* they agreed.

On the other hand, her mind and body were urging her to ignore protocols. With every passing minute, she was increasingly convinced that Trisha's body was hidden in the derelict factory buildings. It made so much sense. And if by some miracle Trisha were still alive and being detained there, immediate action was even more urgent. She could be injured, tied up and abandoned, dying. Finding her today, right now, could save her life. Leaving it until the bosses could be convinced might be a death sentence.

She pulled her phone from her pocket. She should at least tell Derek. But after staring at the screen for several seconds, she put the phone away. He would only start arguing with her, trying to persuade her not to act.

Decision made, she hurried back along the outside of the fence, returning to the second break, the one hidden by the stand of trees. She could access the site from there with little risk of being observed.

However, once she arrived, she hesitated, the same conflicts nagging at her mind as before. What she was considering flew totally in the face of procedure. If she screwed up, she could face disciplinary action or worse. It had taken long enough for her promotion to come through; she didn't want to find herself demoted back to detective constable, or worse, back in uniform.

She pursed her lips, annoyed at herself for conforming, and once again pulled out her phone.

"I'll take that, detective sergeant," said a voice from close behind her.

She spun around, almost dropping the phone in surprise. A man who looked vaguely familiar was standing six feet away pointing a silenced gun at her chest. Then she realised it wasn't so much the man who was familiar, it was the pug dog sitting next to him, her lead lying on the ground alongside her.

"I know you!" she said, as the pieces fell into place. "You were in the pub. What the hell do you want?"

Chapter Forty-Seven

Earlier, after taking his breakfast in his hotel room, Cosimo Graziano Rosselli had sat waiting patiently, as he had done for the past three days.

He had decided to let Detective Constable Brooke sweat for a while. According to the latest update on her website, Mo would be away now for at least another week so there was no urgency to keep his promise to the detective. Not that he had any intention of doing anything with Trisha McVie's body; it would be found as part of a natural consequence of events once he had set his final plans in motion.

Three days. Brooke would be getting more than twitchy. He would have done little except think over and over about what kind of mess he'd got himself into, how the enigmatic stranger, whose name he didn't even know, had taken control of his life, and how he was now a pawn at the beck and call of people he knew nothing about, anonymous people with the power to destroy him.

Rosselli's plan for luring Jennifer Cotton to the factory without squads of police officers being involved was simple. He would give the job to Brooke as a test, with a few tips on how to go about it. He intended to call Brooke the following day, with the news that his bosses had an interest in the detective sergeant in the SCF from her time in the Art Fraud Squad, which wasn't far from the truth. Given who his bosses were, he would say that discretion was optimal and it was of paramount importance that only Brooke should accompany Cotton, and even he would be kept in the background. Rosselli would explain a complete fiction that Jennifer's work in the squad had been *'fluid, shall we say, Gus, far more than you might imagine. There were lines you could cross and those you couldn't, to everyone's mutual benefit.'*

He knew Brooke would swallow it, especially once he also explained that the people to whom Rosselli was answerable regarded this instruction as an important test of Brooke's skills. Succeed and his life would improve; fail and, well, *'let's not think about failure, shall we, Gus?'* He smiled to himself as he thought of the idiot detective squirming in anguish at the difficulties facing him, fearing failure, fearing alerting his fellow officers.

Removing his right hand from where he was idly rubbing the folds of skin on Goccia's head to reach out and pour himself another coffee, he was surprised by a distinctive ping from his phone. The coffee temporarily forgotten, he picked up the phone to see what had triggered the alert.

The screen he called up showed a grid of the displays from the CCTV cameras at the factory, and one of them, now highlighted, immediately caught his attention.

"Goccia, my sweet," he said, sitting up as his mind clicked into full alert, "I think our waiting might be over. It looks as if Detective Sergeant Cotton might have solved our problem for us."

The pug eyed her master's hand, more interested in being stroked than in whatever her master was looking at on his phone.

Rosselli clicked on the screen to isolate and enlarge the display. Thanks to the high resolution camera, he could see Jennifer's face clearly as she stood in front of the factory gates, her arms reaching up and grasping the links while she stared at the factory buildings. Rosselli thought she was about to climb the gates, but a few moments later she stood back slightly to examine the padlock before slowly walking off to the left of the camera's view as she paid careful attention to the condition of the fence.

Rosselli knew that if her examination remained thorough, it would take her well over ten minutes to reach the concealed break in the fence on the far side of the site, more than enough time to be ready to spring, should he need to. He grabbed the two bags he always kept ready, one with his weapons, the other his clothes.

"Come, little one," he said to Goccia as he clipped her lead onto he collar, "we must leave this place and take all our belongings with us. If all goes well, our goal will be achieved today and by this evening we'll be well on our way home."

Exactly twelve minutes after first seeing Jennifer on the feed from the camera pointing at the factory gates, Rosselli had parked his car near Rappington church and was again scrutinising the camera feeds.

Jennifer had just arrived at the point where the fence was broken and Rosselli could see she was examining it carefully. He watched as she started to pull the two sides of the break from each other. But, to his surprise, she paused and pulled the mesh back together. Once the fence was closed again, she continued along the perimeter.

"Thorough or resisting the temptation to go inside?" said Rosselli. "What do you think, tesoro?"

Goccia growled softly from her basket.

"I agree with your sentiments, little one. You know, I think it's time to watch her in the flesh, now we can't watch her on the screen."

He picked up his backpack, lifted Goccia out of the car and locked it.

"We'll move as far as the footpath, shall we? If she's still studying the fence bordering the stream, we'll be able to see her; if she's already turned by the birch trees and is looking along that side of the site, we'll hurry along to the trees. That way we'll be closer but hidden for when she decides to take her next step."

On reaching the path, Rosselli moved to a spot where he could see the factory site a few hundred metres away. There was no sign of Jennifer, who had already started working her way along the part of the fence that would take her back to the gates.

"OK, little lady," he said, as he tightened the straps on the backpack, "we're going for a run."

He checked Goccia's lead was properly attached to her collar and the pair of them headed off along the footpaths behind the village, Rosselli jogging as fast as the struggling dog would allow. On reaching the stand of silver birch trees, Rosselli picked up the panting Goccia and positioned himself in an area of dense vegetation. "Sorry, little one," he said, "I forgot you are not much of an athlete."

While Goccia regained her breath, Rosselli consulted the CCTV feed on his phone and froze as he saw that Jennifer was not only back at the main gates, but she was also taking her phone from her pocket. This was a problem. If she called in reinforcements, the superintendent's body would surely be found along with all the careful modifications he'd made to the equipment in the upper cargo area. Connections may or may not be made to Brooke as trace evidence was found and analysed, but Rosselli's target, Jennifer Cotton, would escape the scenario he had so carefully put in place for her.

A coldness entered Rosselli's eyes. He would resort to a simple kill if he had to, but the thought didn't please him. The way he'd planned was so much more elegant: although the detective sergeant might at some stage fear for her life, when she died it would be without pain and Brooke would be blamed for her death as well as the superintendent's.

Goccia kept quiet, sensing something was wrong. She watched her master out of the corner of one eye, her head down. But then his face relaxed and he smiled.

"She didn't make the call, Goccia! She looked at the screen for a few seconds, but she didn't connect. And look, she's walked off again; she's coming in this direction, only this time her step is far more determined. I wonder what she has in mind; the other way round to the break in the fence would make more sense. Perhaps she's discovered another we don't know about. Let's move closer so we can see what she's up to, shall we?"

Chapter Forty-Eight

"You have a good memory, detective sergeant, or perhaps it was my little friend who reminded you."

Rosselli was standing at the edge of the trees, his eyes registering every nuance of Jennifer's movements. He glanced towards Goccia before nodding at the phone in Jennifer's hand.

"Don't even think of throwing that at me; you would be dead before you even released your grip. Please, just toss it lightly so that it lands in front of me."

Jennifer glared at him, but she knew that for the present at least, he had the advantage. She did as instructed and the phone landed at Rosselli's feet.

Without taking his eyes or the gun off her, Rosselli stooped to pick up the phone and turned it off.

"Good," he said, throwing it into the trees. "Now we can move on. From the expression on your face as I watched you from the bushes, I should say you were hesitating over an important decision. Let me guess. Should you break the rules and go into the factory again or should you call in and seek permission or backup?"

Jennifer said nothing, her mind working hard. Who was this man, his smile apparently benign but his eyes glacially cold? Was he responsible for Trisha's disappearance? Had she been completely wrong about Gus Brooke?

"Well, let me make that decision for you, detective sergeant," continued Rosselli as he pointed with his gun. "If you would like to turn around and pull that damaged fence apart — well spotted, by the way — we can take a look inside. But please remember that if you attempt anything stupid, anything at all, you will die in an instant."

Jennifer shrugged. "You leave me no choice, but will you answer one question first?"

Rosselli raised his eyebrows.

"Is Trisha McVie in there?"

Rosselli nodded, "She is, detective sergeant, she is indeed."

"And is she still alive?" said Jennifer, angry with herself for the desperation she could hear in her voice. She was sure this man would hear it too.

"Let's wait and see, shall we, detective sergeant?"

Jennifer sighed in frustration as she turned to work on separating the fence. As she did, Rosselli quickly gathered up Goccia's lead, slipping the loop over his left wrist to keep his hand free, his right hand controlling the gun.

"Make your way through the fence," he ordered, once the hole was large enough, "and walk ahead until I tell you to stop."

Jennifer walked slowly forward, acutely aware of the Glock pointing directly at her back.

"That's enough," called Rosselli when she was about twenty feet away. "Now, lie face down on the ground with your legs wide apart and your hands clasped behind your head. And remember, my gun will be pointing at you."

Once Jennifer had done as she was told, Rosselli ducked through the gap, making sure that Goccia passed through without getting tangled.

"Very good, detective sergeant," he said, once he was through. "Now, stand up and walk briskly ahead. We'll follow."

They quickly reached the shelter of the inner yard and walked toward the large doors at one end.

"I should imagine that you intended making a rapid search of every room, cupboard and closet on this floor before moving your search to the upper floor, detective sergeant. Am I right?"

"You know you are," growled Jennifer.

"I thought so," said Rosselli. "Well, let me put your mind at rest. Your superintendent isn't down here, so let's not waste time looking. We'll go straight to the upper floor. You know the way; it's through that door and up the wide stone steps."

When they neared the top of the steps, Rosselli ordered Jennifer to stop.

"There's something I need to do before we continue our exploration, detective sergeant, so I must ask you to bear with me. You see the metal handrail next to you, the one running up the steps. I want you to stand in front of it facing the wall. Good. Now, take this cable tie from me, good, and tether your right hand to the fixture holding the rail to the wall."

Jennifer looked at him suspiciously and Rosselli laughed.

"Don't look so shocked, detective, I have no evil intentions in mind."

Jennifer tethered her wrist as instructed and stood facing the wall.

"Now bend and stretch out your left hand as far as it will reach. Good, that's perfect."

In a flash, Rosselli had looped another tie around Jennifer's left wrist and secured it to the railing at a point where it couldn't slide up the rail. He checked the first tie, pulled it a little tighter and stood back to ensure Jennifer was sufficiently spreadeagled and going nowhere.

"Good. Very good," he said. "I shall only be a few minutes. Come on, Goccia."

At the top of the stairs, instead of turning right towards the cargo platform area, he turned left and walked towards the room he had set up as his HQ. Once inside, he removed Goccia's lead and sat her on a pile of sacks he'd found for her when installing the CCTV.

"I'll have to leave you here for a while, principessa. Things might get a bit unpleasant out there in a moment or two, not something a refined young lady should have to witness."

Goccia looked up at him, her high-pitched whine edged with uncertainty.

"Don't worry, little one. Have I ever let you down? I'll be about half-an-hour, after which we'll be off to London and then home. Won't that be wonderful?"

Goccia made no more noises but kept her eyes fixed on her master, watching him as he took his phone from a pocket.

Scrolling down the screen, Rosselli hit Gus Brooke's number. Gus answered on the second ring.

"Yes."

"Yes, Gus, yes indeed. There has been a development. I have discovered your detective sergeant breaking into the Rappington factory. She is here now and at present rate of progress, she will find your superintendent's body within the next ten or fifteen minutes."

"Christ!" hissed Brooke. "Can't you stop her? I mean, you've got your gun, haven't you? Stop the bitch!"

"Now, now, Gus. Let's not get flustered. I have the matter in hand but I do need you to get here from your office as quickly as you possibly can."

"I don't kn—"

"There's no choice, Detective Brooke. You must come or many things will go wrong for you."

"I'll be there within twenty minutes."

"Good. And Gus, remember, all this is our little secret. You tell no one, do you understand? Otherwise the consequences—"

It was Gus's turn to interrupt, his reply terse.

"Of course I understand. Do you think I'm stupid?"

The line went dead in Rosselli's ear.

"Now you mention it, Gus …" he said, and winked at Goccia.

He made a final check that everything in the room was in order and before leaving, he gave Goccia a biscuit as he rubbed her head fondly. "Good girl."

He closed the door quietly and hurried back towards the steps.

"Right, detective sergeant, let's get you out of that uncomfortable position. I want you to grasp the rail with your left hand, good, now I am going to cut the tie, but I want you to continue gripping the rail. Excellent. Now, do the same with the right hand. Snip. Perfect. You may stand up now," he said, as he stepped out of Jennifer's reach.

Jennifer stood, rubbing her wrists and walked to the top of the steps. Rosselli waved her forward with the gun. "That way, towards the open area."

As soon as she reached the large cargo platform, Jennifer stopped. Something had changed; it was not how she remembered it. It was cleaner, tidier, and there were two metal chairs near the edge of the platform overlooking the loading bay. Maybe it was cleaner because the forensic team had been through, but even allowing for that, there was something else. She let her eyes wander around the area. The floor around the storage bins at the rear was definitely clearer than before. She thought she could remember more ropes lying around.

Ignoring Rosselli, who was standing a few feet behind her, she took a step towards the storage bins while looking up at the array of rails above her head. Were they that clean before? She wished she had taken photos as soon as she'd set foot in the area the first time; she would have been able to make a direct comparison. Or at least she would have done if the madman hadn't taken her phone. Wrinkling her nose, she sniffed the air and worked out what was so different. It wasn't the relatively untidy collection of ropes, pulleys, broken packing cases and pallets, it was the smell. Previously there had been an overriding stale, dry mustiness, a sense of neglect and abandonment. That was still present, but woven into it now were other smells, oil particularly. The place smelt more like a car workshop, a place where lubricants were liberally splashed around. Jennifer was certain it had been absent during the earlier searches.

Why? Were the owners of the factory gearing up for a renovation? Were they perhaps intending to remove the remains of the old fittings and sell them for scrap? Getting the overhead rail system working again would make such a job far easier. But the owners had made no mention of this happening. Surely with all the conversations between the SCF and the owners it would have come up.

Puzzled, she turned to face Rosselli.

"Well, where would you like me to go now?"

Rosselli stretched out an arm towards the two chairs near the edge of the platform. He wanted things to be in place when Brooke arrived.

"I want you to sit in one of those. The one on the right. There's a show to watch."

"No!" yelled Jennifer. "You said I could see Trisha. I want to know if she is still alive. Do me the courtesy of telling me that, at least, instead of playing these stupid games."

Sighing, Rosselli looked at his phone to check the progress of Gus's car and decided he would indulge her for a few minutes. He pointed at the bins. "She is very close, detective sergeant."

Jennifer made her way to the rear of the platform area and turned her attention to the storage bins. This time she was in no doubt about things having changed. She could distinctly remember the row of bins along the back wall, but there had been no ropes spread along any of the lids.

She stood in front of the bin with the lid partially obscured by ropes.

"Is she in this box?" she yelled at Rosselli. "Did you kill her and put her in here?"

"Your superintendent? Why do—"

"She's got a name!" snapped Jennifer. "Trisha McVie. She has a name!"

"I apologise, Detective Sergeant Cotton, you are right, the unfortunate lady has a name and yes, her body is in the bin. But while you were right to correct me, you were also wrong. I didn't put her there and neither did I kill her. Why should I possibly want to do that?"

"Then who did kill her?" demanded Jennifer.

When Rosselli shrugged in an exaggerated way that was so characteristic, so stereotypical, the pieces of the puzzle in Jennifer's head began to fall into place. And as they did, a cold fear flooded her body.

"I'm told, and I think it's true," continued Rosselli, oblivious of Jennifer's thoughts, "that she had an accident. That she fell."

Jennifer was only half listening. She was thinking again of when she first saw this man in the Horse and Hounds. He had looked completely different. Had he been in disguise? And he was right, it was the dog, Goccia, that had triggered the memory. Goccia! That was it. An Italian name, and now … an Italian shrug. She had been distracted by his perfect English.

Jennifer fought to keep her voice calm, to maintain an illusion of control she didn't feel, while at the same time feeling stupid for taking so long to work it out.

"Lei è italiano," she said, speaking rapidly, her eyes burning into his. *You are Italian.* It was a statement, not a question.

Rosselli said nothing. He wanted to continue with his plan, to ensure that all blame fell onto Brooke. Which is why he didn't follow his instinct and immediately shoot Jennifer.

"My nationality is irrelevant," he said, answering in English. "Now, I have shown you where your friend is, so will you please do as I ask and move over to the chair? I don't want to keep repeating myself."

Jennifer still didn't move. "It's relevant to me," she continued, the words growled in Italian. "What is an Italian with a gun doing in a derelict factory in the middle of England? How are you connected to Trisha McVie?"

Rosselli straightened slightly. The torrent of fast Italian from Jennifer was unexpected. She had transformed into another person.

He sighed and reverted to his native tongue.

"Signorina, I have no connection to your Trisha McVie and as I told you, no involvement with her death."

"You have every involvement with her death!" shouted Jennifer. "You knew she was hidden here in this box and you did nothing about it. Any decent person would have reported it. An anonymous phone call was all that was needed."

Rosselli was shaking his head. "Signorina," he sighed in exasperation, but Jennifer hadn't finished.

"But you didn't," she continued, "which makes you an accessory. Who was responsible if it wasn't you? Was it Gus Brooke? Why are you protecting him?"

Rosselli held up the hand that wasn't holding the gun.

"Signorina Cotton! Stop these accusations, please. I had, indeed I have, every intention of making sure your authorities know of Detective Brooke's actions. He is a fool and acted badly. He needs to be punished."

Jennifer felt a chill course through her. She had been listening as much to how this man spoke as to what he said. And she had worked it out: he was Sicilian. Which confirmed her earlier thoughts: his presence here meant only one thing. But she daren't let on that she knew. Her only hope was to stall for time in case … in case. In case nothing, she thought. No one knew she was here. She'd misled Derek, promised him she wouldn't enter the factory, and now she was going to suffer the consequences of her stupidity in even being near the place.

Still ignoring Rosselli's instructions, Jennifer turned to the metal storage bin.

"I need to see her; I need to see my friend. It breaks my heart to think she has been dumped here like so much rubbish. She was a warm, kind, intelligent human being with a profound sense of right and wrong, which is why she was such a good police officer. This …" she said, her voice cracking as her arm reached out towards the bin, "this is so … disrespectful. I can't believe that Gus Brooke would do such a thing."

She took a step towards the bin, reaching out for one of the ropes partly covering it.

"Signorina," said Rosselli, "That is not a good idea. It has been many days now. She … she would be—"

Jennifer cut him off with a snort of disdain.

"You forget, signore, I am a police officer. I have seen plenty of bodies. I'm not about to get squeamish or throw up."

She paused, her voice trailing into softness. "I just want to stroke her hair, tell her she was loved. Is that too much to ask?" She tugged angrily at the rope.

Rosselli found himself torn. For the first time in his long career, he felt genuine compassion. Here was a young woman whose dear friend, not a lover but a firm, bonded friend, had been cruelly snatched from her. An image of Giorgio, his lover, flashed across his mind. If Giorgio had been killed and stuffed into a metal box, he would want to see him to say his goodbyes. But … but this young woman was about to die herself, something he strongly suspected she had already worked out. There was no choice in the matter; it was why he was here, why he had been paid a large sum of money. Would seeing the body of her friend change anything?

"There isn't time for this, signorina," he said.

Jennifer had just tossed a rope to the floor and was reaching for another. She stood up straight and turned to Rosselli.

"What do you mean there isn't time?" she said. "Are you expecting company, because I'm not? As I think you are well aware, no one knows I'm here. I'm entirely at your mercy, so what's the hurry?"

As if in answer to Jennifer's question, a ping sounded from Rosselli's phone. He raised his gun towards Jennifer, an instruction to stop what she was doing. He pulled the phone from his pocket and held it up so he could see the screen while still keeping an eye on Jennifer. The alarm had been triggered by the camera focussed on the factory gates. Previously, Jennifer's car had been the only vehicle there; now it had been joined by a second: Gus Brooke's. And it appeared that Brooke had a key to the padlock: the gates were wide open and Rosselli just caught a glimpse of Brooke running along the concrete road leading from the gates to the factory before he disappeared from the camera's field of view.

Rosselli smiled and moved backwards away from the bins towards a large packing crate standing by the wall. Once in its shadow, he would be hidden from the view of anyone crossing the cargo platform.

"As it happens, signorina, you are right. I *am* expecting company."

Chapter Forty-Nine

Two mornings after Sonia's confession to Connie about what she had told the man she knew as Gianpietro Tebaldi, at about the time Rosselli was forcing Jennifer towards the factory, Henry took a call from his agent.

He and Connie were sitting at the computer where Henry was still working on the images of Tebaldi.

As Connie watched Henry's face while he listened to the agent, she became increasingly concerned. There was none of the normal joviality in Henry's eyes, and little more than brief grunts in response to whatever his agent was telling him.

Henry closed the call and turned to Connie, his face now dark with concern.

"Busted flush," he said. "Nothing. Ted has spoken to everyone he can think of in the industry in the UK, the US and here in Italy. There's not a journalist anywhere with the name Gianpietro Tebaldi that anyone's ever heard of. He's not registered with any journalists' union or association, nothing. Whoever that man was, he wasn't a journalist."

"So if he's not an art dealer, not a journalist, who the hell is he?"

"I don't know, but I'm convinced there's something about his face, something familiar. I've tried everything I know on Photoshop but so far, it hasn't helped."

"Where do you think you've seen him?"

"God knows. Locally, maybe. I don't know."

Henry drummed his fingers on the desktop. Connie leaned forward and took his hand.

"I think we should run this through Massimo Felice," she said. "I should like his take on it."

"Good idea," said Henry, picking up his phone from where he had put it on the desk. "I'll call him now."

After the briefest of preambles, once he had heard of their progress so far and the elimination of the possibility of Tebaldi being a journalist, the head of Rome's Art Fraud Squad went on full alert. While Connie explained the details, Henry screen-grabbed the enhanced images of Tebaldi's face and emailed them directly to Felice.

Both sides of the conversation were on speakerphone and as soon as Felice called up the images, he could be heard yelling for several of his squad to come into his office.

Listening to the background babble of voices and exclamations, Henry could imagine a number of Felice's officers gathered around his desk offering their opinions. He was both encouraged and worried to hear, "Madonna, non lo credo," — *I don't believe it* — and a few similar expressions of surprise and concern.

Finally, as the babble subsided, Felice's voice boomed through the speakerphone.

"Henry. Connie. This is both amazing and very worrying. We have been after this man for a long time, but he is extremely cunning and manages to remain invisible. His name is Cosimo Graziano Rosselli. He is an assassin for the mafia in its various manifestations, but only for very exclusive, high-cost cases. His reputation is interesting. He's not the average cold-hearted killer, a man without emotion or connection to the human race. This man prides himself in killing his victims painlessly if at all possible, and making their deaths look either like an accident or the work of someone else."

"Shades of Olivia Freneton," said Henry. "The framing part,

that is. Tell me, Massimo, if you know so much about him, how come he's not in prison."

"It's all speculation and rumour. There has never been any evidence against him and of course he's protected by the mafia which means at a certain level, many public officials will leave him alone too. He is known melodramatically in mafia circles as The Shadow, like the baddie in some trashy novel from the 1950s. But it does reflect what he is like. He operates under the radar, is never seen anywhere near the scenes of his killings and there are always many alibis. We think he uses disguises a lot to get close to and gather information on his targets. He is known to use a dog as a prop to make himself seem harmless."

"What sort of dog!" yelled both Connie and Henry together as they remembered the man in Bar Fulvia.

"A pug," replied Felice, surprised at the forcefulness of their response.

"We've seen him, I'm sure of it," said Henry, and proceeded to fill in the details for Felice.

"So, he was focussing on you, gathering information."

"Listened to music all the time," added Connie. "On an iPod."

"Probably a disguised amplification device," commented Felice. "He would have been tuning into your conversations. From the information about the photographs, it looks as if he was trying to identify Jennifer. He's probably been recruited by the Cambronis. Or Ettore Cambroni, at least. The old man died in prison a few weeks ago. Although I say it myself, we did a good job of erasing all traces of Ginevra Mancini and her connection with Jennifer. He would have come up against a brick wall with that, so perhaps he tried another way. Once he found out about Jennifer's connection to you, Henry, or perhaps Connie's connection to the gallery, he will have decided to go down that route."

"We must contact Jennifer immediately," said Henry.

"How long ago was it that he was in your area bewitching your gullible young lady?" asked Felice.

"At least two months, maybe longer, wasn't it, Connie?" said Henry.

"Yes," replied Connie, "it was about that long ago we saw the man with the pug in the bar. But that man was far older than the one in the photo."

"Of course!" exclaimed Henry. "He was in disguise. That's what was familiar about him. The overall head and body shape. God, I'm so stupid! I'm an actor; you'd think I would have noticed something. I'll do some more work on the computer."

"Two months?" repeated Felice, his tone serious. "We know where this man lives, we're just powerless to do anything about him. I'll get some eyes out, see if he's still here. We might be able to hassle him, worry him enough to make him back off."

"And if you can't find him?" asked Connie.

"Then Jennifer needs protecting."

"In that case, Massimo," said Henry, "we should take action right away. I'm calling Jennifer now."

After repeated attempts to speak to Jennifer, Henry called Derek, who was still waiting for his turn in court. He answered immediately.

"Derek," said Henry. "At last. Have you any idea where Jennifer is? I've been trying to get hold of her and there's no answer."

"She should be at home by now. It's late afternoon and … why? Is something wrong?"

"Don't know, but there could be. Let me explain."

Henry hurriedly summarised what had happened with Sonia two days previously and the result of their conversation with Felice.

"Christ!" exclaimed Derek. "An assassin! She has been following up hunches about Trisha's disappearance. She was going to snoop around Gus Brooke's cottage, just the outside, she promised, and then the factory. Again she said she would only … oh, shit! I've just remembered. There was some bloke in the pub opposite the SCF. One evening after work. A couple of weeks ago. He had a dog with him, a pug with what Jen explained was an Italian name. Let me think. Yes, some wag made a play on the name in English."

"What was it?" asked Henry.

"Gotcha," said Derek.

"Goccia," repeated Henry. "A drop. It would be suitable for a little pug."

"Yes," replied Derek, his voice barely more than a whisper. He was no longer interested in the dog.

"Listen, Henry, I think I know where she is. She's inside that bloody factory. I'll call you back."

Chapter Fifty

Gus Brooke ran cautiously across the factory yard, not wanting to announce his arrival. He didn't know what to expect, but he wanted to maintain the element of surprise.

He stopped at the foot of the main stairs to the upper floor and listened, but he could hear nothing. Treading lightly, he ran up the stairs, stopping at the top to listen again. Nothing. Where the hell was Rosselli? Had he walked into a trap?

Listening for any sound while his eyes swept the area ahead of him, Gus edged slowly forward along the short corridor leading to the large cargo platform. As he came level with the entrance, he saw Jennifer standing by the metal storage bins along the rear wall. She was holding a length of rope.

"Shit!" he muttered through clenched teeth. What was she doing? Waiting for him? She certainly wasn't moving. He needed to take decisive action, protect his back.

His jaw set, he strode forward, his eyes fixed on Jennifer.

"What the hell's going on, sarge?" he said, as he walked into the cargo area.

"You tell me, Detective Constable Brooke," replied Jennifer. "How come you're here? Has the boss ordered a new search of the place? Do we have more troops on the way?"

"I, er, I was going to ask you the same thing, sarge."

"Which one of those were you going to ask me, detective constable?"

Brooke ignored her questions and instead asked one of his own.

"Why are *you* here? Thyme said you were off today."

"I was, but curiosity got the better of me. After mulling over all the possibilities and impossibilities and getting nowhere, I decided to take a look at the improbabilities."

"I don't understand,"

"That doesn't surprise me. And neither does that fact that you're standing here, trying to appear the picture of innocence when you know full well that Trisha McVie's body is lying in the bin behind me."

"What? I don't know what you're talking about. Have you seen the body? How do you know it's there?"

"Because I told her, Detective Brooke," said Rosselli, stepping out of the shadows.

Gus jumped in shock as he whirled around to face Rosselli.

"You bastard!" he yelled. "You said you'd—"

"She had already worked it out," snapped Rosselli, holding up his hand. "I had no need to tell her anything."

He waved the gun in Jennifer's direction.

"Go and stand next to your sergeant, and Gus, remove your phone from your pocket and toss it over to me."

When Gus didn't move, Rosselli fired a shot that whistled past him.

"Do it!" growled the assassin.

As the phone hit the floor in front of him, Rosselli nodded. "Thank you."

He picked up the phone, switched it off and tossed it aside.

"Now, I think it's about time we moved on to the next stage of the day's proceedings," said Rosselli as he glanced at the images from the CCTV cameras on his phone. "I want you both to walk over to those chairs and sit down. The detective sergeant on the right, and you, Detective Brooke, on the left. And please, both of you, do not even think about diving off in different directions and then trying to rush me. I can assure you that if you were to do that, you would both be dead before you'd taken more than half a step."

"Signore," said Jennifer, "have you forgotten what we were talking about before Brooke turned up? I should still like to see my friend's body."

"Jennifer," said Brooke, "I really don—"

"Don't you dare called me by my first name, Detective Constable Brooke," snapped Jennifer. "You lying, duplicitous bastard!"

Turning her back to him, Jennifer fixed her eyes on Rosselli. "Well?"

Rosselli's eyes flickered back and forth between his two captives as he made a decision.

"You, detective," he sighed, waving the gun at Brooke, "clear the rest of the ropes from the top of the bin behind you, lift the lid and pull aside enough of the ropes hiding the superintendent for your sergeant to see her head. You, detective sergeant, stand to one side of the bin."

Realising the futility of resisting, Brooke turned and pulled the remaining ropes from the lid and with great hesitation in view of the smell he was expecting, he opened the bin. Jennifer glanced to her side but could see nothing yet of Trisha's body.

Groaning with reluctance, Brooke leaned into the bin and hauled at the ropes. After tossing a number of them aside, he stood back, the sweat pouring from him.

"Say what you want to say to your friend, signorina," said Rosselli in Italian. "But make it quick."

Taking a deep breath, her mouth quivering with emotion, Jennifer turned and looked into the bin. When she saw Trisha's battered, lifeless face, she felt her legs start to give way beneath her. Gus Brooke was watching and automatically took her elbow to steady her.

She glared at him but didn't resist.

"I'm not all bastard," he muttered.

"But you're responsible for this."

Gus shook his head. "It was all a terrible accident. She fell in my bathroom. I was asleep in bed. I—"

Jennifer held up a hand to stop him. She didn't want to hear any more.

Turning her attention to her friend's body and using one hand to steady herself further on the edge of the bin, Jennifer leaned over and gently stroked Trisha's hair.

"I don't know that I'm going to be in much of a position to change any of this, Trish," she whispered, her voice so quiet that neither of the men could hear her. "I'll do my best, but I have a sneaky suspicion that wanker with the gun has plans for me to join you. Either way, I want you to know that you were the bestest piss-artist friend in all the world and I'll never forget you."

She kissed her fingers and pressed them against Trisha's cold forehead. "Love you," she said.

She stood up straight and took a step backwards. "Close the lid," she said to Brooke.

As Brooke did as she instructed, Jennifer stole a look at his face. The cocky, self-assured womaniser was nowhere to be seen. He had aged ten years in as many minutes, his features sagging, his eyes hollow, but still she found it hard to have any sympathy for him, not when Trisha McVie was lying in the bin beside them.

She turned towards Rosselli. "Thank you, signore," she said.

"Prego," replied Rosselli. *You're welcome.*

With Rosselli still pointing the gun at them, Jennifer and Brooke walked away from the bins towards the open edge of the platform area and the two metal chairs. Apart from being sure she was going to be shot, Jennifer couldn't work out the man's plans. It was clear to her now that he was a mafia hit man, an assassin, and that she was his target. Why was he taking so long about it? And what role, apart from collateral damage, did Gus Brooke play in the proceedings?

"I should like you both to sit in the chairs as I instructed just now," said Rosselli. "You will have ringside seats for the show I've set up for you."

Jennifer looked ahead, wondering if he was intending to make them jump or whether to expect a bullet in the back of the head. She estimated the drop into the loading bay was about five metres.

Unlikely to be fatal, but the injuries could be bad. So it was probably a bullet.

Rosselli stood to one side, offering them no chance of making a grab at him. Jennifer paused and turned to him.

"You didn't answer my question, signore," she said, reverting to Italian again.

"Question?"

"Who are you? Or more specifically, what is your name? It can surely do you no harm to tell me that. Not now."

Rosselli narrowed his eyes. Jennifer Cotton was a brave young woman. He was pleased that even though she knew he was going to kill her, there would still be the element of surprise. She wouldn't see or hear it coming. She would simply stop existing.

He took a deep breath. This was new territory for him. "Rosselli," he said, finally, his accent reverting to the strong Sicilian of his youth. "Cosimo Graziano Rosselli."

Jennifer nodded and walked on.

"Please sit down and wait," called Rosselli as they reached the chairs. "The show will begin in a moment. Keep your eyes on the wall opposite."

He watched as they sat down, almost surprised by their obedience. But sitting wasn't enough.

"Detective Brooke," he called. "Before you get too comfortable, on the floor to your left are some plastic ties. Be so kind as to take two of them and secure the detective sergeant's wrists to the chair arms."

When Brooke hesitated, Rosselli took several steps towards him. "Now, detective!" he commanded.

Gus stood and reached for the ties. Selecting two, he followed Rosselli's instructions, although he carefully didn't tighten the ties as far as possible, not wanting to hurt Jennifer.

But Rosselli was onto him. "Tighter!" he insisted, watching as Gus complied.

"Good," he said. "Now sit again and secure your own right wrist to the chair arm."

Sighing angrily, Gus did as he was told.

"Excellent," said Rosselli as he moved closer.

"Hmm, I think yours could be a little tighter too, Gus," he added as he peered at the tie. "Pull on the end, please. That's right. Now, keep your other wrist firmly on the chair arm while I secure it too."

He looped a plastic tie around Gus's left wrist and pulled it tight.

"Good, I think we're ready."

The appeal of the rail and hoist system to Rosselli was that it could so easily be modified for his purpose. It comprised two pairs of rails running in parallel from the rear of the cargo platform to the void over the loading bay, on which hoists ran on wheels on one pair of rails or the other. Crates of goods could be hung from the hoists for lowering into the loading bay. The rails were inclined at a few degrees from the horizontal to allow the hoists to roll from one end to the other under the pull of gravity.

Given the length of the rails was some twenty metres, this arrangement would be dangerous without something to brake the hoists carrying the goods since over that distance they would pick up substantial speed. Hence the designers had included rubber pads to slow the hoists on their journey every two metres to ensure the rolling hoists would never be moving too fast.

But with time and neglect, the pads had deteriorated, making them easy for Rosselli to remove. Now, once a hoist was allowed to run unchecked the full length of a rail, the angle of tilt was such that it would be rolling at more than twenty kilometres an hour before being stopped by the substantial buffers at the far end, more than enough to cause instantly fatal injuries to any head that happened to be in the way. Rosselli had chosen two old and rusty metal blocks he'd found lying in the cargo area as the heavy loads to hang from the hoists. Both had jagged projections from their surfaces that would make them even more effective.

Releasing either of the two loads was a matter of pressing one or other of two buttons on a remote control. Each would trigger a small battery-powered heater aligned under a length of nylon fishing line that held its load in place. Once the line had melted, which would happen three seconds after the remote button was pressed, the load would be on its way from the rear of the cargo area towards the loading bay.

The only problem with the loads accelerating along the rails was that in spite of extensive cleaning, oiling and greasing, they weren't completely silent. There was still an underlying rumble from the wheels that would forewarn his victims. In the end, the solution was simple: compensating noise. Rosselli hated any form of pop music; he saw it as trite, repetitive and often painfully noisy. But for his purposes today, noisy was good. With one hundred and fifteen decibels blasting from large, battery-powered bluetooth speakers he had positioned only metres from where they were sitting, neither Jennifer Cotton nor Gus Brooke would hear the rumble of pulleys on rails. And the final distraction? A light show from a portable projector of abstract flashing lights pulsing in time with the dreadful music.

Rosselli made one final check of his equipment before pressing a button on a second remote control. The projector burst into life and a mesmerising montage of abstract and semi-abstract images flooded the wall opposite the platform. He saw his two victims' heads lift as the images distracted them. Seconds later, the relative silence of the factory buildings was shattered by the jarring scream of heavy metal music, chosen deliberately for its atonality and acoustic assault. Rosselli smiled as he saw the pair twitch as if they had been electrocuted.

He waited ten seconds for the noise to torture their ears before cranking up the volume to maximum. Five seconds more and he hit one of the buttons on the main remote control to release the first of the hoists.

Gus Brooke was confused. He had fallen for Rosselli's story and was resigned to the fact that for the rest of his working life he would be an informer to organised crime. But at least he would be alive, and he would have a wife and a home. He wouldn't be in prison for the way he had handled Trisha McVie's death.

The involvement of Jennifer Cotton had taken him by surprise. When Rosselli had called that morning to summon him to the factory, hearing Cotton's name blindsided him. But it turned out she knew all about him and blamed him for the death of McVie. Which made her in many ways a more dangerous adversary than Rosselli: he was a crook while she was a no-nonsense honest cop.

And now Rosselli intended to kill her, that much was obvious, even though they seemed to have a rapport going on in Italian.

So why was Rosselli going through this whole pantomime of sitting them down facing across the loading bay? And now, out of nowhere there was a disorienting light show, with enough flashing to bring on an epileptic fit. And if that wasn't enough, the worst music he had ever heard, a cacophony that could hardly be called music, was blasting his ears from speakers close to where he was sitting. He winced, the noise was physically painful, and just as he thought he could cope, it became louder.

He dropped his head and tried to push his left ear against his shoulder in an attempt to block out the sound. As he did, there was something else, a low frequency vibration he could feel through the chair. Was the floor about to collapse? He twisted in his chair. Jennifer was hunched over, her eyes screwed shut. Forcing his body further round, Gus glanced backwards and in the glare of the projector light saw a large metal block hanging from a hoist racing towards them.

Without a second thought he pushed his feet hard against the floor and launched himself sideways, screaming Jennifer's name as he did.

Chapter Fifty-One

Already disoriented by the mind-splitting cacophony blasting from the speakers, Jennifer hardly registered her name being screamed before she found herself hurtling sideways. A split second before, as Gus Brooke collided with her, there had been a heavy thud of metal on bone and blood had spattered onto Jennifer's face and upper body.

Unable to control how she fell, Jennifer and the chair to which she was tethered skidded across the platform until she came to rest on her side.

She looked up, but there was no sign of Gus Brooke or the chair he had been sitting on.

Without warning, the flashing from the light show vanished and the unbearable assault of jarring music ceased, a vacuum of silence engulfing the factory. As the residual echoes in her ears faded, Jennifer slowly became aware of a different sound coming from elsewhere in the building, the sound of a dog barking.

Registering the metallic taste of blood in her mouth, Jennifer spat in disgust as she worked out the blood wasn't hers. She had no idea what had happened, but it seemed that Gus Brooke had been hit by something large and heavy, something intended for her.

She twisted her head to look up, expecting to see Rosselli standing there with a large weapon in his hand, something like a baseball bat. But he wasn't; he was standing twenty feet away looking angry, the Glock still in his right hand pointing at the ground.

"What the hell just happened, Rosselli?" growled Jennifer.

Rosselli's eyes focussed on her. "The young detective saved your life and in doing so, sacrificed his own."

"Yes, but what happened? What did you hit him with?"

Rosselli ignored her question and walked over to the edge of the platform. As he peered down into the loading bay, he nodded his head slowly.

"Yes," he said. "If the block didn't kill him, the fall did."

"Block?" yelled Jennifer. "What block?"

Rosselli turned to look down at her. "The metal block that was intended for you. It's a pity; it's such a painless and unexpected way to go."

"I don't understand, but since I'm still alive for the present, would you please stand this chair up so I haven't got my face in the dirt?"

Rosselli lay the two remote controls he was holding on the ground behind him, bent over to grab the chair back and yanked the chair and Jennifer with it into an upright position.

"I tried to make it comfortable for you, detective sergeant, an instant death, like being shot in the back of the head."

"So why not just shoot me in the back of the head? Why set up this ridiculous performance?"

Rosselli weighed the gun he was still holding in his hand. "It may have to come to that, although I'd still rather not. You see, it's always easier for me if someone else gets the blame."

Jennifer was nodding as she worked out the sequence of events. "Now I understand. You caught Gus in the act, found out his connection with Trisha's death and how he was trying his hardest to worm his way out of it."

"More or less, detective sergeant. It was such ungentlemanly behaviour. It showed no respect for your poor colleague."

"So you decided he should pay?"

"I decided he should not get away with it, yes. The full sequence of events together with the evidence will be made available to your colleagues, and, of course, to his wife."

"Judge and jury," said Jennifer, not even trying to hide her disdain. "And since he would be dead, he'd have no chance to explain his actions, to defend himself."

"I am surprised, signorina, you sound almost sorry for him."

"On the contrary, I think the way he behaved was despicable, but I don't see why he had to die."

"He wasn't supposed to, not at this point."

Jennifer was staring at the man's eyes, trying to follow his reasoning.

"Yes, I see now. You wanted to have him blamed for my death as well as Trisha's. The story would be something like: after realising I had worked out what had happened, he knew I wouldn't hesitate in having him arrested, so he decided to kill me too. You would have been invisible in the whole thing."

"Brava, signorina! You have a good mind. But there is no 'would have' in it, I will remain invisible. What will be found along with your superintendent's body will be Detective Brooke's and—"

"Mine," interrupted Jennifer. She hesitated as the fear she was feeling began to overtake her self-control. She knew she had to keep talking, just in case someone was on the way. She didn't see why they should be; she had well and truly screwed-up, but it was her only chance.

"Do you honestly believe you haven't left evidence of your presence here? Our forensic people are excellent; they will find something."

Rosselli shrugged. "What if they do? What are they going to compare it with? I exist on none of your databases, and these buildings have been overrun with your police officers all looking for the superintendent. I suspect anything I have left will simply merge into the background. White noise. The presence of a third party won't occur to them since they will be far too angry with their own dead detective constable and too eager to blame everything on him. I think I am safe."

Jennifer knew he was right. Why should anyone suspect that someone apart from her and Brooke had been at the factory? If Rosselli set up things carefully, Gus's death could be made to look accidental, a slip-up when he was intent on killing Jennifer. Rosselli could easily put Gus's fingerprints on the buttons of the remote control she'd seen him place on the ground; it would look like he released another load by mistake. She knew there was another; she had looked along the rails and seen it lined up and waiting. All Rosselli had to do now was to reposition her and the chair in its path.

"You seem to have thought of everything, Signor Rosselli," she said in Italian. "You are clearly very professional in what you do."

Rosselli tilted his head in appreciation of the flattery. "I am the best there is, signorina," he said. As far as he was concerned it was a statement of fact; modesty was irrelevant.

Jennifer nodded her head. "Tell me," she said, still trying to stall for time. "What am I worth?"

Rosselli frowned, not understanding the significance of her question. "Are you making me an offer, trying to outbid my client?" he replied, amused at the idea.

Jennifer rolled her eyes. "As if …" she said. "No, I meant, what did you get paid? From what you say, you are an assassin and from your accent, you must work for one or more of the Italian mobs. If you are the best, you would expect a high fee. I just wondered how much I cost your client."

Rosselli laughed. "A lot of money, signorina. My client paid me a lot of money."

"And your client was who? Let me see … Maurizio Cambroni is dying or perhaps even dead by now, although he might have ordered it. I'm guessing Ettore Cambroni. Am I right?"

Rosselli didn't answer. He had decided it was time. Goccia was still barking in the distance and he wanted to go to her, calm her down. Besides, he was finding the conversation difficult. It broke all his rules. He never engaged with the target, never got close, and this exchange with Jennifer Cotton reminded him why. He liked her. She was brave, she was clever and she wasn't going to capitulate to him. Not like the spineless Gus Brooke who had been putty in his hands. No, although she knew exactly what was coming, he would make it quick and she would still feel nothing.

He picked up one of the two remote controls and punched the buttons on its panel. Immediately the factory space was filled with the same deafening discordant cacophony of sound he had played earlier. He saw Jennifer flinch at the onslaught to her ears as the lights flashed along with the noise.

Rosselli tossed the remote control to the floor and grabbed the back of the chair to which Jennifer was tethered, dragging it across the platform to align with the path of the second rust-encrusted hoist and block. Not wanting to see the fear that he was sure would be in her eyes, he remained behind and slightly to her left as he reached down for the second remote control.

Part Seven

GOCCIA

Chapter Fifty-Two

In the storeroom where she'd been left with one meagre biscuit, the normally patient and unflappable Goccia was pacing the floor in canine anguish.

Several minutes earlier, wrenched violently from her slumbers by the painful bombardment of sound pulsating through the entire factory buildings when Rosselli switched on the discordant music, she had leapt in fear from her blanket, her eyes wild. The noise battering her hypersensitive ears was inflicting physical pain, as terrifying as it was disorienting.

She had barked frantically, bouncing around the room in an attempt to distance herself from the attack, while at the same time, she feared for her master. She was desperate to find him, to be reassured by him; she needed his gentle, human contact.

She was still barking when the sound abruptly stopped, but she kept barking and kept bouncing. She wasn't stupid; she knew about doors. She had opened them in the past. Not without difficulty, but with persistence, she had succeeded. And this door had a handle rather than a round knob.

However, try as she may, even though she managed to pull on the handle several times in her attempts, her efforts were insufficient; the door remained closed.

Although exhausted with the effort, the agitated Goccia kept pacing. Up and down, up and down, her eyes hardly leaving the door handle, barking at it with every pass.

She was starting to flag when the onslaught of sound started again, as loud if not louder than the first time.

With a screech of terror as she jumped in shock at the renewed attack on her senses, her ears flattened and her gums receded to bare her teeth. She had to get away. Throwing herself at the door, she groped furiously at the handle, trying to grab it in her mouth or catch it with her feet.

On her third crazed attempt, she succeeded. The door flew open. With the metal barrier of the door removed, the wall of sound was now even louder, but nothing short of annihilation would have daunted the pug's determination. She raced along the corridor from the storeroom, her nose following her master's smell as if drawn along by an invisible line.

When the corridor opened onto the wide platform, her eyes fell immediately onto Rosselli. She skidded to a halt, barking as she saw him drag a chair with a person in it across the wooden floor. But the noise was too intense; her bark, although loud, couldn't compete.

She could smell blood, which disturbed her. Something was wrong; she had to help her master.

Bounding across the platform just as Rosselli finished positioning the chair, she saw him half turn and reach out for something lying on the floor. His hand had almost found it when the pug racing towards him came into his peripheral vision. He paused in shock.

"Goccia! How did you get out?"

Extending his arms towards his beloved dog, Rosselli's immediate thoughts were that someone had opened the storeroom door and released her. Probably taken by surprise to find a dog, whoever it was would have turned to watch her bound off in the direction of the platform. But there was no doubt in his mind that whoever it was would soon recover their equilibrium and there was also no doubt in his mind who the person, or worse, persons might be. The police.

Thinking rapidly through his alternatives as Goccia bounced in excitement in front of him, Rosselli focussed his eyes on the area around the entrance from the corridor. He could see no movement, but if they were good, they would be carefully but rapidly working their way along the corridor, one covering the other as they alternated their advance, any noise they made totally masked by the barrage of sound coming from the speakers.

He reached for the sound-and-light-show remote control only inches from Goccia's paws. The dog bent her head to his hand, licked it and playfully jumped backwards, delighted to have found her master once more. After picking up the remote control, Rosselli straightened up, feeling for the buttons as he once again looked towards the corridor, the Glock still in his hand ready to shoot in an instant. Focussed as he was, he didn't notice that in jumping backwards, Goccia's rear paws landed on the other remote control that was still lying on the floor, her broad pads depressing both buttons.

The first button of the pair had already done its work in dispatching the hoist with the metal block that had shattered Gus Brooke's skull, but the other was ready for action.

Twenty metres from where Rosselli was standing, the metal coil of a tiny heater started to glow, softening and finally melting the taut nylon line running two millimetres above it. As the line snapped apart, the wheels of the trolley bearing the load of the second hoist began to roll.

With his eyes fixed on the entrance from the corridor, Rosselli's fingers pressed the remote control buttons to stop the deafening noise and switch off the light show. In the split second before the hoist and its heavy load reached him, the assassin heard the rumble of wheels on rails. His head turned sharply to his right, his eyes looking upwards in the direction of the sound. The same split second was long enough for him to work out what had happened but not long enough for him to complete his final cry.

"Gocc—"

Resigned to her fate in the hands of a professional assassin, Jennifer had offered no resistance when Rosselli had yanked the chair to which she was tethered across the platform into the exact place for the remaining block to hit her. She slumped in the chair, hoping he might have miscalculated the height, hoping the speeding load would fly past above her head. But she knew it wouldn't; this man wasn't an idiot. He had every last detail accounted for and factored in. It would smash into her head with the same bone-crushing efficiency that had killed Gus Brooke. And with the awful noise, she wouldn't hear it coming.

A kaleidoscope of emotions flashed through her brain, but the dominant one was regret that she had let Derek down. She had gone out on a limb and paid the price. He would never know that she was about to call in reinforcements; he wouldn't know that Rosselli had caught her and forced her into the factory. He would simply think she had been her normal impetuous self, that she had felt compelled to risk everything in the hope of finding Trisha alive, that in her reckoning every second wasted could have been crucial to Trisha's survival.

What he would eventually know was that the risks he thought Jennifer had taken were a waste of time. Trisha had been dead for days, dead since the night of her disappearance, dead since a stupid, avoidable accident had snatched away her life, dead and dumped like so much garbage by an insensitive man in fear for his own survival.

She felt a tear roll down her cheek and she angrily shook her head. As she did, on the edge of her vision she saw Rosselli bend to one side. He was on her left and far closer than she thought. She twisted her head farther to her left and now in the corner of her eye she saw a flash of the excited form of Goccia jumping in front of Rosselli.

This made no sense. Rosselli had shut the dog away somewhere. Had she escaped? Something had gone wrong which meant that not everything was going to plan. She already knew what was about to happen if she remained still, but if Rosselli was distracted, she might be able to change that.

Without warning, the discordant cacophony ceased and the lights stopped flashing.

Hunkering down as far as she could in the chair, Jennifer shifted her weight to the right and pushed as hard as she could against her feet, launching herself sideways away from Rosselli.

As the metal block flashed past only millimetres from her head, she heard a strangled cry that sounded like it could be 'Goccia!' interrupted by the sickening thud of metal on bone. For the second time in a few minutes, a thick spray of blood spattered onto her face and body.

The eerie silence that followed Jennifer and the chair skidding to a halt on the wooden platform was quickly shattered by two bewildered barks. From her almost upside down position, Jennifer turned her head awkwardly towards the sound and saw Goccia standing on the edge of the platform looking plaintively down to the loading bay below. There was another bark as Goccia sat herself down, followed by mournful whimpering, the sound horribly similar to the crying of a distressed child.

"Goccia!" called Jennifer. "Goccia! Good girl. Come here. It's all right, no one's going to hurt you; you're safe now."

The pug turned its head towards her. Not many people apart from her master addressed her by name. But this person had and her voice was soft and kind.

She looked back down at the twisted form of her master lying half on top of another man in the loading bay below. Instinctively she understood that although there was something terribly wrong, there was nothing she could do. Standing up, she let out a final long, mournful whimper, took a last look down and walked sadly over to Jennifer.

Try as she may, Jennifer couldn't persuade Goccia to come any closer than a couple of feet. Initially, as the pug approached her, she thought the dog would come right up close and perhaps even lick her face. But then she remembered she was covered in blood, its harsh smell overlaid with the sweat of fear that would have soaked into her clothing and now be confusing the dog's senses. But the dog made no attempt to run away. Instead she sat and stared sadly into Jennifer's eyes while Jennifer talked quietly to her.

"We've got something of a problem, Goccia," she said. "I can't really move very far."

The pug looked at her suspiciously, not understanding.

"Of course," said Jennifer and switched to Italian. "Your owner spoke to you in Italian all the time, didn't he?"

The dog's expression changed, her ears lifting slightly as she recognised the sound of the language, if not the words, and was calmed by it.

"You see," explained Jennifer as she continued in Italian, "although my legs aren't tethered to this damn chair, I'm attached to it in such an awkward position that they might as well be. I've tried standing up and the rest of the chair just gets in the way. I might, with some effort, get to an upright position, but even if I manage to move around a bit, there's no way I'd be able to get down those stone stairs. I'd probably fall and break my neck."

Goccia continued to stare at her, but gradually, now she no longer felt threatened, the tiredness brought on by her efforts to escape overtook her and her eyes closed.

"It's all right for you, Goccia, my friend, you think I'm going to save you, but to do that, I've got to save myself. You see, no one knows we're here."

Feeling ridiculous to be lying upside down on the ground, constrained by a chair and talking in Italian to a sleepy dog, Jennifer exhaled angrily.

"Bugger it, I'm going to get this thing upright."

It was easier said than done, but after several minutes of easing herself along the floor away from the danger of falling over the edge of the platform, she arrived at a wall she could push against. She squirmed and wriggled the chair around until finally it was standing upright.

She slumped in it, tired from the effort.

Looking down at her wrists, which were chafed from the continual rubbing of the tight plastic ties against her skin as she was manoeuvring the chair, she pulled a face at Goccia, who had moved with her and was now stretched out at her feet.

"I'm going to have to work on these things with my teeth," she said, nodding towards the ties. "It's the only way I can think of to get free. I'm afraid it will take a while."

To reach the ties with her mouth involved bending over awkwardly, making progress painfully slow. Jennifer had no idea how long she had been slowly and laboriously filing at the tie on her right wrist with her teeth, but it wasn't until Goccia suddenly sat up and barked that she noticed the daylight was starting to fade.

"What is it, Goccia? What can you …"

Then she too heard it, heard a siren, two sirens, and ahead of them, far closer, she heard the sound of boots running on gravel and of several people pounding up the stairs, followed by shouted, insistent commands.

"Armed police! Put down your weapons at once!"

Chapter Fifty-Three

After three days of intensive debriefing that included several sessions with a police force psychologist, Jennifer was exhausted. On their drive to London the following Friday afternoon to meet up with Henry and Connie at Henry's Hampstead house, Derek had let her sleep.

Henry and Connie greeted them at the door.

"I'm not sure you should be allowed out on your own," said Henry as he gathered Jennifer into his arms, his voice breaking with emotion. "We were far too slow to make the connections. Thinking about what nearly happened is the stuff of nightmares that will haunt me for as long as I live."

Jennifer hugged him and then Connie before turning and bending to pick up the small pug now sitting patiently behind her.

"Yes, I have this young lady to thank for everything," she said. "Her timing on pressing the buttons on the remote control was perfect."

"Goccia the superstar," said Henry, squeezing the wrinkled folds of skin on Goccia's head.

Goccia looked up at him, suspicious at first, but her finely tuned instincts quickly told her she was in the company of yet another friend. She had made many over the last few days and was rather overwhelmed by all the attention.

"Let's go inside," said Connie. "If you are hungry after your journey, there's plenty of yummy food along with tea and coffee, and for later we have Henry's finest bubbly to toast Goccia."

As they turned to head indoors, there was a cry from the gate to the street. "Carissima!"

Jennifer turned, a warm smile spreading across her face. She passed Goccia to Derek and held out her arms to greet Sofie Lukina, who was running towards her.

"Jennifer, I can't tell you how relieved I am to see you. You poor thing; this nightmare has been awful. As soon as I heard about Trisha, I wanted to take leave and join the search with you. But Paul said there were more than enough capable hands on the job. He also said he would act as liaison with Trisha's squad in the Met for updates and insisted I didn't pester you."

"I know," said Jennifer, "but Paul's version when I spoke to him briefly yesterday in between one grilling and another was that he'd had to tie you to your desk to keep you there."

"Not too far from the truth," laughed Sofie, squeezing her friend again before turning to Goccia.

"So this is the little heroine. Will she be getting a police bravery award?"

"Several, according to Hawkins," said Derek. "We're thinking of hanging them all from her collar."

"Wow!" exclaimed Derek as he lowered himself into one of the deep sofas in Henry's sitting room, his eyes soaking up the huge array of edible goodies Connie had ordered from Fortnum and Mason which were now occupying every inch of the coffee table in front of him. "This looks amazing."

"Tuck in," laughed Connie, "just as long as you tell us what you can about developments this week."

"We can tell you everything," said Jennifer as she reached for a slice of fruit cake. "We're all involved and we know whatever we say won't go beyond these walls."

"What have you managed to piece together," asked Henry. "How did Gus Brooke get mixed up with Rosselli, a mafia assassin?"

Jennifer smiled wistfully. "By chance, we think. We know that Rosselli had been recruited to kill me. He told me as much himself, although he wouldn't say how much he'd been paid. I'm actually quite peeved by that.

"When we saw him in the Horse and Hounds, he was searching for me, probably plotting how he would bump me off. We think his encounter with Gus was pure chance, that he was following us on the day Trisha disappeared and somehow got wind of Gus being involved.

"According to Massimo Felice, Rosselli liked to set up elaborate plans for disposing of his targets so the deaths either looked like an accident or like someone else was to blame. Discovering the factory, which he must have checked out, and with Gus dumping Trisha's body there, he developed a plan to kill me and have Gus blamed.

"We know from a whole host of photos on his phone and computer that Rosselli discovered exactly what went on with Gus and Trisha and then used the information to blackmail Gus. He probably intended to persuade Gus into luring me to the factory, but in the end he didn't need to since I turned up snooping around the fence.

"There were surveillance recordings on Rosselli's phone from a bunch of sophisticated cameras he'd placed in the factory buildings. He was staying only a few minutes' drive away, probably spotted me on the video feed and hotfooted it to intercept me, summoning Gus as he did.

"We think he intended to bump off Gus with the hoist-and-block-railway arrangement, making it look as if Gus had accidentally triggered the load, much like what actually happened to Rosselli himself. He hadn't accounted for Goccia escaping and getting in his way."

"You're sure it was Gus who met Trisha on the road?" asked Connie.

Jennifer nodded. "Yes. As well as all Rosselli's photos, forensics have found a load of evidence at the cottage. There were Trisha's hairs in a brush in the downstairs bathroom and in the shower drains of two bathrooms that match not only in DNA but in the colour she'd had applied the afternoon she drove up to Nottingham. It was a rather stylish ash blonde. Probably couldn't wait to see the surprise on my face when she walked in with it.

"There were also Trisha's fingerprints and DNA on a perfume bottle in the downstairs bathroom. On top of all that, there were fresh body fluid stains on the underside of the mattress in the master bedroom, mixtures of Gus's and Trisha's DNA."

"Underside?" questioned Sofie.

"Gus must have turned the mattress when he cleaned up," said Jennifer, "hoping forensics wouldn't think of looking there."

"I wonder what would have happened if Rosselli hadn't come along," said Sofie. "Do you think Brooke would have got away with it?"

Jennifer shook her head. "I doubt it. Derek and I were thinking strongly along the lines that he must be involved, which means as well as his house being searched once we'd persuaded Hawkins, the factory would also have been searched again and Trisha's body found. Forensics also found bits of shredded plastic gloves with Gus's DNA on them snagged on ropes near the body. We would have caught him."

"How is his wife?" asked Sofie.

"Gutted, even though she knew what he was like. She loved him and was prepared to forgive him a lot. Although this might have been a stretch, even for her."

Henry was studying Jennifer's face as she spoke. "There's something else, Jennifer, isn't there?" he said. "There's something in your eyes; something you don't understand."

Jennifer sighed in capitulation. "Just as well I don't play poker. But yes, you're right. There's a bit of a mystery around whether Rosselli actually went inside the Brookes' cottage. If that were the case and Gus were still alive, it could have blurred the evidence, even with all the DNA and so on putting him and Trisha in bed together."

She smiled at the look of anticipation in everyone's eyes. Even Goccia had lifted her sleepy eyes to her.

"Rosselli was certainly outside. We know that from the photos on his phone and, interestingly, from a few Goccia prints at the end of the garden."

"He brought Goccia along?" Sofie was incredulous.

Goccia glared at her, a soft whine of dissent sounding in her throat.

"Shush, Goccia," said Jennifer. "She's on your side."

Sofie reached out to reassure Goccia by stroking her much-petted head.

"Trisha's body was missing an earring," continued Jennifer. "When forensics searched the cottage, they found one that matched in the drawer by Gus's bed. But the strange thing is that among the photos Rosselli took of Trisha in the garage, when, incidentally, he must have unwrapped the towels from Trisha's body, towels we see in place in later photos of the body, among those shots were several where Trisha is wearing earrings in both ears."

Henry frowned. "So you're saying that he took one of the earrings and later gave it to Gus? Why would he do that?"

"Not sure," said Jennifer. "Maybe it was all part of the black-mail. But there's a possibility he planted it in the drawer where we found it. If that were the case, it begs the questioned of what else he planted."

"He certainly wasn't your run-of-the-mill assassin," said Sofie. "And although I'm beside myself with gratitude that he was clearly rather eccentric, I still can't understand why he didn't just shoot you."

"Probably his fallback position," agreed Jennifer, "but it looks as if he didn't want me to anticipate the precise moment of my death. I mean, all the noise and the lights, he must have used them to stop me hearing the hoist thundering towards me."

"But Gus heard them," objected Sofie.

"No, he didn't. He felt them," said Jennifer. "Rosselli didn't anticipate that. I felt them too but I was slower to react. When Gus felt them, he pushed me out of the way and took the full force of the impact himself."

Connie shuddered and reached out to squeeze Jennifer's shoulder. "Doesn't bear thinking about."

"You're right," said Henry. He stood and walked over to where several bottles of Cristal champagne were chilling in ice buckets. "Nevertheless, we should thank our lucky stars that Signor Rosselli was a professional who enjoyed adding his own personal flourish to his work. That it finally failed thanks to his dog is poetic justice."

A cork popped. "It's time to celebrate," continued Henry as he filled champagne flutes and passed them round.

"To serendipity," he said, as they all raised their glasses.

"And eccentric assassins," added Sofie.

Jennifer smiled as she bent over to kiss the top of Goccia's head. "And," she said, "pretty little pugs."

Chapter Fifty-Four

Giorgio di Bari, Cosimo Graziano Rosselli's lover of seven blissful years, was sitting in Cosimo's favourite swivel leather recliner in the book-lined study where Cosimo had hatched so many of his plans.

He stared through the rain-streaked window of the wet autumnal Rome day, but he saw nothing. His face was a crumpled wreck from more than a week of almost constant weeping, his mind a turmoil of distressed agitation. Cosimo's daily calls had stopped, which could mean only one thing: his lover was dead.

Tacit confirmation had arrived two days previously in the form of a Polizia anti-mafia squad who had made a brash, heavy-handed search of the apartment. They had told him nothing except that they would be back once they had decrypted Cosimo's computer, after which he'd better have some answers.

"Answers to what?" he had asked, but they simply sneered and left.

Giorgio's smile had been bittersweet as he stared at the door the angry police officers had slammed shut behind them. They would find nothing on the computer; it was a decoy designed to fool them. Rosselli's real computer was long gone along with the phone Giorgio had used to speak to his lover. He had destroyed them both, the wealth of information they had contained now irretrievable. His obligation to Cosimo's memory now was to remain strong enough to resist the interrogations he knew would follow, to face the Polizia down and give up nothing. At least having his highly connected lawyer present would prevent any brutal tactics.

It helped that he could tell the truth in answer to at least some of the potential questions, since although he knew much about his lover's activities, there were also important details that Cosimo had deliberately kept from him, details about which Giorgio could honestly say he knew nothing. If more than one person knows a secret, it is no longer a secret. That had been Cosimo's credo and even with his lover and close confidante Giorgio, he had kept to it for the finer points of his strategies.

But before the Polizia returned, there was one final instruction from Cosimo for Giorgio to follow, a procedure that Cosimo put in place at the very beginning of all assassination contracts, to be deployed in the event of failure.

It was a simple enough process: a telephone number and a name to commit to memory, and instructions on where and how to make the call.

However, for Giorgio it was harder than climbing the highest mountain, since by carrying it out he would be admitting to himself that his lover was dead, that everything in his life he cherished had gone forever.

Cosimo's rationale for the instructions was more dispassionate. He was the best at his trade, probably the best there had ever been, which meant that failure was unacceptable. To his warped way of thinking, should he ever fail, it would be owing to circumstances beyond his control, circumstances for which the client must therefore accept responsibility and, like Cosimo himself, pay the ultimate price.

Giorgio dragged his feet to the bathroom and looked at himself in the mirror. "No," he said, shaking his head at his reflection, "I can't go out looking like this." Then he thought about it some more and realised he no longer cared. He splashed some water onto his face, pulled on a hoodie and headed for the street.

· · ·

The security boxes were in a grubby shop fifty metres down a dingy side street from the river Tiber. There were no keys to the boxes, only six-digit combination locks.

Giorgio went to the smaller boxes at the rear of the premises and dialled six numbers into one of the locks. 7-0-3-3-9-1. Five of the numbers corresponded to the positions of letters in the alphabet, the sixth, which was the second of the series, zero, kept the identical form to the letter it represented, the letter 'o'. It was easy to remember. Goccia. 703391.

Inside the box was a push-button Nokia phone left uncharged for months. Giorgio removed it and attached a portable charging block he pulled from his pocket. Once the phone had enough charge to fire up, he punched in the telephone number he had so reluctantly committed to memory.

The answer came after several rings.

"Si." The voice was gruff, coarse.

"Di Bari," said Giorgio.

"Si."

Giorgio paused for the briefest of moments before repeating the second piece of information, since he knew that in saying the words, he would be sealing a man's fate.

"Ettore Cambroni."

"Consider it done," growled the voice.

The phone disconnected immediately.

Clutching the phone like a grenade with its pin removed, Giorgio hurried back along the dingy street to the brightness beyond and without a pause, hurled it into the Tiber.

Afterword

I hope very much that you enjoyed reading this book as much as I enjoyed writing it. If you did, I should be extremely grateful if you could spend a few moments posting a review on Amazon or Goodreads (or both!). It needn't be long; one word will do — preferably a favourable one! Genuine reviews, however short, are worth a lot.

And equally as important, please recommend The Cambroni Vendetta to your relatives, friends and colleagues. While word of mouth is very helpful to the cause of any author, it is particularly so for self-published authors for whom marketing is that much harder. If you tell a few people about this book or any of my other books, and they in turn others, the word will spread.

You can find more information about all my books and other book-related stuff on my website at davidgeorgeclarke.com. If you are on FaceBook, Instagram, Twitter and/or Goodreads, I'm there too:

facebook.com/davidgeorgeclarkeauthor

twitter.com/clarkefiction

instagram.com/clarkefiction

goodreads.com/davidgeorgeclarke

Acknowledgments

This novel was originally self-published under the title of 'The Assassin's Dog' with a different cover. However, following a general review of my books that has resulted in new covers for all seven of them and new titles for four, this tale now bears what I think is a more relevant title: The Cambroni Vendetta. New title and new cover, but there is one constant in all of this: it could not have been completed without the help and encouragement of many people.

First and foremost, my wife Gail is a source of constant support and encouragement. She is always there as a sounding board for ideas, a critical, constructive and patient reviewer of drafts, and an enthusiastic supporter as each book develops from isolated ideas into some sort of coherency. More than anyone, this book is dedicated to her, with love.

In addition, I should like to thank my editor Susanna Moles for her incredible dedication in ensuring that as many rough edges as possible are polished out from the first draft onwards. Never afraid to criticise, she doggedly weeds out the waffle, the clunk and the irrelevant, invariably improving on the original. And the bits she likes, she raves about, which is wonderfully encouraging!

I should also like to thank a number of people who read through drafts at various stages of development, everyone of them helping in the quest for sneaky typos, contextual slip-ups and readability. Thank you, Anne and Sanford Foster, Luci de Nordwall

Cornish, Zoe O'Reilly, Jill Pemberton and Simon O'Reilly (still the fastest copy editor in the East) for your invaluable help, advice and criticism, together with your expert editing and proofreading.

Finally, I should like to thank various readers for their positive feedback, encouragement and reviews for my earlier books. I hope that you enjoyed this third instalment in the lives of Jennifer Cotton and Henry Silk. There will be more!

About the Author

After more than thirty years as a forensic scientist, most of which were spent in Hong Kong, David Clarke retired to the more bucolic pastures of Tuscany where, after dabbling in art restoration, he took up full-time novel writing. Drawing on his experiences in the scientific investigation of numerous serious crimes, he has written The Dust of Centuries series, the Cotton & Silk thriller series and An Imperfect Revenge.

He now spends his time mainly in Tuscany, Italy and Phuket, Thailand.

The Cambroni Vendetta is David's seventh novel.

Find out more from David's website at clarkefiction.com or from the links below.

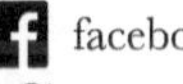 facebook.com/davidgeorgeclarkeauthor

 twitter.com/clarkefiction

 instagram.com/clarkefiction

 goodreads.com/davidgeorgeclarke

AN IMPERFECT REVENGE

If you would like to listen to a free audiobook version of AN IMPERFECT REVENGE read by the author, scanning the QR code above with the camera on your phone will take you to a link to sign up to the clarkeFiction newsletter and download the file. You will also be guided to the BookFunnel app for listening to the book.

Synopsis of An Imperfect Revenge

On assignment to review Villa Brocanti, an up-market agriturismo resort in Tuscany, travel writer Evie Lorrigan explores the dense forest surrounding the Brocanti estate and finds the boarded-up ruin of a palatial villa.

Her journalistic antennae piqued, she breaks in and what she finds is chilling. Prevented from leaving by doors with no handles closing behind her, she has little choice but to make her way through one room after another, each one decorated with extraordinary trompe l'oeil paintings. Lured onwards and upwards, she finally becomes trapped in an attic room with the gruesome remains of a man from a bygone era.

And no one knows she is there…

Enjoy!

A Final Word

Do you have kids or grandchildren, a favourite godson or goddaughter, a class of kids you teach or support in some way? My wife Gail is an author and illustrator who has published ten beautifully illustrated children's books. They are written in rhyme that children from 3–9 years just love reading or having read to them.

Patrick's Birthday Message
Searching for Skye — An Arctic Tern Adventure
Cosmos the Curious Whale
The Chameleon Who Couldn't Change Colour
Ndotto — An Elephant Rescue Story
Mischief at the Waterhole
Dormouse Snoremouse
Meerkat's Excitinmg Adventure
Sharks - Our Ocean Guardians
[The Shark Guardian Series Book One]
Jed's Big Adventure
[The Shark Guardian Series Book Two]

You can find more details on Gail's website and YouTube channel:

www.gailclarkeauthor.com
www.youtube.com/c/gailclarkeauthor

www.ingramcontent.com/pod-product-compliance
Lightning Source LLC
Chambersburg PA
CBHW060736190726
48285CB00001B/225